A DOUBLE BLAST OF BEAUTIES AND BULLETS FOR ONE LOW PRICE!

RED APACHE SUN

"Two of our boys was plugged by the Apaches," the bounty hunter told the Kansan. "An' we owe it all to yer Injun friend."

"Now, hold on a minute."

"You're in big trouble, boy."

"Listen, Mister," Davy said, raising his open hands as he started toward the bounty hunter, "let me try to find Soaring Hawk. I'm sure I—"

Davy's words were cut off abruptly, as one of the men brought the butt of his rifle down upon the base of the young Kansan's skull. The last thing that Davy Watson heard was Consuela Delgado's scream....

JUDGE COLT

Davy Watson's eyes traveled over the weather-beaten faces of the Texans, led by Bart Braden. "This here's Miss Delores Fernandez," he told them, hugging the pretty *chicana* to him.

"Onliest greaser I'm lookin' to meet around here is ol' man Mirabal hisself," Braden sneered.

Davy's nostrils flared. "That ain't no way to talk in front of a lady," he told the Texan.

"I got a piece of advice fer ya, Watson," Braden continued. "Light outta New Mexico, pronto! 'Cause if ya don't it's a good bet you'll catch you a see-vere dose of lead poisonin'!"

It was the Kansan's turn to sneer. "Mister, I been known to trade my share of lead poison too," he shot back.

The *Kansan Double* Series from *Leisure Books:*

**SHOWDOWN AT HELLS CANYON/
ACROSS THE HIGH SIERRA**

DOUBLE **THE** EDITION!

KANSAN

RED APACHE SUN/JUDGE COLT
ROBERT E. MILLS

LEISURE BOOKS **NEW YORK CITY**

Dedicated to my dear friends
Paula Rosenberg and Two-Gun Marty Sobel

A LEISURE BOOK®

December 1992

Published by

Dorchester Publishing Co., Inc.
276 Fifth Avenue
New York, NY 10001

DOUBLE **THE** EDITION!

KANSAN

RED APACHE SUN

Chapter One

Davy Watson shifted in his saddle, thrust back his broad-brimmed hat and mopped his brow with a blue polka-dotted handkerchief. Then he glanced down at the big Walker Colt holstered at his side, and winced as the image of the Arizona sun glared back from the metal surface of the weapon.

Riding at his side through an ancient and arid landscape composed of mountains, dry river valleys and desert plains was his Pawnee blood-brother, Soaring Hawk. The Plains Indian's copper skin had been tanned several shades darker by the southwestern sun, and he wore a red cloth band at his hairline, in the manner of the Apaches.

It was the winter of 1868-69, slightly more than a year from the day that the young Kansan had set out on that strange and perilous odyssey which took him over the face of the American West. Across the great plains of Kansas and eastern Colorado he and Soaring Hawk had ridden; into the high ground of northern Colorado and eastern Utah; across the Great Salt Desert and Nevada's forbidding Great Basin; as far north as the Idaho Territory's awesome Hells Canyon, and as far west as the Pacific Ocean, to the bustling young metropolis known as San Francisco.

In the fourteen months since they had ridden away from the Watson farm by Pottawatomie Creek, in Anderson County, Kansas, Davy and his blood-brother had encountered desperadoes, made fast friends, spent passionate nights in the arms of women throughout the West, and risked their lives more than once.

Following the trail of vengeance that first took them out of the Sunflower State, Davy Watson and Soaring Hawk had found themselves smack in the middle of the Battle of Beecher's Island, that unprecedented stand wherein a handful of brave men under the leadership of Major George A. Forsyth stood off a combined force of Cheyenne, Sioux and Arapaho hostiles numbering over a thousand. And following this, the two young men then survived the bloody and desperate shoot-out in Hells Canyon, by the raging waters of the Snake, where the score was settled at last with Ace Landry, the man who had shot Davy Watson and gunned down his beloved father.

On that dangerous and difficult quest, the bloodbrothers were assisted by two formidable men. Jack Poole was a government scout, and Big Nose Vachon a mountain man; both lost their lives in the showdown, as did Ace Landry and his entire gang of desperadoes.

After the ordeal was over, Davy and Soaring Hawk, both severely wounded, limped back to the rough young town of Boise with several pack mules in tow—mules bearing the gold that the Landry Gang had taken from the miners of the Boise Basin.

6

Welcomed as heroes in Boise, the two recuperated at the boarding house of one Carmela Mudree, a widow with three grown daughters. The Mudree girls were young women with full bodies, dark, gypsy looks and hot blood. Davy soon got to know them . . . in the Biblical, as well as the social, sense. In fact, the sisters contributed a degree of refinement to a love life that had begun over a year earlier, in the arms of the lissome, blonde Deanna MacPartland; they took to bed with Davy in a drunken and delightful carouse, and what went on there awakened the young Kansan to a vision of the rich potentiality of a full and active sex life. It would be a long time before he forgot the six caressing hands and three ardent mouths of Faith, Hope and Charity Mudree.

Things grew wild once more, as the three sisters were kidnapped by the huge and obscene Harvey Yancey.

Barely recuperated from their wounds, Davy and Soaring Hawk rode out in pursuit of Yancey and his pack of ruffians.

The trail led south, across Nevada's Great Basin, and into the wild boom town known as Virginia City, home of the famous Comstock Lode. There they were befriended by a young reporter, Marcus P. Haverstraw, who became their guide as Davy Watson and Soaring Hawk searched the many brothels of Virginia City's red-light district, in the knowledge that Harvey Yancey intended to sell the Mudrees into prostitution, or worse, white slavery.

Yancey led them a merry chase and eventually escaped, but not before Davy had become embroiled in an affair of honor with one of the giant's associates. Malcom Shove, an Alabama procurer, had been angered by the young Kansan's bluntness . . . and had challenged him to a duel.

Pistols at twenty paces, on the windswept slope of Mount Davidson; just after sunrise, high above a sleeping Virginia City. The rising wind worked in Davy's favor, and he survived the duel—against all odds . . . while Malcolm Shove lost his life. Davy lost his left earlobe.

After that, the pursuit was resumed, with Marcus Haverstraw smelling a good story and accompanying the bloodbrothers. And riding along with them as well were U.S. Marshal Fred Klingebiel and his two deputies, E. J. Karioth and Bradford N. Swett. The marshal was an old and sworn enemy of Yancey's.

The little band rode into the easternmost reaches of the Sierra Nevada mountain range, heading across the great natural barrier that separates Nevada from the California plain. And in the steep and snow-filled Donner Pass, the pursuers were bushwacked by Yancey and his bunch.

Marshall Klingebiel and his deputy, Bradford Swett, lost their lives in the ambush. But Davy's quick thinking enabled him to save the lives of the rest of the party. He instructed them to direct their gunfire on the snowladen ledges at the summit of the pass, thus creating an avalanche . . . which came roaring down upon the heads of their attackers.

Digging their way out of the Donner Pass a day later, the pursuers discovered that Yancey had escaped the avalanche, taking the Mudree sisters with him. Across the High Sierra they rode, following Yancey's trail down onto the Plain of California, and ultimately across the breadth of that young state, until they came to the wild and incredible city of San Francisco.

In 1868, San Francisco was a city of extremes, a place where unbridled optimism stood beside suicidal despair, where princely luxury contrasted with appalling poverty; a place of bright gaiety and dark, savage violence. And none of that city's districts better personified its dual nature than the Barbary Coast—the place where Harvey Yancey had taken the Mudree sisters, intending to sell them into white slavery there.

The Barbary Coast was a wild and lawless place, policed loosely by a bought constabulary and offering within its precincts every kind of gambling and vice known to civilized men. And it was within this maze of corruption, debauchery and violence that Davy Watson and his companions had to find the Mudree sisters.

Marcus Haverstraw's journalistic abilities and connections stood them in good stead in the course of the search, and they were ultimately led to a sporting house known as Covent Garden, a place owned by the dapper and ruthless gambler, Bertram Brown, one of the central figures in the Barbary Coast's white slave trade.

When Davy and his companions entered Covent Garden, Bertram Brown was not to be found. Instead, they were met by Della Casson, the black enchantress who was, although they did not know it at the time, Bertram Brown's mistress.

They were told that Brown was away for the day . . . but Della Casson, whose beauty had attracted the companions, seemed herself drawn to Davy, and offered the young men her hospitality. This they gratefully accepted, and retired to a suite of rooms with Della and two other young women.

Later that night the couples paired off, and Davy made love to the black Louisiana beauty . . . finally going to sleep in her arms. A short while later, Bertram Brown appeared, gun in hand, while the huge and fearsome Harvey Yancey stalked down the landing outside, preparing to kill Soaring Hawk and Marcus Haverstraw. Davy and his friends had been lured into a trap.

What saved the young Kansan's life was the intervention of Brown's mistress, who had earlier been deeply moved by Davy's loving kindness and willingness to share. Della was then shot by Brown—at exactly the same time that Yancey began to move on Soaring Hawk with murderous intent.

After the smoke had cleared, two men were dead . . . Harvey Yancey and Bertram Brown. Davy had been creased on the ribs and his forearms had been slashed with a broken champagne bottle, but he was saved by the timely arrival of the reporter, who shot Brown. At the same time, Soaring Hawk did away with the giant. The Mudree sisters were then located in the cellars of Covent Garden, and immediately freed.

Davy, Soaring Hawk and Marcus Haverstraw were held in police custody for several days, while the details of the Covent Garden affair were being sorted out. Recovering from her wound, Della Casson testified in their behalf, as did the abducted and sold Mudree sisters, and the three were promptly acquitted of any wrongdoing.

After another glorious night in the six arms of the passionate sisters, Davy saw them off the next morning, as they departed for Boise town. Then he and Soaring Hawk said farewell to Marcus Haverstraw, who had gotten his dream story, scooping even the San Francisco locals in the process!

It had been a long, hard trail that Davy Watson set out upon fourteen months ago, one that had led him farther and farther away from the arms of his beloved Deanna MacPartland. She was waiting for him at the end of that trail, waiting for him to ride in to the town of Hawkins Fork and take her out of Mrs. Lucretia Eaton's bawdy house.

Davy had been impatient to return to Deanna, the first woman who had ever slept with him, and the one who mattered most in his life, but he was unable to return home as directly as he wished.

It was January, and winter had fallen over the mountain passes and prairies that lay between California and Kansas, and men on horseback, riding exposed to the elements, would have little chance of survival following that trail. Two alternatives were open to Davy and Soaring Hawk: either to spend the winter in California, or to head back to the Sunflower State by a more southerly route. Since the Pawnee was as anxious to return to his people as was Davy Watson to return to the arms of Deanna MacPartland, the blood-brothers left the boisterous metropolis of San Francisco and rode south.

Down the coast of California they rode, marvelling at its great natural beauty, both equally entranced by the Pacific, since neither of them had ever seen an ocean before.

Southward they rode along the coast, through Pescadero, Davenport and Santa Cruz, swinging around the edge of Monterey Bay, then riding through groves of pines and past the dwarfed, windswept Joshuah trees, skirting the Monterey Peninsula, and coming down until they reached the rocky coastline and rugged magnificence of Big Sur.

Further south the blood-brothers rode, down to Piedras Blancas, skirting San Simeon and the Santa Lucia Range to the east, riding along the shore of Estero Bay to Point Conception, where the warm waters of the Pacific flow into the Santa Barbara Channel.

Then through the towns of Santa Barbara and Ventura, across the Oxnard Channel, past Port Hueneme, and into the small, sleepy town the Spanish had named the City of the Angels. There they stayed for several days, resting their horses and replenishing their provisions for the next leg of their great overland journey.

Leaving Los Angeles, Davy and Soaring Hawk rode east through the foothills and stunted forest near San Bernardino, through Joshuah Tree and Twenty Nine Palms, skirting the great Mojave Desert on its southern edge. Then, following the course of the Colorado River, the companions went through the towns of Rice, Vidal and Crossroads, after which they left California and entered into the Territory of Arizona.

Into Arizona they came, riding up from the banks of the Colorado, out of the heat and sun and into the cool welcome of Coconino Forest. Before them to the north, loomed Bill Williams Mountain, named for the mountain man and horse thief who had discovered it. And behind it, still farther north, lay Humphreys Peak, the highest spot in all Arizona.

12

Pink in the sunset and purple at other times, Bill Williams Mountain dominated the landscape for some time. And as they rode farther into the territory, the blood-brothers were overwhelmed by the harsh and abrupt change that nature had wrought. They saw before them an arid land, a place of wrinkled earth and parched rivers, whose surface was occasionally accented by mountains timbered with conifers and mesas dotted with junipers. And to the far north lay the great chasm that had been carved out of the earth by the constant rush of waters millennia ago.

Davy Watson had an uneasy feeling about Arizona. It was a place of violent extremes, a place hostile to man and all his works; it was not pleasant and welcoming like northeastern Kansas, he reflected, but a place wherein man had to struggle constantly to survive.

From Prescott they headed in a southerly direction, down to the valleys of the Gila and Salt Rivers, where the greater part of the territory's sparse population was to be found. Crossing the Hassayampa River, the blood-brothers rode along the banks of the Salt—*El Rio Salado*, the Spaniards had named it—and headed eastward toward the Salt River Valley.

Although the young Kansan was disturbed by the weathered grandeur and dry, wrinkled sprawl of Arizona, he was already feeling the benefits of its climate. In the course of his adventures Davy had lost an earlobe, been slashed across both forearms, and been shot in the shoulder and side. His wounds had bothered him greatly in the damp winter climate of San Francisco, and he had spent much of the time there in considerable pain. But

13

now, he realized, the hot sun and dry air of Arizona had baked the pain out of his bones.

Freed from the nagging presence of physical discomfort, Davy turned his thoughts to more pleasant matters, such as the memory of the women he had known and loved along the train that had taken him far from his native Kansas, and into the great open spaces of the American West and Northwest.

His ears burnt and he felt a stirring in his groin as he recalled Faith, Hope and Charity Mudree, the dark, gypsy sisters who shared a predilection for taking the same man to bed—at the same time!

Like to drove me wild, he told himself, shifting in his saddle. *Them three gals a-playin' with me all at once't was like a three-ring circus. Ever'where I looked they was lips an' hands; big, firm titties an' hot, juicy honey pots. Hoo-wee!*

Soaring Hawk darted a look at his fidgeting blood-brother. The Pawnee was a sharp-eyed observer whose judgments had the rare quality of being considered as well as quickly rendered. Like his people, the young brave lived in harmony with nature and preserved a stoical objectivity. He was an astute student of human behavior.

"You got fever?" he asked, his face expressionless, as he studied Davy's face and posture. "Ears all red."

"Uh, well . . . no, I ain't got no fever," Davy mumbled in annoyance, the rest of his face suddenly going the color of his ears, as he slouched down along the neck of his horse. "I was jus', uh, recollectin' my last night with the Mudree gals."

The Pawnee shook his head. "Too much fuck no good," he asserted. "Make man weak. Then he die soon." Like the Greeks of old, Soaring Hawk believed in the principle of moderation in all things.

Davy smiled wryly. "Well, them three li'l ol' sweeties came durn near to doin' me in, I can tell ya!"

Soaring Hawk nodded slowly, a knowing look spreading over his stolid countenance. "You pussy crazy," he informed his blood-brother.

"What the hell d'ya mean by *that?*" Davy exploded, bridling at the thought of being considered obsessed with sex.

"White boy no get to fuck 'til seventeen, eighteen," the brave told him, looking around and running his eyes over the surrounding landscape of riverbed, cactus and mesquite, and the low, distant mountain ranges.

"I don't get the point of what you're sayin'," Davy told Soaring Hawk.

"Indian boy fuck once he get to be thirteen, fourteen," the Pawnee replied. "Then soon take squaw. After that, fuck when want."

Davy straightened up in his saddle and studied the Indian's face, noting his jet black hair, strong jaw, aquiline nose and high cheekbones.

"Make white boy wait too long," Soaring Hawk explained. "All years between thirteen and time he get fucked, he think heap much about pussy. Then he go hog-wild when finally get chance." He shook his head. "No good that way."

Davy sighed, took off his big hat and fanned himself with it. "That's one of the blessin's of Christianity, I reckon. I do believe you heathens has got it all over us there."

15

The Pawnee nodded. "White man think too much about pussy. Make him crazy."

"Yeah, I know what you mean," Davy muttered, turning his head away as he put his hat back on. Then he pulled its brim down over his eyes. "But there's worse things'n that to think about, ol' son," he mumbled, feeling the warmth of the sun penetrate his body as he returned to the memories of the women he had known.

From a vision of Marcy Jean Gebhardt, the slender young hooker from Greeley, Colorado, who'd had oral aptitudes and a muff like an aroused porcupine, Davy's thoughts roamed through the bedrooms and bawdy houses he had visited since the beginning of his frontier odyssey.

He remembered the face, but not the name, of the honkytonk blonde with whom he had spent a night in Boise, and the way that her dormant tenderness had been awakened. The young Kansan's honesty, openness and gentleness had a singular effect upon women of all types. And then Davy remembered Bright Water, the ardent young Pawnee whom he had loved during his sojourn at the camp of Soaring Hawk's people.

But his consciousness was dominated by the images of two women, each as different from the other as night is from day. There was the elegant and long-limbed Della Casson, the passionate black beauty from Lousiana . . . and there was the fair and delicate Deanna MacPartland, whose colors were gold, ivory and rose, the lissome enchantress who waited for him at the end of the trail, back in Hawkins Fork, Kansas.

Davy's mind strayed back to the Barbary Coast for a moment, to the lamplit vision of Della

16

Casson, lithe and full-bosomed, her black body glistening with the sweat of consummated desire, opening her arms and legs wide once more to receive him. . . .

"Settlement ahead," the keen-eyed Indian said tersely, jarring Davy Watson out of his sexual reverie.

The young Kansan looked up and saw a small settlement ahead, its adobe houses strung out around what the Spanish called a *zanja madre*, or mother ditch, dug for the purpose of irrigating the land with the water of the *Rio Salado*. Patches of cultivated land ran out from both sides of the irrigation ditch. Davy estimated that there were well over a hundred such plots in the area.

As he and Soaring Hawk drew closer, Davy made out the vestiges of other irrigation ditches, those long dried up, the sign of ancient inhabitants who had farmed the area long before the coming of the white man. Even then someone had possessed the vision to water the dry soil.

Himself the product of a farm, Davy Watson studied the yield of the plots adjoining the *zanja madre*, noting with some wonder the burgeoning crops and exotic melons, some of which he had never seen before.

At the edge, or sometimes in the center of many of the plots, stood single-storied houses made of adobe brick, whose sparse number confirmed Davy's opinion that the rough settlement's population numbered no more than several hundred souls.

"Judas Priest," he grumbled, turning to Soaring Hawk. "An' I thought Prescott was a hole-in-the-wall. Wonder what they call this here nickel-dime operation?"

"This good size town for white man," the Pawnee told Davy. "If not get bigger." A nomadic Plains Indian himself, Soaring Hawk had no love for permanent settlements or towns. The frenzy, squalor and overcrowding of San Francisco's Barbary Coast had made a deep impression upon the brave, confirming his deepest suspicions regarding the self-destructive tendencies of the white man.

"Le's head on over there," Davy told Soaring Hawk, pointing to an old Indian ruin that lay about half a mile ahead. "There 'pears to be a bunch of fellas a-settin' on them broke-up walls, passin' around a jug of somethin' or other."

The Pawnee frowned. "Men get drunk, mebbe. Then act like asshole." He loosened his heavy-calibre Sharps rifle in its sling.

"Aw, drunks ain't so bad," Davy told him. "They gen'lly ain't no threat. Can't fight worth a shit, an' most of 'em can't hit a buffalo's backside at ten paces with an Army cannon."

His hand went up to his left ear, as he fingered the place where his earlobe had been shot off in the duel at Virginia City.

The sounds of merrymaking reached the ears of the riders, as they walked their horses up to the Indian ruin. Someone was playing a harmonica for all he was worth, and the steely, nasal twang of a Jew's harp could be heard cutting through the plaintive wail of the first instrument. The sounds of hand-clapping could also be heard, in company with a strange nobbly clacking that Davy could not identify until he saw a man playing a pair of

18

spoons, holding them between the fingers of one hand while he beat them against his other hand and his leg.

The music came to an abrupt halt once the celebrants caught sight of Davy and Soaring Hawk. And when they realized that the young Kansan's companion was an Indian, the men all put down their jugs and instruments and scrambled to their feet, each of them coming up with a rifle or a pistol.

"Now, you jus' raise your hands up high, like I'm doin'," Davy instructed Soaring Hawk through the clenchedtoothed smile he presented to the armed men, as they drew near to the outer adobe wall of the Indian ruin. "Judas Priest," he swore. "They's more'n a score of men behind them walls, an' every mother's son of 'em's got his gun trained on us. "That's a fine way to say 'Howdy.' " Davy twitched as he felt a rivulet of sweat course down his cheek.

"You boys come in real easy-like," a froggy voice with a southern accent boomed out from behind the wall. "Y'all jus' keep yore hands as high as if you was a-goin' to pick God's pockets."

"Yessir, we'll do jus' that," Davy replied through his beartrap smile.

"What kinda Injun's that there?" the possessor of the froggy bass called out once more. "I never done seen me one like 'at afore."

"He's a Pawnee, sir," Davy answered, still smiling like a dead man, able now to stare into the gaping mouths of all the rifles and pistols that were levelled at his chest. "From out Kansas way," he added.

The horses were almost to the wall. Davy made

out the features of the man who addressed him from the far end of a Winchester barrel. He was a thickset man with brown, bushy hair and beard, and hot little eyes that flashed like sparks from a blacksmith's anvil.

"What you doin' with that savage, boy?" his interrogator inquired. "You some kind of renegade?"

"I ain't no kind of renegade, sir," Davy told the angry-looking man, as his horse came to a halt before the outer wall of the Indian ruin. "His name is Soaring Hawk, an' he's a true friend to the white man."

"Onliest Injun what's a true friend to the white man," the froggy-voiced man croaked back as he glared at Davy's companion, "is the one that's a-moulderin' 'neath six feet of earth. I ought to know. I done shot me enough of 'em."

Davy winced when he heard this, and he darted a quick glance at his blood-brother. The Pawnee's face was like a stone carving, but Davy was fully aware that the brave had already calculated his next move, and figured out how many whites he would have time to take with him if the angry-looking man decided to fire his Winchester. . . .

"Oh, I say, Eli, that's a bit sharp!" a voice called out from behind the wall, in an accent totally unfamiliar to Davy Watson's ears.

"You know what William Blade had to say about unalterable opinions, don't you?" the voice went on as Davy sighed with relief, seeing that the angry-looking man had lowered his rifle and turned in its direction.

"I don't know what t'hell you talkin' 'bout, Darrel," the froggy voice boomed, overlaid with tones of annoyance and perplexity.

"Why, here's what Blake said, Eli: 'The man who never alters his opinion is like standing water, and breeds reptiles of the mind.' D'ye see?"

"Goddammit all, Darrel," the froggy southerner croaked angrily, "we's dealin' with Injuns—not rep-tiles! I swear I don't know what-all you jabbrin' 'bout."

"Well, what I am saying, Eli," the other man said in his pleasant baritone voice, "is that perhaps you might do well to find out a bit more about these chaps before you pepper 'em."

"Yeah, le's find out who they are, an' what they want," another voice, this time to the other side of the angry man, called out.

Davy sighed with relief as this opinion was seconded by a chorus of male voices.

"Mind if'n we put our hands down, sir?" he asked the man behind the Winchester.

"Oh, all right," the man grumbled in his harsh bass voice. "But if'n either of you tries anything, I'll blow you out'n yer saddles."

"Oh, for the love of heaven, Eli," the man with the strange accent called out. "Make the gentlemen welcome, and offer them a drink."

The bearded man puffed out his cheeks and blew a whistling stream of air through compressed lips as he stared at the strangers, a thoughtful expression on his face.

"All right," he grunted, waving them on with his Winchester. "Come on in, an' set a spell."

As he dismounted, Davy Watson saw for the first time that the settlement had recently been rebuilt. Piles of charred adobe and ashes sat behind some of the houses, and the ground near them was covered with a fine, sooty film, Davy realized as he made his way around the ruined wall that separated him from the inhabitants of the little settlement.

When he got to the other side, the young Kansan saw before him a group of men seated upon packing crates of diverse sizes, which had been laid out in a rough approximation of a circle. The men sat in the shade of several cottonwood trees that lined the bank of the irrigation canal behind them. And as they did, the men passed around a large earthen jug.

"Gentlemen, gentlemen," the man who had originally taken the part of the blood-brothers called out cheerfully, rising to his feet as Davy and Soaring Hawk came into view.

He was a tall, lean man with dark hair and skin tanned by the Arizona sun to the color of leather. He wore blue denim pants, a navy-blue shirt, a belt whose buckle was hammered silver, and a black, wide-brimmed hat with a flat crown. And while he looked much like any of the frontier Arizonans around him, the man's accent immediately marked him as a foreigner.

"Albert, pass our friends the jug, won't you? That's a good chap," he said, turning to the present holder of the vessel.

"Sure 'nuf, Lord Darrel," the man replied in a squeaky voice, after having swigged at the jug and wiped his mouth on the frayed and dirty cuff of his flannel shirt.

"Bryan Philip Darrel Duppa at your service," the man with the foreign accent told Davy and Soaring Hawk, proffering his hand as he approached them.

"David Lee Watson, of Anderson County,

Kansas, at *your* service, sir," Davy replied courteously as he took the man's hand and shook it heartily.

"Wasson?" the man asked. "I say, isn't that a German name?"

"Watson's *my* name, Mr. Duppa," Davy told him.

"Oh, *Watson*," the man repeated smiling now. "A good English name. Indeed."

"My friend an' blood-brother here's called Soaring Hawk," Davy continued. "He's from the Pawnee nation, an' his people rides over the plains of Kansas an' Colorado."

"I say," the man exclaimed enthusiastically, letting go of Davy's hand as he turned to Soaring Hawk, "the Pawnee are a friendly people, are they not?"

"Friendly to the white man," Davy told the stranger with a grin on his face as he did. "But not so friendly if you's Cheyenne, Arapaho or a couple of other tribes."

"Well, it's reassuring to know that this Indian gentleman is not hostile to whites," the man said, his smile tightening as he felt Soaring Hawk's firm handshake. "We've got all we can do to look out for the Apaches, these days. They're on the warpath again, you know."

"Don't rightly know much about Apaches," Davy said, taking the jug from the man with the squeaky voice.

"You will," the man told him quietly, "if you spend any time in the southern half of the Arizona or New Mexico territories."

"Ooof," Davy grunted, rolling his eyes as he lowered the jug. "That's a right strong drink."

23

"You bet'cha 'tis!" a tubby man wearing a straw hat and overalls called out as he nodded solemnly. " 'At's the way it's s'posed to be."

The friendly man flashed Davy a bright smile. "Bascomb distills his spiritous liquors to a level of extreme refinement. He adjudges his product seasoned when it is capable of melting down a horseshoe."

"That ain't 'zactly the way I does it, Lord Darrel," the tubby man corrected. "Ac 'chooly, I sets my standard by *how fast* the durn stuff can melt down that there ol' horseshoe."

"Well, this last batch must have dissolved the bloody thing in nothing flat," Darrel Duppa said. "I rather fancy that drinking your little beverage is much like imbibing quicksilver, Bascomb."

"Might go in like quicksilver," the tubby man mumbled shyly from beneath his straw hat. "But it comes out like molten lead."

The men in the circle laughed.

"No, it certainly is not the smooth, velvet distillate of the Scottish highlands," Darrel Duppa told him. "But it does possess a certain robust uniqueness all its own. A true native spirit."

"Gawd, that man can shore talk him some fancy talk!" exclaimed one of the other men.

"They ain't nobody more el-o-quent an' reetorical in the whole of the territory," volunteered a burly man who wore a black patch over his right eye.

"Yep," affirmed the man on his left. "An' he's a bona fi-dee English gennulman. A lord by birth, don't'cha know. Onliest one in the whole southwest, I 'spect," he told Davy Watson proudly.

"You don't say," the young Kansan replied, himself somewhat awed by the revelation. "Is that a fact?"

"Actually," the Englishman told him, smiling shyly, "I belong to the minor nobility, but they make such a bloody to-do about it here, you know. My ancestral home is in England, at Hollingbourne House, in County Kent. My actual place of birth was in France, where my father was serving his country as a diplomat.

"As a youth, I travelled with my father," Duppa went on, "and received a classical education befitting a young gentleman of my rank. That was primarily in France and Spain, whose languages I mastered, along with German, Italian, Latin and ancient Greek."

"You ought to hear him talk in Eye-talian," the tubby man muttered. "Sounds right purty."

"Go ahead, Lord Darrel," urged the burly man with the eyepatch. "Talk some Eye-talian fer these here fellas."

"*Lasciate ogni speranza, voi che entratta,*" the Englishman declaimed in his sonorous voice, gesticulating in the manner of the stage actors of the day, his features assuming a stern and forbidding aspect.

"What's it mean?" whispered Davy, impressed by the man's flamboyant theatricality.

"It's from Dante," Duppa told him. "The words graven on the gate of Hell: 'Abandon all hope, ye who enter.' That could apply as well to getting caught by the Apaches on Superstition Mountain, I suppose."

"Superstition Mountain?" parroted a fascinated Davy Watson.

"Yes, indeed," replied the Englishman. "It is an awesome conglomeration of cliffs, peaks and mesas, borne high atop a huge plateau." He pointed into the distance. "It lies a mere thirty-five miles from where we stand."

Duppa smiled knowingly at Davy and Soaring Hawk. "The area bears such colorful names as Pichaco Butte, Tortilla, Fish Creek, Black Mountain, Bluff Springs, Miner's Needle and Geronimo's Head. The Spaniards who first explored this land referred to the range as the *Sierra de la Espuma*—the Foamy Mountains. And today, the entire range is referred to as Superstition Mountain, because, when seen from the southwest—the Apache point of view, one might say—it all looks like one big, bloody mountain."

Duppa paused to take a swig from the earthen jug as it came his way. Then he held it out, offering it to Soaring Hawk, who declined with a shake of his head.

"Darrel, don't you know no better," the angry man called out suddenly, "than to give strong drink to Injuns? Once't them red divils gets likkered up, they'd jus' as soon scalp you as look at you."

"You don't much care for Injuns, do ya, Mister?" Davy asked pointedly, angered by the man's unrelenting hostility toward Soaring Hawk.

"Damn right I don't," the man growled back, his gimlet eyes boring into Davy's. "Them red dogs done scalped my boy, Grover."

"Apaches, he means," the tubby man muttered from beneath his straw hat.

Davy took a deep breath before he spoke again. "I'm plumb sorry 'bout that, Mister," he said finally. "I truly am. But Soaring Hawk ain't no Apache. He's a friend to the white man."

"He's a Injun, ain't he?" the man said bitterly, shooting the Pawnee brave a dark look. "That's enough fer me."

"*Uh-hnnnh*! Well, as I was saying," Darrel Duppa interjected after loudly clearing his throat, his hearty, resonant voice warming the icy silence that had followed the angry man's declaration. "Superstition Mountain is indeed a fearsome place. Many men have gone there, only to lose their lives in the bargain."

Relieved at Duppa's interjection, Davy turned to face the Englishman, after having smiled reassuringly at his impassive blood-brother.

"And it is the focus of great, raging thunderstorms," Duppa went on, pointing toward Superstition Mountain, "which send torrents down onto the jagged face of the mountainside and plateau, constantly coarsening the terrain by creating new barrancas."

"Land sakes, the jug's gone dry," one of the men called out in a disappointed voice.

"Well, if'n that's the case," rumbled the man with the black eyepatch, "git off'n yer butt, an' git you another one over to Eli's place."

The other men mumbled in agreement with this last statement.

"It is a particularly inhospitable place," said Duppa, resuming his narrative, "partly because of its inaccessibility, and partly because of other, more sinister reasons." He raised his hands in the air. "Every bloody sort of cactus and thorny plant imaginable grows upon Superstition Mountain, and the way over its crags and peaks is perilous in

27

the extreme.''

The Englishman grew solemn. "More than that, it is the sacred mountain of the Apaches. They believe the place to be the abode of their Thunder God, whose manifest presence is the storm, and whose voice is the thunder.''

"Here comes ol' Toby with the new jug," one of the men called out.

"When Coronado first led his *conquistadors* into this area, they began to explore the range. But the moment any of them strayed from the group, he disappeared—only to be found dead later . . . with his head cut off.''

"Hot damn," Davy whispered. He glanced at Soaring Hawk, and saw that the Pawnee was staring at Darrel Duppa as he listened intently to the man's story.

"After a while," Duppa went on, "the *conquistadores* no longer ascended the peaks of the range. In fact, they even quit the area. Coronado himself dubbed the range *Monte Superstition* . . . Superstition Mountain.''

"Well, then," guled Davy, "why the hell would a body care to mess around up there, anyway?''

Darrel Duppa leaned toward Davy. "Well, believe it or not, my friend, aside from the Apaches, many men—Mexicans and *gringos*— have made their way up to Superstition Mountain.'' He paused for effect. "And many of those men have never come back," he added in a whisper, rolling his eyes melodramatically.

"And do you know *why* they risked their lives in that awful place—and continue to do so to this very hour?'' the Englishman asked with theatrical emphasis, his voice rising as he finished asking the question.

"No," croaked Davy. "Why?"

Duppa raised his eyebrows and shot an inquiring look at Soaring Hawk. The Pawnee frowned and shook his head.

"Gold," was Darrel Duppa's whispered reply. "The mountain is reputed to contain a vein of gold rich beyond the dreams of Croesus."

"Of who?" asked Davy.

"Croesus. Last king of ancient Lydia," Duppa told him. "You'll find mention of him in Herodotus. He was reputed to be the wealthiest man of his time."

"Oh, yeah," mumbled Davy, impressed with the Englishman's erudition.

"The early Spanish explorer, Cabeza de Vaca, told of the fabled Seven Golden Cities of Cibola, after he had explored the Southwest in 1528, thereby firing Spanish imaginations with a lust for gold," Duppa continued. "Then, in 1540, Coronado came here in search of Quivara, one of the legendary Seven Cities.

"He was told by the local Indians of a mountain full of gold. And when he tried to force those Indians to help him explore the range, they would not go with him . . . even though many of them were subsequently tortured. Their medicine men had told them that the Thunder God would visit a terrible punishment upon them if they did."

The jug came around to Duppa, who took a swig and then handed the earthen vessel to Davy Watson.

"Several centuries later—just twenty-five years ago, in 1845, a ranchero from Sonora, a man by the name of Don Miguel Peralta, discovered gold on Superstition Mountain. He returned in the early fifties with a force of several hundred *peones*, and began to work his claim in earnest, taking millions of pesos worth of rich gold concentrate out of his hidden mine.

"All we know—to this very day," Duppa said emphatically, "is that the gold mine is located somewhere in the vicinity of a towering mass of basalt now called Weaver's Needle, which was named after Pauline Weaver, the frontiersman who carved his name upon it."

"Pauline?" Davy asked in disbelief. "That's a woman's name."

"Somebody should'a told that to his maw," one of the men said. "But weren't no one 'bout to tell ol' Pauline hisself. He was one tough hombre."

"A man got hisself a name like Pauline," the tubby man muttered, "he better be tough."

"Anyway," Duppa interjected, rescuing his narrative once more, "Peralta called Weaver's Needle Sombrero Peak. But the name never took hold. What did stick was the name given to that great, black, jutting mass by the peons who worked the claim: the Finger of God."

Wide-eyed, and thinking about the Apache Thunder God, Davy Watson nodded. Impassive as ever, Soaring Hawk watched Darrel Duppa through narrowed eyes.

"But this happy state of affairs was not to last. The Apaches greatly resented the Mexicans' defilement of their sacred mountain. And they also greatly resented the fact that the *peones* were frolicking with their lasses." He raised his eyebrows at this, and then shook his head.

"In 1848 the Apaches struck. Led by their great

chieftain, Mangas Coloradas, and the present-day leader, Cochise, the Indians surprised the Mexicans and wiped them out. Peralta's body was never found, although the skeleton of a pack mule, its saddle bags filled to bursting with gold concentrate, will turn up from time to time."

"Judas Priest!" Davy Watson exclaimed. "Them Apaches don't fool around, do they?"

"Ain't no Injuns alive that's tougher, meaner or more dangerous." the man with the black eye patch told Davy.

"They are absolutely ferocious," Darrel Duppa seconded. "Mangas Coloradas means Red Sleeves, a name which the chief received after emerging from a knife fight—wherein he had killed several Mexicans—with his forearms covered with blood. The Apaches get their name as a result of such exploits. They are not chaps to be taken lightly, I assure you."

"That's fer shit-sure," growled a man who sat under one of the cottonwoods.

"We have been speaking of the particular band of Apaches native to the Chiricahua Mountains," the Englishman told Davy and Soaring Hawk. "But what Waldo said applies equally to all Apaches.

"Their ordeals and trials are grueling in the extreme. An Apache brave must be able to run a distance of four miles carrying a mouthful of water, which he then spits out at the end of his run. They are trained to fight and endure all manner of hardship, and have been known to run up to seventy miles a day. Raiding and looting are a way of life with them, and an Apache becomes a man when he brings back his first scalp."

The fresh jug came around to Duppa, and he paused to drink from it.

"They are perfectly adapted to life in the mountains and the desert," he went on, passing the jug to Davy. "The men do not work at all. They are warriors. That is their sole occupation. All the menial work is done by their women." The Englishman smiled wistfully. "Apache females are among the most beautiful of all Indian women—they are absolutely ravishing as maidens. But marriage finishes 'em as beauties, for they're worked like dogs by their husbands, and consequently age at a frightening pace." He sighed. "Rather a pity, you know."

"The men don't help 'em none?" Davy asked incredulously, reacting from his background of egalitarian experience at the Watson farm.

"Apache braves don't do no more work than lootin', shootin', scalpin' an' stealin' horses," the man with the patch over his eye told Davy. "For Apache squaws, bein' married ain't much different from bein' a pack mule."

"Hell," said the man with the squeaky voice, "pack mules is treated better by the Apaches."

"That's a fact," agreed the man with the eye patch, as he turned his good eye on Davy and Soaring Hawk. "But them leetle brown gals is sure tough. Why, when they becomes widders—a thing that happens frequent-like with Apaches, some of 'em takes their dead husband's rifles an' goes out a-ridin' an' a-fightin', jus' like the braves."

"An' yet," the tubby man muttered shyly from beneath his big straw hat, "afore they gits hitched up, them gals is jus 'bout the purtiest l'il things you ever did lay eyes on."

"The women ride with this Mangas Coloradas?" the young Kansan asked the Englishman.

"Mangas Coloradas met his end at the hands of the United States Army several years ago," Darrel Duppa informed Davy. "But Cochise is very much alive today . . . and still at large, in the Chiricahua Mountains."

"Anybody work gold mine today?" Soaring Hawk asked.

"Men keep risking their lives to find that bloody vein," said Duppa. "Why, only six years ago, in 1863, a man named Jacob Walz—a German, I believe, although he's called "The Dutchman"—went to Superstition Mountain, and came away with a king's ransom in gold. He's not been there for some time; but when he goes, he's able to elude all those who attempt to follow him. And no one follows him too closely, I daresay, for old Jake Walz is a crack shot with both carbine and Colt .44."

'How'd he do it?" Davy asked, thinking of the Apaches.

"He did it with the aid of his sweetheart, a beautiful young Apache lass named Ken-Tee, which means Sunshine. She smuggled his nuggets out of the camp. But the Apaches eventually caught and punished Ken-Tee . . . by cutting out her tongue. She died in Walz's arms. He was heartbroken."

"Don't think I'd want to meet up with them Apaches," Davy muttered.

Nodding solemnly, the Englishman went on with his story. "After Walz came down from Superstition Mountain, word spread about his find. It became known as the Old Dutchman mine, and many men went looking for it.''

"Anybody ever find it?'' Davy asked.

"No one who has ever lived to tell the tale,'' said Duppa. "I tell you this merely to indicate to you gentlemen, as visitors to this area, that the Apaches are not to be trifled with.''

"I can see that,'' Davy agreed. "Oh, by the way,'' he said, rising to his feet and stretching out his arms in the air, "what's the name of this here place?''

"It used to be called Swillings, after Lord Darrel's partner, Jack Swillings,'' the tubby man told him. "But the place damn near burnt down a little while back, an' we's jus' settin' things to rights again.'' He pointed to the charred remains of several buildings on the far side of the *zanja madre*. "We been talkin' 'bout renamin' the place, but I don't reckon it's got a name, right now.''

"No, it don't,'' rumbled the man with the black eyepatch. "But we got to settle on one right soon—so's we can have us some more farmin' an' irrigatin' equipment sent down here.''

"*Eureka*!'' exclaimed Darrel Duppa, thrusting the jug at Davy and rising suddenly to his feet. "I am visited by inspiration!''

He turned and began to climb the ruined adobe wall. Then, as he reached the top, Duppa turned to face the onlookers, weaving back and forth precariously as he did.

"As the mythical phoenix rose reborn from its ashes,'' he cried, "so shall a great civilization rise on the ashes of a past civilization.''

Davy stared goggle-eyed at the flamboyant Englishman. Never in his life had he met anyone like Darrel Duppa.

"I name thee Phoenix!" Duppa cried out exultantly, spreading wide his arms in a gesture that took in the land on both sides of the canal.

"Phoenix, by God!" cried the squeaky-voiced man. "Lord Darrel, that's a hot one!"

"Leastways it's better'n Swillings," replied the man with the black eyepatch. "With all due respect to ol' Jack, that name allus made me think of stuff you throw in a bucket afore goin' out to slop the hogs."

"Phoenix!" Darrel Duppa cried out once more, as he came down from the wall.

"What d'ya think?" the tubby man asked Davy Watson.

"Well," replied the young Kansan, "it's a damn sight better'n Swillings."

"To Phoenix!" the Englishman called out, taking the jug and raising it aloft.

"To Phoenix!" chorused the men sitting on the packing crates.

"To Phoenix!" Davy Watson cried out, just as the jug came around to him. Then, Darrel Duppa sat down beside Davy and Soaring Hawk, and told them the story of the newly-risen town of Phoenix.

The place had actually been founded by Duppa's partner, the aforementioned Jack Swillings, a native South Carolinian who entered the territory in 1857. He worked on the Gila Trail, joined the Gila City gold rush, and later headed the Gila Rangers, a local militia formed to deal with the raids of the Yavapais Indians.

Swillings was a daring man who was driven by a lust for gold. And while he was pursuing that lust in the area of Pinos Altos, having gained the friendship of the Apaches there, Swillings betrayed

35

the great chief, Mangas Coloradas, handing him over to a company of Union soldiers who would later murder him.

Following that, the Carolinian struck gold near Prescott, and squandered it shortly thereafter. His next move was to work in the Salt River Valley, as a hauler of hay to Fort McDowell. Swillings constantly risked his life in that position, his last three predecessors having been murdered by the Tonto Apaches. And on occasion, it had even been rumored, the southerner would tie a bandana around his face, pick up a shotgun, jump on his horse, and ride off to hold up a stagecoach.

While Jack Swillings was an adventurer, the man was also a visionary. He realized that the ancient Hohokam Indians, whose name he did not even know, had been the first to irrigate the land, reclaiming it from the desert. And it was he, along with Henry Wickenburg and a number of others, who founded the Swillings Irrigating Canal Company, with the intention of growing barley and other crops, which they would then sell to the U.S. Army at the military posts in the area.

Following the path of an old Indian canal at the outset, the *zanja madre* was dug, running north and west. Thirty farmers settled along its banks; and by the time that Davy Watson and Soaring Hawk had come to Phoenix, several hundred more lived with their families on the patches of land that bordered the canal's present network of waterways.

In 1867, Darrel Duppa met Jack Swillings, and the Englishman became the Carolina adventurer's main partner in the irrigation company. Both men lived in the new settlement, Swillings sharing an adobe house with Trinidad, his new wife whom he had met and wooed while visiting Tucson.

Duppa, or "Lord Darrel," as he was called locally, had also spent a number of years in wandering and diverse ventures. He had been an explorer in South America, survived a shipwreck, and then joined his wealthy uncle George in New Zealand, where they jointly developed a sheep station and prospered, acquiring a considerable amount of land in the process.

In 1862, Duppa appeared in Prescott (which was then part of the New Mexicao Territory), investigating some mining shares for his uncle. Living on Bank of California remittances for the sale of his New Zealand sheep, the Englishman lived the life of a prospector and Indian fighter. Shortly thereafter, he moved south, to the Salt River Valley. There he stayed, and it was in that area he was to meet his future partner.

By general agreement, Phoenix became the little settlement's name, due largely to the great respect the locals had for Duppa's erudition. Some of them had wanted to name the place Mill City; others, Salina, referring to the salt marshes along the Salt River. Confederate sympathizer that he was, Jack Swillings had opted for the name Stonewall. And a group of farmers had even wanted to call the place Pumpkinsville. But the new settlement that rose from the ashes of Swillings was to face the future, for better or for worse, as Phoenix.

Evening came, and the men left the shelter of the cottonwood trees and made their way home. The genial Englishman invited Davy and Soaring Hawk to spend the night at his home. This was agreeable

37

to the young Kansan, who had been on the trail for several days. But the Pawnee brave, as always, received the invitation with mixed feelings, disliking as he did the soft beds and food of the white man.

The settlement of Phoenix was a rough-hewn affair, and Darrel Duppa's house was no exception to the general state of affairs. Its walls were thin and unplastered, made of ironwood interlaced with strips of rawhide; the roof was made of bent and tied clumps of willows. The floor was dirt; the furniture sparse and unpainted. Hanging down from joists and beams at various points throughout the house, Davy saw saddles, whips and spurs, guns and cartridge belts.

The house was a sprawling, noisy and bustling place where dogs and mules roamed as freely as the two-legged inhabitants. The mingled scents of beans, chili, onions and spices filled the air. And in the kitchen, a bearded dwarf called Nicky Nunnemaker prepared dinner for "Lord Darrel" and his guests.

"Hash pile! Come a-runnin'!" the dwarf called out in a voice that reminded Davy Watson of the grunting of a razorback hog. *Bam-diddy-bam-diddy-bam*! went the pots and pans that the cook rattled as he summoned all in the house to dinner.

To Davy's great surprise, the meal was well-cooked, and a joy to eat. And by the time he sat over pie and coffee, smoking a stogie and drinking raw Mexican brandy with Darrel Duppa, the young Kansan was in high spirits. Soaring Hawk, as was his custom after a meal in anyone's house, had gone out for a stroll.

"Me'n my pal's headin' back Kansas way,"

Davy told his English host. "But with winter whippin' over the plains right now, we decided to take a southern route."

"I see," replied Darrel Duppa. "But it is my duty to caution you at this juncture," he said solemnly, his smile suddenly fading, "to ride no farther south than you have already, Mr. Watson. For if you do, you do so at great peril. The Chiricahua Apaches have been stirred up lately, and Chief Cochise has them playing hob with all the settlements between here and Tucson."

"Bad, hah?" Davy asked, picking loose bits of tobacco off his tongue.

"Extremely so," Duppa told him, a grave expression on his face. "The Apaches are a fierce and warlike people, and when they raid, they give no quarter. Cochise has never forgiven the whites for their, uh . . ." he shrugged helplessly, "treachery . . . as regards Mangas Coloradas, and he has reached the limit of his patience with us."

"What *did* happen to this Mangas Coloradas?" asked Davy.

"Well," Duppa told him uneasily, "the story goes that Jack—my partner, connived to hand Mangas Coloradas over to the U.S. Cavalry at Apache Pass. The chief came there thinking he was about to parley with one Captain Shirland, but he was subsequently taken prisoner." Duppa shook his head.

"Then it seems that the commander of the local garrison made it known, obliquely, that Mangas Coloradas was too dangerous to live." The Englishman sighed. "That night, the chief was shot . . . allegedly trying to escape."

"They killed him?" whispered Davy.

"One assumes so," Darrel Duppa replied. "I have heard a great many stories to that effect. The Army has always taken an extremely dim view of Apache activities. In fact, during the Civil War, the order had even been given to exterminate all Apaches. But Kit Carson (who was serving here at the time) told his men, to his eternal credit, to disregard the order and even to refuse to obey it."

Davy Watson nodded solemnly. "Ol' Kit's a man who respects life."

"There are some left, thank God," his host replied. "The Confederates, who controlled this area for a time at the beginning of the war, also attempted to exterminate the Apaches."

Davy shook his head. "That don't make fer a heap of trust," he muttered.

"No, it certainly does not," agreed Duppa, as he leaned over to refill Davy Watson's brandy snifter. "So consequently, the Apaches have little love for the 'White-eyes,' as they call us, and even less for the Mexicans, who used to send scalp-hunters out after them. In fact, there are still a number of bounty hunters about in the territory. Dangerous men they are, whose company is to be shunned; cold-blooded killers, whose allegiance goes invariably to the highest bidder."

"You folks sure got your hands full, in these parts," remarked Davy.

Darrel Duppa nodded as he smiled wanly. "Yes," he agreed. "And to top it off, I've just heard that some reckless fools are searching for the Dutchman's gold mine on Superstition Mountain, which will be sure to drive the Chiricahua Apaches absolutely insane."

"You sure hear a heap about Apaches in these

parts, Mister Duppa."

"Let that be the full extent of your acquaintance with the subject, Mr. Watson," the Englishman told him in a low voice. "Pray that you never run across them in the flesh."

Davy looked up suddenly as Duppa's attractive housekeeper held the tin coffee pot over his mug. She gave him an inquiring look, smiling what seemed to him to be a smile of invitation.

"By George, Mr. Watson," Darrel Duppa cried out merrily, "I do believe the lass fancies you. Isn't that so, Consuela?"

As she turned and left the room, the young woman was smiling.

Davy looked from the departing housekeeper to the English aristocrat. "S'posin' she does fancy me, Mr. Duppa," he said. "Jus' what can I do about it?"

Soaring Hawk was walking along the *zanja madre*, near the center of Phoenix, when he made out a cloud of dust in the gathering twilight, a cloud that heralded the approach of a band of horsemen. And as the riders came into sight, the sharp-eyed Pawnee observed two Indians, surrounded by a group of eight white men.

The Indians were of a type that Soaring Hawk had never encountered before. They had round heads, broad cheekbones, fine, straight noses and dark eyes that burned like coals. Their skins were tanned to a deep bronze, and their long, black hair was lustrous. Both of the Indians were dressed almost identically, wearing bright headbands, cotton shirts, loincloths, leggings and leather moccasins. Both were short and muscular, with thick necks, broad shoulders, and the legs of men accustomed to running great distances.

As the riders walked their horses up to the adobe buildings at the center of Phoenix, a crowd began to form around the spot whcre Soaring Hawk stood watching the procession. And by the time that the riders dismounted and began to lead the prisoners, who were shackled hand and foot, toward the jailhouse, the brave was in the front row of onlookers.

"Land sakes," an old man behind Soaring Hawk muttered. "Ain't that Paul Hutzelman a-leadin' them two Apache bucks?"

"Reckon so," replied his companion, an even older man. "Brung in some Injuns alive, fer a change."

"Yup," agreed the first old man. "That ain't his custom. He don't usually tote back nothin' more'n a brace of scalps."

"Well, looky there, an' you'll see why Hutzelman didn't bring him back no scalps this time out. See there, he got ol' Delbert Palmer, the territorial marshal, with him.

"Yup," agreed the other. "An' Delbert was probably under orders to bring them Apaches back in one piece."

"Shore 'nuf," affirmed the second old man in turn. "'Cause that Paul Hutzelman's 'bout the meanest, sneakiest, most bushwhackin' sum'bitch in these parts. He don't never bother to bring back no prisoners, if'n he can help it."

Listening to this conversation with interest, Soaring Hawk stared at the man who was the subject of discussion. Paul Hutzelman was a burly, round-shouldered man of average height, with watery blue eyes, and a red, bulbous nose, and a thin slit of a mouth.

The man grasped the end of a length of chain in each hand, as he led the shackled Apache prisoners into the heart of Phoenix. The bounty hunter walked at a rapid clip, followed closely by the seven men who attended him, all of them cradling Winchester or Sharps rifles in their arms.

Hampered by their shackles, the captives struggled with great difficulty to keep up with Hutzelman. But despite the ignominy of their present circumstances, the bearing of each Apache reflected an innate dignity.

"Stop draggin' yer feet, ya red dogs!" Hutzelman roared, tugging fiercely on the chains that he held in his hands. "Keep up with me, or by God, I'll string the pair of you up to the nearest cottonwood!"

He tugged at the chains again, sending the two Apaches sprawling face-down in the dust of the unpaved street.

Jeers and cat-calls arose from the crowd.

"Drag them thievin' Apaches through town until their hides is rubbed raw!" a young woman beside Soaring Hawk cried out.

"This here's white man's land, now," bellowed a basso at the rear of the crowd. "It's high time we taught them savages a lesson!"

"There's only one kind of Injun you can live with," croaked an old man. "An' that's a dead 'un!"

The foremost Apache struggled to his feet and gave a hard, sudden tug on the length of chain that connected him with Hutzelman. Caught by surprise, the bounty hunter cried out and spun around, his left arm twisted behind his neck.

Dropping the chain, Hutzelman pivotted, stepped in, and lashed out at the offending Apache with his fist, driving the Indian down to his knees in the dust. Then, as the dazed prisoner shook his head to clear it, Hutzelman drew back his booted foot and prepared to kick the man.

"Simmer down, Paul," one of the men flanking the prisoners called out in a flat, nasal voice. "I mean to bring in two able-bodied Apaches—not no piles of walkin' chop meat."

"Delbert, you seen what that red bastard done to me," Hutzelman growled. "Now, I'm goin' to teach him a lesson in respect."

"Sorry, Paul," the man said, just as Soaring Hawk noticed the star on his chest. "I can't let you do that. Jus' simmer down."

Then, just as the bounty hunter made an angry face and turned away from the territorial marshal, the fallen Apache raised his head and looked up, his eyes meeting those of Soaring Hawk.

A current of electricity passed between the two men, as they stared at each other, Indian to Indian, and man to man. The Apache had fierce, deep-set eyes, dark, leathery skin and a bulldog jaw. Soaring Hawk's eyes narrowed as he attempted to decipher what he had seen in the man's eyes.

"All right, Delbert," the bounty hunter grunted. "Have it your own way." Then he bent over and picked up the lengths of chain that he had dropped earlier, grasping each one firmly as he prepared to lead the Apaches off.

The Apache's penetrating eyes flashed once more as he got to his feet. Then he looked away, raised his head proudly in the air, and strode off behind Hutzelman.

The prisoners were taken into the largest of the adobe buildings. Once the door had closed behind the captives, the crowd began to disperse. Soon the dusty street was silent in the gathering dusk, empty except for a lone figure that stood and stared at the building into which the two Apaches had disappeared.

Davy Watson spent little time thinking about his blood-brother that night, for he passed it in the arms of the dark-eyed Mexican girl who had smiled so invitingly at Darrel Duppa's table.

Her name was Consuela Delgado, and she hailed from the Mexican border state of Sonora. Once again that day the subject of the Apaches came up, as the young woman told Davy that they had made her a widow, not so long ago, at the age of twenty-two.

She had moved with her husband, and both their families, to a border settlement near the Rio Grande, just below the southwestern edge of the New Mexico Territory. There they had struggled with the land for several years, and had just begun to achieve a measure of prosperity. But one day, sweeping down upon the rancho with all the sudden fury of a flash flood, a band of Apaches attacked.

Having taken the initiative in the battle which ensued, and making the most of the element of surprise, the Apaches made short work of the Mexican defenders, and it was not long before all of the men at the rancho were either dead or seriously wounded. Cradled in Davy Watson's arms as she sipped the brandy of her homeland,

Consuela told the young Kansan in a small, sad voice that her husband had been killed and scalped before her very eyes.

"It was done by the one called Geronimo," she whispered, hatred causing her voice to go suddenly hard. "He hate *Mexicanos* more than all other Apache."

After the slaughter, Consuela went on, the Apaches had looted the rancho, rounded up all its horses, and then ridden off as swiftly as they had come. The women and children were spared, but not a single man had been left alive . . . not even Consuela's seventy-six year-old father.

Davy recalled what Duppa had told him at the dinner table. "The Apaches were devious and cruel, even among themselves. But they were no match for the Spanish. The *conquistadores*—as well as many of the Catholic priests who accompanied them—were the most ruthless and greedy lot ever to set foot upon this continent. In order to survive, the Apaches of the sixteenth century divided themselves up into little bands and took to the mountains. And as a result of that move, today they are the best raiders and hit-and-run fighters in the world. They come and go like shadows, and are able to live off the land indefinitely."

Consuela's female relatives had gone back to the poverty of their former lives in the crowded south, the young *Mexicana* went on, snuggling up within Davy Watson's arms. But she, being of an independent cast of mind, headed north, into *Yanqui* country.

"You know why this Geronimo fella hates your people so much?" Davy asked Consuela.

She shook her head.

From what Duppa had told him earlier, Davy learned that the Mexican government had never been able to put a stop to the depredations of the Apaches. They had, as did the *gringos* to the north, occupied lands that the Apaches had considered theirs since time beyond memory; and therefore the Indians, who had adopted the lifestyle of nomadic warriors over the centuries, thought it only proper to plunder those intruding frontier settlements.

The Mexican cavalry was regularly dispatched in reprisal, but the elusive invaders would generally head back into the territory of the United States. Plagued by this ever-present menace on its frontier, the Mexican government had recourse to a number of extremely vicious methods in its attempt to rid the country of the Apaches. Of all these harsh and desperate methods, the most notorious was scalp-hunting.

A bounty was paid for each Apache scalp, regardless of where it had come from—the head of man, woman or child. Scalp hunters were recruited from among the ranks of the border desperadoes, many of them gringos from the north. While productive of scalps, the scheme was finally halted when the Mexican government became aware that the grisly tokens of extermination often came not from Apache men, women and children, but from Mexican men, women and children. At the present time, by the terms of the treaty signed at the end of the war with the United States, the responsibility for the pacification of the Apaches had devolved to the gringos.

"They sound like real devils," Davy whispered in Consuela's ear, as he drew her down onto his

47

bed.

"They are," she agreed. "*Diablos colorados*. Red devils. Do you know what the name Apache means?"

Davy kissed her neck and then whispered, "No. What?"

"It comes from the language of the Zuñi Indians. 'Apache' means enemy."

"Well, that may be," Davy Watson whispered in Consuela's ear, as he ran his fingers over the silken smoothness of the insides of her thighs. "But you'n me's friends, ain't we honey?"

"*Si, querido*," she whispered back, turning to Davy and brushing his lips with hers.

She was an extremely beautiful woman: Davy had realized that from the very first instant he'd set eyes on her. But just *how* beautiful he was not to imagine until, with a becoming mixture of shyness and grace, Consuela Delgado stepped out of her clothes and stood naked before him in the lamplight.

The flame of the kerosene lamp spluttered as it danced on its wick, making a sound that reminded the young Kansan of a moth drumming its wings against a screen door on a hot summer's night. It cast a gentle, wavering light upon the naked, statuesque body of the young woman before him, taking his breath away as the shifting levels of illumination continually revealed new and bewitching aspects of the young *Mexicana's* beauty.

She had straight hair that fell to the small of her back, hair as black as the obsidian blade of an Aztec sacrificial knife. Her face was a long, delicate oval, framing dark eyes and features that partook of the best of both sides of the Mexican heritage, Indian and Spanish alike. Her limbs were long and slender, with a dancer's muscle tone. Her firm flanks swelled gently at the hips, which were themselves surmounted by a supple, narrow waist. Above the upward curve of that palm tree waist, past her rib cage, there appeared the sudden, full swell of her breasts, their dark nipples contrasting with the rich, caramel color of her skin.

Gleaming as they reflected the lamplight, the *Mexicana's* dark eyes were set off by her bright smile. As he pulled her down toward him, Davy Watson felt the nails of her long, tapered fingers grazing his skin, as they travelled through the dense hair on his chest. Then he felt his nipples come erect, as her fingers lightly ran over them.

Consuela leaned forward, her lips parting as she did. An instant later their mouths had met, and their questing tongues were darting toward one another in an ardent, salamandrine dance of courtship.

Davy's hand travelled up Consuela's thigh, stroked the basin formed where it joined to her pelvis, and then brushed the full, pouting nether lips, ruffling the thick black thatch that so abundantly covered her mount of Venus.

"*Ay, querido*," she gasped, as Davy stroked the fires of her passion.

His fingers seemed to have a life of their own, and as his hand travelled over Consuela's trembling body, the changes in texture and shape thrilled him as if he were a blind explorer. His hand went up from her thick pubic hair, up to the firm and gentle rounding of her slim belly. Then up again, over her ribcage, which rose and fell to the tempo of her growing arousal; up to her breast, whose warmth and firmness excited Davy even further. He sighed and closed his eyes as he felt her long, thick nipple grow erect between his fingers.

"*Dah-veed,*" Consuela sighed, after she had drawn back her head and taken her lips from his. Then she hovered above him like an angel on a Spanish alterpiece, an angel of Latin passion and mystery, gazing down with narrowed, feline eyes at his handsome, square-jawed face.

She shifted her weight to her left hand, and with her right traced a course down his chest and over his belly, until it came to his groin, where she stroked his throbbing rod from head to root, tenderly cupped and squeezed his balls, and then made him moan like a worked-up bobcat as she grazed his perineum with her long fingernails.

"Oooh," Davy murmured, as Consuela's warm fingers suddenly encircled the shaft of his sex in a firm, velvet grip. She leaned toward him once more, and they kissed, their tongues dancing to the measure that she beat on his instrument of pleasure.

"*Te quiero,*" she murmured after their kiss had ended, giving voice to her passion in the tongue of her people. "*Te quiero mucho.*"

Davy Watson understood no Spanish, but Consuela's supple body translated her desire and willingness into a language common to all men and women. His rod throbbing and swollen with the heat of his desire, the young Kansan felt a churning in the pit of his groin, a stirring that was the harbinger of the volcanic eruption to come.

Moving his hand down to Consuela's narrow waist, Davy applied a gentle pressure, one that communicated his desire to roll her off him and onto her back.

After one final and lingering kiss, the lovely *Mexicana* responded willingly, rolling over on her back and artfully sliding into position beneath him as he rose above her. Then, as his shadow fell over her trembling body, Consuela parted her thighs and reached out her hand, narrowing her eyes and smiling an Aztec smile as she did.

Davy snorted like a stallion when he felt her fingers encircle his shaft once more, and he drew back gently, taking his weight on his forearms as she guided him into the sweet, musky grotto that lay between her thighs. And he snorted a second time, like a young stallion catching scent of an aroused mare, as he began to enter her. He felt an initial tightness, an instant of resistance, which eased a moment later, as her fluids facilitated his passage, and he penetrated her as smoothly as a mole snugs into its burrow.

"*Dios!*" the Mexican beauty gasped as Davy Watson entered her to his full length, the impact of their suddenly butted pelvises stilling her voice and closing her eyes as she smiled a blind, instinctual smile of pleasure.

Then he withdrew . . . slowly, evenly, until only the head of his sex was gripped by her snug pussy. Then, back inside her again. *In . . . and out. Back . . . and forth.* Slowly he stroked, as slowly and evenly as he possibly could, running the length of his shaft, hearing her groan each time he did, lulling her into a sense of regularity and predictable security.

Then—after a number of even strokes—a sudden, swift lunge that sent him deep inside her, abruptly butting their groins and lightly smacking his balls against her squirming flesh.

"*Oh, Dios mio!*" she cried suddenly, arching her back as she strained to rub her groin against his.

Then back to the long, slow strokes for Davy, until he broke the lulling rhythm once more to rock the young beauty with another deep and rapid thrust, causing her tensed thighs to quiver, and eliciting a moan that originated somewhere in the depths of her being.

Occasionally, Davy would alternate several darting, shallow strokes with a deep and aggressive lunge, after which he would lie against Consuela's shuddering body, his groin fused to hers, their tongues dancing as their midsections ground one against the other, as the mortar grinds against the pestle.

Suddenly, David heard Consuela catch her breath. Then he felt her body begin to twitch. Soon it was jerking uncontrollably, as she surrendered her consciousness to the overwhelming, oceanic swell of her approaching orgasm.

"*Santa Maria!*" she gasped, her pelvis hooking spasmodically toward Davy's, as he began to quicken and intensify his strokes. "*Dios mio! Mi corazon! Oh! Ooh! Ai-i-i-eeeee!*"

Gasping himself by now, Davy Watson looked down and saw that Consuela Delgado's beautiful face was swollen with passion, that her full lips were parted and her tongue was protruding, her mouth set in the rictus of self-forgetfulness, as her insticts assumed full control of the *Mexicana's* beautiful body.

Then he had no more time in which to contemplate the passion transformation, as a sudden catch in his groin caused his own pelvis to buck. Pressure and congestion were what he felt in the crucible of his loins as his climax approached, burning his thoughts away as a prairie fire consumes the sagebrush.

Davy Watson cried out as he came, feeling a sudden, fiery rush through body and mind alike, feeling himself slide into the primal darkness that lay just below the thin mantle of his waking consciousness.

Together the lovers bucked and shuddered, tossed like rag dolls in a Kansas twister, helpless in the maelstrom of their passion.

"God! God!" he cried, his voice coming from a place deep within the temple of his body.

"Dios!" she cried, worshipping the same power in a different tongue.

When it was over, they lay like children in each other's arms, hugging and kissing gently.

And then, spent by the intensity of their passion and the depth of their feelings, their limbs still entwined, the sweat of their bodies mingling like the freshets that run down from Superstition Mountain in the spring, they fell asleep.

The fierce-eyed Apache whom the bounty Hunter, Hutzelman, had cuffed to the ground sat bolt-upright in his cell in the adobe jailhouse, while the two guards beyond the bars dozed fitfully in their chairs. The night outside was still, and only the spluttering of the kerosene lamp's wick could be heard as it washed the room in wavering alternations of light and shadow. The second Apache was at the rear of the cell, squatting on the floor, knees drawn up and back against the bars, fast asleep.

While his features were set in such a way that they gave the appearance of having been carved out of the quartz of the Chiricahua Mountains, the first Apache's darting brown eyes were rarely at rest, reflecting the intense activity of the mind that directed them. He had been sitting in this fashion for many hours, and many possibilities had been explored . . . and as many rejected. The enemy had him fast; escape seemed impossible this time. His dark eyes narrowed as the Apache thought of the way that Mangas Coloradas had met his end at the hand of the White-eyes.

A sudden tapping on the jailhouse door interrupted the prisoner's bitter reverie. The dozing guards stirred in their chairs, but neither of them opened his eyes. The Indian's own fierce eyes darted from the guards to the door.

Tap-tap-tap-tap.

"God A'mighty," one of the guards, a tubby man in a weathered brown Stetson grumbled. "Who is it?" he called out.

There was no answer.

Tap-tap-tap-tap. The persistent knocking sounded again on the ironwood door.

"Shit, whose turn is it?" the tubby guard muttered, shifting uncomfortably in his seat.

"You know damn well whose turn it is," his fellow guard, a lanky, bearded man in overalls, told him. "Git off'n yer butt, an' see who's knockin'."

The tubby man groaned, opened his eyes, yawned, stretched and rose to his feet awkwardly. Then he picked up his shotgun and shuffled over to the door.

Across the room, from behind the bars of his cell, the Apache watched the man like a hawk.

"Who is it?" the tubby guard asked when he reached the threshold.

Again, no answer came from beyond the ironwood door.

"Speak up," grumbled the guard impatiently. "I can't hear ya."

Still no answer came.

"Land o' Goshen," the tubby man muttered, stepping aside and hefting his shotgun in his left hand while he threw open the bolt with his right. Opening wide the door, he stepped back and raised his weapon. Then, seeing no one in the doorway, he stepped forward and slowly stuck his head outside.

"Who is it?" the lanky guard asked a moment later, awakened by a scuffling sound, but not bothering to open his eyes.

Noiselessly, the fierce-eyed Apache rose, turned, and laid a hand on his sleeping companion's arm. In an instant the second brave was on his feet, looking as alert as if he had been awake all the while.

"Dammit, Earl," the lanky man grunted in a deep voice, opening his eyes as he did. "Who the hell is it?"

When no answer was forthcoming, the guard got to his feet, holding out the shotgun that had been resting upon his thighs.

"Sweet Jesus," the man grumbled. "This ain't no time to be a-playin' kiddie games, Earl. Now, I *know* it can't be time for them to fetch us our breakfasts."

Holding his shotgun at the ready, the guard slowly stepped out through the doorway, into the dark, open night of Arizona.

From their cell, the two Apaches watched him intently.

"Where the hell are ya?" the lanky guard asked, after having looked both left and right.

His query was greeted by silence.

"Earl, I'm gonna kick your big fat butt," the guard muttered as he turned to his left and began to walk around the side of the jailhouse.

The moment that he was out of sight, the two Apaches exchanged meaningful looks and got to their feet. And both nodded in confirmation a moment later, as they heard the unmistakable sound of a body hitting the ground.

A second after that, they made out a sound which was virtually imperceptible to white men: the gentle scuffing of leather moccasins against packed earth.

The fierce-eyed Apache smiled a tight, grim smile as Soaring Hawk appeared in the doorway. And when the Pawnee stepped inside the jailhouse, the light from the kerosene lamps glittered on the ring of keys that he held in his hand.

A moment later, the Plains Indian was at the door of the cell, trying to fit the proper key into its lock. And when the lock clicked open, the fierce-eyed Apache smiled a smile of wolfish exultation.

Soaring Hawk stepped back as he swung the cell door open. The two Apaches came out and made a bee-line for the gun rack that stood by the wall to the left of the cell. Seeing that the rack was locked, the fierce-eyed man turned and gestured for Soaring Hawk to give him the ring of keys.

The Pawnee walked across the room and handed the keys to the Apache. A moment later the rack had been unlocked, and the Apaches had removed two Winchester carbines from it. The first Apache turned to Soaring Hawk, holding out his rifle, offering it to the Plains Indian. But the brave shook his head and then pointed toward the door, indicating that the prisoners should flee.

The Apaches nodded as they went over to a desk by the door, and went through its drawers until they came across several boxes of cartridges. Then they proceeded to load the Winchesters, after which they stuffed their shirt pockets with the remaining cartridges.

Then the fierce-eyed Apache straightened up, staring into the Pawnee's eyes, after which he made a curt gesture with his head, indicating that he wished Soaring Hawk to accompany him outside the jailhouse.

Two clicks sounded in the quiet room, as the Apaches worked the levers of their Winchesters, sending cartridges into the receivers of those weapons. Then, rifles held at the ready, they ducked out into the night.

The moon shone brightly overhead, and there was a chill in the air. The Apaches looked around in all directions as they filled their lungs with the dry air of Arizona. Seeing two horses tied to the hitching post outside the jailhouse, the first Apache smiled his wolfish smile once more.

Soaring Hawk accompanied the two braves over to the hitching post and watched them untie and mount the horses. After that, he stepped back and looked up into the eyes of the first Apache.

The man spoke to Soaring Hawk in the Apache

tongue. The Pawnee shook his head.

Next, the Apache tried Spanish. Again his deliverer shook his head.

The Apache frowned and shook his own head. Then he expressed his gratitude to Soaring Hawk in sign language, through a series of eloquent and graceful gestures.

Understanding the man at last, the Pawnee nodded and smiled. Then he reached out his hand, drew it slowly toward his body and placed it upon his chest, pointing at himself with a finger of the other.

"Soaring Hawk," he said slowly. "Soaring Hawk. Pawnee."

The fierce man's eyes glittered in the moonlight as he nodded his head. "Soaring Hawk," he said slowly. "Soaring Hawk. Pawnee."

Davy Watson's blood-brother smiled at the Apache.

"Nah-kah-yen," the other said, indicating his mounted companion. "Apache."

"Nah-kah-yen," Soaring Hawk repeated. "Apache."

The first brave nodded. Then he flashed the Pawnee a bright smile and pointed to himself.

"Geronimo," he told Soaring Hawk. "Apache."

The Pawnee was about to repeat this when a sound in the night interrupted him.

He wheeled around in the direction of the sound, suddenly recoiling and shielding his eyes as a door opened across the street and a bright light flared in the darkness.

Several men's silhouettes could be seen in the doorway of the adobe house across the street from the jail, as they began to file out into the street, following a man who held a kerosene lamp.

An instant later, as Soaring Hawk blinded his eyes and focused on the men, the Pawnee heard the sudden crack of rifles, as the Apaches began firing at the newcomers.

Two of the men fell to the ground, one crying out in a shrill voice that he had been shot. The others immediately ducked back inside the building and slammed the door shut behind them.

Soaring Hawk cast an alarmed glance up at the fierce-eyed man, as the other lowered his rifle. The Apache narrowed his eyes and nodded, as if in answer to some unspoken question. Then, reaching down from his horse, he held out his hand to Soaring Hawk. The Pawnee grasped it and swung himself up on the back of the horse, behind the man who called himself Geronimo.

A moment later, the three Indians rode out of the settlement which Darrel Duppa had christened Phoenix, and disappeared into the sheltering night.

Chapter Two

When Davy Watson awoke, he was still in the embrace of the beautiful *Mexicana*. He had suddenly been awakened by the sounds of men's voices—harsh, angry voices, and it took him a moment to realize that what he had heard came not from the depths of a dream, but from grim reality.

The voices of men were raised in anger just beyond the bedroom which harbored Davy and Consuela Delgado. Darrel Duppa's voice was to be heard as well, as Davy's host attempted to exert a calming influence upon the angry mob that had gathered before the door to his house.

"It's no use stallin' us, Darrel," a gruff voice called out. "We know the other one's in there. We want the varmint."

"Gentlemen, gentlemen," the Englishman called out over the angry rumble of the crowd, "let us not be hasty. Let us gather together the facts of the matter at hand—before we do something rash."

"Give way, Darrel," another voice rang out in the darkness outside, as Davy Watson saw that the moon was still in the sky. "We aim to take that dirty dog."

Consuela awoke with a start, sitting up in the bed beside Davy and looking around with wide, frightened eyes. He put his arm around her shoulder and hugged Consuela reassuringly. She leaned against him, shivering, and whispered in his ear.

"I had a dream. The Apaches came out from caves and *barrancas*—killing and burning. And then it began to rain . . . but as the rain came down and fell upon the ground, it turned red as blood." She moaned and lay her head upon Davy's chest.

"It's all right, Consuela," he whispered, stroking her long black hair. "It's all right. But they's a heap of folks a-gatherin' outside Lord Darrel's door, an' each one of 'em's madder'n a hornet."

"Give way, Darrel," some outside growled menacingly.

" 'Pears they're after someone who's stayin' here with Mr. Duppa," Davy told Consuela. "Who else is in the house?"

She looked up at him uncomprehendingly.

"What other guests are in the house?" he asked once more.

"You and your friend are the only guests," Consuela whispered back, a frightened look coming to her face once again.

Davy felt the hairs stand on the nape of his neck as he suddenly realized whom the angry men outside had come for.

"Judas Priest!" he exclaimed, springing out of bed and fumbling in the dark for his trousers.

"Davy—what is it?"

"Damned if I know," the young Kansan grunted, pulling on the denim work pants he had purchased at the emporium of the San Francisco clothing merchant, Levi Strauss. "But I'm gettin' a funny feelin' that them boys has come fer me."

The men outside roared in unison, and Davy heard Darrel Duppa cry out in anger and

61

frustration. Then he heard the sound of bootheels and the tread of feet in the hallway beyond the bedroom. Davy turned pale as he went for his gunbelt, which hung over the post at the foot of the bed.

Crash! The door to the room burst open suddenly, causing Davy to stop dead in his tracks.

"Git away from that gun, boy," someone called out from the hall. "Or I'll cut ya in half."

Davy stared into the darkness beyond the doorway and felt his skin crawl, as the dark, gaping barrels of a shotgun were suddenly highlighted by the moon that shone in through the window behind him. He knew, indeed, that at close range, a blast from the man's double-barreled shotgun would tear him apart. He sighed and slowly raised his hands in the air, resigning himself to the fact that he would not be able to defend himself if the mob got out of hand. He would be at their mercy, but there was nothing he could do about it.

As he stood there, helpless and frightened in the face of the angry mob, Davy recalled the words of the prayer that he said each day when he first awoke.

God grant me the serenity to accept the things I cannot change, the courage to change the things I can, and the wisdom to know the difference.

By the time that he had concluded the silent prayer, the room was filled with angry and suspicious men, all of them carrying rifles or pistols.

"Dash it all, Hutzelman—you can't go barging into a man's home like this!" Darrel Duppa said sharply as he fought his way through the crowd and went up to the red-faced man who stood beside the fellow who held a shotgun trained on Davy Watson's midsection.

The man Duppa had addressed lowered his Winchester and turned to smile at the Englishman. "Well, I'm right sorry about that, yer lordship," he replied with heavy sarcasm. "But it jus' so happens that you're harboring a criminal."

"That's utter rot, Hutzelman!" Duppa shot back angrily. "Mister Watson's been here all night."

"What about the Injun with him?" the bounty hunter asked, still smirking at the Englishman.

"Why, ah, his room is right down the hall," Duppa replied, suddenly growing uneasy as he realized that Soaring Hawk was nowhere to be seen.

"Take a look-see, Sims," Hutzelman told one of the men behind him.

Davy Watson caught his breath as he speculated upon the mysterious absence of his blood-brother. He caught Darrel Duppa's eye, and they exchanged anxious looks.

"They ain't nary a soul in there, Paul," the man called Sims informed Hutzelman when he had returned from Soaring Hawk's room.

"Funny thing, yer lordship," the bounty hunter said, after casting a cold eye upon Davy Watson. "But ain't it curious that some strange-lookin' Injun frees the Apaches an' then rides outta town with them . . . an' *your* strange-lookin' Injun jus' happens to be missin'? Now, ain't that odd?"

Duppa's jaw dropped at this.

"What happened?" Davy asked in a hoarse whisper.

"Your Injun pal freed them two Apaches we done brung in earlier, boy," the bounty hunter told him through a frosty smile. "One of them prisoners was Geronimo, who's just 'bout the nastiest little bastard of 'em all, in case you didn't know. Two of our boys was plugged by the Apaches." His smile fadded. "One of 'em's dead. . . . An' we owe it all to yer Injun friend."

"Now, hold on a minute," Davy said as he lowered his hands and stepped forward.

"You're in big trouble, boy," the bounty hunter told Davy in a voice that chilled his blood.

The young Kansan blinked his eyes, suddenly confused as the meaning of what the bounty hunter had just told him began to make itself felt. He had heard much about the Apaches and their savagery ever since he had ridden into the Arizona Territory. *Why had Soaring Hawk freed those two prisoners? Why had he become involved with the sworn enemies of the white man?*

"Listen, Mister," he said, raising his open hands as he started toward the bounty hunter, "let me try to find Soaring Hawk. I'm sure I—"

Davy's words were cut off abruptly, as one of the men who stood beside Darrel Duppa and Hutzelman brought the butt of his rifle down upon the base of the young Kansan's skull. The last thing that Davy Watson heard was Consuela Delgado's scream. . . .

Southward the three fugitives rode, all night and through the morning, Soaring Hawk seated on a roan stallion, behind the brave called Geronimo, as they made their way into Apache territory.

When they finally stopped to rest it was late

morning, and the bright sun of Arizona stood high in the sky. Having reached the foothills of the Chiricahua Mountains, the Apaches dismounted and led their horses into the cool shade of an overhanging rock ledge.

Soaring Hawk, dismounted, took to the shade, and looked on as the brave known as Nah-kah-yen tended to the horses while Geronimo threaded his way past boulders and *barrancas* until he came to a large cactus plant. Then, drawing out his knife, the Apache proceeded to cut into the cactus. A few moments later, he returned with sections of the plant which had been cut from its tender insides, and offered them to his companions.

Soaring Hawk looked down at the cactus, and saw that a clear liquid was contained with the bowl-shaped section of the plant. Geronimo said something in Apache, and the Pawnee looked up to see the Indian drink from the cactus section that he held in his hands. He looked to Nah-kah-yen, and saw that he did the same.

Soaring Hawk promptly followed suit, and found the juice of the cactus refreshing and not at all unpleasant to the taste. "It is good," he told the Apaches in the Pawnee tongue.

Geronimo wiped his lips and then smiled at Davy Watson's blood-brother, his dark eyes twinkling as he spoke to Nah-kah-yen in Apache.

"Geronimo asks if Soaring Hawk the Pawnee speak the tongue of white man," the brave informed him in English.

Soaring Hawk nodded, his eyes meeting those of Geronimo, as the latter spoke again.

"He say you look different from all Indian he ever see," translated Nah-kah-yen. "He want know where Soaring Hawk come from, where his people live."

The Pawnee looked up at the sun, shielding his eyes as he got his bearings.

"Many days ride to the north," he told Nah-kah-yen. "And many more to the east. That is where my people live. They ride the great plains and hunt the sacred buffalo, who provides for all our needs."

Soaring Hawk noticed a look of puzzlement spreading over Geronimo's face while the Apache listened to the translation of his words.

"What is buffalo?" was the translation of Geronimo's next question, the Chiricahua Apaches never having laid eyes on the beasts.

"It is big, like bull," Soaring Hawk answered. "And hairy, like bear. Its meat and fat nourish my people. Its hide clothes us, and makes our tents."

Geronimo then asked Soaring Hawk about his tent, and the Pawnee described the construction of a teepee. The Apache, in turn, explained about hogans and wickiups. Soaring Hawk was much impressed by Geronimo's curiosity and keen, probing intelligence.

"My people hunt the buffalo, and some of the time they work the land," the Pawnee informed the Apaches. "What do your people do?"

Geronimo nodded solemnly as he listened to this. "Our people go to war," he said. "We take whatever we need . . . from anyone—Indian, Mexican or gringo. An Apache hunts if he must, but he never works." Nah-kah-yen nodded emphatically in agreement with this statement. "Work is for women."

"Do the Apache take scalps?" asked Soaring

Hawk.

"Does the rain fall on the mountains?" Geronimo's smile was bright, in contrast to his deeply bronzed skin. "It is our way. We have many enemies. Sometimes we even go on the warpath against other Apaches."

"Why were you in chains?" the Pawnee asked Geronimo. "What did you do?"

The Apache's eyes narrowed. "We were tricked," he said in a low, cold voice. "The Indian agent at the Fort Burnside reservation promised us many horses, many blankets, and much food for the winter, if we would stop raiding the white settlements on the Salt and Gila Rivers. We thought that man spoke the truth, that he was a friend to the Apaches." Geronimo and Nah-kah-yen exchanged scornful looks.

"Cochise had told me to say that only if the whites gave up their settlements near the Chiricahua Mountains," Geronimo continued, "would we agree to this. The Indian agent agreed to this condition, in the name of the white chief in Prescott. But when we went to smoke on it, he betrayed me to a bounty hunter," his face contorted with anger at the recollection, "a great enemy of our people, a man who has collected many Apache scalps for the Mexican chiefs."

"What will your people do now?" Soaring Hawk asked Geronimo.

"We will go to war," the fierce-eyed brave replied, eliciting a nod of agreement from Nah-kah-yen. "We will show no mercy. We will kill many white men. We will drive the White-eyes from our lands, once and for all."

Geronimo rose to his feet. "We have rested long

enough," he said, walking over to the horses. "It is time we rode up into the mountains."

"Were are we going?" asked the Pawnee.

"To the camp of the great chief, Cochise," was Geronimo's terse reply.

When Davy Watson regained consciousness, the strange perspective which greeted his eyes and the jolting motion that he felt in the pit of his stomach brought him the startling revelation that he was lying across the back of a horse.

His head pounded like a hammer on a blacksmith's anvil when he raised it and attempted to look around, and Davy saw that he was slung across the back of his own horse, riding in the midst of a large band of horsemen, every man-jack of them armed to the teeth. The sun was high overhead, and the chill of morning had already been baked out of the desert.

"He's comin' 'round, Paul," a froggy voice called out at Davy's left.

"Well, so he is," the young Kansan heard the man called Hutzelman reply. "Fer a while there, I done thought you stove in his skull, Martin."

"Oh, t'warn't that serious," the gruff-voiced man said. "I've got so's I can feel it when I whop somebody over the head. When you stove in their skulls, you can sorta feel things give. But this lad here's got him a head like a granite boulder."

"Say," grunted Davy. "How 'bout untyin' me, so's I can sit to horse proper-like."

"What about it, Paul?" the man asked. "Do you trust the whippersnapper?"

"Shore I trust him," the bounty hunter replied cheerfully. "An' if'n he goes ahead an' abuses this trust of mine, why, I'll jus' blow his kneecaps off, an' leave him to bleed to death out here in the middle of nowheres. Go 'head, untie 'im.''

Once Hutzelman had said this, two of the horsemen rode over to Davy Watson and proceeded to untie his hands and feet.

The young Kansan winced as he swung himself up into the saddle; his head began to throb painfully, reminding him of the blow from the gun butt that he had taken in the bedroom of Darrel Duppa's house.

Next, he straightened up in the saddle as he remembered the last sound that had reached his ears before he lost consciousness: Consuela Delgado's scream. During the time they had spent together, Davy and the *Mexicana* had become intimate in more than one way, having shared confidences and hope, as well as their flesh.

He shook his head and looked around, pressing his knees into the sides of his horse, gently guiding it over to the side of Hutzelman's mount. The sun had begun to come up on Davy's left hand, revealing the flat, arid landscape ahead, its brown monotony broken occasionally by dots of cactus or creosote. In the distance, Davy made out the bed of a dry river.

"What about Consuela Delgado?" he asked, reining his horse in beside that of the bounty hunter.

Hutzelman turned to glance at Davy, an odd smirk on his face. "Oh, she's jus' fine," he said pleasantly, a sudden warmth infusing his rough baritone voice. "It's you we's got to be worryin' about, young fella."

"What d'ya mean?" Davy asked.

"Well, we're takin' you to Fort Burnside," the bounty hunter informed him. "An' soon you're gon' meet one ol' boy who'll make you wish you never done laid eyes on that purty li'l Mex."

"I don't follow you, Mister," Davy told the man, shaking his head. Then he studied Paul Hutzelman's face, marking well the cold eyes and cruel, sullen mouth.

"Oh, you'll see soon enough," was the bounty hunter's only reply.

Davy straightened up in the saddle, jolted by a surge of anger.

"Now, look here, Mister . . . whatever-your-name-is," he began, speaking in a voice colored by his anger.

"Hutzelman's the name," the bounty hunter informed him quietly. "Paul Hutzelman."

"Hutzelman, then," Davy said, nearly shouting as he saw the mocking expression on the man's face. "Jus' what right have you got to go a-bustin' into Mr. Duppa's place like that, an' carryin' me off against my will?"

Hutzelman turned to Davy Watson and smiled a sharp, cruel smile. "Why, boy, you's a accessory to a crime. Didn't you know that? Your Injun buddy jus' helped two Apaches bust outta jail. An' that's a serious offense in any white man's law book. Know who your buddy cut loose?" the bounty hunter asked, pausing for emphasis after he did.

"Geronimo. That's who. Jus' the biggest Apache bad-ass of 'em all."

Davy shook his head. "I can't believe that. Soaring Hawk's a friend to the white man."

Hutzelman's smile registered his cynicism.

70

"Only time an Injun is a friend to a white man is when he a-pushin' up daisies. When he can't do nobody no more harm."

"But what have I got to do with this whole business?" Davy asked the bounty hunter.

Hutzelman shook his head. Then he began to speak very slowly, as if he were addressing a retarded child.

"Why, you're his buddy, now ain't you?" he asked softly. "Y'know, jus' bein' a Injun-lover done made you guilty already. Don't you see that, boy?"

"Injuns ain't no different from other folks," Davy shot back, glaring at the bounty hunter.

Hutzelman shook his head again. "Oh, you're gonna learn *jus' how different* they is, boy. An' it's gon' be one hard lesson. You'll see when you meet ol' Jock Forbes." He began to chuckle. "Wait 'til we get to Fort Burnside."

"Listen, Mister," Davy said, his temper flaring up in response to the man's smugness, "you ain't said shit—y'hear me? Now, I want to know what the hell's goin' on around here!"

"Boy," the bounty hunter said softly, in a small, cold voice that was barely more than a whisper, "you keep on raggin' me like that, an' I'll have one of these here gentlemen," he indicated the riders flanking them, "knock out yer teeth an' break a couple of yer bones. I reckon that's what I'm gonna have to do, less'n you show some respect."

Despite the man's bantering manner, Davy realized that he meant business. And when he looked from side to side, the young Kansan saw that the other riders were all glaring at him.

71

He nodded tiredly, slumping down in his saddle. *Yup,* he told himself. *It's dollars to donuts these boys'd like nothin' better than to whale the tar out of me.*

His only course of action, Davy decided, was to bide his time. Hopefully, when the riders reached Fort Burnside, he would be able to plead his case before reasonable men.

After all, Davy thought, yawning as he stretched himself, warmed by the hot sun of Arizona, *the people at the fort are United States soldiers. They work for the government . . . an' that means that they're lookin' out for the citizens' best interests. So everything's gonna be all right, once't we get to the fort. . . .*

At a remote spot near one of the peaks of the range known as Superstition Mountain, within sight of the dark looming mass of rock that the old Mexicans called the Finger of God, the crisp air rang with the sounds of pickaxes chunking as they penetrated the granite body of the mountain, and the hollow, clunking sound of rocks tumbling and cracking into each other.

Three burly men in overalls and flannel shirts puffed and grunted as they wielded their pickaxes, attacking a broad shelf of rock beneath a projecting ledge of granite. At their feet lay several sizeable piles of rubble, the fruits of their labor. And beside each pile there lay a rifle.

From time to time, when the men would lower their tools, wipe their brows and step back, taking a brief respite from their mining, a fourth man, dressed in the same manner as the others, would take their place. He carried a big canvas sack with him as he began to rummage through the piles of stone. The stone was ore, and it was rich in gold concentrate; it was the fourth man's job to select and bag the most promising pieces of the mountain's yield. And once he had filled the sack, the man dragged it away, after which the three men would pick up their tools and resume work.

Apart from all this activity, a fifth man sat on a flat boulder, a Winchester cradled in his lap, watching the work with interest. He was further distinguished by his clothing, which differed from that of the other men, and indicated that he was not a man who earned his living by working with his hands. From time to time he would heft the rifle and glance nervously down the side of the mountain.

His name was Ernest Shackleton, and he was the Indian agent at the "Strip," that narrow section of land which sat under the eye and guns of Fort Burnside, and had been set aside to house and support the friendly Indians of the region.

On the Strip, through those center ran the Gila River, the Indians had been taught to cultivate the soil with great skill and efficiency, thereby enabling them to produce crop yields of an abundance never before seen in that arid land, yields which impressed even the agriculturally-oriented Pima Indians. But the Pimas, who had their own domain, called by the whites Pimeria, had not settled on the Strip in any appreciable numbers. However, many other Indians of the southwestern part of the Arizona Territory had come to live on the fertile Strip.

Residing on that federal reservation were Zuñis, Papagos, Maricopas, and even a number of

Apaches, who had experienced much hardship in the past decade. But the latter had been blessed by their acquaintance with Doctor Abraham Thorne, a white physician who lived among them and learned their language.

From Thorne, their medicine men learned many modern techniques, such as the setting of broken bones and the cleaning of wounds with soap and water. But the greatest by far of all his gifts had been the easement of the pains of childbirth by the judicious application of chloroform and the use of the forceps in delivery.

The doctor was one of the few white men whom the Apaches had ever trusted, their confidence in the race having been continually eroded by the betrayals perpetrated either by the Spaniards or the United States Army, or by the Arizonan settlers themselves. He lived on the Strip with those of the Chiricahua and White Mountain bands who had come to the reservation. Thorne had even been called brother by Cochise, after having delivered the great chief's favorite wife of a healthy boy, after she had lost two earlier children at birth.

In fact, Cochise and Geronimo had even spent some time on the Strip, between what had come to be known as the "Cochise Wars," those breaks in Apache-white relations which were generally engendered by duplicity or irresponsibility on the part of government representatives or the Arizonans themselves.

As fierce as the Apaches were, they had tried several times to reach an accommodation with the whites, due in part to a grudging respect for the awesome fire-and-manpower that the enemy was able to muster, the resources of the United States government being vastly greater than those of the traditional foe (along with the Comanches), Mexico.

Shackleton, the Indian agent, had worked closely with Doctor Thorne and the Apaches, and he had been highly esteemed by both parties, a thing uncommon indeed, as regards government officials. But the man was not what he seemed: beneath his veneer of compassion and concern, Shackleton was actually a cold-blooded opportunist. He chose to veil the dark side of his character with an appearance of integrity, religious piety and humanitarian idealism. The main reason for the Indian agent's pretended friendship for the Apaches was his lust for gold. Shackleton knew that the Chiricahuas held the secret of the location of the Lost Dutchman mine . . . and he intended to learn it from them one day.

Located in the heart of Superstition Mountain, in the place where the Apaches believed that their Thunder God had his abode—their holy of holies—the mine was a shelf of gold whose yield was incredibly high and of unbelievably easy access, being located virtually on the surface of the mountainside.

In the early days, the gold itself had meant nothing to the Apaches, and it had lain undisturbed until the 1840s, when it was discovered by one Don Miguel Peralta, a Mexican *ranchero*. He returned to Superstition Mountain with a force of *peones*, and began to dig for gold in earnest.

This state of affairs did not go unnoticed by the Indians, who became outraged on two counts. Not only was the dwelling of the Thunder God being violated daily, but their women were being seduced by the gay and smiling Mexicans, who gave them trinkets and sang them serenades to the accompaniment of their guitars.

One day, having realized that his men were being picked off one by one, Don Miguel loaded all the rich gold concentrate he had mined onto the backs of burros and, under the protection of an armed escort, led his company away from the gold mine.

He did not get far. The Apaches, having developed and refined the art of *guerilla* warfare, lay in wait for the departing Mexicans and massacred them. Peralta's body was never found. The ore-laden burros ran off and became lost in the inhospitable terrain, later dying of thirst. Years later, daring prospectors would occasionally come across the skeleton of one of Peralta's pack animals . . . with the gold concentrate still in the dead burro's saddlebags.

For fifteen years after the Peralta massacre, the mine had remained an Apache secret. Once during this period, the Chiricahuas had blindfolded their benefactor, Dr. Thorne, and led him to a place in the shadow of the Finger of God where they rewarded him for his many kindnesses by giving him a sack filled with gold concentrate. But other than that, no Mexican or gringo came near the mine until the "Old Dutchman" found it.

The Dutchman was Jake Walz, formerly Jacob von Walzer, a native of Westphalia and a former member of the Prussian Army. He was a trained miner, and became a prospector, quitting his native land to join the rush to California. Years later he returned to Germany, penniless and disillusioned. But it is not in the nature of prospectors to remain discouraged for long, and Walz set out for America once more, this time heading for the territory of Arizona.

He worked in several mines there for a grubstake, and was thrown out of one when he was suspected of "high-grading"—smuggling valuable ore and nuggets out of the mine in his clothing or lunchpail. It was never proved that he had done this, although several of the men who worked with him were caught and hanged by the mine owners. Several weeks later, Walz deposited a large sum of money in a bank in Prescott.

At that time, the Dutchman fell in love with a beautiful young Apache girl named Ken-Tee. She returned his love and grew devoted to him, and it was from her that Walz learned the secret of the mine on Superstition Mountain. He immediately went up into the mountains and, with Ken-Tee's help, began to haul the rich gold concentrate down to his camp in the foothills.

In this manner he amassed a considerable amount of wealth, and deposited great sums in the bank at Prescott. But the Apaches, finally taking revenge for Walz's desecretion of their holy place, raided his house one day. Finding only Ken-Tee there, they seized the young Apache girl and rode off with her.

Walz's neighbors got word of the raid, and rode off in hot pursuit of the Apaches. Realizing that the only way to avoid capture would be to free Ken-Tee, the Apaches promptly did so . . . after cutting out her tongue. An hour after she had been reunited with her lover, the beautiful young Apache died from loss of blood in Jake Walz's arms.

This broke the Dutchman's spirit, and thereafter Walz stayed away from the mine, which had already become legendary. For years after, men attempted to pry the secret of the mine out of Jake Walz. But the Dutchman was not a man to be trifled with, rumor having consequently attributed the deaths of eight potential bushwhackers to his credit.

The Lost Dutchman Mine, as it became known not only in Arizona but throughout the world, due to the newspaper journalism of the day, remained a secret for years . . . in spite of the efforts of the gold-crazed legion who sought it out.

Ernest Shackleton, the Indian agent on the Strip, was the next white man to learn the location of the fabulous mine. It was revealed to him by a dying medicine man, one Sabe Mucho, who had been a bitter rival of Dr. Thorne's. Year earlier, during a falling out with his tribe, Sabe Mucho had challenged the progressive Thorne and lost.

He would have been ostracized by his fellow Apaches, but for the intercession of Shackleton, whom the band all respected. The medicine man was deeply grateful and, several years later, when he was on his deathbed, revealed the location of the secret gold mine to his white benefactor.

Now Shackleton sat and watched anxiously, Winchester on his lap, as his men worked the Lost Dutchman mine, their presence thus far unknown to both Apache and white man. Digging for gold at the abode of the Thunder God was risky at best, the Indian agent realized. But events had taken a turn in his favor, and Shackleton felt that he had a good chance of coming away from Superstition Mountain a wealthy man. The Chiricahua Apaches were currently too preoccupied to take much notice of the goings-on at the mine. Shackleton had seen to that personally. . . . .

Chapter Three

As the horses cleared the rim of a hill, Soaring Hawk caught sight of the Apache camp. But before he did, guards had brought word of the coming of the horsemen, and the site was a-buzz with speculation as to the identity of the strange Indian who rode behind Geronimo, that mysterious brave who wore his hair in long braids and adorned it with the feathers of birds unknown to the Apaches.

The men studied Soaring Hawk's face carefully as he approached the camp, and when he dismounted they took note of the way he moved, and of the glittering, razor-sharp scalping knife that he wore on his belt.

"Oh, look," a young Apache girl whispered admiringly to the other maidens of her tribe. "See how tall and straight of limb he is!"

"And how he moves!" exclaimed another maiden in a hushed, breathy voice. "With the grace of a panther!"

"He is tall and lean," commented a third. "And handsome of face."

"And look at his bold, dark eyes," the youngest of them said in a thin, reedy voice. "I wonder if there is fire in his embrace?"

The other girls laughed.

"Be careful, lest you get burnt, little sister," one of them cautioned. "For he has the look of a fiery man."

The youngest nodded, her dark eyes suddenly flashing. "That is the fire which consumes, and then replenishes," she whispered.

"And *how* would my sister know of such things?" the other asked teasingly.

The youngest looked away shyly. "I do not know of such things personally," she said hesitantly. "Only what I have overheard. But I would learn." She closed her eyes and began to shiver at the thought of anticipated delight.

The maidens all began to laugh.

"What manner of man is this?" an old Apache asked his crony, as they stood in front of the chief's wickiup. "I have not seen his like before."

"He does not look like us," the other old man answered. "Nor like any Indian I have ever seen. He must come from far away."

The first old man nodded. "But I think it is all right that he is here. For after all, he is not of the gringos or the Na-ha-yay."

"That is well," agreed the other. "Better an Indian of any kind than those."

"He is tall and handsome," an old woman named Francisco said to her daughter, as they tended a cooking fire. "He has the look of one who would make a fine husband," she went on, scrutinizing the Pawnee with a practiced eye.

Her daughter, Cho-ko-le by name, merely blushed at this and cast down her eyes as Geronimo and Soaring Hawk strode by. But her mother noted that the young woman repeatedly glanced up at the retreating form of the handsome stranger.

"How many White-eyes do you think he has killed?" one Apache boy asked his playmate, a tone of excitement coloring his voice.

"Many, many, I bet," the other boy replied. "For look how sharp and long is the knife in his belt."

"I bet he could not kill Geronimo," the first told him.

"Nobody can kill Geronimo," the second boy replied solemnly.

The Apache wickiups were of a different shape than Pawnee teepees, and the smells coming from the cooking fires behind them were also different, Soaring Hawk realized as he came into the mountain camp. But the brave felt at home, all the same. He had developed a respect for the austere, stoical Apaches, and found them an extremely resourceful and tenacious people.

"Come here, Soaring Hawk," Geronimo said in his strange Apache accent, taking the Pawnee by the arm and leading him over to the chief's wickiup, before which there stood a cluster of Apache dignitaries.

The man who stood at the center of this assemblage was by far the most impressive-looking among them. Soaring Hawk estimated that he stood well over six feet tall. The man had broad shoulders and a frame that, despite its leanness, had the musculature of an athlete. His lustrous black hair was held in place by a scarlet headband, and he wore a fringed doeskin jacket. He had dark eyes, a high forehead, extremely wide cheekbones and a nose that was high in the bridge. He regarded the newcomer out of clear eyes that took his measure as a man.

"This is our great chief, Cochise," Geronimo told Soaring Hawk as they stood before the big man.

"Who is this stranger from far away?" Cochise asked in a deep, resonant voice.

"He is called Soaring Hawk, of the Pawnee tribe," Geronimo told his chief while Nah-kah-yen

81

whispered a translation of his words into Soaring Hawk's ear. "But," the fierce-looking little man went on in his gruff voice, "I call him Brother, for he saved my life, and the life of Nah-kah-yen, as well."

The chief's eyes widened almost imperceptibly, in the sole register of his surprise.

"I was betrayed into the hands of the White-eyes," Geronimo went on, "betrayed by one who calls himself our friend: Shackleton, the Indian agent."

"Why did he do this thing?" asked Cochise, his face darkening like a stormcloud.

Geronimo shook his head. "I do not know. He sent word for me to meet him at Blanco Canyon, where he would smoke on our treaty with the white chief in Prescott. But when I got there I did not find Shackleton. Suddenly, Nah-kah-yen and I were surrounded by many White-eyes with rifles, led by the one called Hut-zel-man."

Cochise's deep voice rumbled angrily within his deep chest. Then he uttered something in Apache, spitting on the ground immediately afterward.

"What does Cochise say in such anger?" Soaring Hawk whispered to Nah-kah-yen.

"Killer-of-Apaches is what the chief said," the translator told Soaring Hawk. "That is the name given to our great enemy, the bounty hunter, Hut-zel-man. He has taken many Apache scalps in the last twenty years, both for the Mexicans and the White-eyes."

Soaring Hawk nodded, feeling totally justified in having freed Geronimo and Nah-kah-yen.

"Nah-kah-yen and I were taken to the place the White-eyes call Swillings," Geronimo told

Cochise. "We were led there in chains. Killer-of-Apaches laughed much and told us that we would dance at the end of a rope in the morning." He shook his head. "There was no hope for us then. I had prepared myself to die."

Nah-kah-yen nodded in agreement.

"But as they took us to the place where prisoners were kept like sheep in pens," Geronimo continued, "I crossed the path of this man." He turned to Soaring Hawk and smiled at him.

"Later that night, he knocked out the two White-eyes who guarded us, and then let us out of the pen. We took rifles, and then went out to get horses. More White-eyes came. We shot two of them. But they had seen Soaring Hawk. So we took him here."

"It is well," Cochise said, nodding slowly and turning his dark, grave eyes on the Pawnee. "The brother of our war chief, Geronimo, is welcome at our campfire. May he live long."

Once Nah-kah-yen had translated this, Soaring Hawk expressed his thanks to the chief.

"Now come to the fire," Cochise told his guest. "We will eat. Then we will smoke together."

Chochise led them behind his tent, where a great fire was tended by several women who were cooking something in a large clay pot.

The women were of different ages, and the older ones looked at Soaring Hawk with great curiosity, more or less openly; the younger cast shy, sidelong glances at the brave, with the exception of one young beauty who caught his eye and held it for a moment before she turned away.

She was tall for an Apache, and stood straight as an arrow, Soaring Hawk observed, feeling a sudden pang of regret as she went off to fetch some wood and brush for the campfire. Her figure had been trim, yet surprisingly full at the same time. She had dark, sparkling eyes, an oval face, and lustrous black hair. And the brief, tentative smile that she had flashed him contrasted with her bronzed skin like a snow cap on a dark mountain peak.

The young Apache was very beautiful, Soaring Hawk told himself, as beautiful, in her own way, as Della Casson, the black enchantress whom he had met in San Francisco, and the fair, blonde Deanna MacPartland, the woman who had captured his blood-brother's heart.

The Pawnee felt a twinge of regret as he thought of Davy Watson, but he trusted to the common sense and good judgment of Hammer Hand, as he called the young Kansan in the language of his tribe. Then, as Cochise, Geronimo, the warriors and elders of the Chiricahua Apache band were seating themselves around the fire, Soaring Hawk turned to Nah-kah-yen.

"Who is that woman?" he asked Geronimo's companion, pointing to the young beauty.

Having taken a look at the young woman in question, Nah-kah-yen gestured for Soaring Hawk to sit down between himself and Geronimo.

"You like her?" he asked.

Soaring Hawk nodded solemnly, his nostrils flaring as he did. At this, the Apache brave nudged Geronimo, who then turned his ugly face to the Pawnee, and grinned broadly at him.

"Her name is Cho-ko-le," the Apache told him, after having exchanged a few words of Apache with Geronimo. "She is the niece of our chief,

Cochise. Because she is very beautiful, she has been given a special name. Most women are not given a name of their own, since they are inferior to men. We merely call each of them 'woman,'—Ish-tia-nay.''

"How do men get their names?" Soaring Hawk asked, curious to learn more about this austere and warlike people. What had initially aroused his interest, as he walked through the Apache camp, was the fact that none of the babies could be heard crying. Then the Pawnee noticed that whenever an infant was about to cry, its mother would place a finger on its Adam's apple, thereby stilling the child. The procedure was not painful in itself . . . except when the infant attempted to cry.

"Men get their names," Nah-kah-yen told Soaring Hawk, "after the Thunder God sends incidents which reveal what those names should be. Or else the medicine man, our shaman, gives a name based on a youth's character or physical appearance. Before this happens, we call each youth Ish-kay-nay, which means 'boy.' "

The Apache pointed to a warrior seated across the campfire from them. "That one is Nah-tanh—Corn flower. He got that name because he escaped capture by the Mexican cavalry, on a raid into Sonora, by hiding in a cornfield."

Nah-kah-yen pointed to a brave on Soaring Hawk's left. "That one is Too-ay-yay. It means 'strong swimmer.' He is the greatest swimmer among us. And that one over there is called Gian-nah-tah.'' The warrior smiled. "It means 'always ready,' because," he held up a forearm topped by a clenched fist, "he is always ready for a woman. His name in Mexican is *Muy macho*. And my name means 'keen sighted,' because I can see further than any of the other warriors."

At that moment, Cochise cleared his throat loudly, and the gathering of warriors fell silent. Then, after having looked into the eyes of each man present, the great chief began to speak.

"This man," Cochise said in Apache, while Nah-kah-yen whispered a translation in the Pawnee's ear, "has delivered our war chief Geronimo from the prison of the White-eyes. He has become the brother of Geronimo. It is my wish that he now become brother to all Chiricahua Apaches."

The men all murmured their approval and nodded their heads.

"Geronimo was deceived, delivered into the hands of Killer-of-Apaches," the chief went on solemnly. "And the perpetrator of this treachery was one who calls himself our friend, the Indian agent, Shackleton."

Angry mutterings arose from the circle of warriors.

The chief turned his face to Soaring Hawk. "Mangas Coloradas was betrayed, and then taken captive by the white soldiers. Later, they killed him, on the order of their chief."

Soaring Hawk met the grave eyes of Cochise, and saw the chief's expression harden into a mask of anger.

"I, too, have experience of the treachery of the White-eyes," Cochise said in a cold, low voice. "I heard that a boy named Mickey Free was missing, and that I was supposed to have taken him."

He shook his head. "I did not take him. In those days, I did everything in my power to keep the peace with the whites." He smiled bitterly. "I was still their friend. I did not know their true nature."

Geronimo nodded, a scowl on his face.

"So I rode over to Apache Pass, where the white soldiers were camped, intending to palaver with them."

Cochise smiled his bitter smile and looked into Soaring Hawk's eyes. "I spoke to the young white chief, and offered to help find the missing boy. He invited me into his tent. I went in with six of my warriors, but the young chief did not follow me. Then he called out, and I heard the scuffle of feet, as soldiers began to surround the tent. Suddenly, I realized that I had been deceived."

Soaring Hawk nodded slowly, his eyes still meeting those of the Apache chief.

"The young chief of the soldiers called out to me, saying that he was going to hold me and my warriors. But I took out my knife and cut through the tent. Then I ran through the ranks of the soldiers, who were all surprised to see me. They fired many bullets."

Cochise nodded, his bitter smile turning grim. "I was shot three times. But I managed to get to my horse and ride off. The soldiers hanged my six warriors. Soon after that, I led a raid and killed many soldiers. Ever since that day, I have sworn to make the white man pay for his treachery. And I have."

"He has made the White-eyes pay," agreed Geronimo in Apache, and Nah-kah-yen in English.

"Where are you from?" Cochise asked the Pawnee.

"Far away to the northeast," Soaring Hawk told the chief. "Many moons ride from here. My tribe hunt on the Great Plains."

"There is one thing I do not understand," Cochise said as the women began to serve the evening's meal. "You are a stranger, an Indian from far away. What is it to you whether Geronimo and Nah-kah-yen live or die? Our name means 'enemy,' and all men are against us. Why did you free them?"

All eyes were on the Pawnee now, and Soaring Hawk was aware of the great curiosity in them. He noticed Geronimo especially, and saw that the war chief waited eagerly for his reply.

"I freed Geronimo and Nah-kah-yen," Soaring Hawk told the men simply, through his translator, "because they were men. And men should not be in chains, nor behind bars of iron. A man is born free, and he should die free."

The Apaches nodded approvingly.

"Soaring Hawk speaks with much wisdom," Cochise told the Pawnee. "And henceforth, he will be called Brother by all the Chiricahua Apaches."

"Brother," the men all chorused, their voices rising above the crackle of the campfire. "Brother."

Soaring Hawk placed his hand over his heart. "The Apache people do me much honor," he told the assembly. "I will always seek to be worthy of their friendship."

"It is well," said Cochise. "Now let us eat."

The chief waved his hand, and immediately several women came forth with steaming bowls that had just been filled from the big clay pot on the fire.

Soaring Hawk inhaled the seductive aroma of the Apache food, and discovered a moment later that its taste was even better than its smell. The mouthwatering dish was, he concluded, a stew made from rabbit and various vegetables and roots, many of the latter totally unfamiliar to the Plains Indian.

After the meal, a large clay pipe was passed from hand to hand, as the men smoked. Soaring Hawk was accorded the signal honor of smoking second, right after Cochise.

"Once, long ago, we were one great and numerous people," Cochise told the Pawnee, as the latter puffed on the pipe. "But the Spaniards came with their guns and horses, and soon they enslaved all the Indians around us. But not the Apache. We broke up into bands and clans, and took to the mountains and canyons of the southwestern desert. In this way we remained free, and stay free to this very day."

"I have seen the spread of the white man all over the face of the land," Soaring Hawk told the Apaches, with a gesture that took in all points of the compass. "They came from the east, I have been told—from across the great water there. They are as numerous as the sands of the desert. They have many guns, and strange and powerful machines like the iron horse." He paused and looked down at the ground.

"I have travelled much and seen much," the Pawnee went on. "And I do not think that the white man will be stopped. Already he has crossed this wide land, and built cities by the edge of the great Western water called the Pacific Ocean. In those places live more white men than there are Indians all across the length and breadth of this land."

"But they do not live in harmony with the earth," protested Cochise. "Men who lie, cheat, poison and steal—men who are driven by greed—cannot exist for long. The land itself will expel them."

"And so shall the Apaches!" Geronimo cried out fiercely, his dark eyes glittering in the firelit.

"I hope that they will leave your people in peace," Soaring Hawk told Cochise.

"Peace is not our way," the Apache chief told the Pawnee. "We have always been warriors. We have always taken what we needed from other men."

"The white man will give you war as long as you desire it," Soaring Hawk replied.

"We have taught the White-eyes to fear and respect us," snapped Geronimo, as he took the pipe from the Pawnee. "Now, they will learn to avoid us."

"To be an Apache," Cochise told Soaring Hawk, "is to be an enemy to all men. The greatest man among us is he who outwits the most people. To him go the favors of our maidens and our greatest rewards. Greatness in battle is our highest standard."

"No man alive can endure cold or heat, hunger, thirst, or lack of sleep better than an Apache. He who complains is disgraced among us. He who dies in battle is honored above all others."

The warriors muttered their affirmation of this credo.

"Since many of us die in battle," Cochise went on, "we are permitted many wives. And the brave who fathers many papooses is respected by all. Our women work hard. They know their place, and are always ready to fight beside us—a thing which many widows have indeed done."

He paused to puff on the pipe, after it had been handed to him by Geronimo.

"Women desire to be chosen by braves who can afford many wives," the chief continued, "for the more there are, the less work there is for each of them. They pity the only wife of a brave, because she has to do everything for her husband.

"War and plunder are our work. Labor and daily tasks are for women. An Apache might hunt if he has to, but he would rather go hungry than work like other men."

"Tell our brother how the world was made," urged Geronimo, "and of the Apache's place in it."

"When Usen—the Creator, made the earth," began Cochise, "he created a home for each of the tribes of men. He created all the tribes of men, and his purpose in creating them was righteous."

"Righteous," muttered the old men and warriors at the campfire.

"Usen created the Apaches and their home in the West. Then he provided them with the things they needed: grain, fruit and game to eat; herbs and plants to prepare medicine to restore their health; a pleasant climate and everything that was required in the way of clothing and shelter.

"So it was," Cochise said, waving his hand as he completed the series of eloquent gestures that had accompanied his narrative. "The Apaches and their home: each created for the other. And when the Apaches are taken away from these homes, they will surely waste away and die."

The chief's expression grew solemn. "Even now, we are disappearing from the face of the land. But I do not think we are useless, or Usen would not have created us . . . for he creates nothing that is useless."

Cochise sighed. "Yet we are disappearing. How long will it be until it is said, there are no more Apaches?"

"That is how it was, and how it is," translated Nah-kah-yen, as Cochise finished his tale.

The Pawnee nodded. "We are all children of the Great Spirit," he said as Geronimo handed him the clay pipe.

"My brother keeps gazing off into the distance," Geronimo said through his interpreter, smiling a gargoyle smile at the Plains Indian. "Does he send his spirit out after Cho-ko-le?"

Soaring Hawk looked into Geronimo's eyes. "My spirit is with her now," he admitted to the Apache war chief.

"Then may your body follow, my brother," said Gernimo, his terrible smile softened by the warmth of his friendship for the Pawnee. . . .

Davy Watson was hungry as he rode through the gates of Fort Burnside, surrounded by the well-armed horsemen of Paul Hutzelman's band. But food was not uppermost in the bounty hunter's mind as he and the others dismounted and hitched their horses off to the near side of the stockade's central compound.

"Come on, Watson," Hutzelman growled as Davy secured his horse's reins to the scarred wooden post. "Git a move on."

"Where we goin'?" Davy asked.

"In there," the bounty hunter told him curtly, pointing to a big adobe building at the far side of the compound. "Now, git a move on."

Then Hutzelman strode off, with Davy Watson following close behind him, and the other men in the group bringing up the rear. Across the compound, a sergeant bawled in a gravelly voice as he drilled a platoon of new recruits.

Entering the adobe building, Hutzelman came to a halt before a desk, where there sat a blue-uniformed corporal.

"Yessir, what can I do for you?" the young man asked.

"My name's Hutzelman," the bounty hunter informed the apple-cheeked young soldier. "I do some scoutin' for Major Forbes. I got me some important news for him—regardin' the disposition of Apache forces in this area."

The young corporal's eyes went wide when he heard the word, "Apache."

"I'll inform the major you're here, Mr. Hutzelman," he said, rising from his seat and turning to knock on the door to the right of his desk. A moment later, a voice called out for him to enter. The corporal disappeared into the room beyond, closing the door after him.

A second later he reappeared in the doorway. "Major'll see you now, Mr. Hutzleman," he told the bounty hunter.

"In you go, boy," Hutzelman said, pushing Davy Watson toward the door to the office. "An' step lively, for Major Forbes is waitin' to see you." He turned to his followers. "You boys wait out here," he told them.

The men nodded as Davy, followed by Paul

Hutzelman, entered the office.

Two soldiers dressed in blue, who wore the insignia of the United States Cavalry, flanked Davy Watson as he stepped into the office. The room was large and square; on the far wall were stretched two banners: Old Glory and the standard of the Tenth Cavalry. And below those two banners, a man sat at a polished wooden desk, glowering at the newcomers.

"Major Forbes," Hutzelman said respectfully. "Ol' Geronimo's done gone an' kicked over the traces again. I was bringin' him back to you, all wrapped up in chains, an' I'd stopped for the night in Swillings. I dropped the Apache and another buck off at the jailhouse there. . . ." The bounty hunter looked down at the floor and raised both his hands in a helpless gesture. "In the middle of the night, some strange Injun—not from hereabouts a-tall—breaks into the place an' ups an' frees Geronimo an' his sidekick."

"Damn it, what kind of Indian was it, Hutzelman?" the major asked in a flat, harsh voice. "Where the hell did he come from?" He shook his head and stared contemptuously at the bounty hunter. "Now what the Sam Hill is going on, Hutzelman?"

The bounty hunter looked up with a sheepish grin on his face. "I know it kinda sounds far-fetched, Major Forbes, sir. But it's the gospel truth. This kid here," he jerked a thumb in Davy's direction, "happens to be the Injun's pal—says he's even his blood-brother. So I thought you'd want to palaver some with him."

The major glowered at the young Kansan.

"An' you'll never guess where I found him,

Major," the bounty hunter told the commander of Fort Burnside. "He was holed-up at Darrel Duppa's place, jus' as snug as you please . . .shackin' up with Consuela Delgado."

At the mention of the *Mexicana's* name, the major's nostrils flared, and his eyes narrowed until they were mere slits in his face. The man's clenched hands began to tighten, until the tips of his fingers went livid from the pressure.

Major Jock Forbes was a thickset man with red hair and a receding hairline. His pale blue eyes were cold and angry as he glowered at Hutzelman and Davy Watson.

"This Indian a friend of yours?" the major asked gruffly, the trace of a Scots burr coloring his speech.

"Yessir, he is," Davy replied after clearing his throat. "But I don't—"

"Just answer my questions, Mister!" the major barked, his eyes going wide as he suddenly pulled his hands apart and brought his two fists smashing down on top of the desk.

Hutzelman snorted derisively as he cast a sidelong glance at Davy Watson.

"Who are you, and where did you and this Indian come from?" demanded Forbes, resuming his interrogation.

"I'm, uh, David Lee Watson, from Anderson County, Kansas, sir," Davy muttered. "An' the, uh—"

"Speak up, by God!" the choleric officer roared, his face going red. "Or I'll have you horsewhipped!" He slammed a fist down on the desk to underscore his threat.

Davy was getting angry, too. *Just who in the hell*

does this high-handed sum'bitch think he is? he asked himself. *What's goin' on in this crazy place? I'm gettin' a mite tired of bein' booted around by every dumb galoot who comes my way!*

"David Lee Watson, from Kansas," he repeated in steely tones, raising his head and looking the glowering, intimdating cavalry officer right in the eye. "The Injun's name is Soaring Hawk, an' he's a Pawnee from the Great Plains."

"Is he your blood-brother, Mister?" the major asked next, narrowing his eyes.

"I don't see what that's got to do with—" Davy began.

"Answer my question, damn you!" the major bellowed, his angry eyes still on the young Kansan. "I'll have no more of your discourtesy."

Davy took an involuntary step backward, recoiling as if he had been slapped. "Yeah, he, uh, he's my blood-brother," he mumbled, feeling his ears burn.

"How does he come to know Geronimo?"

Davy shook his head. "Ain't no way he could know any Apache. Soaring Hawk ain't never been in the Arizona Territory before."

"You expect me to believe that?" the major asked scornfully.

His throat constricted by the pressure of his own anger, Davy said, "I don't give a hoot in hell *what* you believe. Mister. 'Cause that's the plain, unvarnished truth I'm tellin' ya."

Suddenly the officer sprang to his feet, overturning his chair.

"You're a goddamned rebellious, disrespectful, snot-nosed kid, aren't you?" he said in a voice as hot as his eyes were cold. Then he nodded to the two troopers who flanked Davy Watson. After that, Forbes strode purposefully around his desk and came up face to face with the man he was interrogating.

"Hey!" Davy grunted in surprise, as the troopers grabbed hold of his arms. And when he began to struggle, the soldiers wrenched them behind his back.

"All right," the major gloated, once the troopers had subdued Davy Watson. "Now, perhaps I'll get some proper answers out of you, Watson."

"Now, you look here," Davy shot back angrily, grunting in pain as the troopers increased the pressure on his twisted arms, "I don't know why the hell you think you've got the right to go pushin' civilians around. You ain't got no ju-risdiction over me. So, you'd jus' better—"

Blap! The major cut short Davy's speech with a vicious backhand slap to the side of his head.

"I *told* you to speak when you're spoken to," Forbes said through clenched teeth. "You're in the Southwest now, Watson—on the frontier, where the lives of all the white people are hanging in the balance, threatened by blood-thirsty savages like Geronimo and Cochise. And I'm the man responsible for safeguarding those lives. So just get it out of your head that I have no jurisdiction over you, because anything that concerns the Apache menace is my business."

"Yeah, but that don't mean—"

"It means," the major interrupted, "that I can have you horsewhipped if I see fit. So you'd better watch your step and keep a civil tongue in your head, *Mister* . . . or I'll have you stripped down

97

and flogged in the compound, in sight of everyone on this post."

Davy's face was now redder than the major's, and his rage strangled the words in his throat. And the fires of that rage blazed even higher when he looked at Hutzelman, and saw that the bounty hunter was smirking at him and shaking with suppressed laughter.

Blap! "Look at me when I'm talking to you, dammit!" the commander of Fort Burnside roared, after having delivered another backhand slap to Davy's jaw.

Straining every muscle in his body, the young Kansan tried to throw himself at the cavalry officer, but the troopers held him fast. And as they did, each wrenched his arm higher behind his back, causing Davy to cry out, despite his resolve not to afford his tormentors the slightest satisfaction.

"Now, how does this . . . Pawnee come to know Geronimo?" asked Major Forbes, reverting to his earlier line of questioning.

Red in the face, his body quivering, the muscles of his arms twitching reflexively in response to their violation, Davy Watson clenched his teeth and glared angrily at Forbes, a scornful smile on his lips as he slowly shook his head from side to side.

"You'd better tell me everything you know, Watson," the major growled. "Or by God, I'll break you."

"You'll have to kill me first," Davy grunted defiantly, tasting a sharp, salt tang upon his lips and realizing for the first time that he was bleeding.

The major laughed a harsh, scornful laugh. "I've broken better men," he told the young Kansan in a cold voice. "And stronger men. And tougher men. Watson, I'd just as soon break you as snap a matchstick in two. Keep that in mind."

"If'n I could get loose," Davy told Forbes, "we'd see who'd be breakin' who."

He grunted, and his knees buckled, as the major drove a fist into his stomach. Then the man leaned over until he was face to face with the prisoner, glaring at him as he spoke in a voice that shook with anger.

"I don't know what Consuela could have seen in trash like you," Forbes said between clenched teeth. "You're nothing but a saddle tramp who drifts from town to town, stealing from honest citizens. The West is crawling with scum like you."

At this point something snapped inside of Davy Watson's brain, and he responded to this further violation in the only way remaining to him. He pulled back his head and let fly a gobbet of spit that caught the cavalry officer smack between the eyes.

Major Forbes' response was instantaneous. He uttered a low growl and glared at Davy, while he addressed the two troopers who held the young Kansan.

"Take this prairie trash out to the compound," he said in a voice that quavered, "and tell Sergeant Reagers to sound the assembly. Then lash him to a post, and give *Mister Watson* fifty of the best."

Chapter Four

Coyotes howled at the moon from the desert below, while Soaring Hawk sat at the campfire of Cochise and smoked with the Apache warriors. He told his hosts of the ways of the Pawnees, and they in turn told him of the customs of the Chiricahua Apaches.

They told him as well of their beliefs—of their myths and legends, and of the dread Thunder God, whose abode is among the peaks of the range known to the whites as Superstition Mountain.

"Strangers persist in violating our holy place," Cochise informed Soaring Hawk. "They come in search of gold. For there is much gold in the mountain." He shook his head. "Mines have always been the Indian's curse. Long ago, after innocently revealing the location of a gold or silver mine to the Spaniards, the Indians would then be tortured by the soldiers and priests, in order to get them to tell of further mines. And if they did not know of any, they were tortured all the same, because the Spaniards were blinded by greed. They were not interested in finding out that their victims were innocent. They served a greedy chief and a greedy god."

He took out a doeskin pouch and handed it to the Pawnee. Opening it and emptying the contents into his palm, Soaring Hawk looked up from the nuggets that gleamed in the light of the Apache fire. His eyes met those of the great chief.

"That is gold from the Thunder God's mountain," Cochise told him. "I personally led the raid in which Peralta the Mexican and his *peones* were massacred. They were about to take away the gold. And then we hid all traces of the mine, and I swore all the surviving braves to silence, upon pain of death by torture."

Soaring Hawk nodded solemnly.

"But we cannot always watch the mountain," the chief went on. "And occasionally someone like the white man known as the Dutchman will take away gold from the place of our Thunder God."

Cochise smiled wryly. "But the Dutchman came only once or twice. He was not greedy, although we made him pay by cutting out the tongue of the Apache girl who had become his squaw after betraying the secret of the mine to him." The braves around the fire all nodded approvingly.

"Most of those who came in search of the gold have been killed by us. Their bones litter the mountainside, along with those of Peralta's *peones* and burros."

Soaring Hawk looked wonderingly at Cochise. "The Apaches do not wish to use the gold for their own benefit?" he asked.

Cochise shook his head. "One time we gave some of it to Doctor Thorne, the man who took pain out of childbearing and taught much good medicine to our shamans. He did not know where the gold came from, but many white men kept trying to persuade him to take them to the mine. The White-eyes are very greedy, and if they saw the Chiricahuas with much gold, they would not rest until we had been totally exterminated."

Soaring Hawk saw the truth in this.

"The White-eyes have already stolen our best land," Cochise told him. "And they would not hesitate an instant before stealing our gold. Then they would justify the theft by making it appear that we are savages and killers, when it is really they who are guilty of those crimes."

"But the Great White Father in Washington has sent agents to watch over the Indian," the Pawnee told the Apache chief. "Do they not work in your interest?"

Cochise frowned. "They are often corrupt, and cooperate with the wolves who have stolen what was ours. Even the present Indian Agent, Shackleton, a man we trusted, has now betrayed us. He is in league with the bounty hunter, Hutzelman, the man we call Killer-of-Apaches."

He shook his head. "I am puzzled by why this should be. But what we must do now is go on the warpath once more. There is no other way for the Apache."

"We will make them pay for everything, this time!" Geronimo cried, his eyes glittering in the light of the campfire.

"Geronimo is a great war chief," Cochise told Soaring Hawk. "When he goes on the warpath, many Apache warriors go with him."

Nah-kah-yen and the others all seconded this.

"I have no blood quarrel with the White-eyes," Geronimo said to Soaring Hawk. "I go on the warpath only when they force me to." He narrowed his eyes. "But it is different with the Mexicans. I always go willingly to kill them. Whenever I can."

Seeing the terrible look on the war chief's face, Soaring Hawk asked, "Why should this be,

Geronimo?"

The other Apaches, Cochise among them, all averted their eyes and stared into the flickering campfire.

"I will tell you, Brother," Geronimo answered in a low voice, pausing to toss some brush and ironwood on the fire. And as it flared up, Soaring Hawk noted the look of fierce determination and implacable hatred upon the war chief's face.

"Many years ago," Geronimo began, "in 1846, when I was seventeen years of age, I was made a warrior. Before this, I had lived quietly in the country which lies by the headwaters of the Gila. I desired to serve my people in battle. Up to that time, I had never seen a white man."

The fire crackled loudly as the dry brush was consumed.

"At that time I took to wife Alope, a fair and slender girl who was the daughter of No-po-so. Now that I was a warrior, I could marry Alope, although we had long been lovers." Geronimo's fierce expression softened as he spoke of his bride.

"Her father asked many ponies, for Alope was as dutiful a daughter as could be. But within a week I appeared before his wickiup with a herd of ponies I had stolen from the Mexicans, and No-po-so gave Alope to me. Thus we were married, after the manner of my tribe. At that time, Mangas Coloradas was our chief."

He paused to scratch his head vigorously. "I made a new home for us, a fine place of tanned hides. Inside it were many trophies of the hunt—bearskin robes, lion hides—and my spears, bows and arrows. Alope decorated with much beauty, hanging beads and decorations of buckskin drawings, as well as pictures she herself had drawn upon the walls.'' Geronimo lowered his head, nearly overcome by his memories.

"Alope was not strong," he continued after clearing his throat. "But I loved her, and she was a good wife. We lived in the manner of our fathers. We had three children. We were happy."

Soaring Hawk watched the war chief carefully, amazed by this sudden revelation of the man's love and tenderness.

"Twelve years later, our band went down into Mexico to trade. We were then at peace with the Mexicans. We passed through Sonora, heading toward Casa Grande, and stopped on the way at a town we called Kas-ki-yah. We camped outside the city and went into it to trade, leaving our women and children, arms and supplies under a small guard.

"Coming back from Casa Grande one evening, we were met by some women and children who were bloodied and wounded. They told us that Mexican troops from another town had suddenly attacked the camp and killed all the guards. They took our ponies, arms and supplies.'' Geronimo's face grew dark as a thundercloud. "Then they massacred as many of the women and children as they could."

Soaring Hawk watched the man's mouth twitch as he relived the horror of that day.

"We split up and concealed ourselves. At nightfall, we met at a thicket by the side of a river. Then we stole back—one by one—to the campsite.

"Many had been slain by the treacherous Mexicans," Geronimo whispered bitterly. "I found the bodies of my old mother, my three children . . . and my beautiful Alope."

Soaring Hawk looked around, and saw that all the warriors sat with downcast eye and bowed head.

"That night," Geronimo said, "at the council of warriors, it was decided that, being almost unarmed as well as too few to fight, we should return to Arizona. Mangas Coloradas gave the signal to leave, and we left the bodies where they lay.

"I did not speak again until after we had returned to our camp. As is the custom of our people, I burnt my mother's wigwam and property. Then I even burnt Alope's things, the playthings of our children—even our home. It was not required to do that, but I did not wish to see them any longer."

He took a deep breath and straightened up, the flames of the campfire dancing in his eyes. "Then I went to my kinsmen, the Chokonen Apaches, and spoke to them, saying: 'Kinsmen, you have heard what the Mexicans have recently done without cause. You are my relatives—uncles, cousins, brothers. We are men the same as the Mexicans—and we can do to them what they have done to us. Let us go forward and trail them —I will lead you to their city. We will attack them in their homes. I will fight in the front of the battle—I only ask you to follow me to avenge this wrong done by the Mexicans. Will you come?' "

He paused, smiling grimly as he looked around the campfire at his listeners. Then he nodded, taking up the thread of his story once more.

" 'It is well. You will all come,' " he said, reliving the moment with great intensity.

" 'Remember the rule in war: men may return or

they may be killed. If any of these young men are killed, I want no blame from their kinsmen, for they themselves have chosen to go. If I am killed, no one need mourn for me. My people have all been killed in that country, and I, too, will die there if need be.' "

Geronimo was smiling now. "The Chokonen agreed, and then I made the same appeal to the Nedni Apaches who live to the south. They, too, agreed to go on the warpath.

"Nearly a year after the massacre, the three tribes met at the Mexican border. I guided them along mountain tracks and river courses, the better to hide our movements. Along the way, we skirmished and killed many Mexicans, and on the day that we drew near to Arispe, we captured a supply train, which brought us provisions and many guns."

Soaring Hawk nodded and tossed a handful of brush upon the fire.

"The next morning, a great force of Mexicans came out after us—two companies each of infantry and cavalry. My heart leapt as I recognized the murderers of my people among the horsemen. And when I told the chieftains, they gave me the honor of directing the battle."

Here Geronimo paused as he held his nose between thumb and forefinger, leaned forward, and blew his nose into the campfire.

"I was determined to prove myself worthy of that great honor," he told Soaring Hawk as he wiped his hand on a buckskin legging.

"I gathered the Apaches in the timber by the river, arranging them in a semicircle. Two lines of Mexican infantry advanced upon us, while the cavalry was held in reserve. They halted four hundred yards away from our position, and opened fire upon us."

The war chief's eyes flashed. "I gave the signal to charge, also sending a number of warriors to attack from behind. I led the Apaches. My heart was full of fury as I remembered what the Mexicans had done to Alope, my mother, and my little ones.

"We fought for two hours, and I killed several of the enemy. In that time, we killed many—many more than our number." He sighed. "But we, too, were killed. Soon our guns were empty, our lances thrown, our arrows all loosed at the enemy. I found myself in the center of the battlefield— together with only three other Apaches. But all who had faced us lay dead."

Geronimo wore a solemn expression on his face. "Suddenly, two soldiers bearing rifles came toward us. They shot down two of us, and the remaining warrior and I fled back toward our braves. One of the soldiers dropped his rifle and pulled out his sabre, cutting my companion down. But when I got near our warriors, I picked up a lance and turned on the soldier behind me, killing him with it."

The war chief smiled his wolfish smile. "Then I picked up his sabre, and rushed at the other Mexican. After killing him, I rose to my feet, waving the bloody sabre in the air as I looked about for more of the enemy to kill.

"But these were all there were; we had wiped the Mexicans out completely. The deaths of our loved ones were avenged!" There was a look of wild exultation upon Geronimo's ugly face.

"And all the Apache warriors had seen the deeds

I did that day," he said proudly, in a quiet voice.

Soaring Hawk watched in fascination as Geronimo seemed to grow larger before his eyes.

"Still covered with the blood of my enemies, still holding my conquering weapon, still hot with the joy of battle, victory and vengeance, I was surrounded by the braves and made war chief of all the Apaches. Then I gave orders for the scalping of the slain."

Geronimo sighed, and Soaring Hawk watched him shrink back to normal size, as the war chief slumped over, leaning in toward the warmth of the campfire.

"I could not call back my loved ones," he told the Pawnee in a voice that was little more than a whisper. "I could not bring back the dead Apaches. But I could rejoice in this revenge. The Apaches had avenged the massacre of Kas-ki-yeh."

"So it was," spoke up Cochise, "how Geronimo became war chief of all the Apaches." He raised his eyes, and met those of Soaring Hawk. "This is the man that you have saved from the treachery of the White-eyes."

"But enough of war for tonight," Geronimo said loudly, clapping the Pawnee on the back. "For I am sure that my brother's lance is ready to spear fairer game than soldiers."

Nah-kah-yen chuckled as he translated this for Soaring Hawk.

"What does Geronimo mean?" Cochise asked.

"This hero," he said, cocking a thumb at Soaring Hawk, "has found favor in the eyes of an unmarried Apache woman."

"And what woman is that?" asked Cochise.

"Cho-ko-le," Geronimo replied.

Cochise nodded. "Then let him go to her," he replied, smiling at the Pawnee brave.

Crack. Chunk. Crack. Chunk.
The sound of pickaxes penetrating stone, and of sections of rock shelf tumbling down rang out loudly in the clear, morning air atop Superstition Mountain. The crew of four worked energetically in the early light, while Shackleton sat on his rock with Winchester held at the ready, scanning the slope below for any sign of the dreaded Apaches.

The sight of a rider brought the Indian agent to his feet, raising the rifle to his shoulder and peering along its barrel as he got the newcomer in his sights. A moment later he lowered the weapon and smiled, a relieved expression on his face.

Shackleton went over to the edge of the rock, gripped his Winchester just below its mouth and rested its butt on the stone, as he peered over and observed the rider's progress up the side of the mountain.

Before long the terrain had become completely inhospitable, and the newcomer was forced to dismount and lead his horse up the slope. Stumbling into craters and sliding into barrancas, skinning his elbows and knuckles on sharp spurs of rock, pricked continually by the spikes and needles of a multitude of cacti and thorny plants, the newcomer swore in frustration as the ascent became progressively more difficult.

"Dad-blast it, you spavined bag of bones!" he roared at his shying horse, tugging at its reins as he attempted to guide it through a bed of prickly plants. "Over here—God damn your ass!" he cried, losing patience with the bridling mare.

"By Gad, you ain't got the good sense of a plow-horse, you sway-backed, skittish son of a jackass! Come along, I say!"

The mare shied again, and then whinnied loudly as the man gave a final, brutal tug on the reins, pulling her through to the other side of the obstacle.

"That's better, that's better," the man murmured, suddenly tender as he stroked the mare's flank and spoke in her ear. He took off his hat and wiped his forehead with a forearm. And then he peered into the distance, looking up the side of the mountain, toward the looming and ominous black peak known as the Finger of God. He caught sight of Shackleton standing atop his boulder. Holding his brown hat in his right hand, the newcomer waved it back and forth over his head, repeating this action until he had done it three times.

When he had finished waving, the man watched as Shackleton returned his signal, waving his own grey Stetson back and forth three times. Nodding with satisfaction, the newcomer began the final stage of the difficult and laborious ascent.

"It's about time you got here," Shackleton said as the other man led his horse around the boulder. "I was expecting you yesterday." He hefted his Winchester. "I was beginning to think that your old friend, Cochise, had gotten hold of you."

Paul Hutzelman smirked his crooked smirk. "Now, don't you fret none 'bout them Apaches, Ernest," he told the Indian agent. "I done got things stirred up real good now. It's gonna be all them red devils can do to hang onto their own hides, let alone come pokin' 'round Superstition

110

Mountain."

"Well, what have you been up to, Paul?" the Indian agent asked. "Did you take Geronimo into Swillings, on your way to Prescott?"

The bounty hunter scratched the salt-and-pepper stubble on his chin. "Yep, I did that, all right," was his reply. "And by the way, Swillings ain't Swillings no more. The place is called Phoenix nowadays."

"Phoenix?"

"Yep. Phoenix."

"Who the hell thought *that* one up?"

"Ol' Darrel Duppa."

The Indian agent shook his head. "Leave it to him. That's a name out of classical antiquity. Did you know that?"

The bounty hunter looked bored as he shook his head.

"It was the name of an old Greek bird that was supposed to have died in flames, and been reborn from its ashes. Hmmm. I suppose it *is* rather appropriate."

"Ernest, I don't give a shit about no old Greek birds," Hutzelman said impatiently. "Don't you want to hear what I done to stir things up?" The bounty hunter looked hurt.

"Well, *sure* I do, Paul," Shackleton replied hastily. "Of course, I do. Nothing could interest me more."

Hutzelman nodded. "Okey-doke," he said, breaking into a self-satisfied grin. "Y'see, what happened was that I done slapped the shackles on ol' Geronimo and that other buck, Nah-kah-ken." Hutzelman's grin was transformed into a knowing smirk.

"Boy, was that frog-faced little shit hoppin' mad when he found hisself covered by my boys. An' when he seen me, he was fit to be tied. They call me Killer-of-Apaches, y'know," he told Shackleton proudly. "Ol' Geronny jus' cussed me out in Spanish an' Apache—up an' down, high an' low, north, east, south an' west."

He chuckled. "An' then I took holt of his chain, an' drug his ass off to the Swillings—uh, I mean Phoenix calaboose. I'd've strung that little shit up on the spot, if'n Delbert Palmer hadn't been there."

"What was the amount of the reward?" the Indian agent asked.

Hutzelman scratched his big red nose. "Don't rightly know, Ernest. It don't matter now, anyways."

Shackleton's eyes widened. "What do you mean by that, Paul?" he asked.

"Well, it seems that this here strange Injun from back east a-ways—Pawnee, I believe he is, was hangin' round town when we brought the prisoners in. An' late that same night, he done busted into the calaboose an' sprung ol' Geronimo an' Nah-kah-yen. They was spotted comin' out. Then they shot two men, an' high-tailed it outta town, takin' that strange Injun with 'em."

Shackleton looked horrified. "Oh my God," he said in a hoarse whisper. "Do you realize what this means?"

"Well, sure," Hutzelman answered. "It means that ol' Geronny is on the loose again."

"Dammit man!" the agent squawked, panic sending his voice up into the falsetto register. "What it means is that Geronimo will be out for blood—*my blood*! I was the one who led him into your hands—*and he knows that*!"

Paul Hutzelman rubbed his big, pitted nose and beamed at the frightened Shackleton. "Jus' simmer down, Ernest," he said, reaching out to pat his associate's shoulder. "You ain't got no cause to worry. I done took care of everything for ya."

"Oh yes—you certainly did!" the agent shot back accusingly, in a voice colored by bitterness and fear.

Hutzelman smiled and shook his head. "Now, you ain't to worry yerself none, Ernest," he murmured soothingly. "You always was a high-strung soul. But I tell ya there's nothin' to fear."

"W-What does this m-mean?" stammered the frightened Indian agent.

"Y see, it's like this, Ernest," the bounty hunter said, opening his big, callused hands and throwing wide his arms. "This here Pawnee had him a white buddy—a blood-brother, can you believe that? Well, folks knew he was spendin' the night in Swillings—excuse me, Phoenix—so word got back to me right after ol' Geronny's jailbreak."

"But *what* does this have to do with the fact that Geronimo is now *at large*, Paul?" Shackleton asked anxiously. "My God, you *know* how bloodthirsty he is. And now, he'll be coming—"

"No, no, Ernest," Hutzelman interrupted, grabbing hold of the shoulder of the Indian agent's jacket and tugging on it. "You got nothin' to fear. Now, listen to me."

Shackleton took a deep breath. "All right, Paul," he sighed. "I'm listening."

"Good. Now, what I done was to bust into Lord Darrel's place, an' get holt of the Injun's buddy—some young squirt name of Watson. Then I brung him to Fort Burnside, to see ol' Major Forbes.''

The bounty hunter paused to hawk up a mouthful of phlegm and spit it out, leaning over to follow its course down the side of the mountain. "Y'see, when I told Forbes that I was gon' to bring Geronimo to the fort, but that young tad, Watson, done let him loose—why, he done jus' 'bout lost his mind. He done got up an' whomped the shit out'n that boy. An' then he had him stripped to the waist in the post compound, an' done made Watson a present of fifty stripes 'cross't his back.''

Hutzelman smirked. "'Course, it didn't help the tad's case none when I let drop the news that I found him in bed with that Delgado woman. Major's been layin' siege to her for more'n a year now, but he ain't got nowheres. But I know he's itchin' to put his brand on that purty l'il Mex.''

"But what about Geronimo, Paul? What about Geronimo?''

"Don't get yer balls in an uproar, Ernest,'' the bounty hunter told his associate. "I'm comin' to that.''

Shackleton gulped, nodded, and took several deep breaths.

"Well, Major Forbes, he got hisself all fired up by what young Watson an' his Injun friend done, an' he's holding the tad captive, figgerin' to get to the Pawnee through him—an' from him to ol' Geronny. What I done really set him off, an' he's a-musterin' up all the available troops 'twixt here an' Fort McDowell, makin' ready to go out after Geronimo an' Cochise. He's playin' fer keeps this time, make no mistake about it. This one's goin' to be a full-scale expedition. He's already asked me'n my boys to scout fer him."

Shackleton narrowed his eyes. "And you're going to lead him to the Apache camp, aren't you, Paul? By God, if anyone can, you're the man."

The bounty hunter nodded, beaming proudly now. "I reckon if any white man could find old Cochise's hidden camp, it'd be me. An' I don't mind messin' 'round in the Chiricahua Mountains . . . not if'n I got me a couple of hundred bluecoats behind me."

"But won't it be dangerous?"

"Not fer me, if'n I can help it, Ernest. I'm leadin' Forbes an' his troopers in, but I ain't intendin' to git all that close, myself. I ain't about to git in the way of no bullets nor arrows. Let the blue boys make pincushions out'n themselves. That's what they get paid for."

He leered at the Indian agent. "An' then, when they's scrappin' an' mixin' it up—knifin', fightin', an shootin' the shit out of each other—why, I reckon I'll jus' skeedaddle outta there an' head back here to Superstition Mountain. You ought to have all the gold you can carry in a couple of days' time, oughtn't you, Ernest?"

Shackleton nodded. "All I need is two or three more days," he told Hutzelman. "Your little strategy should certainly keep the Apaches bottled up for some time to come, Paul."

"Damn tootin'," the bounty hunter agreed. "For even if'n we don't manage to wipe out all of them red dogs, it'll be a long time afore ol' Cochise an' Geronny dares to stick their snouts out'n the Chiricahua Mountains."

"You figure that's where Geronimo is now,

Paul?"

"Ab-so-lutely, Ernest. Cochise's hidden camp is up there somewheres, an' it's 'bout the only place safe enough fer Geronimo, these days."

"That's good news," the Indian agent reflected with growing confidence.

"Shore is, Ernest," his partner agreed. "You ain't got nothin' a-tall to worry 'bout." He flashed Shackleton a sly smile. "'Less'n you git yerself into trouble with that ol' Apache Thunder God."

"That, I assure you, is the least of my worries."

Hutzelman narrowed his eyes and smirked at his partner. "Or the Dutchman," he added softly.

Shackleton's expression grew sombre. "I never even thought of the Dutchman," he whispered.

"Well, it is his mine, after all," the bounty hunter rejoined, amused by the Indian agent's reaction.

Shackleton hefted his Winchester, "My God, what if he *should* show up here?" he said in a voice that shook.

Hutzelman laughed. "I was only funnin' ya, Ernest," he told the other. "Ol' Jake Walz ain't been back to Superstition Mountain fer years, now. An' it ain't likely he's gonna show up now." He shook his head. "Besides, he ain't too keen on runnin' into Apaches, not after what they done to his l'il Ken-Tee. Nor is he 'bout to go up agin five guns. You know that, Ernest. So you got nothin' to worry 'bout. Nothin' a-tall."

"I suppose you're right," Shackleton said with a sigh. "I do tend to worry overmuch, sometimes."

"Jus' start a-figgerin' out how much all this here gold'll bring us. That'll keep ya in a good frame of mind."

116

"You're right, of course," Shackleton admitted as the bounty hunter walked over to the rock shelf where the men were working with their pickaxes.

The rubble of the digging covered the ground by their feet, and the gold concentrate gleamed warmly as it reflected the light of the morning sun. There it was, littering the ground in a strip twelve feet long, like the carpet to Midas' throne—the fabled gold of Superstition Mountain, the world-famous yield of the Lost Dutchman Mine.

"By Gad, that's rich ore," Hutzelman whispered, hypnotized by the gleaming carpet before him.

"Howdy, Paul," one of the men said, lowering his pickaxe and turning to the bounty hunter.

"Howdy, Everett," Hutzelman replied, never taking his eyes from the gold, as the other men stopped working and proceeded to exchange greetings with him.

When he finally looked away, the bounty hunter said, "Well, I reckon you boys stand to make out a mite better than you done when you was mustered out of ol' Jeff Davis' army."

"Hell, ah sholy hope so," the man called Everett replied cheerfully. "All ah got fer my troubles then was a bagful of Confederate money, for to plug up the holes in my boots."

"You'll be pluggin' up them holes with U.S. greenbacks soon, ol' fella," Hutzelman told him.

"Plug 'em up, hell," Everett exclaimed as he scratched his bushy brown beard. "Why, ah'm gon' be so damn rich, ah'll nevah have to walk again."

"Yeah, we done more than our share of walkin' when we served the south," a thickset blond man asserted in a bass voice. "Covered the country from Louisiana to Pennsylvania, and back."

"Well, them days is over, boys," Hutzelman told the miners. "'Cause we's gonna be millionaires within the week . . . soon as we give them Apache sum'bitches what-for."

"I, for one, will be glad to quit this place," said Shackleton.

"Why is that, Ernest?" asked the thickset blond man, smiling at Hutzelman as he did.

"Because it spooks me," was the Indian agent's reply.

In his cell in the prison stockade at Fort Burnside, Davy Watson awoke with a groan, and his shame stung with an intensity at least the equal of the searing pain that came from the raw stripes on his back. He was animated by hatred now, and if he had been free to act upon his desires, the first thing that Davy would have done was to kill Major Jock Forbes.

The violation and outrage resulting from his first meeting with the brutal commander of Fort Burnside, who was as well his rival for the affections of Consuela Delgado, had been intense. But these feelings were surpassed by the awful ordeal of his public flogging.

After Forbes had ordered Davy taken out to the compound, stripped to the waist and tied to a whipping post, the major had his bugler sound the assembly. Within a minute's time, the troopers of Fort Burnside had formed themselves in a square whose center was the whipping post to which Davy Watson was bound.

Then the captive heard voices chattering in

Spanish and English, as the fort's civilian personnel straggled out into the compound, motivated by curiosity, eager for something to happen, something that would cut through the grey monotony of life on a frontier military post.

Sergeants barked commands, and the civilians babbled excitedly in the post's two tongues. Several moments later, a drumroll cut through the hubbub, silencing all in the compound.

Looking over his shoulder, Davy made out the form of a big man coming up behind him. The newcomer was hatless, and naked to the waist; his trunk and arms were heavily muscled. He wore brown leather boots and the blue twill trousers of the U.S. Cavalry.

Davy knew that this was the man who would administer his fifty lashes. This opinion received chilling confirmation when the young Kansan caught sight of the whip in the man's hand—a collection of rawhide thongs that ran out from a bound leather handle. The man's approach set the civilians to babbling once more.

Another drumroll sounded, and the crowd fell silent. The soldiers all stood at ease in their blue square, each man watching Davy Watson and the man with the lash. Davy suddenly felt his throat go dry, as a tremor of fear shook his body. Then he gritted his teeth, straightened up, and raised his thoughts in silent prayer.

Suddenly, Major Forbes' voice rang out in the compound. "I have summoned you all here," he began, "to witness an example of military justice and discipline. The man you see before you is a renegade. He is connected with the successful attempt to free Geronimo, after that rebellious savage had been taken into custody by territorial officials and a United States marshal.''

Davy strained at his bonds, turning in the direction of the major's cold, metallic voice, but he could not see him.

"This man is now a prisoner of the army," Forbes went on, "and is being punished for the flagrant disrespect he has displayed toward a representative of the government of the United States of America, as well as for his refusal to cooperate with duly constituted authority. While in the toils of his recalcitrance and rebelliousness, the prisoner even had the temerity to attempt an assault upon my person. So it is for all these reasons that I have chosen to make an example of this man . . . an example for all to see and heed.''

Standing thirty-five paces behind Davy Watson, Major Jock Forbes looked slowly around the compound, once he had finished his speech. The mass of civilians regarded him watchfully, eyes wide in expectation; and the eyes of the troopers darted in furtive runs toward the position of the commander of Fort Burnside.

Pausing a moment longer, to milk the situation of all its dramatic possibilities, Forbes slowly raised his hand in the air. Then, after holding it up for a long time, he brought it down sharply. The moment he did, another drumroll sounded, and the burly man behind Davy Watson raised his whip. Then—suddenly—as the drumroll ended, he brought it down sharply, across the young Kansan's bare back.

"*One*!" a sergeant-major called out from the square in stentorian tones, beginning the count.

"*Uunh*!" grunted Davy Watson as the rawhide thongs scored his flesh. The pain made him catch his breath, and he felt a sudden, chill rush in the pit of his stomach.

"*Two*!" the sergeant-major called out with the second stroke.

The civilians began to mutter among themselves anxiously and look from the suffering prisoner to the cause of his suffering.

"*Three*!" Jock Forbes smiled a thin smile as he watched Davy Watson's body shudder and stiffen as the third stroke landed upon his back.

"*Four*!" The new recruits among the soldiers winced as the rawhide thongs smacked against the prisoner's quivering flesh. Here and there an old enlisted man would frown and shake his head almost imperceptibly, having first ascertained that his commander was not watching.

"*Five*!" Waves of pain seared Davy's back, and his nerve ends seemed to scream in response to their continual violation.

"*Six*!" Davy grunted loudly—against his will—as the pain of the lash drew forth this anguished reaction. And with each succeeding stroke, the pain grew and multiplied in its intensity.

By the twenty-eighth stroke, Davy Watson cried out, his voice echoing through the compound.

By the thirty-nineth stroke, his back was streaming with blood.

By the forty-ninth stroke, he had passed out.

And when the fiftieth stroke had been delivered, and the punishment was at an end, Major Jock Forbes gave the order for salt to be rubbed in Davy Watson's wounds before the Kansan was cut down.

After that, the commanding officer of Fort Burnside spun on his heel and strode out of the compound. And by the time that he had returned to his office, Major Forbes was whistling *The Bonny Blue Flag*.

Chapter Five

The winter moon of Arizona shone down with a pale light, bathing the peaks and wooded slopes of the Chiricahua Mountains in its ghostly radiance. It was a thin, silver light, of the kind that the Indians associated with the visits of spirits, as those disembodied entities wandered between worlds.

Seen in this eerie light, inanimate objects appeared pregnant with revelation, scarcely containing the great potential that seemed to resonate within them. It was as if the outer world were a mere play of shadows that barely covered the pulsating energic heart of things.

All Arizona lay beneath that patina of moonlight, as it silvered mountain and desert, valley and settlement alike, draining the territory of all color as it rendered the landscape in monochrome. And its argent beams entered the quarters of friend and foe alike, indifferent to the human qualities of goodness or evil. And as the moonlight united all whom it shone upon, so thoughts and dreams of Davy Watson united people in diverse places and circumstances that night.

As the moonlight entered the window of an adobe house in the newly-risen settlement of Phoenix, and fell upon the recumbent form of Darrel Duppa, the Englishman tossed in his sleep and mumbled, "Look here, Hutzelman—you can't break in like this!'' In his sleep he was reliving the humiliating events of the past day, re-enacting the mob's violation of the sanctity of his home. But this time, as he writhed and tossed in troubled sleep, Duppa won his point and turned the mob out of his house . . . thereby saving his guest, Davy Watson from the fury of the outraged Arizonans, and rationally allowing him a fair chance to explain his part in the Geronimo business. . . .

Duppa, anguishing over the seizure of his Kansan guest, was united in spirit with Consuela Delgado, as the latter lay wide-eyed and unblinking in her own bed, kept awake by her concern for the virile and tender young man who had been her lover the night before.

The moonlight silvered her brown skin and gleamed in her dark eyes, as the handsome *Mexicana* shifted her long, graceful limbs uneasily, disturbed by the knowledge that Paul Hutzelman had gone to turn Davy Watson over to Major Forbes, the hard, cruel man who had been paying court to her for months. She feared the worst if Forbes learnt that Davy had been found in bed with her. She knew how jealous and possessive the cavalry commander was; and how ruthless and fully capable of cold-blooded murder, as well. . . .

At Fort Burnside, Paul Hutzelman, the man known as Killer-of-Apaches, sniffled and chuckled in his sleep, immensely pleased about the way he had used the Watson kid to his own advantage. The bounty hunger snorted, moaned, licked his chops, and chuckled again, secure in the knowledge that he and his partner, Shackleton, would be able to descend unmolested from

Superstition Mountain, their burros staggering under the weight of a king's ransom in gold concentrate.

He felt secure indeed, now that Major Forbes had been goaded into launching an ambitious, large-scale expedition into the Chiricahuas, one whose objectives were the defeat and subjugation of Geronimo, Cochise and all their tribemen, those formidable *guerilleros* who stood in the way of all who would work the rich vein of gold located within the precincts of their Thunder God's dwelling place. . . .

Also on the army post, sharing the restless sleep brought by that strange, pallid moon, Major Jock Forbes sighed and stirred, his prominent jaw thrust out and his lips set in a grim smile of satisfaction as he dreamed of the humiliation and public flogging of that impudent young pup called Davy Watson.

The major drew his strength from controlling others, and therefore he throve upon their discomfort and submission. He had derived great pleasure from the spectacle of Davy's corporal punishment, and welcomed it as an opportunity to impress once more the seal of his authority upon the hearts and minds of his soldiers.

Even more gratifying than that was the widespread fear and resentment aroused by the news of Geronimo's escape. Like his contemporary, George Armstrong Custer, Major Forbes eagerly sought honor, advancement and glory on the field of battle. He would no longer have to chafe under the restraints of President Grant's peace policy, because public sentiment would soon give him a mandate over the territory, and he would be free to wage a war of extermination—starting with the Chiricahuas, and, once they had been wiped out, extending to the Tonto, White Mountain and Mescalero Apaches.

Forbes sighed as he shifted in his sleep. Soon his great ambitions would be realized; soon he would set out on the same trail of glory as his rival, Custer. Soon he would be called to Washington, and honored by U. S. Grant himself, as the savior of the Arizona Territory, the man who had provided a final solution to the Apache problem. . . .

High in the fastness of the Chiricahua Mountains, the Apache war chief, Geronimo, lay on his blanket, his ugly face a silver mask in the moonlight that flooded into his wickiup, grinding his teeth and moaning as he relived his betrayal at the hands of the white man he had trusted, the Indian agent, Shackleton.

He dreamt as well of his new brother, Soaring Hawk, that strange Indian from the plains far away to the east. And he shared the Pawnee's concern for the fate of his white blood-brother, wondering what would happen to him once the angry inhabitants of Phoenix associated him with the rescue of the dreaded Geronimo.

The war chief hoped fervently that Soaring Hawk's white brother would not fall into the hands of the man his people had named Killer-of-Apaches, for the bounty hunter was a man without honor, a treacherous dog who would stop at nothing to get what he wanted, a man far more devious and savage than the Apaches whose scalps he collected. . . .

Cochise tossed fitfully beside his young wife, groaning so loudly that he woke his children several times in the course of that strange, silver night. Things had come to a head with Soaring Hawk's daring rescue of Geronimo and Nah-kah-yen, the chief of the Chiricahua Apaches had realized; soon the White-eyes would take drastic action against his people. Soon it would be total war—with no mercy shown by either side. And Cochise was certain that the first casualty of this impending war would be the white blood-brother of Soaring Hawk. . . .

In a ghostly cell whose bars appeared to be cast from silver, Davy Watson lay face down on an army cot, sleeping in that position because his wounds would not permit him to lie on his back.

He, too, was restless; and his sleep was disturbed by kaleidoscopic dreams of violence and revenge. He dreamt of hunting down and shooting his captor, Hutzelman. But more than that, he dreamed of the various ways in which he would avenge his great humiliation and kill the man who had violated his being—Major Jack Forbes, the man he hated above all men . . . .

Closer to the moon than any of the dreamers, thinking of Davy Watson, but fully awake in the pale, silvered landscape of the Chiricahua Mountains, Soaring Hawk made his way up the mountain peak where Geronimo had told him that the lovely young Cho-ko-le would be found.

The Pawnee was deeply concerned about the safety of his blood-brother. And while he realized the enormity of his "crime" in the eyes of the white Arizonans, in his own heart the brave was secure in the knowledge that he had done the right thing. Indeed, he considered himself a friend to the white man, who had helped his people hold their own against the Sioux and Cheyenne—but not at the expense of his loyalty to his brothers.

After having listened carefully to the talk of Cochise and the other Apache warriors, the Pawnee had gauged the temper of the Chiricahuas, and realized that their main concern for some time to come would be self-preservation. The whites would shortly be taking the offensive. Therefore, he could not count upon the aid of the Apaches in riding back to Phoenix and rescuing Davy Watson.

Geronimo would, of course, ride with him, Soaring Hawk knew, assembling a band of warriors to accompany them. But such a move was far too dangerous for the Apaches at the present time. The Pawnee knew he would have to rescue Davy Watson alone. . . .

Cho-ko-le stood in silence beneath the moon, looking like the spirit of a maiden who had returned to earth after the death of her physical body. Her black hair glowed with a silver tint, and Soaring Hawk could see the young Apache's face as he drew near, marvelling at the beauty of her strong profile.

When she became aware of his presence, Cho-ko-le turned in the Pawnee's direction, and the brave was intoxicated by the beauty of her oval face, with its black, vaulting eyebrows, high cheekbones, dark, shining eyes, fine straight nose and strong, sensual mouth.

When she stood before him, Soaring Hawk's breath caught in his throat, as he observed the swelling, womanly fullness of Cho-ko-le's supple body. The young Apache was the most beautiful woman he had ever seen. All of a sudden, he ached to take her in his arms, and felt a stirring in the pit of his groin. Several paces behind the Pawnee came his translator, Nah-kah-yen. Since Cho-ko-le spoke no English, and Soaring Hawk no Spanish or Apache, he had asked the warrior to introduce them properly and interpret until he and Cho-ko-le became comfortable with each other.

He nodded to Nah-kah-yen, as the latter came up beside him, and then turned to the beautiful Cho-ko-le, his face a stolid mask while his eyes were eloquent of his desire.

"This is Soaring Hawk, Geronimo's newfound brother," Nah-kah-yen told the young woman. "This is the great warrior who rescued the war chief and me from the hands of our great enemy, Killer-of-Appaches. Make him welcome, Cho-ko-le."

Lowering her eyes modestly, the young woman spoke in a soft, sweet voice. "Cho-ko-le welcomes the brave warrior from far away, and considers it a great honor that he should come and speak to her."

"Our eyes have already spoken," replied Soaring Hawk, after having heard the translation of her words.

For an instant, Cho-ko-le's eyes met his. Then she lowered them once more.

"Does Soaring Hawk, who speaks a tongue unfamiliar to me, understand the language of the eyes?" she asked shyly.

Nah-kah-yen was grinning as he translated this.

"I am told that the eyes speak more truly than the tongue," was the Pawnee's reply.

"I would not know," she said coyly. "What do the great warrior's eyes say to Cho-ko-le?"

Nah-kah-yen grinned again.

"Soaring Hawk's eyes," the Pawnee answered, staring intently at her face, "say what is in his heart. He wishes to know Cho-ko-le. He wishes to share himself with her."

As he translated this into Apache, Nah-kah-yen nodded, impressed by his friend's eloquence.

"This is a great honor," the young woman whispered, shifting nervously from foot to foot.

"Does this mean," the Pawnee asked, "that Cho-ko-le wishes to share herself with Soaring Hawk?"

Even though her skin had been tanned to a dark bronze by the sun, Soaring Hawk could tell that she was blushing. And, as the two men waited for Cho-ko-le's reply, Nah-kah-yen rolled his eyes and showed his strong teeth as he smiled at the Pawnee.

For an instant, the dark young beauty raised her eyes and looked searchingly into those of Soaring Hawk. He met her glance, and smiled back at her. Then Cho-ko-le, still shuffling from one foot to the other, lowered her eyes again.

All three fell silent beneath the ghostly moon, and Soaring Hawk waited patiently for the young woman's reply, staring at her beautiful face and listening to the night sounds of the Chiricahua Mountains.

When Cho-ko-le finally replied, the Pawnee and his interpreter had to strain their ears to hear her.

"What Soaring Hawk wishes at this moment," came the translated reply, "Cho-ko-le wishes as well."

"Then it is time for us to be alone," Soaring Hawk told her, eliciting a nod from Nah-kah-yen, as he translated this.

"It is well," replied Cho-ko-le, in the last Apache words that Nah-kah-yen would translate that night.

"I thank the Apache warrior for his kindness," the Pawnee told his translator.

"Much is owed to you," Nah-kah-yen told him before he went off into the night. "Whatever Soaring Hawk asks of me, that will I do."

The two men nodded to each other in mutual respect. A moment later, Nah-kah-yen was gone.

Soaring Hawk turned back to Cho-ko-le, and saw that the bronze beauty had turned, and was staring up at the pale silver moon.

"Cho-ko-le is fortunate," he whispered in her ear as he drew near, speaking in his own language. "She has the beauty of a doe and the grace of a wild mountain cat."

He reached around her back and placed one of his hands upon her shoulder, gently squeezing and caressing it as he turned her to him.

"Cho-ko-le fills Soaring Hawk with wonder," the brave went on. "She draws him as if she were a spirit sent to lure men to the place of darkness. She has stirred my heart and laid claim to my feelings. She is the sister of my heart."

She snuggled up to Soaring Hawk, looking up at him with wide and trusting eyes.

"Soaring Hawk does me much honor," she murmured as he smiled down at her, his eyes alight with feelings both tender and grave. "And gives me much pleasure by his presence. I see beauty in his form, and goodness in his eyes."

"Cho-ko-le's voice is clear as the running stream," the Pawnee replied in his own tongue. "And her eyes bring the starry skies close to me.

131

Her scent is the fragrance of the open prairie, at the time when life comes forth anew.''

"Soaring Hawk is the handsomest of men," the Apache beauty murmured, casting down her eyes, even though she knew he could not understand a word of what she had told him. "He is the tallest, and most graceful young man I have ever seen. He is lean and quick as the mountain lion; tall and strong as the stallion ridden by great Cochise."

"Soaring Hawk wishes to take Cho-ko-le in his arms," the brave whispered. "And then make love to her."

"Cho-ko-le has long dreamt of being intimate with such a man as Soaring Hawk," the Apache whispered back in her own speech.

Then, without having understood a single word that the other had spoken, their desires by now fully communicated through the agencies of facial expression, gesture, intonation and touch, Soaring Hawk and Cho-ko-le embraced.

When they finally came out of that first ardent and tender embrace, Cho-ko-le turned and took Soaring Hawk by the hand.

"Let us go now to the wickiup which Geronimo has provided for us," she whispered, looking over her shoulder and flashing him a bright Apache smile.

"Where Cho-ko-le goes," the Pawnee replied in a voice colored by the great emotion that he felt, "Soaring Hawk will follow. . . .

As Soaring Hawk and the doe-eyed Cho-ko-le started toward the place of delight where they would give physical expression to their desires, and to the feelings that each had aroused in the breast of the other, Davy Watson rolled over on his back reflexively, and awoke a moment later with a start and a groan.

Opening his eyes wide and gritting his teeth in reaction to the pain that screamed through the nerve ends of his flayed back, the young Kansan sat bolt-upright on his cot, shuddering and gasping for breath as wave after wave of almost unendurable pain wracked his body.

When the pain began to diminish in its intensity, Davy sighed and recollected the last instants of the dream he'd had before awakening.

It had taken place in the brown and austere compound of Fort Burnside, under a red, burning sun and the eyes of hundreds of blue-uniformed monkeys.

Suddenly the monkeys fell silent, as the hiss and crack of a bullwhip flayed the air. Davy felt a sharp stinging at his back, and when he looked over his shoulder, struggling to free himself from the whipping post to which he was lashed, the young Kansan saw Major Jock Forbes—stripped to the waist, and whirling a bullwhip in the air.

Kshhh-oook! The bullwhip made a whirring sound as it snaked through the air toward Davy's back. *Smack*! He screamed as it cut into his quivering flesh. The monkeys in blue began to jump up and down, chattering in excitement.

"That's enough—goddam you!" Davy Watson cried out to his tormentor, feeling himself grow in size, as if inflated with hatred and rage.

"I'm making an example of you, Watson," Forbes told him, smiling demonically as he wound up to deliver another blow.

"*Oh, no, you're not*!" Davy screamed at the

cavalry commander, bursting his bonds and turning from the whipping post.

"Get back!" Forbes cried out as Davy advanced upon him like an avenging angel. Then he lashed out at Davy with the bullwhip.

"*No-o-ooo!*" the young Kansan roared defiantly as he caught hold of the lash and began to pull on it, hand over hand, dragging Forbes ever closer to him.

"Seize him!" Forbes screamed, digging in his heels as the grim tug-of-war continued. "I order you to arrest this man," he called out to the legion of chattering monkeys.

But his command was not obeyed. The monkeys continued to jump up and down frantically, chattering and screaming among themselves.

Hand over hand, Davy continued to pull on the whip, his strength growing with each firm tug, until Forbes was within reach.

Just then, the major let go of the rope and thrust himself backward. But it was too late—for Davy had already released his grip, and was lunging at him!

A fraction of a second later, the young Kansan's big hands closed around his tormentor's throat. Forbes tried to scream, but all that came from his mouth was a strangled gurgle as Davy's strong fingers contracted relentlessly.

Davy watched with grim satisfaction as the major's face turned pale at first, and then more livid as he increased the pressure on the man's windpipe. He turned his head away as Forbes began to claw at his neck. He tightened his grip, squeezing even harder than before.

Jock Forbes' eyes bulged out of his head, and a

trickle of blood ran down his chin from the left side of his mouth. His body began to jerk spasmodically, and a moment later, his clawing hands grew still as they flexed and then stiffened, falling to his sides.

When he was satisfied that Forbes was dead, Davy Watson finally relaxed his grip, and allowed the body to crumple to the ground. After that he knelt by the major's side . . . and proceeded to gouge out the man's eyes.

Down they came from the mountain, moving noiselessly in their moccasins, gliding along in the eerie light as if they were disembodied spirits, Soaring Hawk the Pawnee following closely behind Cho-ko-le the Apache. Then, as the ground levelled off, the young woman led Davy Watson's blood-brother back along the tortuous path that led to Cochise's hidden camp in the Chiricahua Mountains.

That camp was located deep in the heart of an almost impassable, aggressively formed mass of cliffs, peaks and mesas, and could be reached only by means of a trail that was virtually invisible to all but the Apaches.

Following the course of a twisting stream that ran down from the heights, Cho-ko-le and Soaring Hawk made their way over to what the Plains Indian took to be the foot of a mountain pass. But what lay beyond it was not at all what he had expected to see.

As he stood looking out from the mouth of the pass, the Pawnee was amazed to see a valley below—a valley surrounded by cliff walls that formed a great natural basin, a veritable amphitheatre. It had trees and a level bottom composed of roughly fifty acres of grassland, Soaring Hawk estimated. Several streams watered the pleasant valley, and its precipitous, craggy walls were easily defended by Apache marksmen.

Now, in the heart of night, the camp was still as the Apaches slept. Only the sentinels remained awake, invisible at their posts on the surrounding cliffs. They were all heavily armed and at the ready, stubbornly determined that no one should surprise Cochise and his people in their hidden valley.

The sentry nodded curtly as Soaring Hawk and Cho-ko-le passed by him, on their way down to the valley. Then he hefted his breech-loading rifle and turned his face to the rocky pass that he was guarding.

When the two reached a cluster of wickiups that sat on the bank of a stream at the edge of the grassland, sheltered by a series of overhanging ledges, Cho-ko-le, still holding Soaring Hawk's hand, pointed to a dwelling that stood apart from all the rest.

"That is the wickiup of Geronimo," the young Apache announced to her companion. "He has put it at our disposal for the night."

Soaring Hawk nodded, although he understood no Apache. The association of Geronimo's name with the dwelling that Cho-ko-le had pointed to made the situation clear to the brave.

Hand-in-hand, the Pawnee and the Apache made their way down to the wickiup. In the moonlight, the stream took on the appearance of a rivulet of molten silver; and as they walked, beads of dew quivered on blades of grass like pearls dancing on the string of a necklace. An owl hooted at the far end of the valley and a colt whinnied briefly, breaking the heavy silence that mantled the secret camp of Cochise.

The wickiup was the basic unit of housing for the Indians of the arid southern half of the Arizona Territory. It was made of posts of trimmed saplings or the larger branches of trees, which were driven into the ground upright. These posts supported rafters, across which branches were bent in the shape of a dome. Bundles of brush were draped over this and tied down, until they formed a thick and uniform surface. The final step in the wickiup's construction was the plastering of the brush with mud, which would then be baked by the strong Arizona sun to a hard adobe finish which excellently withstood both heat and rain.

The wickiup had an oblong open space for a door, and the pale moonlight streamed through it, revealing, as Soaring Hawk entered, the sparse furnishings of the place. Matted brush covered the ground, upon which a blanket of vivid red and blue stripes had been spread. A small jug and an earthen crock stood by the head of the blanket, and across the room the Pawnee saw a blanket roll and a neatly folded pile of clothing.

Her eyes downcast now, Cho-ko-le knelt down on the edge of the blanket, beckoning Soaring Hawk to join her. Then she reached over and picked up the jug, which she held out to her Pawnee guest.

As he sat down upon the bright blanket, Soaring Hawk realized that the young Apache woman was blushing. And then his breath caught in his throat, as he saw how beautiful she was in the moonlight.

He took the jug as she murmured something in Apache. Tasting its contents, he discovered that it contained cool spring water.

After he drank, Cho-ko-le took the jug from the Pawnee's hands and replaced it with the earthen crock, which contained a venison stew. She passed him a bone spoon, raising her eyes to meet his for an instant. Soaring Hawk took a spoonful of the stew, nodded in approval, and then passed it to Cho-ko-le, urging her to eat. They sat on the blanket in silence, sharing the meal.

When they had finished eating, Cho-ko-le knelt over to put the jug and crock aside. Then, as she turned back to Soaring Hawk, the dark and lovely young Apache raised her eyes and met his, as she returned his look of intense longing.

"Cho-ko-le," the Pawnee whispered, each syllable a verbal caress, rising to his knees opposite her, his eyes never leaving the dark eyes of the lovely young woman. "Cho-ko-le," he said a second time, reaching out a hand and gently stroking her lustrous hair, whose color made him think of the darkness that mantles the plains on a cloudy, starless night.

From her thick black hair, he directed his caresses to the graceful column of Cho-ko-le's neck, and from there to her face, running his long, tapered fingers lightly over her high cheekbones and smooth skin.

Soaring Hawk felt an indescribable softness as his fingertips brushed her lips; and when his fingers circled up to her temples, ran over her brows and then grazed her eyes, the movement of Cho-ko-le's lashes made him think of a moth fluttering its delicate wings beneath the prairie moon as it settled onto a stalk of buffalo grass.

Next he ran his hands over the young Apache's arms, feeling the firmness and pronounced muscle tone characteristic of women whose way of life was physically demanding. Then he ran his hands down past her collar bone, gliding over her warm flesh until they came to rest upon her firm breasts.

Cho-ko-le shivered, and sighed like the wind rising in a mountain pass.

Cupping and massaging her breasts, Soaring Hawk rolled the young beauty's erect nipples between his fingertips, their stiffness softened by the flannel shirt that she wore.

"Cho-ko-le," the brave said in a husky voice, breathing heavily now, his hands leaving her breasts and running over her ribcage and belly.

Cho-ko-le gasped, made a sound like the ringnecked partridge at mating time, and then gave a long, whistling sigh as the Pawnee's deft hand continued its descent, caressing her mount of Venus, its palm coming to rest on its base, while his fingers gently compressed the lovely Apache's engorged nether lips.

At this, she gave three short moans, raising her eyes to his, the perfect oval of her face now slightly swollen with passion.

Soaring Hawk looked deep into her eyes as they reflected the moonlight that shone over his shoulder, reminding him of the sparkling pools formed by mountain streams. The brave smiled at her reassuringly as he began to open the buttons of her shirt.

A few moments later she lay naked before him on the blanket, as he removed his own garments. The skin beneath her clothing was the color of copper, never having been exposed to the strong sunlight, and her nipples and areolae were several shades darker, and stood out atop the gentle hillocks of her breasts in bold contrast.

Her flanks and thighs were trim and shapely, and she held her hands modestly over her sex, whose straight black hair and dark, pouting lips the Pawnee glimpsed between her fingers as he shed the last of his garments.

Soaring Hawk leaned forward and lay down on the blanket beside Cho-ko-le, who watched him now with half-lidded eyes. The brave reached out a hand and caressed her body in long, slow strokes, beginning at her temple and ending at the inside of her calf.

"Cho-ko-le," he whispered, passion rising in his voice like the wind that heralds a thunderstorm.

"I have longed for this moment," the dark young beauty murmured in Apache, lowering her eyes as she said this, only to dart a glance up at her Pawnee lover an instant later.

The brave smiled down at her. "It is well," he whispered in his own tongue. "Now we shall merge our bodies and spirits, and be as one."

Cho-ko-le reached up tentatively and ran her fingertips over the Plains Indian's smooth, hard-muscled chest at the same time that his gentle hand began to stroke her black-thatched pussy.

She sighed like the prairie wind as his middle finger parted her outer lips and ran down inside of them in a smooth, breathtaking stroke. Then he curved his finger in and penetrated her to the accompaniment of a soft squishing sound.

When he withdrew his finger, Soaring Hawk breathed deeply of the perfume of Cho-ko-le's arousal. Then he leaned toward her and placed his nostrils close to her hair, sniffing as he revelled in the subtle mixture of scents that emanated from her body. Following a downward course, sniffing like a hound dog in the act of flushing out a possum, the Pawnee covered the young Apache beauty's body with olfactory kisses.

Her hair smelt like prairie flowers, and her skin as fresh as the new spring grass. The hollows under her arms had a sharp, heady aroma, and the musky grotto between her thighs put the brave in mind of summer afternoons and the distant scent of otter at a pond.

She stroked his muscular upper arms and shoulders as he lightly massaged her breasts. And when he stroked the insides of her thighs, she ran her slender fingers through his hair and murmured in Apache, her body quivering with anticipation. Taking his cock in hand, somewhat in the manner of a warrior hefting a lance, Soaring Hawk guided himself into the grotto of delight. Cho-ko-le gasped as he did, and began to moan. And then, as he entered her to the length of his shaft, suddenly butting his pelvis against hers, the Apache beauty gasped and stiffened in the brave's arms.

Slow . . . and long . . . were the strokes that Soaring Hawk used at first, as he revelled in the warmth, wetness and snug fit of Cho-ko-le's pussy. She, in turn, thrust herself up toward him, matching the Pawnee exactly in the speed and intensity of her movements.

"Oh, a fire spreads deep within me," Cho-ko-le whispered in Apache, "like a brush fire in the dry season. And its heat thickens my blood and swells my veins."

"Cho-ko-le," Soaring Hawk whispered ardently.

"Oh, faster. Faster, my warrior," she cried out, urging her lover on with swifter movements of her own pelvis. "Come against me harder, now. Thrust toward me more deeply."

Soaring felt her pussy gripping him tightly, and his blood pounded as it coursed through his veins, keeping time with each wet, enveloping stroke that ran the length of her sheath.

Then he changed the tempo suddenly, causing her to gasp and stiffen beneath him, squirming frantically as she thrust herself toward Soaring Hawk in an attempt to take the brave deeper inside her. But the Pawnee kept only the head of his cock within the grip of her sphincter, barely entering the vaginal vestibule, working back and forth with a series of rapid and shallow strokes.

Suddenly he stopped for a moment, and then entered her with a deep vigorous thrust, running the full length of his stiff and throbbing cock, their groins meeting in a sudden, breathtaking contact. He could feel *everything*, each fraction of an inch, as his cock made its way into the snug, juicy warmth of Cho-ko-le's grotto of delight. He felt that pussy, as it spoke to him in an intimate language of contraction and release, of resistance and acceptance.

Now Cho-ko-le emitted little high-pitched cries of ecstasy, tugging at Soaring Hawk's hair and raking his bare back with her fingernails.

The Pawnee increased the depth and pressure of his strokes, and the Apache beauty matched him with her own complementary movements. Her eyes were closed now, and her mouth wide open. Her body began to shudder, and her pelvis hooked in toward his with sharp, staccato movements. And then she came, wailing "oh-h-h-h," over and over again, tossing, writhing and tugging at Soaring Hawk's hair as she was buffeted by the oceanic swell and breaking waves of her orgasm.

The sweat that ran down the hovering brave's cheeks fell onto Cho-ko-le, and pooled in the hollow of her neck. His eyes were glazed and heavy-lidded as he gazed down at her. Having held his own climax at bay until the lovely Apache was experiencing hers, Soaring Hawk surrendered to the almost unbelievable pressure in his groin and then saw a battery of lights flashing somewhere in his brain, like shooting stars crossing the summer sky. A wrenching groan arose from the depths of his being, and at the moment when he felt his soul take flight, the Pawnee closed his eyes and let the dark, turbulent river of his instincts sweep him away.

Cho-ko-le herself was borne away on the tide of her own instincts, and her cries blended with his in a fervent chorus of release. Once their passion had been spent, there was rest and a state of mindless, floating bliss. Then came a period where the Indian lovers snuggled within each other's arms, and nestled within the golden cocoon of their shared tenderness. And after that, when the fires of their bodies, emotions and spirits had banked and gone out, there was sleep. . . .

Chapter Six

The bugles of Fort Burnside sounded at the crack of dawn and the blue ranks of cavalry streamed through the gates of the post as Major Jock Forbes led his horse soldiers out toward the engagement that would break the power of the Apaches once and for all, and bring him fame and a promotion to colonel.

Riding apart from the long file of troopers, surrounded by the rough frontiersmen who comprised the company of scouts led by Paul Hutzelman, was a bedraggled figure who sat slumped over his saddle. The man looked neither left nor right, but rode with bowed head and sullen countenance, brooding darkly beneath the rising sun.

It was Davy Watson. His wounds had healed sufficiently in the last few days to enable him to travel on horseback, and Major Forbes had ordered him brought along, in view of his possible use as bait to lure Soaring Hawk—and through him, Geronimo—into a trap . . . for surprise was the tactic which the cavalry commander had decided upon.

The major rode at the head of his troopers, with Old Glory fluttering behind him in the morning breeze. He wore an expression of veiled exultation upon his face, the look of a man who has just drawn his fourth ace at the poker table. He was secure in the fact that his two hundred-odd troopers were all combat-ready and loaded for bear. And he was also confident that he held the reins of future events.

Jock Forbes was gloating, secretly pleased that Hutzelman was unaware of the great opportunity for making military and political capital that he had supplied. Not only had the word of Geronimo's rescue created a great public furor which resulted in a mandate to deal with the Apache situation in any way that the major saw fit, but the bounty hunter had further put him in touch with someone who would reveal the location of Cochise's hidden camp in the heart of the Chiricahua Mountains.

Ko-deh-ne was an Apache outcast, a man who had committed a crime so grave in the eyes of his tribesmen that they had chosen to ostracize him. Hutzelman hinted that the Apache's offense had something to do with incest, but no one could say for certain what Ko-deh-ne had done. But what *was* evident, the bounty hunter had pointed out to Forbes, was the man's great animosity toward Cochise, the man who had formally ostracized him.

The Apache had fallen upon hard times, and was living the life of a marauder. Bands of outcasts often formed for the purpose of looting and thievery, but they were eventually exterminated, either by the Mexicans, the Americans, or even other Apaches.

Ko-deh-ne was one of the survivors of a band that had been hunted down by the U.S. Cavalry, and Hutzelman had occasion to hear his story recently at Fort Burnside, where the prisoners were incarcerated. The bounty hunter immediately relayed this news to Major Forbes, and the commander of the post was quick to take advantage of the situation, offering the renegade Apache his freedom in return for leading him to Cochise's hidden stronghold.

Ko-deh-ne agreed without hesitation, never batting an eye at the thought of betraying many men, women and children along with Cochise, so deep was his thirst for revenge. And now, as the Apache rode out at his side, Jock Forbes gloated, realizing that Hutzelman had not been smart enough to seek a share of the glory that would attend the successful completion of this mission. Soon, Forbes told himself, he would be the equal of flashier, better-connected officers such as George Armstrong Custer. . . .

Wincing in pain as his horse broke into a trot, Davy Watson felt a pang of sadness at the thought that he might never see his Pawnee blood-brother alive again. This was one of the two major themes that dominated his consciousness on that morning. The other was how to avenge himself upon Major Forbes.

Davy's misfortune had hit him with all the devastating suddenness of a lightning bolt, and the young Kansan was still in the process of comprehending the enormity of what had happened, and what was going to happen to him. Branded the accomplice of no less a criminal than Geronimo, Davy realized that he would be considered by many a traitor to his country. And the consequent punishment for such a crime would most likely be a prison sentence whose shorter end would consist of something like twenty years' hard labor in a federal penitentiary.

Or it might not even come to a trial, the prisoner admitted to himself grimly. Both Forbes and Hutzelman were utterly ruthless men, and he knew that his life was far from safe while he remained in their "protective" custody. He could not understand why, but he had a feeling that the bounty hunter was using him, playing some strange and secretive game of his own. And Davy Watson was also sure that the worst was yet to come. He had never felt so lost and alone in his entire life. . . .

As Cochise's eyes narrowed and his bronzed face was suddenly drained of all color, Soaring Hawk became aware that the Apache chieftain was being buffeted by a thunderstorm of anger behind the mask of his stoical composure.

Shortly after sunrise, the Pawnee had left the wickiup to which he had retired with the beautiful and ardent Cho-ko-le the night before, taking his leave of the young Apache in total silence, his parting glance far more eloquent than his words could ever be. Then he joined Cochise, Geronimo, and a number of warriors around the campfire for a breakfast served by the women, which consisted of the buds of the cholla plant baked on a bed of coals, and cakes made from the figlike fruit of the saguaro cactus.

The cause of Cochise's anger had been the news that he had just received from a new arrival at the camp, a brave named Ponce. The chief had earlier been disturbed by rumors of white men going to Superstition Mountain and, even though his people were currently in the Chiricahua Mountains, Cochise detailed two of his warriors to observe the

147

actions of any White-eyes who might have the temerity to violate the most holy place of the Apaches.

Ponce had been one of the observers, and he returned to the hidden valley with the disconcerting news that white men were indeed digging for gold in the abode of the Thunder God. And more than that, he had seen Killer-of-Apaches come and speak with the man in charge, who was none other than their former friend, the man who had betrayed Geronimo . . . the Indian agent, Shackleton.

Cochise's features were hard, and his eyes blazed as he spoke. "Now, I understand. Now it is clear to me," he told the Apache warriors. "Shackleton made much trouble for us, and Killer-of-Apaches aroused all the White-eyes in the south, so that we would have to stay hidden in these mountains."

The eyes of Geronimo flashed in the war chief's ugly face. "They are after the gold, those two. They seek to keep us away from the high place."

"There is more, O Cochise," Ponce said, nodding his head and looking around at each of the assembled Apache warriors.

"Red hair rides out of Fort Burnside at the head of many horse soldiers," he told them all, referring to Major Forbes. "They come here after Cochise and his people."

The warriors began to mutter angrily among themselves. Soaring Hawk's eyes travelled over their faces, coming to rest upon the strong features of the Apache chief.

"Let them come," Cochise growled in a deep voice. "We will see if the horse soldiers know how to die, for die they surely will."

"They will know what it is to feel the fury of the Apaches," Geronimo told them with a frightening smile. "Let them come. My knife is sharp, and thirsty for blood."

"Red hair brings a white prisoner," Ponce added.

"The brother of Soaring Hawk," Geronimo told him.

"Why does he bring my white brother?" the Pawnee asked as Ponce nodded, his eyes narrowing as he turned to Geronimo.

"To bargain with, or to use as protection," the war chief answered. "He must believe that we would not kill the brother of the man who saved my life."

"Is this so?" Soaring Hawk asked, turning to Cochise as he realized that Davy Watson's life was in great danger.

The chief's eyes met his. Cochise shook his head slowly, a trace of sadness visible in the set of his mouth. "We must now fight for our lives against the horse soldiers. Your friend is among them. It will be very difficult to spare his life. I cannot promise that."

It was Soaring Hawk's turn to nod his head. "So be it," he said in a low voice. "It is in the hands of the Great Spirit."

"It is time, O my brothers," Geronimo said as he rose to his feet, "to demonstrate once more that Apache warriors are not afraid to die."

"Death to Red hair!" a brave cried.

"Death to all White-eyes!" the war chief cried back in reply.

Paul Hutzelman reined his horse in beside that

of the Apache outcast, Ko-deh-ne. The Indian glared suspiciously at the bounty hunter, fully aware that he was being visited by the dreaded Killer-of-Apaches himself.

"I come to remind my friend, Ko-deh-ne," Hutzleman said in Apache, "that he will gain much honor and money after we vanquish Cochise and Geronimo."

"Ko-deh-ne wants no money and needs no honor," the brave replied haughtily. "All he wants is revenge upon Cochise."

"That he will have in plenty," the bounty hunter assured him.

Staring straight ahead, no longer looking at Hutzelman, the Apache nodded.

"But if Ko-deh-ne speaks with forked tongue and tries to betray us," Hutzelman went on, patting his saddle, "then I will add his scalp to those of his brothers."

The Apache darted a sidelong glance at Hutzelman's saddle, which was fringed on both sides with many Apache scalps. The renegade paled visibly, but said nothing.

Studying Ko-deh-ne's face, Hutzelman broke out into a grin. "And before my friend gives up his scalp," he said quietly, "he will spend a long time dying, in pain greater than any man has ever known. Does Ko-deh-ne understand his friend, Hutzelman?"

The Apache nodded, a tic appearing at the corner of his left eye. "Ko-deh-ne understands."

"It is well," Hutzelman murmured as he wheeled his horse around and rode back along the column of cavalry to where Davy Watson rode, flanked by two of the bounty hunter's cronies.

"Well, Mr. Watson," he said cheerfully, as he reined in his mount beside that of the man on Davy's left, "it looks like we'll be havin' Injun fer dinner. What d'ya say to that?"

Davy just glared ahead sullenly, not even acknowledging the bounty hunter's presence.

"But don't you worry none, Mr. Watson," the man known as Killer-of-Apaches crooned. "I'm a-goin' to find yer Injun friend fer ya. An' when I do, I'll bring ya back his scalp."

"Now, listen here, you sum'bitch," Davy growled suddenly, shifting in his saddle as he turned to face the bounty hunter. But as he did, the man on his right whipped out his Colt .45 and slammed its butt down between the young Kansan's shoulder blades, causing him to straighten up and grunt in pain.

"You got to learn to go easy, Mr. Watson," Hutzelman said mockingly. "'Cause a man who lets hisself get as upset 'bout things as you do is bound for an early grave."

The riders flanking Davy began to laugh.

"An' if I was you," Hutzelman added, speaking now in tones of mock-confidentiality, "I wouldn't tell ol' Major Forbes no more 'bout how we come upon ya when you was a-stickin' it to that purty li'l Mex he's sweet on."

As the men laughed again, Davy stared straight ahead, his face a sullen mask. Knowing full well that he was powerless for the moment, the young Kansan decided to bide his time, waiting to strike with the patience of a rattler, contenting himself with a thorough review of the possible ways in which to kill Paul Hutzelman when the opportunity presented itself. . . .

At the head of the long blue column rode Major Jock Forbes, dreaming of what he would do on the day that he came to Washington to be honored by President Grant as the man who had killed both Geronimo and Cochise and conquered the dreaded Chiricahua Apaches. He was just savoring the vision of a victory parade in his honor, when a fierce cry—unmistakable to those who had ever heard it before—rent the air.

"No," Forbes cried out in shocked disbelief, drawing his Army-issue Colt revolver out of its holster and standing up in his stirrups as he did. *"Apaches! It can't be!"*

At the moment that the wild cry rang out, startling the cavalry commander, the column of horsemen were riding through a pass high in the Chiricahua Mountains. Rock walls towered above them on both sides, and the level ground upon which the troopers rode was open and exposed. As any military tactician could have pointed out, the place was a perfect spot for an ambush.

"Oh, God—the Apaches!" Major Forbes screamed, his face livid, his eyes bulging under the pressure of his surprise and the rage which attended it. By this time, dozens of large rocks were tumbling down the walls of the pass, set in motion by the Apaches above. And by the time that the commander of Fort Burnside cried *"Bugler—sound the alarm!"* Cochise and his warriors had taken aim with their weapons and unleashed a storm of arrows and hot lead upon the heads of the beleagured cavalry.

Half-way through sounding the alarm, the bugler abruptly terminated his call with a screeching high note, as an arrow pierced his throat.

Major Forbes emptied his pistol at the all-but-invisible assailants above, and then wheeled his horse around and rode back along the line of his troops. As he went, the major saw that the ranks were in total confusion, with men swearing and horses whinnying, the screams of men and beasts rising above the din of battle each time a rock, bullet or arrow found its mark. The ground was already littered with blue-coated bodies and the carcases of horses, and Jock Forbes heard screams beneath him as he rode his horse over the dying and wounded.

"Make for the cover of the rocks!" Forbes called out in passing, as he attempted to rally his confused ranks. But there was precious little shelter to be had in the pass. Cochise had chosen the spot well.

Ko-deh-ne's eyes bulged in his head and his jaw dropped as he realized that he and the White-eyes were trapped in an Apache ambush. He was the one who was going to surprise Cochise in his sudden camp. *What was happening?*

The renegade was never to learn the answer to that question, for no sooner had he asked it than his life came to a bloody end.

"You dirty red dog," Hutzelman growled as he leaned over in his saddle, lunging at the Indian. The Bowie knife in his hand shone brilliantly in the sun for an instant, and then it was coated with red, covered with Ko-deh-ne's blood, as the bounty hunter slit the renegade's throat from ear to ear.

His cry of horror and surprise ending in a strangled gurgle, the Apache pitched out of his saddle and fell headfirst to the ground.

Davy Watson never moved a muscle as he watched the murder that transpired only a few feet ahead of him. He never moved at all until a bullet whipped his hat off his head. Then he ducked down in his saddle, just as the bounty hunter sheathed his bloody knife and rode over to his men. Suddenly, Davy felt the first hope he had known in days, as he realized that Soaring Hawk was probably somewhere up above him.

"Jesus, we're trapped, Paul," one of the men flanking Davy cried out. "What'll we do?"

"Listen up," Hutzelman told them, unholstering his .44. "The blue boys is tryin' to make a stand—that's what them damn Apaches expect."

Suddenly, he spun around and fired up at a ledge above the riders. A scream was heard, and an instant later a body came crashing down to the ground.

"But we're gon' bull our way out'n the pass—back the way we come. There's a passel of Apaches gatherin' there, now, but there'll be a shitload more a-comin' to bottle us up. So le's beat the red bastards to the punch."

One of his men cried out and slid from his saddle. The other men looked to Hutzelman anxiously, after they had fired several volleys up at their ambushers.

"What about the Watson kid, Paul? Should I drill 'im?" asked the man at Davy's right, chilling the young Kansan's blood as he did.

The bounty hunter shook his head. "Hell, no," he told the others. "We're takin' Watson with us. He's our insurance policy, such as it is. Now, let's vamoose!"

Saying this, the bounty hunter leaned forward in his saddle, pressing against the mane of his horse as he put his spurs to the animal. Then, as the horse shot forward, breaking into a gallop moments later, Hutzelman's followers took off behind him, the man on Davy Watson's right grabbing the reins of his horse and taking the young Kansan along with him.

Guns blazing, howling like Comanches, Hutzelman's little band fought their way to the head of the pass. Surprise worked in their favor, and they gained it before a force sufficient to seal it off had arrived. Also fortunate for the riders was the fact that the general confusion allowed them to go a good distance toward the head of the pass before the Apaches above were able to get the hard-riding bunch in their gunsights. Scattering the braves who guarded the exit from the pass, the horsemen thundered through to freedom.

Davy Watson crouched low in the saddle as bullets smacked into the flesh of men around him or whizzed past his bare head with the sound of angry hornets. And as the band rode hell-bent for leather in their desperate attempt to escape the trap that Cochise and Geronimo had laid, Davy's only thought was for the moment when utter confusion set in—the moment when he would be able to launch himself at Paul Hutzelman, with the intent of taking his life. But that was not to be.

He groaned in disappointment as the horses shot out of the pass, followed by gunshots and the screams of the frustrated Apaches. Then his heart sank as Davy imagined that he was leaving Soaring Hawk behind, and that he might never see his blood-brother again . . . at least, not in this life.

Hutzelman's bold plan had worked. The bounty hunter and his followers had fought their way out of the Apache trap. But at great cost: Now, only Hutzelman and three of his pistoleros remained, the other four having paid the price of the escape with their lives.

"By God, Paul—we did it!" a pale, lanky man told the bounty hunter, clapping him heartily on the back as they made their way down from the pass. "But we lost Swinson an' Burdett."

Hutzelman looked over his shoulder. "McCoy an' Walpole, too, by the look of it," he muttered. "Well, that's jus' that much more gold we'll have to divvy up 'mongst ourselves."

"Kin I drill the Watson kid now, Paul?" asked the man who held the reins of Davy's horse.

"Not yet," the young Kansan heard Hutzelman growl. "Not 'til we git our butts off'n Superstition Mountain."

"That where we's headin'?"

"You bet your sweet ass it is," the bounty hunter told the man. "Them Apaches is gonna be tied up fer a while, takin' care of ol' Jock Forbes an' his boys, so I figger it's the perfect time to haul ass over to the Dutchman's mine an' finish our business there. Shackleton should be 'bout ready, so's I don't guess it'll take long a-tall to load up an' tote our fortunes away. Then we jus' hightail it out of the territory, an' live high on the hawg fer the rest of our lives."

"You won't live long enough to spend none of that gold, Hutzelman," Davy Watson told the bounty hunter in a voice that rang with hatred and scorn. Then he grunted as the man beside him delivered a sharp backhand slap to the side of his head.

"One thing I know fer sure, Watson," Hutzelman told him, grinning from ear to ear. "I'm gon' be livin' a lot longer than you will. . . ."

The fierce, wild cries of the Apaches grew more exultant as the carnage progressed within the confines of the mountain pass. Jock Forbes, wounded in both shoulder and thigh, had fought his way over to the cluster of boulders that afforded some sparse shelter in the lonely place where he and his men found themselves trapped.

His ranks had been decimated. The cavalry commander estimated that less than a quarter of his troops were still on their feet. Apache losses, as far as Forbes was able to tell, had been minimal. He and his company were trapped, and all that Cochise and his warriors had to do was to pick them off at will, as if they were shooting fish in a barrel.

The major heard a flat, thwacking sound at his elbow, and turned to see what had made the strange noise. As he did, the trooper behind him emitted a long, wheezing sigh, and slid down to the ground, the brightly-feathered shaft of an arrow protruding from his chest.

The major wheeled back around, squatted down behind the rock, aimed his Colt at an overhang by the opposite wall of the pass, and fired twice. He grunted with satisfaction as a man cried out.

In response to this, the Apaches intensified their fire. Three more of Forbes' cavalrymen fell to the ground.

"Damn those filthy savages," the major muttered to himself as he put his last five bullets into the Army Colt. He clenched his teeth as a wave of searing pain broke over his body. And as he caught his breath, tears streaming down his cheeks, Major Jock Forbes involuntarily recalled the raw, bloody back of Davy Watson.

Then, as he finished loading his revolver, Forbes had a fleeting vision of the glory and honor that the Apache ambush had cost him.

Instead of a victory parade through the heart of his nation's capitol, on boulevards overflowing with worshiping crowds, the major found himself trapped in a grim and desolate place, boxed in by a foe who was noted for his lack of mercy and the severity of his retribution. In the space of a few short hours, he had lost everything.

Groaning with the pain of his deep wounds, Forbes fired two shots up at the rocks overhead, narrowly missing the Apache warriors who were closing in on him.

"Damn them, damn them," Jock Forbes sobbed, laying his head on his arm after firing off another shot. A moment later, the answering fire of the Apaches came crackling back from above and across the pass.

He realized bitterly that, instead of returning to Washington as the Victor of Arizona, he would end his life in this desolate place, and his scalp would soon adorn one of Cochise's lodge poles.

"Major Forbes," one of his troopers called out in an anguished voice. "We're out of ammunition, sir. What'll we do now?"

Jock Forbes did not answer. And then, when the trooper cried out in desperation, repeating his question, the commander of Fort Burnside still did not reply.

Major Jock Forbes did not bother to reply, for he was a man who preferred to lead by example.

There were two bullets left in his Colt. The first he fired at the Apaches. And the second, by way of example, he put into his own head.

Chapter Seven

The drab brown floor of the mountain pass was accented by areas of blue and red, the colors of the fallen soldiers' uniforms and blood. Bodies of men and horses littered the pass for the greater part of its length. With the exception of the escape of Hutzelman and his scouts, Major Forbes' entire expeditionary force had been trapped in the Apache ambush. The embattled troops had been able to hold out for several hours, but their numbers had steadily diminished under the deadly cross-fire from above.

Cochise stared down at the grim scene, his dark, hawk's eyes scanning the battlefield, as he calculated the magnitude of his victory and the worth of the spoils that had fallen to him.

It had been a major victory, no question about that. The Apaches had decimated the ranks of the United States Cavalry troops stationed in the area and killed Red hair, their great enemy, the horse soldier who had vowed not to rest until the last Apache had been exterminated.

One or two more victories like that, Cochise reflected, might be sufficient to panic the white settlers south of Prescott, and stampede them out of Apache Territory once and for all.

The Apache triumph was rich in the spoils that attended it. Red hair and his horse soldiers had come well-equipped to the Chiricahua Mountains,

Cochise knew, for only a fool or a madman—unless he were an Apache—would not do so before daring to enter such rugged and forbidding country. And what the bluecoats had no further use for, the Apache chief reflected ironically, would arm and sustain his people for some time to come.

Some horses had been killed in the encounter, but many survived; and a great number of pack mules as well. In the saddlebags of those animals would be many things that the Apaches could use. And the food and supply wagons of the cavalry were still intact. His people, the chief told himself, would be provisioned for many moons.

Then there were the coarse blue uniforms of the fallen troopers, which were much valued as winter wear by the Indians. Cochise's warriors liked to wear the blue shirts of the cavalrymen, especially those of the sergents, with their yellow chevrons and rockers on both sleeves, and those of the officers, with their gold and silver insignia.

And the solid boots of the soldiers were also prized by the braves, as were the broad, golden-tasseled blue hats of the officers.

More important than all those things, the chief of the Chiricahuas noted with grim satisfaction as he surveyed that place of death and desolation, were the weapons that had fallen into Apache hands. War was the mainstay of the Apache way of life, and its implements were vital to the maintenance of that way of life.

A veritable arsenal was now his for the taking, Cochise gloated, the stolid mask of his face hiding the great and fierce exultation that he felt. There were many carbines and breech-loading rifles;

Army-issue Colt revolvers littered the battleground in profusion. The ammunition required for these weapons Cochise resolved to obtain on his next raid. Perhaps he would gather his warriors and strike directly at Fort Burnside, the last place in all Arizona that the White-eyes would now expect the Chiricahua Apaches to appear.

The chief nodded as he saw the considerable number of sheathed sabres hanging from the belts of the fallen cavalrymen. Those bright, keen blades were much sought after by his braves, as they were also considered to be used by the Gahe, the mountain gods worshiped by the Apaches.

"I'm dying, Mother," a thin voice rose in the air, suddenly cutting through the stillness that had mantled the battlefield. "Oh, Mother. Help me, please."

As if in response to that anguished and delirious cry, a wounded horse whinnied, the sharp register of its pain echoing off the walls of the pass.

All of the Apache braves watched Cochise intently, waiting for a signal from their leader.

The chief looked from side to side as the last echo of the horse's cry of pain and suffering faded away. Then he stepped out from behind the ledge where he had directed the ambush, and raised both hands in the air. Silence filled the pass once more, an expectant silence that pulsed in the air like the collective heartbeat of the Apache band.

Nodding once, a grave expression on his craggy painted face, Cochise brought his arms down with a sudden, sharp motion. Shrill cries of triumph reverberated through the mountain pass, echoing and re-echoing off its walls, as the warriors all rose to their feet, left their positions, and streamed down onto the battlefield.

Moving like locusts over a field of grain, the braves looted the bodies of their fallen enemies. An occasional shot rang out above the general clamor, often heralded by a scream or a pitiful neighing sound, as the warriors administered the *coup de grace* to any wounded troopers or horses they came upon. And as they scoured the field, the braves would call out to one another, making jokes and announcing what they had plundered.

"Look at Gian-nah-tah," one grizzled veteran cried to his comrades. "He looks like a great chief in his new hat."

The warrior referred to grinned broadly as he stood up, releasing his grip on the hair of the lieutenant he had been about to scalp. "It will not be needed by this young white chief any longer," he called out. "Now it will be my victory hat, which I will wear to remind my brothers of our great victory at Arrowhead Pass. It will be big medicine."

"And I have two fine rifles," another called out, holding aloft a carbine in each hand. The warrior was even uglier than Geronimo, and he smiled at the Apaches with the face of a gargoyle.

"With these two rifles, I will kill twice as many White-eyes as before," the man roared.

In response to this, the warriors broke out into that shrill and chilling cry of exultation that is peculiarly Apache.

"I have fine leather boots," another brave crowed, once the last echoes of the wild cries had faded. "They make me look like a Mexican *vacquero*," he said as he strutted proudly before the others.

"And now," he added, coming to a halt and looking around the battlefield, a mischievous expression coming onto his face. "With these strong boots, I can smash the skulls of my enemies," here he drove the heel of his boot into the face of a dead cavalryman, "as a horse steps upon an egg."

"Many Kicks will be your name, hereafter," boomed an older warrior, rising to his feet and pointing to the brave in cavalryman's boots.

"Many Kicks," the other Apaches cried out delightedly. "That is a good name."

"Many Kicks is my name," the man with the boots repeated with a proud grin on his face.

"Many Kicks," chorused the other Apaches.

"Look what I have found," a warrior at the head of the pass yelled back to his comrades. "This man was shot off his horse, and when he fell to the ground, his teeth came out of his mouth."

The other Apaches all turned in the direction of the speaker, and saw the brave holding up a pair of false teeth for all to see.

False teeth were a great curiosity to the Apaches, an emblem of that mysterious technology of the White-eyes, who seemed obsessed with the attempt to mechanically duplicate and improve upon the workings of nature. This technological turn of mind, this ideology of "progress," was an extremely difficult thing for the Apaches, and Indians in general, to understand.

Barring fights and accidents, the Apaches rarely lost any teeth, and were baffled by the white man's clumsy fabrication of the efficient instruments with which nature had endowed men. Their diet was coarse and natural, almost totally lacking in the soft foods favored by the whites, and consequently the Apaches went through life with strong, healthy teeth. They regarded the use of false teeth as a bizarre and degenerate practice, one which confirmed their opinion of the whites as a race out of touch with nature. False teeth, false food, false ideals and false hearts: such, the Apaches believed, was the nature of the men who had invaded their ancient lands.

His heart rising within his breast as the great eagle rises into the morning air from its eyrie on a mountain peak, Cochise strode over the battleground, surveying with immense satisfaction the full extent of his victory. The day of the Battle of Arrowhead Pass was a day that the Chiricahua Apaches would long remember.

"I have taken this for you, O Cochise," a warrior called out as the chief walked past. The man held out a brand new Winchester rifle.

"I thank my brother, Shar Knife," the chief called back, continuing on his way.

"Big medicine for the tent of Cochise," another Apache cried, coming up to his chief, holding the torn and bloodied flag of the United States of America in his hands.

"It will remind me always of our great victory," Cochise told the man, still moving on.

As he made his way through the pass, Cochise was hailed continually by his warriors, who made him gifts of the best of the spoils. These things they gave freely, in token of the great esteem in which they held their chief.

Cochise moved among them, acknowledging each tribute with a nod and a few well-chosen words, never halting until he came to the place he had been seeking.

"Here is what my chieftain seeks," the warrior Nah-kah-yen told him, pointing to the pair of booted feet that stuck out from behind a boulder. Here is the body of the white chief."

"Red hair?" Cochise asked in a low voice, careful not to display his great excitement.

Nah-kah-yen nodded. "Red is his hair, more red now than it was in life . . . for it is red with his blood."

"It is well that he is dead," Cochise said, walking over to the spot that the brave had pointed out and standing over the corpse of Major Jock Forbes. "He will hunt no more Apaches."

"What will he hunt in the dark place?" Nah-kah-yen asked his chief.

Cochise shook his head. "No man knows for sure," he told the brave. "No man can truly say what goes on in the land of shadows."

"Red hair will not be alone," the warrior told his chief, smiling a smile that was as sharp as the blade in his hand. "We have sent many of his soldiers along with him on that journey."

"Perhaps we shall meet him, one day," the Apache chief mused as he knelt down beside the body of the late commander of Fort Burnside, the man who had wished to outdo that other ambitious and arrogant cavalry officer, George Armstrong Custer.

The major had used his last bullet wisely, reflected Cochise, for by blowing out his own brains he had escaped the elaborate and enduring torture that he would certainly have been subjected to by the victorious Apaches, whose hatred of Jock Forbes was surpassed only by their animosity toward the man they had named Killer-of-Apaches, the man who had taken more scalps than any of the Chiricahuas.

That was the only thing to mar Cochise's joy on this occasion, and as he unsheathed his long knife, the chief was chagrined at the thought of Hutzelman's bold escape. For he, as did all Apaches, had a score to settle with the bounty killer.

Red hair had done a good job of killing himself, Cochise thought as he dropped to his knees and leaned over his dead enemy, his shadow falling over the major's face, shading its contorted features.

The major's blood and brains spattered the ground behind his body, and a sticky red pool had formed on the earth beneath his head as he lay flat on his back. The bullet from his pistol had entered his right temple, and emerged on the upper left side of his head, blowing away a goodly portion of his skull.

Red Hair must have died instantly, Cochise told himself as his fingers curled in the auburn locks of Jock Forbes' hair. That was unfortunate, for the warriors would have derived much satisfaction from watching the spectacle of so great an enemey's protracted sufferings.

But that was not to be, Cochise realized, nodding as he pulled on the auburn locks in his left hand and brought down the knife in his right, setting about the business of taking the scalp of Major Jock Forbes. . . .

Davy Watson's blood grew cold as he realized that he had, at best, a few more hours to live. The peaks of Superstition Mountain loomed before him, and the young Kansan knew that once Hutzelman and his associates had taken the gold down from the Dutchman's mine, his usefulness to the bounty hunter would be at an end.

They were using him as a hostage, in case the Indians had come in pursuit of them. But no riders had been sighted on their trail, so apparently no one was about to come to his rescue, Davy told himself, shivering in reaction to the grim finality of that conclusion. Once the riders were out of the mountains, his life wasn't going to be worth a plugged nickel; for Hutzelman would surely kill him before he and his men hightailed it out of the Arizona Territory.

He'd been in tight scrapes before, Davy told himself, but at least he'd had a fighting chance then. Now he sat weaponless among four armed men, going to meet at least as many more, he expected. His hands were bound together with a rawhide thong, and the men on either side of him watched Davy as closely as a fox watches a chicken coop.

There didn't seem to be a thing he could do, the young Kansan reflected sourly, looking up the slope at the man in the gray suit who stood on top of a boulder and waved his gray hat, signalling Hutzelman to come ahead. Soaring Hawk was nowhere to be found in the vicinity; in fact, Davy couldn't even be sure that his blood-brother had been with the Apaches who ambushed Major

Forbes and his troopers. For an instant, an icy, hangman's smile flitted over Davy's mouth as he pictured Forbes at the mercy of the Chiricahua Apaches.

Prospects for the future looked grim, and it seemed to Davy Watson that the only remaining agency which could effect his release from captivity would be a slug from Hutzelman's .44.

"Geey-yup!" the man riding behind him cried out as the ascent grew perilously steep. Davy turned in his saddle and looked down the side of Superstition Mountain, down the rugged, thorny surface that descended at a sharp and dizzying angle.

Everywhere he looked, the young Kansan saw jagged rocks, spiked and bristling cacti and plants whose leaves were as sharp as the points of an Indian lance. It was the most inhospitable landscape he had ever seen; the desolate panorama made him think of a garden plot in hell. But he also realized, as he felt a sinking feeling in the pit of his stomach, that it was also the landscape of his hopes.

"Turn back around, Watson," the rider behind him growled, "or I'll blow off your other earlobe."

Davy turned back around, and as he did, a pang of longing stabbed him in the heart. He thought of his loved ones in faraway Kansas: his mother; his sister, Amy; and Lucius Erasmus, his kid brother. And the pain of loss and regret became even more intense when Davy Watson thought about Deanna MacPartland.

He had ridden so hard, and travelled so far in the past fourteen months, and now, as he was finally about to return to the arms of his sweetheart, his blonde angel of passion, Davy was forced to end his odyssey in the harsh and arid land of Arizona, where his bones would lie out on the windswept desert, bleaching under the merciless glare of the red, Apache sun.

"How's it goin', Ernest?" Hutzelman called out to the man in the gray suit, after he and his men had dismounted to lead their horses up the final stage of the difficult ascent. The man nodded vigorously, in answer to the bounty hunter's question.

Weaver's Needle towered in the background as the men and horses reached level ground, that huge black mass of basalt that the *peones* of Don Miguel Peralta had called the Finger of God.

"We're moving along according to schedule," the man told Hutzelman, taking off his gray Stetson and mopping his brow with a linen handkerchief. "I didn't expect to see you so soon."

"Got out of the Chiricahuas a mite sooner'd I'd planned," the bounty hunter told Shackleton, once he had tethered his horse. "That sum'bitch Cochise bushwhacked us."

"Cochise!" the Indian agent cried out in alarm. "Is he . . . coming after . . . ?" His voice trailed off, and he stared at the bounty hunter, an expression of pure fear on his face.

"No, no, Ernest," Hutzelman replied in a voice whose tone of gentleness surprised Davy Watson. "We pulled a fast one on them Apaches, and shagged-ass out'n their li'l ol' trap."

He paused to spit out a goblet of tobacco juice. "Cost me four of the boys," he went on. "But we done blasted our way out'n that ambush of Cochise's—an' a clever one it was, too. Why, we'd barely gone into the mountains when they'd sprung it on us." He scratched his head. "Wonder how in hell they got wind of us so soon?"

He began to grin wickedly at his partner. "But that don't make no never mind now. An' we done left ol' Jock Forbes an' 'bout two hundred of his blueboys down there to keep the red dogs busy, Ernest. By Gad, there was one hell of a shootout goin' on when we left. I figger even if they come a-lookin' fer us afterwards, we done got us four or five hours headstart on 'em."

"And Geronimo?" Shackleton asked anxiously.

"Shit, I don't know, Ernest," Hutzelman told him with a sigh. "I ain't had no news of ol' Geronny since the frogfaced li'l bastard rode out of Phoenix with this here hombre's Injun buddy." Saying this, the bounty hunter jerked a thumb in Davy Watson's direction.

"And what about *him*?" Shackleton asked in a quavering voice as he put on his Stetson hat. "Why in God's name did you bring him back here, Paul? *Why*?"

"Simmer down, Ernest. I tell you it don't make no never mind. I'll tend to him."

The Indian agent looked stricken. His eyes travelled from Davy to the bounty hunter. "But you know what this means," he gasped, going white in the face. "You'll have to. . . ."

"Now, don't go gittin' yerself in a tizzy," Hutzelman said soothingly. "Ain't no way in hell a body can make a omelette without first he breaks the eggs. That's somethin' you jus' gotta learn, Ernest. But don't worry. I'll take care of

171

everythin'. Jus' leave it to me."

Shackleton stared wide-eyed at the young Kansan for a moment. Then he gulped, blinked his eyes, and turned away.

"We got much more gold to take out'n the mountain?" Hutzelman asked cheerfully.

As Shackleton shook his head, Davy noticed the men working by the mountainside. And behind them, glittering in the late afternoon sun, he saw a shelf of rock shot through with gold. It was the fabulous Lost Dutchman Mine, Davy realized at that moment—the gold that men had sought and died for since the days of the *conquistadores*! There it was before him, the legendary treasure of Superstition Mountain.

"We've got nearly all we can take away now, Paul," Shackleton replied. "I think we ought to get out of here—right away!"

Hutzelman picked his red, bulbous nose as he studied the rock shelf and the gold concentrate lying on the ground before it. When he turned back to Shackleton, there was a wistful expression on the bounty hunter's face.

"Yeah," he sighed. "I reckon you're right, Ernest. No sense in pressin' our luck." He turned to the miners. "All right, boys," he called out in his gruff voice. "Lay down your pickaxes, for your diggin' days is over."

"We finished?" one of the miners asked as he turned and lowered his pickaxe.

Hutzelman grinned as he nodded at the man. "Pack it in, fellas." he said.

"Whoopee!" a second miner cried, throwing down his pickaxe.

"Gawd A'mighty!" yelled the remaining miner,

clapping the man with the canvas ore sack on the shoulder, and doing a little jig after that. "At last!" he cried breathlessly as he hopped up and down. "Now we can get down to the business of con-ductin' ourselves like proper millionaires."

"Cut out the horseshit, an' start loadin' up them mules," Hutzelman ordered. "Let's git whilst the gittin's good."

"Well, how 'bout lendin' a hand, then?" one of the miners groused.

"That makes sense, Paul," Shackleton told the bounty hunter. "Let's all pitch in, so we can get out of this wretched place."

"You still worried 'bout the Thunder God, Ernest?" Hutzelman asked with a grin. "'Cause he's the only damn Apache you'll be likely to find fer thirty mile around."

"Come on," Shackleton told him impatiently, turning as he went toward the pack mules. "Let's get loaded up."

Hutzelman nodded. "All right, boys," he told the men who had ridden to Superstition Mountain with him. "Give them fellers a hand." He unholstered his big .44. "I'll keep an eye on our friend, Watson."

Suddenly the sky was lit by a blinding flash, as a bolt of lightning cut through the gathering dusk. *BA-BOOOM*! A peal of thunder rang out seconds later with a deafening roar.

"Oh, Lord," Shackleton exclaimed nervously. "There's going to be a storm."

"Looks like that ol' Thunder God finally roused hisself, Ernest," the bounty hunter told him. Davy observed that the Indian agent's face had suddenly gone pale.

"Git a move on boys," Hutzelman told the others as the first drops of rain began to patter down on the mountainside. "All hell's gonna break loose afore you know it. 'Cause when it rains up here, it comes down like the devil."

Davy shifted in his saddle, his wrists stinging from the bite of the rawhide thongs that bound them, and looked down at the man the Chiricahuas had named Killer-of-Apaches.

"What d'ya think of our little bonanza, Watson?" Hutzelman asked cheerfully. "That there's a sight you ain't likely to see every day."

Davy just glared down at the man, a sullen expression on his face. He was thinking desperately of a way to save his life, but he was unable to come up with one.

Hutzelman laughed and shook his head. "You poor sum'bitch. Why, you don't even know what hit you, do ya? One minute, you're lyin' 'twixt the thighs of that li'l brown sweetie, Consuela, an' the next, you're strapped to a post at Fort Burnside, gittin' the hide flayed off'n yer back. You poor sum'bitch."

"I don't need no pity, Hutzelman," Davy growled back angrily. "Leastwise, not from no scalp-huntin', baby-butcherin' trash like yerself."

Hutzelman chuckled. "I see you done got yer spirit back, Watson. Well, at least it'll make yer end a mite more tolerable." He grinned up at Davy. "It ain't easy, I'll say that, boy . . . goin' from Consuela's honey-pot to a dried out, unmarked grave in the desert."

"Hutzelman, if I could jus' get loose, I'd—"

"Yeah, an' if my grandmaw had one, she'd be my grandpaw," the bounty hunter told him scornfully. "Save yer breath, Watson, an' make yer peace with yer maker," he counselled. "'Cause you ain't got a hell of a lot of time left to live."

Chapter Eight

By the time that the gold concentrate had been loaded on the backs of all eight pack mules, the rain came down in sheets upon Superstition Mountain, with all the fury of a flash flood. The air had grown damp and chill, darkened almost to the shades of night, except for those moments when a flash of lightning would bathe the area in its ghastly light, bleaching all objects of their color. Thunder rang out on the mountain, pealing like the crack of doom, causing the horses to shy and the mules to bray in fright.

"Goddam it—lash that sack down, an' le's git our butts outta her before we's washed away," Hutzelman roared at two of the miners who were struggling to adjust a sack of ore on the back of a skittish mule.

"For the love of God—let's get out of here!" Shackleton called out in near-panic.

BA-BOOM! A peal of thunder rent the air with the force of a dynamite charge. Several of the horses reared, and one of Hutzelman's men was thrown to the ground.

"Git up, Parry," Hutzelman yelled at the man, pulling his hat down to shield himself from the gale-force winds that had suddenly come up.

Davy Watson sat slouched in his saddle, the sting of the rain reminding the young Kansan of the whipping post at Fort Burnside.

"Stop that fuckin' mule!" another man cried out, as one of the pack animals bolted in panic, heading up the mountain.

"Paul, I don't think we ought to drag this here Watson fella long with us," a big, heavyset man called out to Hutzelman, his long beard dripping water like a beaver's back. "Let's put an end to 'im, here an' now."

Davy heard this, and his blood ran cold. At the same time a flash of lightning illuminated the black, brooding mass that towered above them. The Finger of God pointed to heaven which, Davy reflected, might well be his next destination. *He had to do something right away!*

All he could do, the young Kansan concluded desperately, was to put spurs to his horse, duck his head, and hope for the best as he rode hell-bent for leather at a breakneck speed down the dizzying slope. *If he made a break for it now, in the middle of the raging thunderstorm, he just might have a chance!*

BOOOM! BA-BOOOOOM!

Just as Davy leaned forward along the neck of his horse, ready to dig his spurs into its flanks, he looked around. And what he saw made him catch his breath. . . . There, not two inches away from the bridge of his nose, was the barrel of a Smith and Wesson .44.

"Mind if'n I settle the score with this sum'bitch now, Paul?" the man called out to the bounty hunter through the rain, wind and darkness.

Shielding his eyes with his forearm, Hutzelman turned to look at Davy Watson. His watery blue eyes narrowed as he stared at Davy. Then his lips formed in a characteristic smirk. "Go 'head,

Sims," he told the man with the .44 as he wheeled his horse around and headed back to Shackleton. "He ain't nothin' to me."

"*I'll see you in hell, you lousy bastard!*" Davy Watson roared at the retreating bounty hunter.

Hutzelman looked over his shoulder as another flash of lightning lit the mountainside, turning the Dutchman's shelf of gold to silver. "Well, you jus' save me a place when you get there, boy," he called out to Davy. "An' give my regards to ol' Nick."

BA-BOOM!

"Paul—for the love of God!" Shackleton cried frantically.

"All right, Ernest. I'm comin'," the man known to the Chiricahuas as Killer-of-Apaches said gently to his partner as he looked away from Davy Watson and rode off.

Then, over the sounds of the growing storm, Davy heard the hammer of the huge Smith and Wesson click as the man called Sims cocked it back. He took a deep breath and stared with morbid fascination into the mouth of the weapon. Another flash of lightning followed on the heels of the first, and Davy looked over Sim's shoulder to see Hutzelman, Shackleton, the other men and the train of eight pack mules slowly making their way down the slope.

"Here's some Arizona justice, ya Injun-lovin' scum," the man growled, his voice barely audible above the howl of the wind.

Okay, Davy Watson told himself as he took another deep breath and continued to stare into the barrel of the Smith and Wesson. *I'm ready to die. G'bye, Maw. Emily. Lucius Erasmus.* He thought about his loved ones in Kansas. And then he thought about the woman he cared for above all other women. *G'bye, Deanna.* . . .

BA-BOOOM! BOOOOM!

Suddenly Sims bucked in his saddle and straightened up with a jerk. He dropped his .44 and began to claw at his chest. Davy looked down from the man's agonized face and saw that a knife protruded from his body. Then, as blood gushed from the man's mouth and the light died in his eyes, Sims pitched backward out of his saddle.

Davy wheeled around, just as another flash of lightning illuminated Superstition Mountain. And there, thirty feet above him, clinging to the side of the Finger of God, was Soaring Hawk!

The Pawnee flashed him a bright smile of triumph.

BA-BOOOM! GROAM-ROAM-BA-BOAM!

A growing rumble, louder than the thunder, caused Davy to spin around in his saddle. And as he did, the young Kansan's jaw dropped as he saw a boulder come tumbling down from the peak above—heading straight for the men and animals who were departing with the gold!

The beasts felt the approach of the boulder before the men heard it coming. Horses shied and whinnied, and the mules brayed in a discord of terror.

"Oh, Jesus," one of the riders whispered as he turned in his saddle and saw the boulder bearing down on his party.

Then there was no more time. The huge stone plowed into the rear of the mule train, scattering the bodies of men and animals with the force of its impact, sending them flying into the air, to land crippled or dead upon the ground, lying there in grotesque, contorted postures like broken and discarded children's toys.

Before the boulder had finally swerved off-course, it had crushed or thrown three mules, a horse, and one of Shackleton's miners. The man was dead, and his horse lay on the ground moaning pitifully, its back broken. The boulder's rumble diminished as it rolled down the mountainside and disappeared from sight.

"Paul—what happened?" Shackleton cried, an edge of panic to his voice.

The bounty hunter's rain-streaked face was livid with rage. "I don't know what's goin' on," he growled, drawing his pistol as he wheeled his horse around. "But some sidewinder done rolled that rock down on us."

By the time that the boulder had hit its target, Davy Watson was on the ground, scrambling for Sims' .44. And by the time he had risen to his feet, Soaring Hawk had appeared at his side.

The blood-brothers embraced.

"I never thought I'd see you again," the young Kansan told the Plains Indian. "You done saved my life."

"We are bound to each other by blood," was Soaring Hawk's reply.

Davy stepped back and spun around, .44 held at the ready. "They's a passel of mean hombres down there, my brother," he said tensely.

The Pawnee laid a restraining hand on his arm. "They will not go far," he told Davy.

Ernest Shackleton screamed in terror as the next flash of lightning revealed that it was raining arrows as well as water. The man next to him slumped over the neck of his horse, a brightly feathered shaft protruding from his back. And behind Shackleton, at the rear of the pack train, one of Hutzelman's men slid out of his saddle with a thick, gurgling cry, arrows sticking out of his body in several places.

Lightning flashed once more, and the Indian agent moaned when he saw Apaches emerge from behind clusters of rocks on both sides of the pack train. And then he began to scream again, as he recognized the ugly face and fierce, glittering eyes of the Apache war chief, Geronimo.

Startled though he was, Hutzelman made good use of the brief illumination by gunning down the Apache warrior who had suddenly appeared ten feet in front of him. Then he reined his horse in and faced down the mountain, as he called out to the other men, attempting to rally them to the defense of the gold.

After the rain of arrows, the Apaches fired upon the whites with rifles and pistols. And by the time that Hutzelman had reached the head of the train, only he and Shackleton, of all the defenders, remained in their saddles.

"Oh, God—he's here, Paul! Geronimo's here!" the Indian agent screamed, clutching desperately at the bounty hunter's fringed buckskin jacket. *"Save me, Paul—please save me! I'll give you anything you want. Anything!"*

Having sized-up the situation by this time, Hutzelman knew that only one course lay open to him.

"Git the fuck off'n me!" he roared, swinging around in his saddle to smack Shackleton in the face with a hard overhand right.

The man grunted and fell backward out of his

saddle; and by the time that he had hit the rocky ground, the bounty hunter put spurs to his horse and was off, streaking down the mountainside.

Puffing and blowing and gibbering with fear as he scrambled on all fours toward his fallen Winchester, Ernest Shackleton gagged and reared back on his knees when he saw that someone was standing on the rifle. Then the Indian agent gave a strangled cry when he looked up into the hideous, painted face of Geronimo.

"Don't kill me," Shackleton moaned, his face drained of all color as two braves came up from behind and took hold of his arms. "Please don't kill me, Geronimo," he pleaded suddenly changing from English to Apache. I'm your friend. I've always been your friend. Hutzelman made me do it. For God's sake—don't kill me!"

Geronimo's dark eyes glittered, and his smile was terrible to behold. "Do not worry, Shackleton . . . my friend," he told the panicked Indian agent in Apache, as he drew a long, sharp knife from its sheath. "I will not kill you."

A third brave came up in the driving rain and knelt beside Shackleton. Then Geronimo's smile faded as he turned to the brave and said, "Take down his pants."

"*No-o-ooo!*" the former friend of the Chiricahua Apaches screamed, when he realized what the war chief was about to do. "*Oh, Nooo-o-o-oooo!*"

Fifty yards down the side of the mountain, Paul Hutzelman lay on his back in a barranca, blinking his eyes in confusion as he was brought back to consciousness by the awful screams that arose from the gelding of Ernest Shackleton.

Twelve feet behind him, his horse lay on the hard earth, whinnying with the pain of its broken forelegs. And a few feet behind the crippled animal, tautly stretched between the bases of two cactus plants, was the length of wire that had halted the bounty hunter's precipitate flight.

Hutzelman moaned and attempted to sit up, but nothing happened. After several moments spent scrabbling around on his back like an overturned horseshoe crab, the man known to the Chiricahuas as Killer-of-Apaches lay his head back down on the ground and began to sob.

"Oh, dear Lord," he muttered, tears flowing down from the corners of his eyes and mixing with the pelting rain. "Oh, sweet Jesus . . . my back's broke."

Suddenly, the bounty hunter caught his breath as he became aware that Ernest Shackleton was no longer screaming. He looked up a moment later, and saw a number of Apaches standing over him in a circle. He began to whimper like a whipped dog.

"Killer-of-Apaches," one of them said, in a voice that chilled Hutzelman's blood when the bounty hunter realized who was speaking to him. "Killer-of-Apaches," Geronimo boomed in his own tongue, "the warriors of the Chiricahuas greet you."

Hutzelman stopped whimpering and closed his eyes. "Our father who art in heaven," he whispered in a hoarse voice, while Geronimo knelt down beside him and raised the knife that was still dripping with Ernest Shackleton's blood.

"Hut-zel-man," Geronimo said in a cold voice, just as a blinding flash of lightning lit up Superstition Mountain. "Hut-zel-man. Killer-of-

Apaches. You have reached the end of your trail. Now, you will take no more Apache scalps. Instead, I will bring *your* scalp back as a trophy, to present to great Cochise.''

Hutzelman's eyes popped open as Geronimo's brown fingers tangled in his long, greasy hair. And then the bounty hunter, the man known as Killer-of-Apaches, screamed as Geronimo began to sever the scalp from his living flesh. . . .

The war chief of the Chiricahuas, the forty-year-old Apache who had become the terror of the Southwest, had been responsible for saving Davy Watson from death at the hands of Paul Hutzelman and his men.

Just prior to the ambush, Soaring Hawk had seen his blood-brother riding among Hutzelman's scouts, and he pointed the young Kansan out to the war chief. Then, once the bounty hunter and his companions had fought their way out of Arrowhead Pass, Geronimo resolved to go after them.

"He saved my life," Geronimo told Davy Watson, pointing at Soaring Hawk while a warrior translated his speech from Apache into English. And on Superstition Mountain, the rain stopped as suddenly as it had begun.

Awed at meeting the legendary Geronimo, Davy blushed and mumbled something. Then he turned to his blood-brother.

"Y'know," he began, "what you done opened up a whole other can of worms. Them damn people back there really put me through the wringer."

"It was accident," the brave replied. "I was seen with Geronimo. Then I had to go."

"I guess," sighed Davy, nodding his head, a wistful smile on his lips.

"When a man fights for his land and his freedom," Soaring Hawk explained. "That is not crime."

"Well, I see yer point," Davy agreed. "But them people in Phoenix—or Swillings, or whatever the hell they're a-callin' it now, don't necessarily agree with that."

"White man here for few years," Soaring Hawk told him, "Indian for many lifetime. To who does land belong?"

Just then Geronimo came up, and Davy asked the war chief how it was that Hutzelman had not become aware that the Apaches were on his trail.

"Killer-of-Apaches know one way to get to home of Thunder God; Apache know many." The war chief smiled his chilling smile.

"What about Major Forbes?" Davy asked in a voice that shook, as a wave of anger broke against his innards.

Geronimo was still smiling as his translator said, "Red hair walks with his fathers today."

" 'Vengeance is mine, saith the Lord,' " Davy muttered as he and Soaring Hawk walked away from the gold of Superstition Mountain, the gold which the Chiricahuas were unloading from the pack mules and spilling onto the rock ground.

"Y'know," he told Soaring Hawk, "all our stuff is still back at ol' Darrel Duppa's place. I, uh, I'd like to sneak back there under cover of darkness an' pick it up on the sly . . . an' say goodbye to somebody at the same time. Know what I mean?"

The Pawnee looked at his blood-brother and

185

smiled. "I know," he told Davy Watson. . . .

"Oh, hold me—hold me tight!" Consuela Delgado whispered fervently as Davy Watson put his arms around her waist and drew her lithe, naked body to his.

"*Querido Dah-veed*," she murmured, her lips nibbling his ear, her long, tapered fingere travelling down his scarred back in grazing runs.

Davy felt her taut nipples brush his chest as he leaned forward to kiss her neck, suddenly intoxicated by the heady combination of touch, sight and smell, the warmth of her limber body and the fragrance of her long black hair.

"Hold me," she whispered in a voice colored by overtones of intense longing and desire.

His rod was swollen and distended, and he could feel it pulse as it pressed against Consuela's trim belly.

The *Mexicana* sighed and reached down with one hand, drawing back her midsection at the same time that she took Davy Watson's stiff cock and placed it between her thighs. Then, as they kissed, his tongue fluttering in her mouth, Consuela hooked her pelvis toward him, rubbing the throbbing and engorged lips of her pussy along his shaft.

When their kiss ended, she tangled her fingers in his blond hair and gently pulled his head back. She emitted a low, feline purr and smiled, still moving back and forth, her nether lips still brushing his sex, while he stared into her dark, gleaming eyes.

Davy's left hand was at the small of the lissome brunette's back, and his right travelled up from her belly, halting when it encountered her full, firm breasts.

"*Ay, te quiero mucho,*" she whispered deliriously, as Davy gently massaged her breast, cupping its warm fullness or tracing circles around her thick, stiff nipple and dark areola. Consuela's skin broke out in goose bumps as Davy caressed her sensitive breasts, and she continued to rub the lips of her swollen pussy against his thick shaft, whispering to him now in some wordless, private language of desire.

Looking up from the sweet flesh of Consuela's neck, past the black, scented curtain of her hair, Davy caught sight of the bed behind the sighing, squirming *Mexicana*.

"Hang on honey," he whispered in her ear, drawing back slowly as he did, his rod coming out from between her trim thighs, its head tracking a slow, moist course between her lips as it withdrew. Then he brought down his arms, opened wide his big hands, and grasped Consuela's pert buttocks.

"*Que paso?*" she asked in mild surprise as Davy lifted her up and began to walk toward the waiting bed.

"Don't you worry none, Consuela," he whispered reassuringly. "I jus' got to feelin' we should set a spell."

"Sit down?" she whispered back, still at a loss as to what her lover was about to do. "*Porque?*"

"You'll see," he murmured, spinning her around gracefully, as if they were two naked waltzers, and sitting down on the edge of the bed.

"*Si. Comprendo,*" Consuela told him, her full red lips parting to reveal her white, even teeth. Then, as Davy, still gripping her buttocks, lowered her onto his knees, the lovely young *Mexicana* opened wide her legs.

In a moment she was straddling his knees, smiling wickedly at Davy Watson, who had now changed his grip, and had both his big hands around her narrow waist.

Consuela wriggled along the tops of Davy's thighs, assisting him as he drew her closer. Then, as he smiled and looked down at his groin, she gave a little, tinkling laugh, said something in Spanish, and reached out to take Davy's hot, rigid member in her slender fingers.

She rose above him, her knees still bent, and smiled both with her pretty mouth and her dark, latin eyes as she inserted the head of his cock into the wet and gripping warmth of her tingling, engorged pussy.

"Oh, Dah-veed," Consuela Delgado gasped breathlessly, as Davy Watson entered her. And then she uttered a little series of delighted cries as he moved her hips back and forth with his hands, entering her more deeply with each smooth stroke.

"*O, es un sueño del placer! Que delicia!*" she exclaimed as Davy began to intensify his strokes, drawing her to him until the masses of their pubic hair joined, the brown of his minging with the black of Consuela's.

He sat there with legs outstretched now, watching her with parted lips and narrowed eyes, watching her fine, full breasts joggle to the rhythm of her passionate movements, watching the dark and swollen lips of her pussy glide along the wet and dully gleaming shaft of his cock, taking him ever deeper inside her.

When he came, Davy Watson's tongue was lolling out of the side of his mouth, like that of a sheepdog on a hot afternoon, and his eyes were on Consuela's beautiful face; and as his jissum came rocketing out of his body with an incredible pressure and force, Davy's soul was immersed in the dark and sparkling pools of Consuela Delgado's eyes. . . .

"Ask the warrior if he will be staying among us any longer?" Cho-ko-le asked Nah-kah-yen, darting a sidelong glance at Soaring Hawk as she did.

"He says he cannot stay," Nah-kah-yen translated quietly as the Pawnee stared at the strong, handsome face of the dark young Apache. "He has been away from his people for a long time, and now he must return to them."

Cho-ko-le bowed her head, a look of ineffable sadness in her eyes and a slight, wistful smile on her lips.

"But," the Apache warrior added, "Soaring Hawk says that he will carry Cho-ko-le in his heart when he goes. And wherever he goes: on the plains, in the mountains, on the desert. Everywhere."

When Cho-ko-le looked up at Soaring Hawk, her eyes were moist, and they sparkled in the firelight like beads of dew gleaming in the morning sun.

"It is well," she whispered. "Tell the warrior that he, too, will always have a place in Cho-ko-le's heart."

While this was being translated, Soaring Hawk and Cho-ko-le gazed into each other's eyes with great longing, and when Nah-kah-yen had spoken, the Pawnee nodded and smiled at the dark and lovely Apache.

"Nah-kah-yen bids his brother farewell," the Apache interpreter said as he rose to his feet before the small campfire that burned outside the wickiup. "But his home is always open to Soaring Hawk, and he is always in his debt."

Soaring Hawk looked up at Nah-kah-yen. "I say to you what I have said earlier to Geronimo," the Pawnee told him, "that if my brother ever comes to the land of my people, there will be much honor in store for him."

Nah-kah-yen nodded solemnly before leaving the campfire. Soaring Hawk looked up into the sky of Arizona and marvelled at the myriad of stars he saw there. Then he turned from the stars to gaze at the firelit beauty of Cho-ko-le the Apache.

After having sat together in silence for some time, hand in hand, alternately gazing up at the stars or deep into each other's eyes, Soaring Hawk and Cho-ko-le retired for the last time to Geronimo's wickiup. . . .

Now the trim and supple bodies of the Pawnee and the Apache were intertwined, as the two Indians made love with an intensity generated by the awareness that they would never again lie within each other's arms.

Cho-ko-le's breasts quivered as the Pawnee's lips brushed her erect, sensitive nipples. Then, after mouthing and kissing the lovely Apache's high, firm breasts, Soaring Hawk proceeded downward to Cho-ko-le's musky grove of delight.

His keen nose traced a course through the subtle and mingled perfumes of Cho-ko-le's body, and the Pawnee revelled in the heady mixture. The air about her groin was suffused with a dense warmth and a pungent, musky aroma. Soaring Hawk stroked the smooth insides of Cho-ko-le's thighs, causing her to moan softly. Then, when he raised and lowered his head in slow regular alternations, blowing a thin, concentrated stream of air along the cleft between her dark and swollen nether lips, Cho-ko-le threw back her head and gasped with delight. And when the Plains Indian's long tongue parted those fevered, pouting lips and ran a skipping, butterfly course down within them, the beautiful Apache's body stiffened and her back arched like a drawn bow.

The lips of Soaring Hawk's mouth met the lips of Cho-ko-le's sex, as the brave began to apply his tongue to her in earnest. Not long afterward, the drawn bow of her backbone quivered and she sounded the bird-like calls which heralded the onset of her orgasm. And finally, as she gasped loudly, the bow was unbent as, jerking and quivering, the young Apache's back came to rest upon the vividly colored woven blanket that belonged to Geronimo.

A moment later, as she spread her thighs apart and mumured tenderly to her lover in Apache, Soaring Hawk entered Cho-ko-le. Then, bearing his weight on his hard-muscled arms, the brave began to stroke at a slow and even pace, gradually increasing his tempo and penetration as he went on. And by the time that he was ready to come, the beautiful young Apache was already bucking and writhing beneath him, deep in the throes of another orgasm.

All that night they lay in each other's arms, still or active, blind with passion or reading the deep secrets they saw in each other's eyes. They made love many times. They made love that was graceful, tender and poignant, and ardent and vigorous, by turns. And in the spaces between their active lovemaking, they held each other with infinite tenderness. In this fashion, they passed the night.

In the morning, as the sun came up in the east, Soaring Hawk parted for Cho-ko-le, each murmuring tender endearments and farewells in a language that the other did not understand.

Soaring Hawk left the wickiup, turning only once to gaze for an instant at the face of the Apache, Cho-ko-le, reading the hearbreaking message in her dark eyes. He turned and proceeded to make his way to the tent of Cochise, where he bid the warriors and elders of the Chiricahuas farewell. After that, he mounted his pony and rode northeast to the place where he had arranged to meet his white blood-brother, Davy Watson.

Two hours later, he met the young Kansan. And as they rode along under the clear, open sky of morning, both were steeped in silence, each listening to the poignant message that came from the deepest recesses of his being, each steeped in the beautiful and healing memories of the night before.

The red, Apache sun shone down brightly upon the two riders as they made their way eastward, over the long, hard trail that led back to Kansas.

DOUBLE **THE** **EDITION!**

KANSAN

JUDGE COLT

1

DEATH ON HORSEBACK

Death was the tenth and last of the plagues of Egypt, and the worst in order of severity of punishment. And as the Angel of Death once flew over the houses of Pharaoh's people in Biblical times, it now seemed that his shadow tracked across the length and breadth of the United States possession known as the New Mexico Territory. But this time the Angel of Death travelled on horseback, and he had traded his terrible sword for a Colt revolver and a Winchester rifle.

Throughout the territory, men shot at each other in the streets of its towns, or lay in wait, hiding in dark and secluded places, ready to bushwhack an enemy, to shoot him in the back. Liquor fueled the fires of anger and hatred, and rampant drunkenness greatly compounded the violence and acts of atrocity prevalent in the territory. In Cimarron, in the space of only one month, eleven men were killed in the same bar. And in the Lincoln County town of Las Vegas, five men were gunned down in the course of one wild, drunken spree. Alcohol was consumed heavily in all American frontier societies, and the results of its abuse were glaringly evident in New Mexico, where the bitter and protracted conflict between white men and Indians, replete with bloodshed and atrocities, had bred the attitude that human life was an extremely cheap commodity.

The territory was wide-open, and men who had grown accustomed to the legally sanctioned bloodshed of the War between the States found little encouragement to renounce their habitual resort to violence. In the eyes of New Mexico's hardened inhabitants, killing was not a serious offense; in fact, it was the generally accepted means of settling disputes. The six-shooter was now a perfected weapon, and it was regularly resorted to in that violent and ungoverned society.

It was a hard land, peopled by hard men. And the hardest of those hard men were the Texans. Daring, deadly, and adventurous survivors of the Civil War, they were men tough as whang leather and hard as a flint hide. The Texans burst violently into New Mexico, seeking their fortunes, riding roughshod over those who stood in their way.

It was into this cauldron of savagery and violence that the Kansan and his Indian blood-brother rode . . .

In the spring of 1870, the semi-arid mountain and desert country of the Territory of New Mexico was the wildest, most lawless place this side of hell. This condition of violent disorder and rampant lawlessness would continue until the turn of the century, and to this very day, it has had no equal in all the history of the United States.

A virtual state of anarchy prevailed in New Mexico: the territory had become a magnet for those who lived outside the law. Looking back upon the fevered and violent life of the period, one observer noted the influx of aggressive and impulsive men who chafed under the restraints of civilization; and even more, noted the wide-open territory's attraction for desperadoes and unprincipled men: "Even from Arizona, Utah, and California, the human refuse found its way to New Mexico, the territory becoming a sort of catch-basin for a certain type of rough, lawless character."

Here American frontier society overlaid the earlier Mexican frontier society, and the merger of the two cultures was less than successful, what with the wounds of the Mexican War constantly being reopened.

In Washington, the general opinion was that New Mexico was a profitless wasteland not worth defending. General William Tecumseh Sherman had remarked that "we should have another war with Old Mexico, to make her take the territory back."

Whereas the California and Nevada territories had turned out to be treasure troves, and were granted full statehood in almost no time at all, New Mexico appeared a troublesome wilderness with nothing to recommend it. Rock-bottom among appointments to federal posts, an official assignment to the territory was considered by the unfortunate appointees as tantamount to punishment or exile . . . or both. And as a result

7

of this low regard by the federal government, New Mexico was staffed by the nation's most incompetent, corrupt, and undesirable officers.

The extensive collapse of law and order was due to the lack of a stable civil authority. Justice was meted out on a political basis, by territorial appointees, rather than on one that was legal and impartial. Judges and officials, great numbers of them, were for hire to the highest bidder.

Local sheriffs played the same game, and quite often those who put themselves under the protection of the law wound up shot in the head by either the sheriff or his deputies, or else were handed over to a band of vigilantes. Further aggravating this condition was the fact that the poverty of the territory's municipalities made it virtually impossible to recruit concerned and competent law enforcement officers.

The law was a joke in New Mexico, and its enforcement was a ghastly travesty of the legal practices prevalent throughout the United States of America. Judges were corrupt, juries were constantly being either bribed or intimidated, and men with money and influence took whatever they wanted, with little regard for decency and fairness.

In an environment such as this, it was inevitable that men should have recourse to violence in their last desperate efforts to obtain justice. The standard for justice in the territory was a man's gun; and his readiness to use it was the court of last resort. Valid or not, the plea of self-defense provided a justification for murder; and in many instances, deep grievances and bitter disputes were adjudicated solely by the gun . . . by "Judge Colt."

The telegraph and the railroad had not yet made inroads into the New Mexico Territory, and the mountain ranges and great open spaces of that land provided innumerable hiding places for those who had committed crimes. The place was a desperado's paradise.

Complicating an already desperate situation, and further augmenting the fear and anarchy which mantled the territory, was the relentless drive of Texas cattlemen to control and occupy the open range in New Mexico. These men, having made their fortune with longhorn herds, supplying the North with beef after the Civil War, began to expand their domains, spilling over into the grasslands of the territory. But the prized areas were already occupied.

Herds of sheep ranged far and wide over the pasture lands, owned by Spanish-Americans whose roots went back to the pioneer stock that had settled Mexico, men whose people were in the area long before Texas became a republic. But this was of little interest to the cattlemen, who were bent upon driving the sheepherders off the land.

At the time, it was the prevalent opinion among cattlemen (although later disproved) that pasture lands were being destroyed by sheep, whose grazing cropped them too short. And in addition to this, adding insult to injury, cattle were offended by the smell of sheep, and would not drink at any water hole which had been recently visited by the woolly creatures.

The Texans, already hated for two previous

attempts to invade the New Mexico Territory, were ruthless in their methods, and consequently there was no love lost between them and the sheepherders. They brought with them, in addition to their lowing herds, a heritage of prejudice and intolerance, and an abiding hatred for those descendants of Texas' old enemies, the Mexicans. In fact, the term *tejano* was applied to all newcomers who displayed the negative qualities of bigotry and intolerance.

Davy Watson, on his way back home to Deanna MacPartland, as well as to his home and loved ones, knew nothing of the conflict between the cattlemen and the sheepherders, between Spanish-American and *tejano*. His only concern, after riding out to avenge his father's death at the hands of Ace Landry, and undergoing a series of incredible adventures in the process, was to return to the sovereign state of Kansas, where he could settle down at last with the woman he loved. He had been away for more than a year and a half, as had been his Pawnee blood-brother, Soaring Hawk, and both men longed to return to their people, and to their homes . . . .

Aspens and stands of conifers were to be seen below the timberline of the mountains, the former pale green in spring, changing to golden yellow in autumn and silver grey in winter, and the latter always a dark, saturated green. And in the desert areas, the sturdy and stunted *piñon* and juniper were to be found.

The dark and light greens of the hardy

vegetation; the greys of chamiso, cactus and stone; the vivid and variegated colors of the rocks; the blue beyond blue of the vast looming sky, accented by the pure, incredible whites of huge, drifting cloudfields; such were the colors of New Mexico.

The valleys of the relatively few permanent rivers were rich in native plants, and rich in crops where men had accumulated. Cottonwoods shaded the river banks, which were alive with a great host of water fowl, freshly arrived from their migration.

Alder, willow and mountain cottonwood abounded in the canyons of the mountains, dotted with a colorful array of ferns and flowers. Deer took to the thickets, and squirrels to the trees, as the riders' approach sent bluebirds darting overhead. Quail could be heard below, whirring as they flitted from place to place, taking on the coloration of their surroundings.

In the more arid areas, the hardy mesquite grew in lacy treelike blooms. And in strong contrast to the darker cactus, the white candles of yucca blooms stood tall and gleaming in the light of the intense southwestern sun.

"Biggest damn sky I ever did see," Davy Watson remarked to his Indian companion, awed by that open and blue immensity, which made its presence felt with an elemental and commanding power.

Soaring Hawk nodded, acknowledging the Kansan's statement. Despite his stoical demeanor, the Plains Indian shared his blood-brother's feeling about the incredible sky of New

Mexico.

It was a strange, almost surreal land, a place whose intense features had the look of a hallucinatory landscape. But at least it appeared calm and peaceful, which was a welcome change from the harsh contrasts and red Apache sun of the Arizona Territory.

That was where the two riders had come from, after having holed up for several weeks, waiting for Davy to fully recover from the wounds he had sustained at the hands of Jock Forbes, the cavalry commander, and Paul Hutzelman, the bounty hunter. But both foes were dead now: Forbes' carcass had been picked clean by the kites in a pass in the Chiricahua Mountains; and Hutzelman's bones lay bleaching beneath the harsh, hot sun that glared down upon the gold-flecked walls of Superstition Mountain.

Davy Watson shook his head. It had all seemed like a strange and fevered dream. From the arms of the beautiful Consuela Delgado, to the fifty lashes he had received at the whipping post in Fort Burnside; from the moment Soaring Hawk had freed the dreaded Geronimo from the jailhouse at the new settlement of Phoenix to the Apache ambush at Arrowhead Pass, led by Cochise himself; to the spectacle of the shelf of gold on top of Superstition Mountain: the entire journey had possessed an eerie, unreal sense of dream and hallucination. But as strange as it seemed, the adventure had been real.

He had the scars on his back to prove it, Davy Watson thought as he tilted his hat forward, shielding his eyes from the glare of the New Mexico sun. But through pain, he remembered the warmth and passion of the lovely *Mexicana* who had been his lover in Phoenix.

Soaring Hawk had his memories too, Davy realized, recalling his blood-brother's account of the idyll with the beautiful young Apache girl, Cho-ko-le, whom he took as his lover in the wickiup of the war chief, Geronimo, the man who called him *Brother*.

It had been a strange and perilous odyssey, from the plains of Kansas and eastern Colorado to Idaho's Hell's Canyon, where Ace Landry met his end at the hand of Big Nose Vachon; from young, rough Boise town to sprawling, cosmopolitan San Francisco; down the length of the California coastline and then across the anvil of the southwest. He had seen great natural wonders: the awesome spectacle of Hell's Canyon, with the raging Snake River at its center; the fabled gold of Superstition Mountain; the rugged splendor of the Idaho Territory, which was perhaps the wildest spot on the face of the North American continent; the sea of grass that ran west from Kansas to the mountains of Colorado; the vast, shining expanse of the might Pacific Ocean, and the avalance-plagued Donner Pass.

There were man-made wonders, and horrors, as well, the mechanical marvel of the Union Pacific Railroad, on its way to meet with the Southern Pacific in Promontory, Utah, and thus link the United States with bands of steel from coast to coast; the infernal smelters and pits, the ghastly luminescence of the Burning Moscow mine, in Nevada's Virginia city, home of the legendary Comstock Lode; the unbelievable and

13

phantasmagoric display of vice and degradation in San Francisco's notorious Barbary Coast; and the skill and ferocity of the world's greatest hit-and-run fighters, the Chiricahua Apaches.

They had known high old times, as well, the Kansan reflected, thinking of the women he had met in the bawdy houses and gambling halls of the West, on the trail and in the towns, in *adobe* houses and Indian teepees. And those women had been of many races and colors. Consuela Delgado, whose white teeth and flashing eyes contrasted with the rich caramel coloring of her skin; Bright Water, the Pawnee whose hair was as black as the underside of a raven's wing; Desirée, the Southern belle, the bawdy house girl who had mesmerized Soaring Hawk by giving him his first sight of auburn pubic hair, Della Casson, the black Louisiana beauty who had the eyes of a doe and the grace of a panther; and the lissome, blonde, blue-eyed Deanna MacPartland, the woman who waited for Davy Watson to come to take her out of Mrs. Lucretia Eaton's bawdy house in Hawkins Fork, Kansas.

There were good men and boon companions, too: old John Ketcham from Boise, who took Davy's side against Harvey Yancey, and later died at the obscene giant's hand; Nah-Kah-Yen, the Apache companion of Geronimo, and the man who aided Soaring Hawk's wooing of the dark-eyed, copper-skinned young Cho-ko-le, translating the Pawnee brave's English into the speech of the Chiricahua Apaches; Marcus Haverstraw, the lively Virginia City newspaper-man whose extravagant swearing sent sailors and muleskinners running for cover; Jack Poole, the

14

wry-humored, gritty Indian scout, and the formidable trapper and mountain man, Big Nose Vachon, both killed in the showdown at Hell's Canyon, where Davy and his companions had wiped out the entire Ace Landry gang.

They were all good men, the living and the dead, Davy told himself while the creak of leather sounded above the wind that came soughing through the grasslands as the Kansan shifted in his scarred and dusty saddle.

The day was sunny and mild, in sharp contrast to the high winds the two riders had encountered earlier. It was March, the windiest month in New Mexico, and they had already been buffeted by gale winds whose peak velocity must have reached fifty miles an hour.

New Mexico's dry climate was subject to drastic atmospheric shifts, and the wind whipped freely over the great flat expanses which characterized a large section of the territory's topography. In addition to this, the light dry soil was picked up by the high winds, resulting in severe dust storms. And it was now spring, the time when the dust storms were at their peak, when they often lasted for days. The blood-brothers had encountered a heavy storm several days ago, upon their entry into the territory, and they were still brushing it off and spitting it out of their mouths.

"The dust penetrates everything," an early traveler to New Mexico had written. "You eat it, you drink it, you breathe it, you wear it like a coating, and the last handkerchief at the bottom of the box in your trunk is gritty and smells of alkali."

This statement articulated Davy Watson's feeling about a New Mexico dust storm. He realized that he was now in the heart of a land of extreme contrasts, whose changing moods, could be as sudden and capricious as those of a drunken hanging judge. *That was the thing about the territory,* the Kansan realized. *You never knew what was going to happen next.*

Looking down at the grass and realizing that it was no longer full and singing in the wind, Davy remarked to his blood-brother, "From the look of this here grass, I'll bet'cha we's in sheep country. Ain't no cattle chews it down that close."

Beside him the Pawnee nodded, staring down at the cropped grass as he thought with longing of the great buffalo herds that roamed the plains of his homeland.

"Very close," agreed Soaring Hawk. "Buffalo not graze like that."

They rode on in silence through the pastureland, making their way eastward. The sun was high in the sky, and the day was clear and still and windless. And in that vast open land, beneath the blue, endless sky, Davy Watson felt as if he and Soaring Hawk were the only two men alive on the earth.

Mesas, mountains, parched rivers, deserts, ranks of saguaro cactus standing like giant sentinels, composite rocks of rainbow colors, spiders and evil-looking lizards, snow-capped mountains merging blue with the blue sky above, white sands of gypsum and dark stark beds of lava: the Southwest was a land of extremes, of harsh contrasts, and its sights still made themselves felt to the Kansan in an ominous and unsettling way. It was as if the land had once been a habitation for colossi, for some great and demonic race which had sprung up in the days when there were giants in the earth. Now the land was inhabited by the race of men; but it dwarfed them, for its scale was too big. It was as if God had never intended it for men.

Soaring Hawk reined in his pony and pointed ahead, off in a northern direction. Davy's horse came to a halt, and the Kansan leaned forward in his saddle, squinting as he looked off into the distance, to where the keen-eyed Indian had pointed.

The Pawnee's eyesight was exceptionally sharp, and Davy sighed with frustration as he strained to make out what lay ahead. It was always this way, he thought ruefully; Soaring Hawk would stop and point something out . . . but at such a great distance that only he could distinguish what it was.

White mounds, not too big, and spaced out at irregular intervals: *what the hell could the things be?* Davy Watson asked himself, rubbing his eyes as he looked away.

He was curious to know what the strange objects were, but he'd be damned if he'd ask Soaring Hawk. It had become downright embarrassing for him to query the Pawnee about what he had seen, each time the latter had called a halt to their progress.

So he clenched his teeth and flicked his reins, swaying in his saddle as his mount went forward. Then he cloaked himself in silence and inscrutability, in the manner of his blood-brother. He had decided not to depend so much on Soaring Hawk, and to learn to trust his own senses and instincts. After all, his eyesight had improved greatly over the last year or so, and his other senses had been sharpened as well. As it was, he realized with a feeling of deep satisfaction, he could almost make out what the mounds were.

As the two companions drew closer, they soon discovered the identify of the white objects. They were the corpses of sheep: lying mute and awkward, a glaze of fear and pain over their wide-staring eyes; their white fleeces accented by thin scarlet lines, as blood trickled down from the bullet holes in their hides.

"Blood still run," Soaring Hawk told Davy. "Not be long dead."

Shaking his head, the Kansas looked across the pastureland ahead, noting the profusion of white mounds that dotted the green grass and brown earth.

"Judas Priest," he muttered. "Why in the hell anybody'd want to gun down a passel of sheep is beyond me." The farmer in him was revolted by the sight of such wanton bloodshed. "They had no call to shoot all them sheep," he said softly. "Sheep don't never do nothin' to deserve shootin!"

"Not take wool or meat," reflected the Pawnee. "Just shoot and leave dead." Beneath the expressionless mask of his features, the brave was puzzled.

"It don't make sense," Davy muttered, as they rode on through the pastureland littered with the white and fleecy corpses of sheep.

"Now men die," Soaring Hawk said a few minutes later, as they came over a knoll.

"Oh, Lord," Davy Watson said in a husky voice. "They wasn't content to murder sheep."

Ahead of them in the distance, at the edge of a clump of cottonwood trees, the Kansan made out a group of men on horseback. Then, as he squinted in an attempt to deepen the focus of his eyes, Davy saw that several men stood on foot within the circle made by the surrounding horsemen. And when he looked up from the circle, he became aware once more of the sight that had greeted his eyes when he first glimpsed the cottonwoods.

Stiff and contorted, a man's body dangling from a rope that had been slung over one of the nearest tree's stouter branches. The other end of the rope, Davy saw now, was attached to the saddle horn of the horseman farthest from the cottonwoods.

"Too late to do anything for him," he said in a hoarse voice, his throat gone suddenly dry.

"Two more left," the taciturn Indian replied.

"What d'ya think we oughta do?" Davy asked Soaring Hawk. "What if them fellas on foot is rustlers?"

The Pawnee shook his head. "Men on horses not sheepherder. Look like cowboy. Like cattlemen."

"Mebbe it's a range war," Davy said in a hushed voice. "One of them sheepmen-cattlemen feuds."

The brave nodded, as a horseman slipped a noose over the head of one of the prisoners.

"But we jus' can't stand by, whilst they

strings up them two boys."

Soaring Hawk met Davy Watson's eyes.

"Guess we ought'a ride over an' palaver with them cattlemen, huh?"

Just as he said this, the rider whose lariat was attached to the neck of the prisoner gently urged his mount forward until all the slack was taken up on the hanging rope.

"Well, you know what to do, ol' son," Davy told Soaring Hawk, his eyes never leaving the clump of cottonwoods.

Without a word, the Pawnee drew his heavy-caliber Sharps rifle from the sling that hung from his pony's side and raised it to his shoulder. Then, squinting as he took a breath and exhaled gently, the brave began to slowly squeeze the trigger.

The Sharps was a powerful weapon, and, in slightly higher calibers than Soaring Hawk's, was the preferred weapon of buffalo hunters. One shot could drop a bull buffalo at unheard-of distances, and it was unusual for the animal to rise to its feet after taking a bullet from a Sharps.

Davy had always been impressed with the uncanny accuracy of the Pawnee's aim. And while his weapon was not a markman's rifle (whereas Davy's own Henry was), the Indian's calculation of distance, windage, and the like, combined with an intimate acquaintance with his breech-loading Sharps, enabled Soaring Hawk to perform wonders of marksmanship.

He remembered especially the incredible feat the Pawnee had performed on the plains of Kansas, in the days when they first rode out after Ace Landry, the man who had gunned down Davy

Watson's beloved father, John Jacob.

Approaching them in the distance, strung out in a line and coming into the sun, had been four mounted and heavily armed Kaw braves, hereditary enemies of Soaring Hawk's people. They were outnumbered two-to-one, Davy recalled, and he was sure that the braves would not let a Pawnee pass with his scalp intact.

The Kaws must have been close to a mile off, Davy had estimated, exaggerating the distance somewhat, he realized in retrospect, when Soaring Hawk shouldered his rife and fired off a booming shot at the enemy. They waited for several seconds while the whistling slug travelled through the air, Davy staring wide-eyed, not comprehending why the Pawnee should bother to fire across such a great distance.

And then, to his utter amazement, he watched one of the riders in the center of the line fly backward out of his saddle and tumble onto the ground. A moment later, two of the Kaws picked up the wounded brave and slung him across his own horse. After that, to Davy Watson's surprise, the startled Indians rode off into the distance. Now *that* was shooting!

Would the Pawnee be able to duplicate that feat? the Kansan asked himself, calculating the distance between them and the horsemen at the edge of the cottonwoods. And perhaps shooting someone down was beside the point this time, he reflected as the Pawnee's rifle discharged thunderously. It would be better merely to shake the horsemen up a little, just enough to save the life of the man with the noose around his neck. Then there would be time to talk things over.

The heavy slug from the brave's rifle smacked

21

into the hanging tree, sending out a hail of chips and splinters, which caused the frightened mounts of the four riders to whinny loudly and rear back upon their hind legs.

The potential hangman was thrown out of his saddle, and another rider clung to the side of his horse, desperately trying to scramble onto its back, while the beast circled and skittered. The shock of this sudden intervention gave the prisoner time enough to reach up with both hands and withdaw his neck from the noose.

Soaring Hawk quickly reloaded his rifle, and Davy drew his Henry from its boot. Then the blood-brothers put spurs to their horses and rode out toward the cottonwoods.

"By Gawd," Davy cried as their horses shot forward, "you got yerself one helluva eye. Why, I'll bet you could outshoot Bill Tilghman, or even ol' Bill Cody, hisself."

The horsemen by the cottonwoods were no slouches themselves, Davy realized when he saw their reaction to Soaring Hawk's metal calling card. For while two of the horsemen were temporarily out of action, the remaining pair had wheeled their horses around and were at that very moment streaking toward the blood-brothers, hell-bent for leather, pistols drawn.

"Git down!" Davy cried to Soaring Hawk, pulling his mount up short, having decided to alter his strategy when he saw the riders charging at them full-tilt.

An instant later, the Pawnee reined in his pony and leapt down out of his saddle, joining Davy Watson on a sparse bed of scrub grass.

Up ahead, the two riders continued to bear

down upon them, their charge not checked in the least by this new tactic. And by the time the Kansan and the Pawnee had raised their rifles and squinted into the gunsights, the onrushing horsemen had already begun to blaze away at them.

Them boys ain't the ones to scare easy, Davy told himself, his finger tightening gently and evenly upon the trigger of his Henry.

BOOM! The Pawnee's Sharps roared like dynamite in a canyon, causing the Kansan's ears to ring. He winced and caught his breath. Then he began to exhale slowly, his finger resuming its interrupted contraction on the trigger of his rifle.

CRACK! The Henry discharged with a crisper and lighter sound than the Sharps, and Davy looked up to see his target go down. He aimed at the rider, but had hit the horse. The slug tore into its skull, and the palomino heeled over on its right side, going down heavily onto the grass.

As for Soaring Hawk's shot, Davy had only seen the empty saddle which resulted from it. The Pawnee had caught his adversary square in the upper part of the chest, blowing the man backward out of his saddle, to land on the ground in a twisted, motionless heap.

Davy's man kicked free of the fallen horse and rose to his feet unsteadily, backing off with a pronounced limp in his right leg, as he trained his gun on the blood-brothers.

CRACK! Davy fired off a second shot, but it went wide. By that time, the man had the Kansan in his sights, and was about to fire his Colt.

BOOM! The Sharps roared again, and the man flew backward, part of his shoulder blown away by the big slug.

"That's one I owe ya," Davy crowed to the sharpshooting Indian.

By this time, the remaining two horsemen were in full control of their mounts, but seeing what the newcomers had done to their companions, they were having second thoughts about charging head-on. And when the next slug from Soaring Hawk's rifle blew apart a large overhanging bough, causing the hanged man's body to turn and sway, the horsemen spurred their mounts and rode off into the blue distance, where the vast sky merged with the far-off ghostly mountains.

Then the Kansan and the Pawnee brave remounted and rode over to the cottonwood trees. The two former prisoners were engaged in cutting down the body of their hanged companion when their rescuers drew near. Davy saw that the two sheepmen were short and brown-skinned, with dark eyes, lustrous black hair, and bright grateful smiles.

Having cut through the hanging rope, the first sheepmen lowered the dead body in his arms, grunting something in Spanish to his companion, upon whose shoulders he sat.

The man on the bottom grunted in return and lowered the other to the ground. Immediately following that, he ducked his head out from between the man's legs, straightened up and stretched his arms, and then gave his comrade a hand with the dead body.

When the corpse had been reverently laid upon

the grass, the two crossed themselves and then turned to face Davy Watson and Soaring Hawk. The Kansan and his blood-brother sat tall in their saddles, each hefting his rifle, waiting for the men they had rescued to break the silence.

"My name is Jesse Santacruz," the older of the two men said with a heavy accent. "My fren' Ramon an' me, we give you *muchas gracias* for savin' our lives, *Señores*. We owe you much."

"Just who was them shit-kickin', hard-ridin' fellas?" Davy asked, jerking a thumb over his shoulder, in the direction of the two fallen cowboys.

"*Tejanos*," Jesse Santacruz replied tersely, a disgusted scowl on his face.

"What's '*teh-hanoz*'?" Davy asked, struggling to pronounce the Spanish word.

"In your language, they are called men from Texas," the sheepherder replies.

"Oh," said Davy. "Texans."

"*Si*. Texans," Santacruz replied. "That's what *tejanos* is."

"What's all the trouble about?" the Kansan asked. "Why was those boys a-killin' yer sheep, an' why did they uh . . . ." here his voice trailed off, and he flushed, gesturing lamely at the corpse of the hanged man.

There were tears in Jesse Santacruz's eyes, as he looked up from the body. "Them *tejanos*, they came up here wit' their cattle herds. They don' care nothin' for sheepmen—nothin' for people like us who got *chicano* blood." He shook his head. "*Tejanos* don't like nobody but *tejanos*. So they come up nort' here, an' start a war wit' the sheepherders."

25

"But we gon' to get them," the man called Ramon added bitterly. "Don Solomon, he no gon' to let them *maricones tejanos* push us aroun'. He gon' pay them back. He done it before."

Jesse Santacruz nodded. "This time, they sneak up on us," he told his rescuers, his eyes hard and cold. "But nex' time, we ride out with our *compañeros,* with Don Solomon leadin' us—mebbe one-two hundred *caballeros.* Then you don' see no more *tejanos* in all New Mexico."

"Who's Don Solomon, Mr. Santacruz?" Davy asked, while Soaring Hawk continued to stare at the New Mexicans, his dark, gleaming eyes the only features in his stoical countenance possessed of animation.

"Don Solomon, he's our *patron,*" Ramon told Davy and Soaring Hawk.

"*Si, Señores,*" added Jesse Santacruz. "An' once we round up our sheep an' get our *caballos,* we gon' to take you to him."

2

THE FIESTA OF
LA CONQUISTADORA

The *rancho* of Don Solomon Mirabal, which lay
to the north of the town of Española, was a huge
and sprawling affair. Apart from the palatial
stucco-and-Spanish-tile hacienda which housed
the *gran patrón* of the area's sheepmen, the
place contained shops, stables, a corral, clusters
of small adobe houses for the workers, pens and
shearing facilities for the sheep, a general store,
a *cantina,* a schoolhouse, and a church. And it
was to the *patrón's* great spread that Jesse
Santacruz escorted Davy Watson and Soaring
Hawk, once he and Ramon had rounded up
their scattered flocks.

By the time the blood-brothers rode through
the gates of *La Rosita,* Don Solomon Mirabel's
vast estate, it was late afternoon. Prior to their
arrival, they had ridden with the two New
Mexicans to the sheep camp where, with the aid
of the sheepmen there, Jesse and Ramon
rounded up their flocks. And after that, they
brought the body of the hanged man, their
companion, one Rigoberto Fuentes, back with
them to *La Rosita.*

Davy Watson was just tying up his roan

stallion at the hitching post outside the big, two-storied *hacienda* when Don Solomon Mirabal rode into sight, coming toward them at the head of a group of horsemen.

The riders were bronzed, wiry men who wore leather chaps, dusty boots, and broad *sombreros*. They had the look of *vaqueros,* and appeared to be rough-riding individuals. Davy noticed the cold, gleaming pistols holstered at each man's side.

In contrast to the workaday appearance of the *vaqueros,* Don Solomon Mirabal was a splendid figure of a man. The New Mexican patriarch was spare and handsome, in his late fifties or early sixties, Davy guessed, with the face of a Spanish aristocrat and a carefully-trimmed white beard. He wore a flat-topped black sombrero, woolen pantaloons, leggings, and a short jacket made of leather. Over his shoulders was draped a colorful and elegant *serapé*.

The Kansan nodded admiringly when he saw the *pàtron's* saddle, which was a hand-tooled work of art, studded with silver. He noticed as well the ornate bridle with its punishing bit, and the sharp, roweled spurs which gleamed like polished silver dollars.

Jesse Santacruz walked up to the Don, took off his hat, gave a little bow, and then began to speak rapidly in Spanish, recounting all that had occurred earlier in the day, with special emphasis on the details of the lynching of Rigoberto Fuentes, and the rescue from the hated Texans.

Davy watched the *patrón's* face, as Don Solomon listened to his *partidario,* as most of the men who worked for him were called. Jesse had earlier explained to Davy and Soaring Hawk that most of the area's sheep were owned by wealthy men, *ricos,* such as the Don. Mirabel then let his sheep out on *partido,* hiring men like Jesse and Ramon to tend them, their labor contracted on shares, whereby at the end of each year the *partidarios* received a stipulated number of lambs, ewes, wethers, and rams. Occasionally, an enterprising *partidario* might accumulate numerous flocks of his own, but the general run of them remained heavily dependent upon the *patrón.*

Mirabal's face grew hard as stone and dark as a thunderhead, as he listened to Jesse Santacruz's account of the depredations of the *tejanos.* And each time that the sheepherder mentioned the name of the hanged man, Rigoberto Fuentes, Davy Watson noticed that a vein pulsed and stood out upon the Don's temple. When the narrative had ended, Jesse Santacruz turned and pointed to the Kansan and his Pawnee blood-brother.

Nodding his head, the *patrón* looked over to the men who had saved his *partidarios* from being lynched by the hated Texans. Davy's eyes met those of the Don, and he felt as if an electric current had passed between them, as if the very force of the man's will had made itself felt.

Don Solomon walked his horse over to where Davy and Soaring Hawk stood. "*Señores,*" he said in a deep, resonant voice, "I wish to express my heartfelt gratitude to you for saving the lives of my *partidarios,* Jesse and Ramon. I hope that you will consent to stay as my guests during the fiesta of *La Conquistadora,* Our Lady of the

Conquest, which begins tonight. My house, my goods, my servants are all at your disposal. *Mi casa es su casa.*"

As the Don indicated his possessions with a sweeping gesture of his arm, the facets of the emerald and ruby rings on the *hidalgo's* fingers caught the rays of the late afternoon sun. Davy Watson saw that a crew of workmen were stringing up decorations and hanging festoons from the adobe buildings which bordered upon the plaza whose center was the big well standing a hundred feet from the entrance to Don Solomon's *hacienda*.

"You're right welcome, Señor Mirabal," Davy told the *patrón*. "Soaring Hawk an' me, we jus' couldn't stand by an' watch your boys get strung up." He shook his head. "Them Texans is sure a mean bunch, ain't they?"

The Don nodded at this, a steely glint in his eyes, but he did not directly answer Davy's question, until the Kansan sat beside him at dinner . . . .

They sat at the center of a huge oak table, carved with the ornate scrollwork of the Spanish baroque style, a table long and wide enough to seat forty people. And it did not go empty, either; for the Don's immediate family was large, and several generations ate together, beneath silver sconces whose candles burnt with a bright, dancing flame.

At the very center of the table sat Don Solomon, flanked by his guests, Davy Watson and Soaring Hawk. Across from the Don sat his wife *Doña* Esmeralda, and his ancient and venerable mother, *Doña* Inés. Around these parties, on both sides of the table, there sat the sons (Anibal, Vicente and Alvarado) and daughters (Ines, Ramona, Delores and Juana) of the *patrón;* and on their far side, running out to both ends of the table, sat an assortment of aunts, uncles, cousins, and close friends of the family.

The food served by the many men and women in attendance upon the Don was no longer exotic to Davy and Soaring Hawk, since the two men had often eaten Mexican food during their journey through the Southwest.

Tortillas made of hand-ground, lye-softened corn, along with *sopaipillas,* both served directly off the hot stone, were the breadstuffs. *Chile con carne,* served out of a deep pot which had simmered for days, rich in herbs, spices, and its unique savory *salsa,* or sauce, came next. After that came courses of mutton, beef, poultry, and venison, complemented by servings of rice, corn, beans and the delicious, thick, and crusty loaves of wheat bread baked by the Indian women.

Soaring Hawk, who preferred the food of the *chicanos* to that of the *gringos,* ate heavily, abstaining only from the rich red wine that constantly made its way up and down the table, drinking instead cup after cup of the rich coffee that the New Mexicans added to boiled milk.

Davy Watson ate with gusto, as he always did after an overland journey, grateful to be rescued from the monotony of trail food, from the grey tyranny of hardtack and pinto beans, of jerked beef, grits, and sourdough biscuits hard as cartridge casings. And he sloshed down the wine, that lip-smacking *viño rojo,* as if it were St. Louis drug store soda pop.

After the luxurious meal, crisp cakes were served, as well as brandy and cigars for those of the men who wished to smoke out on the patio; but none of the sons would have dared smoke in the presence of that formidable matriarch, *Doña* Esmeralda, who reigned supreme, after the Spanish fashion, in her own house.

To Davy's surprise, he noticed that the New Mexican women smoked on the patio beside their men. Taking their strong tobacco from little silver boxes, the *señoras* and *señoritas* wrapped it in cornshucks. And then having allowed the men to light the smokes with the flame of a blazing lucifer, the women smiled as they puffed their *cigarillos.*

The Kansan found this somewhat shocking, as the only women of his acquaintance to smoke in public were to be found in bawdy houses, saloons, and gambling halls. But he was much taken with the grace and beauty of the New Mexican women, with their devilish, flashing eyes and gay, rich laughter.

Don Solomon turned to him and began to speak in a low voice. "Our troubles with the *tejanos* are not new, *Señor* Watson. They go back to the early days of the Republic of Texas. In its fifth year, that government found its treasury empty, and decided to embark upon an adventure which would enrich it."

The Don sighed, stroking his silvery beard

with long, tapered fingers. "The Texans, under Sam Houston's administration, laid claim to New Mexico, seeking to divide it into counties, which they would then annex to Texas proper."

"That so?" Davy murmured, his interest aroused now, recalling the bold and reckless charge of the Texans.

"So they sent an armed expedition to New Mexico," the *patrón* went on, "in order to *protect* us. But it was a fiasco, and failed dismally. The insufficient force was soon vanquished, and many prisoners were taken. They were not adequately led or provisioned, and by the time they encountered our own forces—*chicanos* and *Americanos* together—they were in dreadful condition."

Don Solomon paused to sip at his brandy. "Another expedition followed, a few years later, but that, too, failed. Then the threat of war with Texas loomed on the horizon, as the *tejanos* cast covetous eyes upon our land."

Davy nodded. "They're rough customers," he remarked.

"*Si, es verdad,*" the Don replied, nodding solemnly at the Kansan. "They are hard men, quick to use their guns, and not afraid to risk their lives. The *tejanos* are daring and enterprising and not easily stopped."

"Well, how did ya stop 'em?" asked Davy, leaning in toward Mirabal.

"It was the United States government that stopped them," the *patrón* answered. "By officially proclaiming New Mexico a territory."

"I see," Davy said, nodded as he reached for his wine goblet. "An' now they're back?"

33

Don Solomon shook his head. "They have never stopped coming. Each year, more and more *tejanos* settle in the south of the territory. *The Mexicanos* have a proverb, which says, 'Mexico is far from God, and near to the United States.' "

He smiled wryly. "We feel much the same way about Texas, even though it is now a state."

Davy nodded after emptying his goblet, which a servant promptly refilled.

"We have had much trouble with the *tejanos,*" Don Solomon continued. "They have a great hatred of people of Hispanic descent, owing to their struggles with Mexico. But many of them are also extremely bigoted and intolerant, and they have provoked much conflict with the *chicanos.*"

"It seems like them folks is all over the place," the Kansan sighed.

"Indeed, *Señor* Watson. The world, I am afraid, has its share of fools. But even worse than that are the Texas cattle barons, who have been encroaching upon our pasture lands for years, until they have pushed us to the brink of a range war. You saw what happened with the *tejanos* this morning."

"Yup. I sure did, *Señor* Mirabal."

"Those were the men of Bill Fanshaw, one of the great *tejano* cattle barons who had moved into New Mexico. He now lives in Roswell, to the east of here, and is doing his best to get me to sell him part of my lands."

"Are ya thinkin' 'bout doin' that?" Davy asked.

The *patrón's* eyes flashed. "Not as long as a

Mirabal remains alive in New Mexico," he replied, in a voice both hard and cold. "If Fanshaw presses me any further, I will treat with him across the barrel of a gun."

Davy shook his head. "I hope it don't come to that, sir," he whispered.

"Madre de Dios," the Don whispered back, "so do I, *Señor* Watson."

He was about to say something further, when cheers and applause broke out in the room and interrupted him.

"Ah, here comes the *troubador*," he told Davy, grabbing him by the arm. "Now let us enjoy ourselves. There will be time enough later for the *tejanos*. But now, there is *fiesta*."

The *troubador,* a stocky, white-haired man with a guitar, sat down on a chair fifteen feet from the center of the table, facing Don Solomon and his honored guests.

"He sings of many things," the Don told Davy and Soaring Hawk, "of love, pride, and passion. He makes many of the songs up as he sings. Pepe Jimenez is one of the great *troubadores,* much in demand at the *bailes,* where he sings *fandango* and the old songs of Spain, in addition to his famous improvisations."

"What's he singin' 'bout now?" the Kansan asked, intrigued by the keening wail of the troubador, and the supple, sinuous melody of his song.

"Ah, he sings of *pasión,"* the Don told him, "of how the dark, gleaming eyes and bright smile of a beautiful woman can topple a throne and change the history of nations."

"I never thought of it that way," Davy

muttered.

"He sings that love is bitter and that love is sweet," the Don went on, "that it is beautiful, even when it is turbulent and ruinous, and most beautiful when it is not requited. That way it remains in the realm of the ideal, and is most perfect."

"I see," said Davy, nodding gravely, as he reflected upon what a to-do these folks tended to make of the doings of a man and a woman.

After the *troubador* finished and departed to thunderous applause, a fiddler, guitarist, and accordionist mounted a stand on the far side of the room, and the *baile* began in earnest. With high grace and dignity, the men and women took their places and danced round after round of the swift, elegant dances of Old Mexico.

"Boy, I'll be danged if that one don't look like a schottische," Davy told Don Solomon, suddenly recognizing the steps of the latest dance to be performed.

"Indeed it is, *mi amigo,*" the patron replied cheerfully. "It is called *La Varsoviana*. The dance is said to have come originally from Warsaw, and was taken to Spain by the officers of the *Grande Armée* of Napoleon Bonaparte. From thence it came to Mexico, and our fathers brought it to New Mexico."

After a while, and a few more goblets of wine, Davy Watson was out on the dance floor, delighting the Mirabal clan with his vigor and enthusiasm. And he laughed as loudly as any one of the New Mexicans, each time he attempted an intricate step and wound up looking like a drunk stumbling through a harness maker's shop.

Nodding his head solemnly and keeping time with the music by banging his fists down upon the tabletop, Soaring Hawk sat bolt-upright in his seat, with a show of dignity unlikely to be surpassed by even the haughtiest *grandee*.

Dancing with the dark and lovely *chicano* women set Davy's blood to boiling, and all the wine he had drunk only served to further inflame him. But under the watchful eyes of their *dueñas*, the young beauties of the Mirabal family were more than amply protected.

"Looks like there ain't no chance fer a fella to do a little spoonin' hereabouts," the Kansan mournfully confided to Jesse Santacruz.

"Well, this is the *patrón's* family," the sheepherder told Davy. "But you come outside with me, my fren'," he added with a knowing wink, "an' I make for you to meet some beautiful *muchachitas.*"

"Now, yer talkin'," Davy shot back, reaching for his goblet.

"What about *el Indio?*" Jesse asked, indicating Soaring Hawk with a waggle of his thumb.

"Dunno, Jesse. I better ask 'im." Saying this, Davy got up and sauntered over to where the Pawnee brave sat, stolid and ramrod-straight, still pounding the table with both fists.

"My brother," Davy said in Pawnee, a tongue he had by now thoroughly mastered. "Jesse says there are pretty women outside. Would you like to come with me and meet some of them?"

He waited while the brave reflected upon this.

Indians having different values and social standards from whites, Davy had learned not to take his attitude toward things for granted. He never knew whether Soaring Hawk would choose to do something the way that he, Davy Watson, thought that the Pawnee should. Indians and white folks had very different ways of looking at things.

"Women here dark and graceful like deer," the Indian told Davy. "Make Soaring Hawk think of Indian women."

By the momentary softening of the brave's stern expression, Davy could tell that his blood-brother was thinking of the young Apache, Cho-ko-le, whom he had loved in the Chiricahua Mountains of the Arizona Territory.

"Pretty like Cho-ko-le?" the Kansan whispered to the brave.

"Almost," Soaring Hawk replied, the shadow of a wistful smile crossing his face. "But make me think of her." He sighed. "You go my brother. I stay here."

"You sure?" Davy asked.

The Pawneed nodded. "I am sure," he said in a husky voice. "My heart is with the Chiricahua Apaches. In the wickiup of Geronimo, where Cho-ko-le waited for me."

"Injun ain't the only one to shoot arrows, my brother," he told the Plains Indian. "My people's got a li'l guy name of Dan Cupid, who shoots him a mean bow. Looks like he done scored a bull's-eye on you."

"Who is Dan Cupid?"

"Why, he's, uh, this here l'il fella with wings, who brings love each time he skewers a body with one of his arrows."

The Pawnee nodded. "He is a spirit."

"Yeah . . . sorta." was Davy's reply.

"Then he was one who shoot me," Soaring Hawk replied with conviction. "Right in heart."

"You could always mosey back, Arizona-ways," Davy gently told his blood-brother.

The Pawnee looked down at the table and slowly shook his head. "No. It is not to be that Cho-ko-le and Soaring Hawk will meet again. She is Apache, and she could never leave her people."

"Ken-tee left the Apaches fer ol' Jake Walz," Davy replied, referring to the man who had discovered the gold of the Apaches, the Lost Dutchman mine, on Superstition Mountain.

Suddenly the brave looked up at Davy. "When Ken-tee did that, she sealed her fate. It is not easy for an Apache woman to leave her people." He sighed. "And I long to ride over the plains and hunt the buffalo."

"Well, yeah," Davy said softly. "I reckon you got yerself a point there, ol' hoss. If you, uh, want me, I'll be outside somewheres."

The Indian nodded, looking more melancholy than Davy Watson had ever seen him before.

"See you, uh, around," the Kansan mumbled, his hands flapping awkwardly at his side as he turned and walked into the night.

Outside Don Solomon Mirabal's *hacienda,* the night sky was alight with the flash and glow of fireworks, as the *patrón's* servants celebrated the *fiesta* of *La Conquistadora,* Our Lady of Conquest, a holiday instituted by the *padres* who accompanied the early Spanish *conquista-dores*.

The plaza was filled with New Mexicans, brightly dressed men and women who laughed and sang, danced and drank the *patrón's* wine, crying out in delight each time a burst of fireworks lit up the sky. The music of guitars and fiddles filled the night air, and the gaiety and high spirits of the celebrants radiated throughout the plaza, affecting all who came near. And while the sky was washed with colors, and couples laughed and danced, Davy Watson stalked through the stables of Don Solomon Mirabal on tiptoe, naked as the day he was born.

When the Kansan had gone out of the *patrón's* dining room, leaving Soaring Hawk to his memories of the beautiful Cho-ko-le, he was met outside by Jesse Santacruz. The sheepherder immediately introduced Davy to his friends, male and female, warmly affirming that the newcomer had saved his and Ramon Santiago's life.

Davy was warmly welcomed by one and all. There were many attractive young women in the plaza, and one in particular had caught the Kansan's eye.

"What's that gal's name again, Jesse?" he asked in a whisper, pointing to a short, full-bodied young woman in a bright shawl and tight-fitting red dress.

"You like her, *amigo*?" Santacruz asked in turn, his brown face suddenly lit up by the gleam in his eyes and the wide expanse of his bright smile.

"She's right smart-lookin' " Davy muttered,

flushing as his eyes travelled over the young *chicana's* curvaceous figure. "An' when I smile at her, she smiles back right purty."

"Come on, *Señor Dah-veed*," Santacruz told him. "I take you to meet her."

"Well, uh, sure," Davy mumbled, his ears the color of Maine lobsters. "Le's, uh, jus' mosey on over there."

As the two men crossed the little plaza hung with candles and festooned with bright ribbons, the fiddler and guitarist played a haunting and plaintive melody, accompanying the *troubador,* who sang a *jácara,* a popular folk-ballad, whose words were as follows:

> *Me voy de soldado razo*
> *Y cuando me halle en compania*
> *Muy lejos ya de mi tierra*
> *Sabe morir donde quiera.*

> I go as a soldier of my race
> And when I find myself with others
> Far from my homeland
> I shall prove to them that my race
> Knows how to die anywhere.

Delores Fernandez smiled warmly as Jesse Santacruz introduced Davy Watson to her, obviously taken with the tall, blond Kansan. And Davy himself smiled back with equal warmth, as he beamed down at the volptuous-looking little woman in the scarlet dress who worked in the kitchen of the Don's *hacienda.*

"Dah-veed, he's one tough *hombre,"* Jesse told Delores. "This mornin', he saved me an' Ramon from bein' lynched by four *tejanos."* The sheepherder smiled. "Him, 'n that *Indio,*

41

they come in shootin', jus' as I was about to be strung up."

"*Ay, Dios,*" the *chicana* murmured.

"Boom!" Jesse exclaimed, startling the people near him. "First they shoot this big rifle at the hangin' tree, an' nearly blow it apart. This knocked one of the *tejanos* off his horse, an' made another lose control of his."

Delores was watching him carefully, her eyes wide, scarcely breathing now.

"This give me time to slip out of that noose," Jesse went on. "Then the other two *tejanos* draw their pistols, an' rides out after *Señor Dah-veed* an' *el Indio.*"

The little brunette shot Davy an inquiring look. Davy nodded back in confirmation of Jesse's statement. Delores gasped, shivering with excitement as she pictured the Texans' charge.

"*Bang! Bang! Bangbang!*" Santacruz cried loudly, jerking back his right hand, whose thumb and index finger were held in a position which resembled the barrel and trigger of a pistol. "Them *tejanos* come out firin' like *bandidos,* but they ain't ready for what *Señor Dah-veed* an' *el Indio* does nex'."

Jesse Santacruz flashed Delores Fernandez a sly smile. "They gets off their horses an' goes down to the groun', firing with their rifles. *BOOM! BAM! Boombamboom!*" He chuckled. "Pretty soon, them *tejanos* is eatin' dirt, layin' on the groun', shot full of bullets."

"*Ay coño!*" Delores muttered under her breath.

"Then, *el Indio* shoot his big gun at the other two *tejanos.* This time he nearly blow away the

42

tree they hang Rigoberto Fuentes from." His countenance grew solemn for a moment, as Jesse thought of his murdered comrade. "An' then," he added, smiling once more, "them other two *tejanos* took off like jackrabbits, an' hightailed it out of there. An' that is how *Señor Dah-veed* an' *el Indio* save my life, an' the life of Ramon Santiago."

"You are very brave, *Señor Dah-veed,*" the little brown-skinned brunette said in a breathy whisper, touching Davy's arm with her hand.

"Well, Ma'am," he said, flustered by her praise, to say nothing of her intoxicating proximity and the excellent bird's-eye view he had of her low neckline and swelling breasts, "we, uh, jus' couldn't sit by while ol' Jesse an' Ramon got themselves hanged."

"Now that you two is properly introduced," Jesse Santacruz told the Kansan with a broad grin, "I gonna leave you alone, an' go back to dance with Conchita Ramirez."

"Thanks, Jesse," Davy muttered, feeling his ears burn once more. Then he turned to Delores Fernandez. "Would you, uh, care to dance, *Señorita?*"

"*Si, Señor David,*" she replied, her dark eyes flashing as she shot him a hot and inviting smile. "*Con mucho gusto.*"

So they danced, and danced some more, dancing until the early hours of the morning, as the fiesta went into its second day. Davy's friendliness and adaptability endeared him to the *chicanos,* who already respected the Kansan for his bravery and daring. And with each succeeding dance, Delores grew more affectionate, drawing closer and closer to Davy, staring up at him with eyes that promised intimacy and passion. And when the dancing had ended, Delores offered to show Davy the stables of the *patrón* . . . .

So there he was, naked as a jaybird, padding along noiselessly over the straw and packed earth of the darkened stable in amorous pursuit of the equally naked Delores Fernandez.

The scents of hays, straw, oats, horseflesh, and manure commingled in the stable to produce a heady, earthy fragrance, which caused the Kansan's blood to course rapidly through his veins. Horses snorted and switched their tails, dreaming of the *Llano Estacado,* the Staked Plains to the east, where they once ran wild in herds, direct descendants of the horses brought to New Mexico by the *conquistadores.*

Outside the moon was full, and a coyote howled in the foothills of the mountains to the north, rousing the sheepdogs from their dreams of sheep and men, causing them to bay at the full, cold moon of New Mexico.

Davy Watson stopped dead in his tracks when he saw the long shadow that fell across his path. Then he looked slowly to his right, and his breath caught in his throat as he saw Delores Ferandez' ripe body silhouetted in the moonlight.

The cold, silver light edged her voluptuous form, running down her profile, over the rounding of her shoulder, outlining full, round breast and thick, erect nipple, down over her belly, glistening on the edges of the hair of her full, dark muff, highlighting the curvature of her thigh, and running down to her trim ankles and small, well-formed foot.

She was hiding behind a beam, waiting to pounce upon Davy as he passed. Feigning ignorance of her presence, the Kansan stepped into the moonlight, his ears picking up the sound of the *chicana* catching her breath as he suddenly appeared before her.

They had arrived at this point after a half-hour's foreplay, where they necked and spooned and groped until heated to a fever-pitch with desire for each other.

Then, in delicious mutuality, the two undressed each other, slowly, and with lingering attention to each newly uncovered area. And by the time they were totally undressed, Davy Watson was hotter than a blacksmith's forge. But mischief was Delores' special aphrodisiac, and she wriggled out of his arms, all hot and giggling, calling for him to catch her, promising Davy something special if he did.

He made as if to pass her, appearing totally oblivious to her presence, then suddenly darting to his right as he sprang toward the beam which only partly concealed the shapely Delores.

She uttered a soft little cry of excitement, and stepped backward as Davy lunged toward her. The *chicana's* eyes were wide and her mouth half-open, her white, even teeth highlighted by the moonlight and gleaming in the darkness of her oval face.

As his arms went around Delores, and he drew her to him, Davy Watson emitted a low, involuntary growl. He shuddered as her firm hard-nippled breasts pressed against his naked

45

flesh, and he felt his rod stiffen as her warm, smooth belly made contact with it.

"Ay, Dah-veed," the little woman murmured ardently, as she felt his stiffening sex glide over her belly.

His big hands ran down over her shoulders and back, travelling around her waist and then up to her front, where he palmed and caressed her big breasts.

At the same time he leaned over to kiss her. Delores' full lips parted, and the Kansan put his tongue into her mouth with the alacrity of a salamander darting into a cave.

He snorted like the horses in the Don's corral when Delores wrapped her fingers around the shaft of his now-erect rod and then began to stroke it, her small hand running up and down the length of his sex.

In another minute, the two were down upon the nearest pile of straw, their bodies fused as they bucked and heaved in the grip of the moment's passion.

Delores had parted her legs once she was on her back, and murmured passionate entreaties in Spanish, as she arched her body before him.

"Oh, yes," he murmured as she took him in her hand. "Lord, Yes."

She was wet and fully aroused, and he entered her easily, running the length of his shaft, and coming to rest only when their pelvises were butted together.

Then he leaned over and kissed her, their tongues' frenzy registering the intensity of their arousal. She wriggled beneath him, and he made a sound like a bull at stud, drawing back as he began to stroke.

He kissed her full, red mouth and nuzzled her neck, the smell of her perfume and the sweat of her body merging with the smells of the stable to create a perfume which intoxicated the Kansan beyond belief.

She, in turn, sucked at his lower lip and caught it between her teeth, tugging gently, but firmly. And then, as his strokes began to quicken and intensify, she uttered a series of little whimpering cries and began to lick his face like a cat.

"Ay, Dah-veed! Ay, Dah-veed!," Delores uttered in a drugged, faraway voice, her pelvis beginning to twitch, as her body was lashed by the first surges of her mounting orgasm.

Harder, faster, and deeper stroked Davy Watson, when he felt the passionate *chicana* shudder beneath him. And as he did this, Delores arched her back, the sweat running down her ribcage, the moonlight turning it into streams of quicksilver, as she met the Kansan's feverish strokes with an equal intensity.

"Oh, God Almighty," Davy groaned, feeling as if a geyser was about to erupt in the pit of his groin.

"Ay, Dios," Delores murmured, in a voice that sounded like the wind that ripples through the high grass on the *Llano Estacado*.

"I . . . can't . . . stand . . . no more," Davy moaned, as his pelvis began to hook reflexively toward Delores' moist and gripping pussy.

"Hoo-wee," he groaned, his eyes rolling up in his sockets, his eyelids closed and fluttering, his mind's-eye alight with visions of sky-rockets,

pinwheels, and Roman candles flashing in the
sky, illuminating the dark night of the senses
with fiery bursts of delight . . . .

The sky was glowing with the first light of
dawn, and Davy could just make out the faint
outline of the mountains to the east, as he and
Delores Fernandez tottered out of Don Solomon
Mirabal's stable.

Arm in arm, the Kansan and the pert, dark,
New Mexican *señorita* walked across the
deserted plaza. The only sound heard in the
night, beside the scuff of their feet upon the
dusty ground, was the hoot of some far-off owl.

By the time they had crossed the plaza, and
stood by the draw well, where they drank of its
sweet, cold water, Davy heard sounds which told
him that they were no longer alone.

He looked up, into the distance, toward the
gates of Don Solomon's spread. And there,
dimly seen in the first light, looking like a
gathering of mournful spirits come to haunt the
dreams of the sleeping revellers, was a group of
horsemen.

Each sat tall in his saddle, as if the creature
beneath him were part of his own body, moving
with the horse as surely and confidently as one
being, rather than two; each sat proudly, neck
and head thrust forward, confident and
aggressive in his movements.

They were not New Mexicans, Davy told
himself as he studied the bearing of the five
horsemen. And he was convinced of it when he
made out the high-crowned Stetsons, long
boots of hand-tooled leather, and holstered Colt

six-shooters that each of them wore.

"We got us some Texans come to visit," Davy whispered to Delores. He felt her body stiffen.

As the riders drew nearer, the Kansan was able to make out their features. They were rugged and hard-looking individuals, with a set of the jaw which marked them as men not to be trifled with.

The horsemen drew nearer still, and the fingers of the Kansan's gun hand began to twitch. His earlier meeting with the Texans had made him wary, and the fact that he was outnumbered five-to-one, with a *chicana* standing unarmed and vulnerable beside him, did little to reassure Davy Watson.

With the exception of himself and Delores Fernandez, it appeared to Davy that every soul on Don Solomon's property was fast asleep, including that redoubtable shooter of Texans, Soaring Hawk. The young woman was now trembling; and even though the dawn was chill, Davy Watson had begun to sweat.

What were these five, formidable-looking cowboys doing here, right on Don Solomon's doorstep? the Kansan asked himself. What errand had brought them so casually into the heart of the enemy camp? Were they here to settle a score? Had they come looking for him and Soaring Hawk?

"That's him, Bart," one of the men growled, and Davy suddenly recognized him as one of the two survivors of the Texan lynching party.

The cowboy addressed by the survivor was a tall, broad-shouldered man with brown hair, whose handsome, square-jawed face was highlighted by a Roman nose with the mocking smile beneath it.

"Him, huh," the man said, nodding as he studied the Kansan. Their eyes met for a moment and Davy felt the force of the man's will, much as he had earlier with Don Solomon Mirabal.

"Yup," the survivor replied. "That's one of 'em. T'other was some kinda Plains Injun."

The horsemen drew to a halt, facing Davy across the draw well.

"I hear you an' yer Injun pal done gunned down two of my boys," the man said to Davy with a Texas drawl.

"They didn't give a body no time to palaver," the Kansan answered. "Didn't leave us much of a choice." His eyes narrowed, as the man's mocking smile flashed even more brightly than before.

"Texans is impatient folks, Mister," the man told Davy. "They tends to shoot first, an' ask questions later."

"If'n that's their standard way of greetin' folks," Davy shot back, "it stands to reason there can't be too many Texans runnin' 'round now, can there?"

The man's smile suddenly disappeared, and Davy noticed the cruel set of his mouth. "What's yer handle, Mister?" the Texan asked.

"Davy Watson, from Kansas. The Injun yer friend talked about is called Soaring Hawk. He's a Pawnee." As the man nodded slowly, Davy spoke again. "An' who might you an' yer friends here be?"

"Bart Braden's my name," the man told

Davy, smiling once more. "I'm ramrod for Bill Fanshaw. An' these here's some of my boys."

Davy nodded now, his eyes travelling over the weather-beaten faces of the Texans.

"This here's Miss Delores Fernandez," he told them, hugging the *chicana* to him with his left arm.

Braden's smile turned into a sneer. "Onliest greaser I'm lookin' to meet around here is ol' man Mirabal hisself," he told the Kansan.

Davy's nostrils flared. "That ain't no to talk in front of a lady," he told the Texan.

Braden's eyes were hard, and his smile grew cold, as he stared into Davy's eyes. "Mister, don't press yer luck," he whispered, in a voice both cool and angry. "I already owe you a little somethin' fer pluggin' my boys!"

Davy's fingers began to twitch again.

"You're jus' lucky I got me other fish to fry," Bart Braden went on. "But I got me a piece of good advice fer ya, Watson: Light outta New Mexico, pronto! 'Cause if ya don't, it's a good bet you'll catch you a see-vere dose of lead poisonin'!"

It was the Kansan's turn to sneer. "Mister, I been known to give out some lead poisonin' too," Davy shot back.

"Well, you're jus' the kinda young fella us Texans likes to run into," Bart Braden sneered, "when we feel like a little target practice."

"It's easy to talk big with four guns behind you, Mister," he told the Texan.

Braden's eyes flashed, but he was still sneering when he spoke again. "Boy, I don't need nobody behind me to make the likes of you eat

51

dust. I don't even need me a gun." He nodded slowly. "It's a pity I got some pressin' business with ol' Don Solomon," he went on in mocking tones. "But you jus' stick around these parts a little bit . . . an' mebbe I'll be back to look you up soon."

"Yep. I might jus' do that," Davy replied between clenched teeth. "I'm beginnin' to like it here."

"Well, you jus' think about whether or not you're gonna like pushin' up daisies," Braden said loudly, stirring in the saddle, his own fingers twitching now. "Cause I'm findin' you downright offensive, Mister."

"By god, I'd gun the snot-nose down on the spot, Bart!" one of the men beside Braden exclaimed angrily.

"There will be no shooting here, *Señores,*" a voice called out behind Davy Watson.

The Kansan spun around toward the *hacienda,* and saw Don Solomon Mirabal standing in the doorway, dressed in nightgown and cap, a pearl-handled Smith and Wesson .44 in his hand. Above him, at the windows of the house's upper story, a dozen men with rifles leaned out of the windows which overlooked the plaza.

"This here boy don't make no never-mind, Don Solomon," Braden told the sheepman, sneering contemptuously at Davy Watson. "It's you I come to see. Mr. Fanshaw's got him a little proposition fer ya to consider."

The *patrón* shook his head. "I talk no business during *fiesta, Señor* Braden," he told the cattle barons' ramrod. "But you are welcome to stay as my guest, until it is over."

"That's right kind of you, Don Solomon," the Texas replied. "I think we might jus' take you up on that offer."

"You will please be so good as to unbuckle your gunbelts and give them to my servants," Mirabal told the Texans.

Braden raised an eyebrow as he stared at the Don. "Does that mean you don't trust us, sir?"

The *patrón* nodded, his eyes meeting the Texan's. *"Exactamente, Señor Braden,"* he shot back. "I have learned not to trust *tejanos.*"

Braden's boys started muttering at this, but the ramrod smiled warmly at the Don. "Well, at least we know where we stand," he said. "Unbuckle your gunbelts, boys."

The Don nodded. "Come inside the *hacienda.* I will have breakfast served in a short while."

Nodding, Braden swung a leg over his saddle and dropped to the ground with a display of great agility.

"Stick around, Mr. Watson," he said, smiling his mocking smile as he walked past the Kansan. "Then later, you 'n me can have us some real fun."

3

THE CATTLE
BARON'S OFFER

Breakfast that morning was not the most
pleasant meal the Kansan had ever eaten, what
with Bart Braden and his four Texans glaring
across the table at him. And when Soaring
Hawk came into the big dining room and seated
himself beside Davy Watson, one of the Texans
immediately pointed the Indian out as the other
man who had gunned down his companions.
Don Solomon had acted wisely in requiring the
Texans to turn in their weapons, for they were
boiling mad, and would surely have drawn on
Davy and his blood-brother.

In turn, Davy told the Pawnee whom the
newcomers were. Soaring Hawk looked up from
his plate and coolly met the hot, angry eyes of
Braden's men. And before he looked away,
Soaring Hawk smiled slightly, as if to let the
Texans know that he was unconcerned and
totally unintimidated by their presence. But
Davy was glad when the meal had ended, and he
belched with relief as the five Texans, leather
chaps rustling and rowelled spurs jangling,
strode out of the room.

By ten o'clock that morning, the *fiesta* had resumed, entering its second, and final, day. This time, there were games and athletic contests, and dancing in the afternoon. A children's chorus sang in the plaza, and a morality play of the Catholic Church, *Los Moros Y Los Christianos,* concerning the victory over the Moors in fifteenth century Spain, was performed by the *campeones*.

Whole sheep were roasted over pits filled with burning coals, turned over and over on metal spits, and basted in their own juices by the kitchen staff. And it was with a sigh of relief that Davy ate his lunch in the cool shade of the *patrón's* patio, away from the murderous stares of the Texans.

At dinner, however, the Kansan found himself opposite Bart Braden and his boys once more. But the strain of this touchy situation was considerably eased by the presence of a beautiful woman.

Don Solomon's daughter, Raquel, had come down from Albuquerque, where she attended the convent school of Our Lady of Guadalupe. Having just graduated, Raquel had come home to live with her family once more, until a husband was found for her.

Raquel Mirabal could not have been more than eighteen years old, by Davy Watson's estimation, but her beauty, infused as it was by the first flush of womanhood, was already considerable. Davy's breath caught in his throat when she walked into the dining room, and even the stoical and undemonstrative Soaring Hawk looked up from his plate and stopped wolfing down the chile he was so fond of.

Even the Texans ceased their coarse banter, and Bart Braden's eyes went wide as the Don escorted his daughter into the room. And when the sheepman formally introduced her to his guests, they stood up, to a man, and greeted her with courtesy and smiles.

Her skin was pale as marble, with just the faintest hint of rose in her cheeks. Davy thought that her dark, gleaming eyes reminded him of polished onyx stones, and that her long hair was the same color as the sky on a late summer's night. Her eyebrows formed thin black vaults above and to the sides of the high bridge of her aristocratic nose, and there was a slight, appealing pout to her moist, pink lips.

Her body was trim and lithe, filling out at the hips and bosom; her ankles and wrists were slender, and she had delicate-looking hands with long, tapered fingers. But the whole was more than just the sum of its parts, Davy realized, marvelling at the freshness and youthful beauty of Raquel Mirabal.

When she met the strangers, the *patron's* young daughter glanced at each man for a brief instant before lowering her eyes. Raquel made two exceptions to this practice, her eyes meeting and holding for several seconds in turn, those of Davy Watson and Bart Braden.

The Kansan fumbled for something polite to say, and managed to mumble several sentences to the effect that, while New Mexico had afforded him many beautiful sights, he had not seen the most beautiful of all until the present moment. His palms were clammy as he spoke, and his ears had begun to feel like a pile of smouldering corn husks.

In contrast to Davy's flat-footed eloquence, the tall and ruggedly handsome Bart Braden said nothing at all. The Texan merely looked at Raquel Mirabal, staring with all the concentration of an eagle espying a baby lamb, and smiling a broad, wolfish smile when the Don introduced him to his youngest daughter.

Raquel, in her turn, had murmured greetings in a low, musical voice, reminding the Kansan of the rich contralto of Della Casson, the black Louisiana beauty who had saved his life in San Francisco's notorious Barbary Coast. She might be innocent, Davy told himself, having been carted off to a convent school at an early age, but her eyes, and the way she moved her graceful, womanly body, betrayed an intensely passionate nature.

Don Solomon was overjoyed at the return of his youngest child, whom he doted upon, and that set the tone of the dinner, which was gay and festive throughout. Even the Texans put by their smouldering animosity for the moment, and got into the spirit of things. Despite their bigotry, Braden and his men seemed to hold the formidable Don Solomon in high esteem. What they probably respected, Davy opined, was the man's strength of character, his refusal to be intimidated by powerful men like Bill Fanshaw and his fellow cattle barons.

The *troubador* sang throughout the long and elaborate meal, accompanied by the musicians of the previous day, who had since acquired the services of a trumpeter, and they performed music of Mexico with a ringing and plaintive sweetness.

All throughout the dinner, Davy and Raquel Mirabal stole glances at each other, in an optical choreography of desire, their mutual attraction burgeoning in the manner of flirtatious school children in the classroom of a strict disciplinarian.

Their eyes raised and lowered, flashed and danced, signalling the birth of desire and the subsequent workings of arousal. Through it all, both were the objects of the burning glances of Bart Braden.

In the course of this ocular courtship, Davy and Raquel were careful to avoid the notice of the *patron,* his wife, and Raquel's paternal grandmother, the formidable matriarch, *Doña* Ines. But neither of the two was oblivious to the fact that Braden watched them constantly through his hard and glinting hawk's eyes.

The four Texans with Braden were merry and courteous in Raquel's presence, but their leader was steeped in a cold and brooding silence. Whenever one of his hands spoke to him, which was quite often, the ramrod merely nodded his head slowly in acknowledgement of the speaker, never taking his eyes from either Raqel Mirabal or Davy Watson.

"Denos, Señor, buena muerte," sang the *troubador,* singing the words of a chant sung by the religious order of *Los Penitentes,* known also as the Brothers of Light, *Los Hermanos de Luz,* a stern order of flagellants.

"Give us, Lord, a good death," went the words of the reenactment of the Passion of

Christ. The ceremony would continue throughout the night of Good Friday, accompanied by the sound of moaning and groaning, the lashing of whips, and the noise of rattles and chains. But in the morning, there came a knocking at the door of the ceremonial room.

"Who knocks?" the *Penitentes* would call out.

"Jesu Cristo!" came the answer, bringing with it hope, and light out of darkness, as the door was opened, and candles were lit in anticipation of the beauty and glory of Easter.

"Give us, Lord, a good death." The phrase ran through Davy's head after he'd heard it, momentarily bringing him back to the cold reality of the situation. If Don Solomon did not accept Fanshaw's offer, whatever it was, there was a strong likelihood that blood would flow like water in New Mexico. The territory was a powderkeg, and men like Bill Fanshaw and Bart Braden held burning matches in their hands. The Kansan wondered if those flaming lucifers could be used to light the torch of peace.

After dinner there were fireworks, serenades, and dancing in the plaza, as there had been the night before; but this time, Davy danced almost exclusively with the willing Raquel Mirabal. This earned him a series of dagger-stares from Delores Fernandez, who had expected to spend the night dancing with the Kansan.

Furious at Davy's inattention, Delores mastered her anger and made a play for Bart Braden. But here again she was disappointed, for the Texan ramrod was interested in no other woman than the lissome and breathtakingly beautiful daughter of his enemy, Don Solomon Mirabal.

The pert *chicana* shook with rage, and left the plaza in tears, mortified by this series of rejections. She left hating her new rival, Raquel Mirabal, and vowed to pay Davy Watson back for his indifference to her.

Jesse Santacruz shook his head as he watched Delores Fernandez storm off. "I don't like this, my friend," he said in Spanish to Ramon Fuentes. "*Señor* Watson, he had better take care. Delores won't let something like that go by. She has real Spanish pride."

"*Ay, coño,*" groaned Ramon, nodding in agreement with Jesse's observation . . . .

The night passed pleasantly enough for Davy, as he danced with the *patrón's* beautiful daughter. And later they sat down together, under the watchful eye of Raquel's older female relatives, and spoke long and intensely.

Raquel, whose English was extremely fluent, told Davy of her childhood and youth spent on the Mirabal lands, and of her later years in Albuquerque and the convent school of Our Lady of Guadalupe.

The Kansan, in turn, told Raquel of his life on the Watson farm by Pottawotomie Creek, in Anderson County. And he grew serious, as he recounted the tale of his wanderings since the day he rode out to avenge his father's death at the hand of the desperado, Ace Landry.

The latin beauty's eyes grew wider and wider, as Davy spoke of the adventures he'd had on that long, hard trail; and the handsome blond young man before her grew in Raquel's estimation with each succeeding story. And by the time Davy had concluded his tale, the young woman was absolutely fascinated by him.

"Your life, it has been so very exciting, *Señor* Watson," Raquel said breathlessly.

"More excitin' than I care for, I reckon, Miss Raquel," the Kansan replied. "Uh, d'ya suppose your could see yer way to callin' me Davy."

"*Si, Señor* Watson," Raquel whispered, suddenly blushing and lowering her eyes. "I mean, Davy."

He smiled at her. "Now, I feel at home." He looked around casually, pretending not to notice the eagle-eyed *dueñas* who took in his every move as they peered over their black lace fans. He felt about as much at home under those sharp, piercing stares as a possum in a circle of hound dogs.

Then they danced some more, resuming their covert courtship. But the night ended much too early for Davy's liking, and the beautiful Raquel, like some *Infanta* of Spain, was led away by a procession of aunts, with barely time for a whispered goodbye.

At that point, Davy became aware of Bart Braden's bird-of-prey eyes upon him. He turned sharply and looked the Texan ramrod square in the eye. Braden smiled his cold, mocking smile and nodded at Davy.

The Kansan frowned at first, and then worked up to a sneer. The two men stared at each other for a long time. Then, suddenly, the Kansan spun on his heel and walked across the plaza, to where his blood-brother was sitting.

"He's not like you, my brother," Soaring Hawk told him. "I think mebbe we better kill him soon, before he kill us."

"He's one mean sum'bitch," Davy agreed. "I'll give ya that."

The Plains Indian nodded.

"But we ain't gonna see him no more, after tonight. When the *fiesta's* over, he'll conduct his business with Don Solomon, an' hightail it outta here. An' us, why, we'll jus' hit the trail for Kansas." He sighed. "Like we been doin' fer so damn long, now." He thought about Deanna MacPartland, and prayed that she was still waiting for him in the town of Hawkins Fork . . . .

At two o'clock in the morning, the candles were snuffed out in the plaza, and the last of the revellers staggered off to their beds. And at that time Don Solomon Mirabal met in his study, over brandy, with Bart Braden.

The other Texans waited in the dining room, drinking black coffee and Mexican brandy. For some reason of his own, the *patron* had invited Davy and Soaring Hawk to witness his dealings with the Texan. Davy was later to learn that the clever Don wanted the viewpoint of an *anglo* in his dealings with the Texas cattle people.

"I am now prepared to listen to *Señor* Fanshaw's offer," Don Solomon told the ramrod, putting down his brandy glass.

The Texan nodded, and then swigged down the rest of his own brandy. When he put the glass down, Braden shot a quick glance at Davy Watson and Soaring Hawk.

"All right, Don Solomon," he began, his deep resonant voice barely more than a whisper. "What ol' Bill wants is to purchase ten or fifteen thousand acres of your western lands, up to the foothills of the mountains. He'll pay top dollar, I promise you that."

Don Solomon stared at Bart Braden for several seconds before he replied.

"*Señor* Braden," the patron began, "you are asking me to give a foothold in these grazing lands to the traditional enemy of the sheepman." He smiled coldly. "Is this not somewhat like replacing a sheepdog with a wolf?"

The Texan broke out into a wide grin. "I kinda know what you mean, Mister Mirabal," Braden answered. "But what Bill Fanshaw's after is somethin' different from that entirely."

"Oh?" said the Don, raising his eyebrows. "And what might that be, *Señor?*"

"The name of the game now is the shippin' of beef to the North, Don Solomon," the Texan said in a low, earnest voice, leaning toward the sheepman. "Folks back east is payin' top dollar—they have been ever since the end of the Civil War, when the stock up there got sore depleted. An' if Bill Fanshaw can git a corridor through your land, he can get hisself top dollar . . . . 'cause he'll beat all them other cattlemen to the draw, an' have his herds to market way before anyone else."

The Don nodded slowly, taking this all in. "*Señor* Fanshaw has been known to say one thing, and then do another," he said after a long silence. "The sheepmen in the south of the New Mexico

Territory learned that lesson too late, *Señor* Braden." He drew himself up in the chair, his spine straight as a ramrod. "But Solomon Mirabal has not," he went on, his voice ringing out in the study. "Fanshaw will never run a cow over these lands while I still own them."

Bart Braden shook his head. "That's a mighty unreasonable attitude you're takin', Don Solomon . . . 'cause ol' Bill Fanshaw, he jus' ain't gonna be able to take such a flat-out 'no' fer an answer."

The Don's eyes narrowed. "I think it will be in his interest to take it for an answer in this case, *Señor* Braden," he told the Texan in a low and steely-toned voice. "Tell him that, if for no other reason, he should accept my answer in the interest of his health."

Braden groaned and shook his head again, smiling his icy, mocking smile at the *patrón.* "Bill ain't gonna like that one bit, Mister Mirabal. If'n I was you, I'd reconsider that decision, 'cause Mr. Fanshaw ain't about to let nothin' stop him."

"Then let him ride north. I shall be waiting."

"They's gonna be a lot of blood spilt if he does, Don Solomon," the ramrod said softly.

"It will be *tejano* blood, too," was the Don's reply. "Tell Fanshaw that if he attempts to run his cattle over my land, death will be the only one to welcome him."

The Texan's eyes flashed at this. "Yep," he said through a chilling smile, "I reckon Death's gonna be ridin' roughshod all over this country, Don Solomon, cuttin' a swath through these here pasturelands, like ol' Tecumseh Sherman burnin' his way through Georgia."

A long tense silence followed this exchange.

"I have nothing further to say, *Señor* Braden," the Don told the Texas, rising abruptly from his straight-backed chair.

"I'm right sorry you feel that way, Don Solomon," the ramrod said in a low voice, as he rose to his feet.

Then, after taking several steps toward the door of the study, Braden stopped and turned to face Davy Watson and Soaring Hawk.

"I hope you'll light here a spell, Mister," he told the Kansan. " 'Cause I'd like nothin' better than to fix yer hash when I get back up here again.'

Davy's eyes met those of the Texan. "Well, if'n I do go," he said in a harsh voice, "it won't be on your account, Braden. An' if'n I'm still hereabouts when you get back, why, you jus' feel free to look me up."

"Oh, I'll do *that,* all right," was the ramrod's mocking reply. " 'Cause there ain't nothin' in this world I'd druther do."

"Well, jus' come back this way real soon," the Kansan shot back through clenched teeth. "So's you can get yer chance."

Bart Braden nodded and smiled a menacing smile. "I'll sure do my best," he said in a voice as cold as winter in Wyoming.

The next day, Don Solomon called a gathering of his male relatives and *partidarios,* as well as the neighboring sheepmen. He also invited Davy Watson and Soaring Hawk to attend, valuing their opinions as trusted outsiders who would be more impartial than any of the parties involved. This meeting was to take place the evening of the following day.

Davy readily agreed to stay for the meeting, as it gave him an opportunity to spend some more time in the company of Raquel Mirabal, albeit under the watchful eye of her aunt, *Doña* Ana. The Kansan was enchanted with the young beauty, and she herself was quite taken with the tall, blue-eyed *anglo,* thinking him the most exciting young man she had ever met.

Soaring Hawk had been of a different opinion. "We stay, gonna be heap much fighting. Texans be back, by and by. If we stay, we got to fight 'em."

Davy waved his hands in the air. "Now, that ain't gonna happen, ol' son," he told the Pawnee. "'Cause we'll be long gone afore them Texas rides back this-a-way. Besides, we was asked special-like to stay, by ol' Don Solomon hisself. An' he's been so durn hospitable, that I think we should at least do that little thing fer him."

The brave shot him a sour look. "That not real reason," he said. "You stuck on Don Solomon's daughter." He shook his head. "You go and get balls in uproar over her. Now you not think with brain. Think with dick. That make heap trouble."

"What the hell d'ya mean?" Davy asked in a squawky voice that registered his annoyance.

"Last time you think with dick," the Pawnee replied, "we almost get killed. In white man village by great water."

"Oh," Davy said, exhaling loudly as he did. Soaring Hawk was referring to San Francisco, where his liaison with Della Casson, the black mistress of the gambler, Bertram Brown, had almost cost Davy, Soaring Hawk, and reporter

Marcus Haverstraw their lives at the hands of the huge, obscene Harvey Yancey and Brown himself.

"Well, uh," Davy blustered, going red in the face, "how was I, uh . . . I mean, how was we to know that was a set-up? Ain't no way in hell a body could've told that."

The Indian's eyebrows went up, and he frowned at the same time. "Brown was heap bad man. So what you do?" he asked rhetorically.

"But, but," sputtered Davy Watson, as the brave went on, cutting off his protest.

"Know what you do? You go to bed with Brown's woman—in Brown's sporting house. Then Brown catch you with pants off." Soaring Hawk shook his head. "Not smart."

"Well, uh, *how* was I to know?" squawcked the red-faced Kansan. "I mean, you was in bed with some ol' gal your own self."

The Pawnee looked away. "Not this time," he muttered.

Davy sighed. "All right, I do admit that I'm a mite taken with Raquel. But I solemnly promise you once't that there meetin' is over, we'll skeedaddle. How's that fer a deal?"

Soaring Hawk nodded slowly. "Okay, my brother. Then we go . . . 'cause pretty soon, blood run here like Pecos River."

"Well, I surely hope not," Davy replied. "But if that's the case, we ain't gonna be around to see it, nohow."

"You sure?" the Pawnee asked, looking hard and long at the Kansan.

"Yeah, I'm sure," Davy said, sighing heavily as he did, his mind's-eye suddenly filled with a vision of the lissome, blonde Deanna MacPartland, who waited for him back in Kansas . . . .

That evening, Davy sat beside Raquel Mirabal at dinner. Each time he touched her (upon the pretext of passing her some food or refilling her glass with *viño rojo*), the Kansan saw that the lovely young *chicana* shivered. A flush came to her face, and the skin on Raquel's arms broke out in goose pimples. She was breathing heavily, and her dark eyes were aglitter with a mixture of candlelight and desire. And Davy knew, as sure as he was born, that the young latin beauty was ready and wiling to give herself to him.

If only we was to be alone, he thought ruefully, squinting through gimlet eyes at *Doña* Ana, the ubiquitous watchdog of the Mirabal family.

He admitted that he was stumped by that one. Spanish manners and customs had Davy Watson buffaloed, their elaborate forms confusing the forthright and plain-spoken Kansan.

They's more chance of springin' an owlhoot from Leavenworth Prison than of gettin' little Raquel out'n ol' Doña Ana's sight, he thought. *I reckon it would take a earthquake or a Kansas twister to shake that ol' lady off'n her tail.*

Perhaps some miracle would come to pass and give him an hour alone with Raquel, Davy hoped wistfully. But as it turned out, he did not get the opportunity to consummate his desire before the hour of the Don's meeting.

"Ah, but this is impossible, my friends!" growled Don Enrique Miranda, a neighbor of Don Solomon's, and a sheepman himself. He threw up his hands in exasperation, his eyes burning in his sun-bronzed face, as he looked around the Mirabal dining hall, where a number of New Mexicans were gathered.

"We have always had trouble with the *tejanos,*" the Don went on. "But now that we are *Americanos,*" he said in a voice colored by bitterness, "there is no law to keep them from encroaching upon our lands—lands we inherited from our fathers, lands which have belonged to our people for hundreds of years."

A great murmur arose from the men in the hall. Seated at the great oak table, at the right hand of Don Solomon Mirabal, Davy Watson could feel the crackling anger which spread through the big room like a brushfire fanned by a high wind.

"The *tejanos* are barbarians," Don Enrique went on, pacing up and down before the assembled *patrons* and *partidarios*. "They hate our race, and spit upon our customs. They are murderous brigands who have always coveted our pasturelands, and they will stop at nothing to get them."

"Then we must stop them!" a young man called out.

The crowd began to roar, cheering in response to the young man's passionate cry. Wide-eyed at this, Davy Watson nodded as Alvarado Mirabal, Don Solomon's youngest son, translated the words into English.

"Too long have we taken the insults of the *tejanos*—of all *gringos!*" Don Enrique bellowed angrily, his face livid with rage.

The New Mexicans were upon their feet now, cheering wildly and crying for blood. Almost to a man they were applauding the angry *patrón;* only a handful of those in attendance remained in their seats.

Chief among those who remained seated were Don Solomon Mirabal, and his neighbor to the east, Don Francisco Guzmán. And when the tumult had abated, and the New Mexicans were back in their seats, Guzmán got up and addressed the assembly.

"My friends," the squat, portly Don began in a booming bass voice, "it appears to me that many of you—especially the young men—are too eager to spill the blood of the *tejanos.*"

He looked around the room, a stern expression on his bulldog face. "I do not forget, my friends. I fought under Santa Ana in the war with the United States. And before that," he added, drawing himself up proudly, "I was an officer whose soldiers stormed the Alamo."

Again the Don looked around the big room, his face red and his breathing stertorous. "What my friends seem to forget is what a terrible thing war is," he went on, his voice rasping in his throat. "If we do this thing, many of you, will not be here next year for the *fiesta* of *La Conquistadora.*" He raised his arm and swept it around the room. "And your widows and orphans will go hungry, and become a burden to their more fortunate relatives."

Seated at the head of the big and polished oak table, Don Solomon Mirabal nodded in grim and reluctant agreement with his neighbor's prediction. Looking along the table, Davy saw that, despite the fervor of the *partidarios,* most of the sheep owners were not convinced that a

70

range war was the best policy for the immediate future. Don Solomon had obviously reconsidered his stand of of the previous evening, wishing to avoid a bloodbath.

"I say we try one more thing before our pasturelands go up in flames and the land becomes red with blood," Don Francisco went on. "I say that we negotiate with *Señor* Fanshaw one last time. I say that we give him a corridor . . with the written agreement to this signed in the United States District Court."

At this, one of the young men laughed scornfully.

Don Francisco sighed. "I know we cannot trust the authorities in the territory." he told the assembly. "But once the agreement has been signed, witnessed, and legally acknowledged, we will send it to Washington, with a delegation of our people, and lay our case before *el Presidente,* Ulysses Simpson Grant."

Angry murmurs ran through the audience, clashing with the sounds of approval which had followed Don Enrique Miranda's words. The young men were all for fighting, Davy Watson realized, but their elders, many of them remembering the last war, had decided in favor of moderation.

Don Solomon stood up and raised his arms in the air. *"Amigos,"* he called out over the hubbub of the divided men. "My friends, listen to me, *por favor."*

He called out again, but several moments more were to pass before order was restored among the New Mexicans.

"Where is your respect?" Don Solomon

asked loudly. "This venerable *patrón* knows each of you, young and old, and he is among our wisest of counsellors. I beg you to let him finish."

The assembly moved restlessly, and many of the sheepherders looked away in embarrassment.

"Thank you, my good and respected friend," Guzmán told Don Solomon, resuming his speech. "I have mentioned our legal protection, but I have not yet spoken of our practical protection."

The big room grew quiet as a tomb. Using this sudden silence to his advantage, Don Francisco paused for effect.

"The corridor we will give them *will not* be to the west of Don Solomon's lands, where we are most vulnerable to invasion by the *tejanos* . . . but to the east of *my lands,* where they will be between the mountains and the Jicarilla Apaches." The Don smiled triumphantly. "That way, the *tejanos* will give us *mucho dinero* for two things: the worst grazing land in all New Mexico, and the pleasure of dealing with our old enemies, the Jicarillas."

It took a minute for this to sink in, but when the *partidarios* realized what the canny old *patrón* was attempting to do, they rose to their feet and began to cheer him. It was a brilliant move: the Texans would be far to the west, out of the way, in land which was now under the control of the dreaded Apaches. The men cheered loud and long.

"If a passage to the markets of the north is all that *Señor* Fanshaw truly wants," Don

Francisco concluded, when the cheering finally died down, "then he can take the trouble to clear a path through that inhospitable country. He will be doing us a great service, and the peace will be kept between us."

A grizzled old *partidario* stood up. "What if," he asked, "that is not all the *tejanos* want, Don Francisco?"

The Don nodded his head slowly, his round, mustachioed face darkening. "Then war will come . . . . But at least we will have done our best to avert it." He shrugged. "And then we will have a chance to prove our valor, and make the *tejanos* wish they had never begun this thing."

The hall was quiet as a tomb after the Don had said this, and Davy studied the grave faces of the New Mexicans.

As Don Francisco Guzmán took his seat, Don Solomon Mirabal stood up and addressed the crowd.

"Amigos, compañeros," he began, turning slowly as his eyes scanned the faces of the men in the crowded room. "If we do this, our cause will be a just one, and *El Señor Dios* will cause us to walk in the path of righteousness, no matter what the outcome."

At the mention of God's name, all the New Mexicans crossed themselves.

"This gesture shows that we are fair men. And if Bill Fanshaw is honest in his intentions, he will accept. It would not be a bad thing to have one of the great *tejano* cattle barons as an ally; for by this agreement, his interests and ours will be one."

Davy saw the uneasy look on the faces of many of the listeners.

"I know it has not been our custom to deal with the great enemy of our people," Don Solomon went on. "But if we are to stand united and hold the land of our fathers, then it is in our best interest to divide the *tejanos.*" He nodded. "I know those gringos well. Their only true allegiance is to money. If we grant Fanshaw the exclusive right to cross our lands, he will stand with us against his own countrymen."

The older men in the room nodded knowingly.

"So I will ask you to vote, *mis amigos,* either for or against this plan of Don Francisco's. Those in favor, raise your hands."

All the older men, and a goodly number of the younger, raised their hands.

"All those against," the Don called out, after a count had been taken.

Less than a third of those present, according to Davy's tally, voted against the plan.

"But how will we propose this to *Señor* Fanshaw, Don Solomon?" a sheepman asked the *patrón.* "After you sent his emissary away with such a harsh refusal, he will not be likely to receive a delegation of *chicanos.* He is very proud, this *rico.*"

Don Solomon nodded at the man. "*Sí. Es verdad, Don Antonio.* It is true what you say. But I believe that Fortune has presented us with the means of approaching *Señor* Fanshaw."

"What might that be, my old friend?" asked Don Francisco Guzmán, turning around in his seat to face Don Solomon Mirabal.

"Fortune has sent this man to us," the *patrón* told the assembly, pointing to Davy Watson. "He is an *anglo,* a countryman of Fanshaw's. Surely, the man would listen to our proposal, if it were delivered by someone of his race."

The Kansan stared open-mouthed at Mirabal, taken completely unaware by this sudden nomination.

"But he is no friend of the *tejanos, patrón,*" Jesse Santacruz called out from the back of the hall. "For *Señor Dah-veed* and *el Indio* have sent two of them to hell already."

Laughter filled the room.

"I know that, my friend," the Don replied, once the laughter had subsided. "But that is the way of the frontier. The man called Bart Braden may not forgive our friends here, but a *rico* like *Señor* Fanshaw will not pay much attention to this matter, not when a high profit can be made."

The Don turned to Davy Watson. "Will you do this great service for us, *Señor* Watson? Will you and your *amigo indio* ride to the new settlement of Roswell, and delivery our offer to *Señor* Fanshaw? All the people of the sheep country would be in your debt."

"Judas Priest," Davy muttered under his breath, going red in the face as he turned and glanced sheepishly at his Pawnee blood-brother.

"You heard 'im" Davy whispered to the brave.

Soaring Hawk nodded slowly, a sour "I-told-you-so" look upon his face.

"It's up to you," the Kansan whispered, shifting uncomfortably in his seat and looking around the room. His ears were burning, as he realized that he and the Pawnee were the focus of everyone's attention.

"You want go?" Soaring Hawk asked.

"Well, uh, I, uh," the Kansan stammered, "I, uh . . . . Yeah. Sure. I'll, uh, go."

The Plains Indian nodded. "Then I go, too. To go will win us much honor."

An' maybe a bullet or two, the Kansan thought glumly, recalling the promise that Bart Braden had made concerning any future meeting.

"Will you go as our emissaries, *Señores?*" the Don asked again, looking at Davy Watson and Soaring Hawk in turn.

The Kansan glanced over to his blood-brother, who nodded solemnly. Then Davy rose to his feet and faced Don Solomon.

"It would give me an' my pal a heap of pleasure to do that, Mister Mirabal," he said in an approximation of the Spanish style.

The *patrón* smiled at this, and when Davy's words were translated, the New Mexicans began to stand up and cheer for the Kansan and the Plains Indian.

The cheering continued for a very long time, as the men in the big room expressed their belief at the prospect of avoiding a bloody confrontation with their traditional enemies, the Texans.

"We are all in your debt, *Señores,*" Don Solomon Mirabal told the two men, as he walked over and shook their hands. "You are charged with a very important task."

The *patrón's* eyes met those of the Kansan.

"It is with you that all our hopes ride. And it will be by your actions that we strive to avert disaster and bloodshed."

Oh, Lord, Davy Watson thought, remembering the reckless belligerance of the Texans, *I surely do hope so!*

4

BILL FANSHAW'S DAUGHTER

All the way back, for the entire length of the long ride southeast to Roswell, Bart Braden did not say a word, except to call an occasional halt when the sun was high, or to stop for meals. Such was the ramrod's authority that none of his four companions dared to disturb his reverie.

Competent and cold-blooded, independent and self-sufficient to an extraordinary degree, even among men as self-sufficient and independent as his fellow Texans, Bill Fanshaw's foreman had been smitten by the beauty and loveliness of Raquel Mirabal.

The man was obsessed; thoughts of Don Solomon's youngest daughter filled his mind. She was all that he thought of during the return journey to Fanshaw's headquarters at Roswell. The Texan was intoxicated by the young woman, and being above all a man of action, he was determined to do something about it. He wanted her badly, much as a drunkard wants his bottle, or an opium addict longs for his pipe.

Braden had never been so intensely moved by a woman in his entire life. He determined to make Raquel Mirabal his own, one way or another. Never having known mature love, Bart

Braden equated it with possession. Raquel Mirabal must be his; he wanted the beautiful young *chicana* as he had wanted no other woman—or anything else, for that matter—in all his life.

It was only a question of time, the ramrod told himself, still brooding as his little band of horsemen caught sight of the settlement of Roswell. *When* and *how* were questions that he would answer, the Texan told himself with certainty. There was absolutely no doubt in his mind that Raquel Mirabal would soon be his. Bart Braden had a will of iron, and once he set his mind on getting something, he let no one stand in his way. If need be, the man could be utterly ruthless, and totally without mercy. He feared no man, and it was said of his daring and courage that he would take a potshot at Old Nick himself.

So, as he rode toward Bill Fanshaw's spread, the Texas ramrod had made up his mind to possess Don Solomon's lovely daughter. And, should Davy Watson still be around when Braden returned to the Mirabal lands, Fanshaw's foreman had also determined to gun the Kansan down . . . .

Roswell had only been founded the year before, but in 1870, it was already growing by leaps and bounds. Charlie Goodnight, first of the Texans to reap a fortune by bringing his herds of longhorns up to the territory, had made the place his headquarters, and where the cattle baron hung his hat, there the business interests attendant upon his empire followed.

While Goodnight pioneered the New Mexico cattle trade, Bill Fanshaw came up right behind him, and was currently the cattle baron's chief rival in the territory. Fanshaw had the knack of hiring tough and ruthless men who remained loyal to him. This he did by virtue of his own forceful personality, his strength of will, and the top dollar he always paid his hands.

After the fashion of a feudal lord, Fanshaw ruled his domains with an iron hand, dispensing his own brand of justice. He was bigger than the law in New Mexico, and he knew it. The gun was the only law in which the cattle baron put his trust. When he wanted to settle something, Fanshaw would look his opponent in the eye, and threaten to bring the dispute to "Judge Colt," patting the six-shooter in his holster as he calmly spoke. As a rule, the disputant suddenly became willing to accept Bill Fanshaw's terms . . . . which were never ungenerous, although always in his favor.

He was a big, powerful man in his late fifties, with silver hair and a face tanned to the color and texture of leather by years of riding the range. Bill Fanshaw directed his empire not from a desk, but from the saddle, and he could ride, rope, and shoot with the best of his cowhands. Many men feared him, and even more respected him. He was known as a man of his word, and one not to be crossed.

Fanshaw was fast to use his hands, those great, thick-fingered paws which had clubbed more than a few men to the ground. His grey eyes were cold as winter in the Rockies, and his smile could be more chilling than the wind that howls through the Donner Pass in the High Sierra. But he was a fair man, albeit a hard one, and few men could complain, all in all, about the way he had treated them. The only exceptions to this rule were the men who had either attempted to rival Fanshaw, or those who had stood in the way of the cattle baron's ever-expanding empire.

A knock on the door to his study caused the cattleman to look up from his big, mahogany desk.

"Who is it?" he asked in a high-pitched, throaty voice that sounded incongruous coming from a man of his size and rugged appearance.

"It's Bart Braden, Mister Fanshaw," he heard his ramrod call out from the other side of the door. "I jus' got back."

"Come in, son," Fanshaw called out, leaning back in his swivel chair. Then he opened his desk's top drawer and pulled out a box of long, thin black cigars.

"Have a cheroot, boy," he told Braden.

"Thankin' you kindly, Mr. Fanshaw," the ramrod told him quietly. "But I ain't of a mind to smoke, now."

"That's all right, Bart," the cattle baron said through clenched teeth, as he lit a match and puffed on his cigar. "But I shorely would like it if you was to jine me in a l'il drink." He pointed to a sideboard across the room, which held a number of bottles and decanters.

"Don't mind if'n I do," the ramrod muttered, as he strode over to the sideboard. In a few moments, he returned with tall glasses, each half-filled with Kentucky sour-mash bourbon and branch water. He handed the glass in his right hand to his employer.

"To tall grass, an' big herds," Bill Fanshaw said, raising his glass in a toast.

"To runnin' cattle from the Rio Grande to the Mississippi," was the foreman's reply.

After they drank, Fanshaw motioned for his ramrod to sit down in a chair facing the desk.

"You don't exactly look as if you's overflowin' with good news, boy," the cattle baron said in his rough, high voice.

"No, sir, I ain't," Bart Braden admitted. "Ol' Don Solomon got him a bug up his ass, an' he jus' goes on and on 'bout how the *tejanos* is allus after the sheepmen's land."

"Well, there's some truth to *that*," Fanshaw admitted.

Braden nodded. "He was madder'n a hornet. Made me wait 'til the end of that *fiesta,* Our Lady of whatchamacallit . . . I can't rightly remember now."

Fanshaw nodded. "Yep," he said. "It's all the same. All that Catholic Church rigamarole."

"Yessir," Bart Braden replied. "We went through this here whole *fandango*. You know how them greasers can be."

"Lord, yes!" Fanshaw exclaimed, puffing on his cheroot. "I shorely do."

"An' I had to wait 'round in the company of these here two jokers—a Pawnee Injun an' a white man, so help me God—who done kilt two of my boys."

Fanshaw's eyes narrowed, as he took the cheroot from his lips. "Who was kilt?" he asked from behind a cloud of cigar smoke.

"Charlie Tilden an' George Prentiss, Mister Fanshaw."

There was an angry look on the cattle baron's face. "Damn it to hell, Bart! They was both good hands. How'd it happen?"

Braden took a swig of his drink, then put down the glass on the small table beside his straight-backed chairs. "Seems they was a-terrorizin' some of Mirabal's boys. Done strung one up by the time them two strangers got into it with 'em. Jake Leinninger an' Harold Sofield was with 'em. Said the pair of 'em was like Kentucky sharpshooters. So Jake an' ol' Harold, they backed off, an' let them fellas rescue the two greasers they was a-gonna set to jiggin' in the air. That's what happened, Mister Fanshaw."

The angry look on Bill Fanshaw's leathery face had been transformed to one of intense disgust. "Texans vamoosin' when the odds is even—that's somethin' I ain't never heard of before." He slammed his huge, meaty fist down upon the table top. "You better give them two boys what for, Bart. That was downright cowardly of 'em."

"Well, they was a mite outgunned, sir," the cattle baron's foreman replied. "The Injun was out of range, an' blowin' the place apart with a buffalo gun, so the boys tell me."

"Ain't that a crock of shit," Fanshaw said angrily, his high voice cracking. "Well, why didn't they jus' charge in, until they was within firin' distance of them two fellas?"

Bart Braden sniffed, and then took another pull at his bourbon. "Seems *that* was exactly what poor Charlie and George done, Mister Fanshaw." He paused to wipe his mouth with the back of his hand. "An' them fellas jus' picked 'em off, like as if they was blackbirds on a whitewashed picket fence."

"Shit, piss, an' corruption," the cattle baron grumbled. "What's this world comin' to?" He paused to finish his drink. "So we ain't had no luck nohow, huh?"

The ramrod shook his hed. " 'Fraid not."

"Damn," the big man swore. "An' all I wanted was a little corridor for to run my beef to market. Ain't that the shits? . . . Well, we gonna have to teach ol' Don Solomon a lesson."

Bart Braden smiled an iron smile.

"All right, boy," Fanshaw said. "That's all fer now. But get yer hands all loaded fer bear, an' ready to ride out in the mornin'."

"Yessir," the ramrod answered respectfully.

"Oh, an' by the way, Bart," the cattle baron added, causing Braden to stop at the door of the study, and turn around to face him.

"Y'all go by the house an' see Samantha, y'hear," he told the ramrod. "She's fixin' to give ya something."

"I'll do that, sir," Braden told his boss. And when he left Bill Fanshaw's study, the foreman had a knowing smile on his lips.

Samantha Fanshaw was tall and blonde, tall even for a Texas woman, with a body whose ripeness caused men to stare at her through narrowed eyes. She was Bill Fanshaw's eldest daughter (her fourteen-year-old sister, Violet, was at school in Fort Worth).

Headstrong and impetuous, she generally got what she wanted, being able to wrap her doting father around her little finger. The thing that Samantha Fanshaw wanted most in the world was to become the wife of her father's ramrod, Bart Braden. The man was not easily corralled, she had found that out for herself; but Bill Fanshaw's daughter was not a woman to give up easily.

They had been lovers for more than two years now, unbeknownst to Bill Fanshaw, who tended to regard his strikingly handsome nineteen-year-old daughter as an innocent. But she was far from that, having had carnal knowledge of men since her sixteenth year. Samantha Fanshaw, in contrast to Raquel Mirabal, had been sexually accomplished long before she reached her seventeenth birthday.

Her affair with Bart Braden had been a tempestuous one, for both of them were passionate and strong-willed individuals. Braden had reciprocated the blonde's intense lovemaking, and each seemed to use the other as a drug, as a powerful intoxicant and aphrodisiac, which took them into realms of sensuality and dark feeling normally inaccessible to those who lived a more mundane existence. Their lovemaking was always intense, and it was also characterized by an edge of cruelty; there exists a very fine line between love and hatred, and in some strange and obsessive way, the lovers explored that narrow borderland, and often went beyond it.

A complication had arisen in this relationship, and now it would never be the same. Bart

Braden could think only of Raquel Mirabal, and Samantha Fanshaw took one look at the ramrod and knew that something was wrong.

"I've been waiting for you," she said, her deep blue eyes travelling over his face, lighting on his handsome features and cruel, thin-lipped mouth. Samantha's lips were full and pink, and she moistened them with a long, slender tongue.

"I jus' rode in," Braden answered, as he attempted to gauge her mood.

"You wouldn't have come to see me, would you . . . if I hadn't told Daddy to send you up here?"

The ramrod took off his dusty Stetson and scratched his head, which was covered with brown curly locks of hair. "I ain't really had time to think on it, honey," Braden told Samatha Fanshaw in a low voice.

"If I hadn't've had Daddy sent you over here, would you have come on your own, Bart? Would you?" she persisted.

"Seems to me like somebody got a bee in her bonnet," the foreman and trail boss of the Fanshaw Ranch told the cattle baron's daughter, a crooked smile coming to his lips as he did.

"Would you?" she persisted.

Bart Braden's crooked smile grew wider, as he realized what the name of the game was. Samantha was burning with jealousy, the volatile blonde was already suspicious of him, knowing down deep, at some instinctual level, that his mind was filled with visions of another woman.

The Texan was amazed at how keen and unerring was this instinct of Samantha's. It was as if her jealousy, and the intense nature of her feelings for him, had sharpened her senses to an extraordinary degree. She could sense—from the first instant that he came into her presence—if he was thinking about another woman, picking up such thoughts with the sudden keenness of a hound dog picking up the first scent of coon on a sudden breeze.

"I told you, I ain't had time to think about it."

"Well, think about it!" she demanded, rising from her chair and coming toward Braden, speaking in the imperious manner which she had inherited from Bill Fanshaw.

The ramrod nodded, lowering his eyes and making a show of thinking, as if he were in deep concentration.

He kept this up for a long time, enjoying the fact that he held Samantha's emotions in the palm of his hand. And when he finally raised his eyes, Braden saw that hers were blazing, practically giving off sparks, as she looked at him intently.

"Well?" she demanded sharply, coming up to him until they were face to face.

"After havin' thought about it some," he drawled, speaking as slowly as possible in order to further bait her, "I come to the considered opinion that I jus' might have moseyed over here, after—"

WAP! She leaned in toward the ramrod, and struck him with a stinging, right-handed roundhouse slap that almost knocked his hat off. Braden's eyes went wide, and then almost immediately narrowed to slits; his smile was transformed into a thin, hard line, and his left cheek reddened vividly where Samantha had slapped him.

"Liar!" she spat at him, her voice going suddenly cold, as if the fire of her anger had paradoxically produced a glaze of ice. "How dare you look me in the eye and tell me such a bare-faced lie?"

If a man had treated Bart Braden in such fashion, he would have been dead by now—no matter who he was, a man of God, or U. S. Grant himself. But on account of their intimacy, the ramrod permitted Fanshaw's daughter to take liberties which he had granted to no one else. And in keeping with the stranger side of their relationship, her anger and scorn inflamed his senses in a dark rising of desire.

Samantha sensed this immediately. Trembling with the release which followed the discharging of her rage, the tall handsome blonde smiled a cruel smile of her own. Then she went back to her armchair, walking backward slowly, never taking her eyes off Bart Braden.

"God, I love you," she whispered in a voice choked with bitterness and passion. Then she sat down, still watching the ramrod like a hawk.

The anger in the Texan's eyes became transformed into desire, and the crooked smile returned to his thin lips.

Samantha lay back in the overstuffed armchair, feet planted firmly on the floor, her legs open, her arms on the arms of the chair, her pelvis thrust forward. Watching this, Braden's eyes widened, his desire rising like the wind that wails through the passes of the San Andres

Mountains.

She wore pajamas of Chinese silk, sheer as gossamer, with nothing on beneath them. And the ramrod marvelled at the way the exquisitely delicate fabric clung to the contours of Samantha's body, following the line of her long, trim thighs; flowing up to the sweet place between them, where the outer lips of her sex rose in a gentle, swelling pout; up the rise of her belly, into the valley which led to her ribcage, then up to the full, round breasts, whose capped areolae and blunt, erect nipples jutted out like twin peaks.

"C'mere, Bart," she growled in a husky voice, noticing the contours of the peg of Braden's erect sex beneath the heavy fabric of his denims.

There was fire in the ramrod's cold eyes now, and his hands went to the bucklet of his gunbelt, as he began to walk toward Samantha, who stayed exactly as she was, lying back in the big chair, her pelvis thrust forward, legs invitingly open.

His gunbelt and holstered Colt hit the wooden floor with a thump. Then, stepping over the belt, Braden strode forward once more. When he came up before Samantha, he dropped to his knees, never taking his eyes from her.

Her own eyes were wide, and she spoke in a voice thick with desire. "Do it to me, Bart. Do what you will with me."

As she spoke, he reached out his big, brown hands and began to pull down the pants of her pajamas. Samantha arched her back, raising her sleek thighs and firm, rounded buttocks in order to allow her lover to draw down the soft silken pants.

Down they came, over her small, rounded belly, over the thick, curly fleece of her golden muff, past the *moue* of her nether lips, and the honeyed roundings of her thighs, down over the full, long calves, trim ankles, and delicate high-arched feet.

Taking the blue silk pants in his hand and raising them to his face, eyes still locked onto Samantha's, the ramrod sniffed the crotch of her pajamas, his nostrils flaring like an aroused stallion's.

"Whatever you want, Bart," Samantha murmured, staring at him through glazed eyes.

Putting the pajama pants down, Braden grunted, "Pull off the top."

"Yes, Bart," she whispered, in a voice that reminded him of the wind that swept across the *Llano Estacado*.

He grabbed her ankles and placed her feet together, causing Samantha's leg to close. Then he licked and kissed her, starting from the toes, and working his way up her feet, ankles, calves and thighs, parting her legs wider and wider as he progressed.

"*Aaah, aaah,*" was all that Samantha said, in a voice now like a high wind over the plains.

He was between her thighs now, the lamplight in the room glinting on the fine golden hairs which ran down from the pelvic valley. Braden mouthed, kissed, and bit the insides of those long and well-turned thighs, running up one and down the other. And as he intensified his attentions, the long-limbed blonde moaned and arched her back, thrusting her sex at him.

"Bart, Bart, Bart," Bill Fanshaw's daughter moaned, her body stiffening as he lowered his head, and leaned forward, his arms now resting on hers.

The sharp perfume of her arousal made his nostrils twitch, and his lips began to pucker, as the foreman continued to lower his head, running his tongue down through her golden fleece. And when his lips met the warm, resilient flesh of her nether lips, Samantha Fanshaw gasped.

Working downward, planting firm and impassioned kisses on those pouting lips, Bart Braden moaned like a longhorn steer catching scent of water at the end of a cattle drive.

Then he began to work his way up, starting from her perineum, his long, thick tongue making its way up into the ravine of her vulva, running up the moist, warm flesh of her sex, setting the long, elegant body aquiver from head to toe.

"Oh, Lord," Samantha gasped. "I feel as if I'm like to explode."

As he ran his tongue up and down inside her throbbing lips, with the lightness of a butterfly's wings and the darting accuracy of a gila monster's tongue, Braden felt the motions of Samantha's thighs, as they twitched spasmodically, clapping him about the ears with their silken smoothness.

His tongue began to circle the pink, throbbing length of her erect clitoris, and Samantha gave a swift, sudden yip that sounded like the first notes of a Comanche war cry.

"Aaaah-aah. Aaaa-a-aaaah!" she cried in a high-pitched cracking voice, as the ramrod's tongue made a series of swift, gliding runs up the sensitive mass of her clitoris.

Resuming his deft tonguing of the inside of her lips, and alternating this with heavy vulvic kisses, and an occasional run over Samantha's long, pink clitoris, Bart Braden caused the blonde's pelvis to buck like an unbroken bronco at its first rodeo.

Her mouth was open and her eyes closed, and Bill Fanshaw's daughter emitted a series of breathy little cries, as she was gripped by paroxyms of orgasm. A reddish flush had spread from her breastbone up past her neck, its border reaching up to her high cheekbones. Her hands clasped and unclasped her breasts, nails grazing the pink caps of her areolae, fingers rolling and tugging at her taut, thick nipples.

While he mouthed Samantha adroitly, Braden ran his hands down over her belly and thighs, making grazing runs with his blunt nails, and leaving a trail of red lines over her golden flesh.

Samantha's pelvis bucked even more wildly now, and it was all that the ramrod could do to maintain the attentions of his mouth and tongue. But this situation could not last for long, and its resolution came, as the lissome blonde's entire body grew rigid, and she threw back her head, emitting a long, shuddering sigh. Then she collapsed back onto the chair, the flexed muscles of her arched back suddenly relaxing.

She lay there, not moving a muscle, for a long

time, while Braden gently stroked her breasts and planted small, closed-mouth kisses on the insides of her still-quivering thighs.

When Samantha Fanshaw finally opened her eyes, she raised her head and stared at Bart Braden.

Sensing her eyes upon him, the ramrod looked up, his dark brown eyes meeting Samantha's deep blue ones.

"Bart, I love you," she whispered tenderly, as she gazed into Braden's eyes.

The Texan said nothing, a crooked, triumphant smile coming to his lips.

"I love you,' she whispered once more, her eyes searching her lover's face.

The answering light in the ramrod's eyes was a cold one, and he continued to smile that cruel and crooked smile.

"You run into some little filly, didn't you, Bart?" she asked in a voice now drained of all tenderness. "Though goodness knows where you found the time, busy as you've been with the trip to Don Solomon Mirabal's spread."

Braden said nothing.

"Unless," Samantha whispered, flashing him an accusing look, "you had a chance to get your hooks into one of the Mirabal gals."

Braden continued to stare and smile at her.

"They're all married, or spoke for, as I recollect," Samantha went on, searching his face. "An' you know how jealous those greasers are of their womenfolk."'

"Yep, they sure are," Braden said in a low voice, his smile warming for an instant.

"Unless it was Raquel Mirabal," Samantha

said loudly, studying Bart Braden's face as she did. Her mouth took on a hard set, as his reaction to the name confirmed her suspicions.

Braden said nothing.

"So she's back from that school," Bill Fanshaw's daughter said rhetorically, already knowing the answer to her own question.

She smiled at the ramrod, but her eyes were as cold as winter in the High Sierras. "You ain't had time to be alone with her—I'll bet dollars to donuts on that, Bart Braden," Samantha told him triumphantly. "But if I ever get wind of you seein' her again, I'll kill her." She looked into his cold eyes. "I mean that, Bart. You're mine."

Still looking into her eyes, Braden stood up and slowly began to take off his clothes. Samantha sat bolt-upright in her chair, transfixed by the sight of his lean, muscular body.

Then, when he stood before her totally naked, Samantha reached out and grasped the shaft of his erect member in her hand, going down on her knees as she did.

"You're mine, Bart," Samantha whispered once more, as she lowered her eyes, beginning to tremble as her glance travelled over the ramrod's body.

Standing above her, his fingers now curled in her long blonde hair, Bart Braden smiled a cruel smile of triumph, as Samantha Fanshaw took him into her mouth . . . .

Heading south through the Pecos River valley, with the Jicarilla Mountains at his right hand, distant and blue in the twilight, Davy

Watson rode with Soaring Hawk and Don Solomon Mirabal's two eldest sons, Anibal and Vicente, on his way to head off a range war.

They rode long into the night, and it was well after midnight when they finally camped, the urgency of their mission causing them to dismount only for the sake of their spent horses.

The four men pitched in, and in no time were seated around a campfire, digging into a meal of tortillas and beans, washed down by the strong and bitter coffee drunk on the trail. Tethered and fed, the horses nodded as they dozed, dreaming (or so the Kansan imagined) of the freedom of the sweeping and open plains.

Anibal Mirabal played his guitar, and Vicente sang *jácaras* and Mexican folk songs. In his turn, accompanying himself upon the small ceremonial drum he carried in his blanket roll, Soaring Hawk performed chants sung at marriages and war dances, and before embarking upon that specialty of his branch of the Pawnee nation, the buffalo hunt. And Davy Watson, himself no singer, declaimed in a loud voice (after the fashion of the flamboyant Englishman, Darrel Duppa, whom he had met in the Arizona Territory), with accompanying gestures which characterized the broad dramatic style of the American stage of 1870, the epic and maudlin poem, "The Boy Stood on the Burning Deck."

The Kansan blushed as he received a thunderous round of applause, so overwhelmed by the reception given his recitation, that he did not consider the irony inherent in it.

Nobody understood what the hell he had been

talking about. The poetic diction of the piece was incomprehensible to the Pawnee; and while the English of the Mirabal brothers was serviceable enough for the work-a-day world, it was not sufficient to enter the realm of the arts. But being gentlemen of the Spanish persuasion, the Mirabal brothers smiled and applauded Davy heartily; and the Pawnee joined them out of love for his blood-brother, even though he looked upon Davy's impassioned recitation of the poem as an exercise in gibberish.

The festivities ended with the Mirabals dueting on a serenade, the tune most popular with the latin swains of the New Mexico Territory. By the end of the serenade, Davy found himself humming along with the bright, strong voices of the two brothers, and thinking of the dark, loveliness of Raquel Mirabal.

His applause was cut short by the whinnying of the horses, who had obviously caught the scent of something approaching in the darkness.

Scrambling to their feet, the four men picked up their rifles, each sending a cartridge into the respective firing chambers with a sharp click of the bolt.

Davy bit his lip as he peered into the darkness, his index finger tapping on the trigger guard of his Henry rifle. Here they were in the middle of nowhere, in country frequented by Apaches, Comanches, and hostile Texans. Davy felt that the odds of meeting a friendly party at this moment were in no way in his favor.

"Over there," Soaring Hawk whispered. "By rise."

As the Pawnee said this, the three other men

all wheeled around to their left and trained their weapons upon the spot which Soaring Hawk had indicated.

A sudden creaking sound underscored the brave's words, and there before him, ghostly in the cold light of the moon, Davy saw a Conestoga wagon, drawn by two horses. A moment later, a second wagon, almost identical to the first, came over the rise, its wheels creaking, and the harness of the horses that pulled it jingling as they came down the slope.

Faced with four rifles trained upon them, the drivers of the Conestogas quickly reined in their horses and drew them up to a snorting, jingling halt. Then they clambered down from their wagons and walked toward Davy and his companions, with the unsteady legs of men who had not set foot on solid ground for some time.

The men were not the sharpest-looking fellows he'd ever seen, the Kansan told himself, as he stared at the pair who approached with friendly smiles and open hands held up at shoulder-level. One was squat and thick-set; and one was tall and thin as a split rail. One was a *chicano* and the other an *anglo*. Both were dressed in dusty denims and flannel shirts whose checkered patterns were faded almost to the point of invisibility.

"*Saludos amigos,*" the short, squat man said, looking at the Mirabal brothers and grinning through a mouth full of gold teeth.

"Howdy, gents," said the tall, thin man, smiling at Davy and Soaring Hawk with a smile which made the Kansan think of picket fences.

"It is pleasant and reassuring to meet

gentlemen of quality in this lonely and deserted place," the squat man said in Spanish to Anibal and Vicente Mirabal.

"If you speak English, *Señor,*" Anibal told the man in Spanish, "we would be much obliged if you would converse in that tongue, for the sake of our friends here."

"As the *Señores* wish," the man replied in English, startling Davy for an instant.

"Whom have we the pleasure of addressing?" Vicente Mirabal inquired of the strangers.

"I am Diego Cabrera," the squat man replied. "And this gentleman," he indicated the tall, gap-toothed man with a sweeping gesture, "is my associate of many years, Mister Alton Slagel."

"Right proud t'make y'all's acquaintance," the thin man drawled in a deep bass voice.

"And what is your business, gentlemen?" Anibal asked. "What are you doing in this desolate place?"

"Why, we are traders, *Señor,*" the squat man said with a smile, "bound for Albuquerque." He gestured in the direction of the two Conestoga wagons. "My associate an' I have jus' come back from Mexico with a load of goods to sell to our fellow New Mexicans."

"We got us a passel of dandy leather pieces—belts, gunbelts, chaps, bridles, an' the like," the man named Slagle boomed. "All hand-tooled an' spankin' new."

At this, Anibal Mirabal nodded. He and his three companions lowered their rifles.

"An' we got lots of fine blankets," Diego Cabrera told the men, smiling his golden smile, "wove by the *indios* of Sonora."

Gesturing toward the campfire, Anibal Mirabal welcomed the traders and then proceeded to introduce himself and his companions.

"Here's a leetle somethin' I carries 'round jest in case of snakebite," Alton Slagle told the others, after he and Carbrera had drunk some coffee. He held out a bottle of rye whiskey.

The alcohol was welcomed in the chill New Mexican night by all but Soaring Hawk, who made it a point never to imbibe spiritous liquors. But the three other men drank liberally from the trader's bottle, and they sat around the campfire for more than an hour, before unrolling their blankets and laying their heads down on their saddles.

Soaring Hawk stood guard for the first two hours of the night, and was relieved by Diego Cabrera, who would, in turn, be relieved by Vicente Mirabal.

God grant me the serenity to accept the things I cannot change, Davy Watson prayed silently, *the courage to change the things I can, and the wisdom to know the difference. Amen.*

As he lay his head down on his saddle and tilted his hat over his eyes, the Kansan thought for a moment of the gravity and importance of his mission.

The Texans would soon be up in arms, and it was up to him to see Bill Fanshaw and talk some sense into him. And while Bart Braden, that arrogant and formidable man, might prove to be an obstacle in his path, Davy Watson was confident that the sheepmen's new proposal would be acceptable to the cattle baron.

Acceptable, Davy told himself as he began to drift off to sleep, if Fanshaw meant what he said. The cattle barons and the *ricos* who owned the pasturelands were all playing with dynamite . . . and as far as he could see, that dynamite had one hell of a short fuse. But there was no sense in worrying at this point, Davy reminded himself, as he yawned and stretched out his arms.

So far, so good. He and his companions had ridden long and hard, making steady progress on the first leg of their journey. They'd had the good fortune to steer clear of any of the marauding bands of Apaches or Comanches who roamed the lower Pecos area and the *Llano Estacado* to the east. They had already completed the most difficult and demanding part of their journey, and by sundown tomorrow, at the very latest, they would be in Roswell, where Bill Fanshaw had his headquarters.

So it was with a satisfied mind and a clear conscience that the Kansan went to sleep, expecting no surprises between then and the time he dismounted at the Fanshaw ranch in Roswell. But as the poet, Robert Burns, has known, the best-laid plans of mice and men oft go astray. And when Davy Watson was roughly awakened, only three hours after he had gone to sleep, he opened his eyes to a sight which made the hairs at the nape of his neck stand on end. The camp was ringed by a great number of strangers.

Then, hearing Anibal and Vicente Mirabal call out in surprise, Davy learned who the shadowy figures were. The visitors to the camp were Indians—of a tribe so bold and ferocious that they were feared by the dreaded Apaches themselves. If he possibly could have encountered a greater misfortune, the Kansan could not have imagined it at that moment. He slowly rose to his feet, both hands held high in the air, as he stared into the muzzle of a Winchester rifle.

As he got to his feet, Davy saw a number of Indians pointing their weapons at Soaring Hawk and the Mirabal brothers. But what struck him as odd was the fact that neither Diego Cabrera or Alton Slagle had their hands in the air, nor were any of the fierce and scowling Indians pointing rifles at them.

"What's goin' on?" he croaked, turning to the lanky Slagle.

"Oh, jest a l'il social call," the man responded. "These here's our ol' pals, the Comanches . . . ."

5

PRISONERS OF THE COMANCHES

In the deepest darkness of the night, in the hour which preceded the skyglow that heralded the coming of the sun, Raquel Mirabal stood by the barred window of her room on the upper story of Don Solomon's *hacienda,* and gazed up at the cold, bronze moon of New Mexico, listening to the faint and far-off sounds of a guitar that floated across the plaza.

Some drunken and rejected suitor must be playing that mournful tune, the *patrón's* daughter imagined, listening to the music in the darkness. Alone in the night, but for his bottle and guitar, the poor *hombre* serenaded the cold, unheeding moon with a song of lost love.

Love was uppermost in the young beauty's mind as she stood by the barred window, naked in the moonlight, the wind that came sighing down from the mountains ruffling her long thatch of pubic hair, and causing her nipples to stiffen.

Thinking of Davy Watson, of being alone in her room with him, the door securely locked and their clothing lying on the floor, Raquel leaned against the bars of her window. Her nipples grazed the cold, unyielding metal, and when it made contact with her full breasts, Raquel's skin broke out into goose bumps. A sharp intake of breath occurred when the full and turgid lips of her sex made contact with the cold metal.

"Oh-h-h," she sighed, in a voice that resembled the whispering wind from the mountains, slowly and gently rubbing herself against the stiff length of the bar. And as she moved upward, her breath coming in long, slow gasps, the cold metal caressed the front of her thighs, as well.

She had never made love with a man. No, the Don's youngest daughter had always been guarded as jealously as the crown jewels of Spain. But Raquel and her schoolmates had often fantasized, alone at night in their rooms, when the vigilant nuns were finally asleep, what it must be like to be the lover of some handsome, faceless young man. But this time, the tall and muscular man in the fantasies of Don Solomon's daughter had a face. And she was ready, Raquel Mirabal told herself as she squirmed against the bars, to give herself to him.

That he was an *anglo,* and not a man of her own race did not bother the lovely eighteen-year-old at all, for she was smitten by the Kansan's virile, blond good looks, and his open-heartedness and tender charm. In her eyes, no man was so handsome, nor so noble.

Of course, Raquel thought with a wicked smile, as her wet pussy glided down the bar, that insolent *tejanos* who had never stopped looking at her during the *fiest* of *La Conquistadora* was also a very handsome man. That Bart Braden, who was cool where Davy Watson was warm, thrilled Raquel Mirabal in a different, darker, and only slightly lesser way.

One would be tender, and the other violent. One would be affectionate, and the other challenging. One would be intimate, and the other cruel and remote. And while her better self opted for the warmth and virile tenderness of the Kansan, something dark within the *patrón's* daughter responded to the aquiline fierceness of the Texan.

Fantasy was the way in which the young beauty resolved this inner conflict—at least for the moment. And while her supple body quivered from head to toe as she moved up and down the hard, rounded metal, its dark surface drawing off the warmth of her sex, Raquel visualized the two men, one blond and one dark, standing naked before her at the foot of the bed.

They came toward her, with open arms, and dimly-seen sex organs, whose stiffness and heat she perceived through her nerve endings, rather than her eyes.

Raquel Mirabal gasped as her pelvis began to jerk spasmodically, and she grasped the bars so tightly that her hands went white. Then her plaintive, sighing moans escaped into the darkness beyond her window, and mingled with the drunken guitarist's far-off song, the only sounds to be heard in the night that mantled the plaza. . .

On the floor below, oblivious to the soft, intense cries of his youngest daughter, Don Solomon Mirabal snored in the darkness of his bedroom, with the sound of a bull rousing itself from a dream of the butcher's knife.

Beside him lay *Doña* Esmeralda, a sleeper so sound that not even the taurine snorts of her husband could dent the armor of her slumber. And there was even a little smile upon her lips, as if the *patrónesa* were dreaming of a wedding for her darling Raquelita.

The Don's bullish snorts, as he began to stir beneath the covers, were not unlike the sounds made at times by the herds of Bill Fanshaw, the *tejano* cattleman. And the *patrón* saw those herds in his sleep, watching helplessly as they, in their numbers, spread over his pasturelands, like the incoming tide of some great, dark ocean. And the thunder of their hooves reminded Don Solomon of the great waves which broke on the rocks that lined the shore of Acapulco, in Old Mexico.

In wave after wave, the dark, snorting herds kept coming, flowing over the Mirabal lands, trampling the Don's white, fleecy sheep underfoot, leaving the broken, lifeless bodies behind, like the flotsam and jetsam of the sea cast up on the shore.

The Don watched this from the safety of his *hacienda*, from behind a barred window. He felt paralyzed as the mighty waves of cattle broke over his lands. And when he tried to rally his *caballeros* and *partidarios,* when he cupped his hands to his mouth and made to summon up all his relatives, retainers, and allies, no sound came out of Don Solomon's mouth. And the only sound that could be heard in his nightmare was the thunderous beating of hooves . . . . .

Bart Braden and Samantha Fanshaw made love for close to two hours, acting more like passionate antagonists than tender lovers, locked in a combat whose field of battle was the huge, quilted bed in her quarters behind the ranch house.

The marks of the blonde hellion's nails trailed across the ramrod's chest, back, and thighs; and the bruises that he had inflicted upon her unblemished golden-hued skin stood out in livid contrast to the surrounding fairness of her full and elegant body. In their relationship, Dan Cupid was as ferocious as Geronimo, and his arrows were poisoned and barbed. And even after the fires of lust had been banked, there was no rest for the lovers. Braden's heart was elsewhere, and Samantha knew it; and that knowledge gave her no rest.

"Bart," she whispered in the trail boss's ear. "Make love to me again."

"Well sure, honey," Braden grunted, turning his face to the wall. "Soon's I git my second wind."

"Now, Bart," she whispered insistently, reaching over and taking his flaccid sex in her hand.

Braden compressed his lips and puffed out a whistling stream of air, his muscles suddenly tense.

After stroking the Texan for a while, she leaned over and brought her head down, her mouth opening as she did.

His eyes closed, the image of Raquel Mirabal's dark beauty in his mind, Bart Braden stretched out upon the big cast iron bed and gave himself over to Samantha's ministrations.

Her tongue darted out, running in sharp, flicking motions over the neck and head of Braden's rod.

"Oooh," grunted the Fanshaw foreman, his pelvis shuddering in response to the deft workings of the blonde beauty's long pink tongue.

Then clasping his rod at its base, Samantha took him in her mouth. He moaned and writhed, as her lips parted and his throbbing sex entered the welcoming warmth of her mouth. It was wet there, and her tongue massaged him with firm, intense strokes. And then she bobbed her head up and down, sucking and tonguing in alternation, working the man beneath her up to a fever pitch of excitement.

"Damn, damn," groaned the ramrod, pitching from side to side like a storm-tossed vessel out on the distant North Atlantic. Sweat ran down his forehead, trailing through his thick sideburns to soak into the pillow beneath his head.

Samantha Fanshaw worked and worked on her lover, grasping him tightly, and running her nails up along the underside of his shaft as she raised her head on the upstroke.

Braden was puffing and blowing like a longhorn steer, his teeth clenched and his eyes rolled up in their sockets. "Huh, huh, huh," he grunted, snorting in short, explosive bursts with the sound of a Southern Pacific engine working up a head of steam.

At this point, feeling the ramrod's body stiffen, Samantha Fanshaw opened her eyes and darted a glance at Bart Braden's contorted features. It was not the eye of the dove that she opened to look up her lover's face; no, it was more like the cold, predatory orb of the hawk.

"*Hunh,*" grunted Braden, as the fiery fullness which heralded orgasm began to suffuse the pit of his groin. In another few moments, he would climax.

Just then, her cruel glance having provided her with the exact timing, Samantha raised her head, drew back suddenly from Braden, and released her grip on his member.

"*Hunh! Wha-a-a-?*" the trail boss cried, suddenly thrashing from side to side in frustration, as his body began to react to the blonde's cruel maneuver. He opened his eyes wide, the look on his face that of a man who had just fallen into an icy river.

Samantha Fanshaw's hawk-eyes narrowed, and she smiled a smile that was colder than the barrel of Braden's .45.

"Dammit gal," he whispered, in a voice that crackled with the electricity of his anger. "What t'hell you doin' t' me?"

"You fancy-assed, high and mighty bastard," she hissed in rattlesnake sibilants. "You smug, overbearing saddle tramp. How dare you come into *my* bed, and use *my* body, and soil *my* love—when the only thing on your mind is some other woman. *How dare you!*"

At this, Braden sat bolt-upright in the bed, glaring at the blonde with bobcat eyes.

"By God, you *do* have some little *tamale* in your thoughts," she went on in the low, reptilian voice of her anger. "And either you got you some little wench in the hay, or you're running around all hot and bothered and unsatisfied, with a sweet smile on your face and a stiff pecker, after sniffiñ' around Raquel Mirabal like a lap dog."

"That's enough," he said in an icy voice.

"Enough, hell!" she roared suddenly, causing the rugged trail boss to wince involuntarily. "I've only jus' begun, Bart Braden. It *is* Raquel Mirabal, isn't it?"

"I said that's enough, Samantha," he snarled.

"You ain't never gonna get near her," Bill Fanshaw's daughter sneered. "Not a piece of white trash like you. Her people's real quality, an' there ain't no way a mongrel like you's gonna lay hands on that child." She laughed bitterly. "Why, she's ol' Don Solomon's honey baby, his favorite child."

Braden was silent now. His eyes flashed and his face was livid; his body shook° to the accumulated fury of his rage.

"And if you ever *should* hook up with her," Samantha told him with venomous sweetness, "I'll see to it that you don't get a chance to set her backside down in your bed." She smiled wickedly. "I'll have her killed, Bart. So help me God, I will."

"No-o-o-ooo!" the ramrod exclaimed suddenly, lashing out at her with a sweeping back-handed motion, his anger overflowing like the Mississippi overrunning its banks after the spring rains.

Whap! His big, leathery paw caught Samantha on the side of the jaw. Her head shot back, and she fell across the bed with a deep, strangled grunt.

Braden was shaking all over now, like a man in the throes of Saint Vitus' Dance. He leaned forward, resting his weight on both arms, which were placed on either side of Samantha Fanshaw's head. There was a cruel smile on his lips and lightning flashing in his eyes, as he lowerd his head and looked down at her.

Samantha's eyes were wide and she was trembling now from the shock of the blow. As she opened her mouth, a thin trickle of blood ran down from its right side.

"I ain't *nobody's* whippin' boy, lady." Braden said between clenched teeth. "An' any man who talked that way to me would be thrashin' on the ground by now, with a belly full of hot lead."

"My father made you his top hand," she whispered back in a voice that shook. "And he could knock you off your high horse at the drop of a hat . . . if I told him to."

Braden stared at Samantha out of hard, cold eyes, and smiled his cruel and mocking smile.

"That don't go far to scare me," he sneered. " 'Cause the man ain't been born yet that Bart Braden's afraid of—your daddy included. An' as fer my position, well, that don't amount to a hill of beans, neither." He shook his head. "Y'know, I wasn't exactly starvin' to death my own self, afore I met Bill Fanshaw."

Her eyes met his, and they were equally hard and cold. "You better just rein in, while you still got the chance, Bart," she warned. " 'Cause Bill Fanshaw's twice the man you are, even on your best day.''

Braden sneered again and slowly shook his head. ''You worshippin' your daddy, know that, gal?'' He looked into her eyes, ''Sometimes I git to thinkin' you'd druther be in this here ol' bed with him, than with—''

Whap! Samantha delivered a stinging slap to the ramrod's face.

''You watch your dirty mouth, you shiftless saddle tramp.'' she warned, her face suddenly flushed with a mingling of emotions—anger and something else . . . something which Bill Fanshaw's lovely daughter dared not acknowledge.

''You're mine,'' she told him in a harsh voice. ''An' I'm going to go to any length to keep you.''

The ramrod sneered as he took his hand away from his cheek. ''Lady, nobody owns Bart Braden.'' His eyes narrowed ''And as for what you said about Raquel Mirabal—''

''It is her!'' Samanthan cried out loudly, struggling to rise. But the ramrod's left arm shot out, and his big hand encircled her long, graceful neck.

''You keep your mouth shut,'' he told her in a low, even voice, as she made small gurgling sounds, gasping as his thick fingers tightened around her throat.

''Just mind your own business, gal, an' I'll tend to mine.'' As he said this, she began to writhe furiously beneath him. Then she emitted a high-pitched, strangling sound as he tightened his grip on her throat once more.

''Get in my way, an' I'll ride you down.'' he

went on. "By God, I will. Ain't nobody gonna git in my way. Not you. Not ol' Bill Fanshaw. Not nobody, you hear?"

By this time, Samantha Fanshaw's eyes had rolled up in their sockets. Her face had begun to purple, and when Bart Braden saw this, his eyes went wide, and he immediately released his grip on her throat.

Samantha's body was wracked by a series of convulsions as she began to gasp for air.

Bart Braden stared down at Bill Fanshaw's daughter, his features now as cold and immobile as those of a marble statue. She had almost recovered when someone began to pound on the door to the room.

"Bart! You in there, Bart?" a sandpaper voice growled.

Braden frowned as he turned to the door. "What t'hell you want?" he asked in annoyance.

"Bart, it's me—Frank Reagers," the man on the other side of the door called out.

"I know who it is, ya damn fool," Braden shot back. What ya doin' botherin' me here?"

"I shore am sorry to disturb ya, Bart," the man rasped apologetically. "But we-all got to saddle up an' hightail it outta here."

Braden frowned. "What, *now?*" he asked.

"Yup. Right this very minute. Ol' Bill Fanshaw got hisself madder'n a hornet, an' he done tole me to git you. He wants ever'body saddled up'n ready in five minutes."

"But what's goin' on?" Braden persisted.

"Oh, shit, I don't know, Bart," the man whined. "All's I know's they's blood in his eye,

112

an' he's ready to ride out."

"All right then, Frank," Braden called out to the man. "I'll be by in two minutes."

"Yessir," the man replied, as the ramrod heard the departing scuff of his boots.

Braden dressed quickly, never looking at Samantha, who now sat up in the bed cross-legged, staring at him with angry eyes.

After he had dressed and began to make for the door, Fanshaw's daughter reached out a hand toward the departing ramrod, a stricken look on her face.

His hand on the doorknob, Braden turned in the blonde's direction.

"I reckon this is gon' be the last we-all see of each other," he said softly.

Samantha's jaw fell open and her features seemed to collapse, as a wall of old adobe crumbles under the force of a flash flood. She said nothing, and was not even breathing as the ramrod stared at her.

"Well, I hope y'all can let bygones be bygones," Bart Braden whispered. "Good luck, Samantha," he told her just before he left the room.

Then the door clicked shut. The silence in the room lasted for a long time, and was broken at last by Samantha Fanshaw's venomous whisper.

"Oh, you'll get yours, Mister Bart Braden," she said. "You'll get yours. I promise you that right here and now."

"Madre de Dios!" Anibal Mirabal said bitterly, as Davy Watson listened to the screeches and war whoops of the Comanches. "I

should have known that them two *pendejos* was *Comancheros!*''

"What's that?" the Kansan asked, turning to face the eldest of the Mirabal brothers.

"*Comancheros* is men—native New Mexicans—who trades with the Comanche Indians. This trade is forbidden by the *anglos,* but that don't mean nothin'. These *hombres* is very good at dodgin' your military patrols."

He shook his head and smiled a wry smile. "*Los Comancheros* make them *soldados gringos* look like fools. An' now, since 1860, their trade with the Comanches is bigger than ever."

"You mean they's a kind of alliance twixt these fellas an' the Injuns?" Davy asked.

"It it perhaps," Anibal told him, "the strangest alliance in the history of the southwest. The Comanches are the fiercest *indios*—the mos' terrible of all the Plains Indians. They have always fight against the *tejanos*—an' against our fathers in Old Mexico, too."

"How'd they do against the Apaches?" the Kansan asked, remembering his warlike acquaintances, Cochise and Geronimo.

"Even the Apaches have fled from the Comanches," Anibal Mirabal replied. "There is no one who ride the horse like them—not even the Apache. One historian has call them 'The Huns of the New World.' "

Davy nodded, remembering his readings in the book of his Uncle Ethan, concerning the Huns and their ferocious chief, Attila, who was known as "The Scourge of God."

"They was at peace with the Spaniards for over a hundred years," Anibal went on. "An' then they continued to trade with our fathers, as well as with *los indios de los pueblos.*"

Soaring Hawk took all this in, but his eyes never left the Comanches, who whooped drunkenly as they caroused by the blazing fire before the chief's teepee. In the distance, there could be heard the lowing of the cattle which had been stolen by the Indians and traded to Cabrera and Slagle for rifles, cartridges, and cases of whiskey.

This was in fact, the epitome of the present *Comanchero* trade. Dealing in illegal items, mainly liquor and firearms, and occasionally horses, the mainstay of the Plains Indian, the traders grew rich, as the Comanches rustled cattle from the Texans and Old Mexicans, and traded them off for a song. And while the *Comancheros* easily eluded the small United States Cavalry patrols in the territory, they were not always quite so fortunate when it came to the *tejanos,* whose undying enmity they had earned by inciting the Indians to steal their cattle.

"But when your people came, after 1864," Anibal told Davy Watson, "both the *indios* and the *Comancheros* don't like this, so they work together—against the *anglos.*"

"Your folks don't have nothin' to do with these here scoundrels, do they?" asked Davy.

Anibal shook his head. "Years ago, it was a respectable business, the *Comanchero* trade. But not no more. 'Cause them *indios* gets drunk, an' then goes on the warpath, killin' anyone they come across—men, women, or child."

He shook his head. "Now, if we catch them

Comancheros," he drew a forefinger across his throat, "we make sure they do no more tradin'."

"You fellas sure can talk," Alton Slagle told them cheerfully, as he sauntered over to where Davy, Soaring Hawk, and the Mirabal brothers, their arms bound behind their backs, sat in front of the Comanche chief's teepee, at the center of the raiding party's encampment.

"Well, at least I'm glad y'all's havin' a good time," th *Comanchero* went on in his *basso profundo*. " 'Cause me'n ol' Diego, we got to take that cattle into Arizona, right soon."

As he said this, his partner waddled up behind him.

"Alton is right, *muchachos,"* Diego Cabrera told them, smiling his gold-toothed smile. "We got much business in the Arizona Territory. So we must now say *adios, amigos.*"

He drew back suddenly, as a gob of spit from the mouth of Vicente Mirabal flew past his face.

"That is a very poor way for a gentleman to behave, I think," Cabrera told Vicente, shaking his head, and still flashing his golden smile. "I would like to teach you a lesson, but I think my ol' amigo, Chief Pahanca, will learn you some manners even better than me."

"Haw, haw, haw," Slagle boomed, as the two *Comancheros* walked off into the night, leaving the Kansan and his companions at the mercy of thirty drunken Comanches.

6

BLOOD ON THE PLAINS

"Hai-ee-ya-ya! Hai-ee-ya-ya!" the Comanches chanted, hoarse and off-key, as they wove around the blazing campfire, not a man among them able to walk a straight line.

Bottles shattered against the rocks, and the Comanches paused only to open fresh ones, as they staggered and shuffled in the harshly flickering light of the fire, discharging their carbines into the air, shrieking like a legion of fiends from the deepest part of hell.

"Them boys is really gittin' shit-faced," Davy observed.

"Indian get crazy from firewater," Soaring Hawk replied in a low voice, his features composed into a mask of inscrutability. "Not good. Make 'em heap mean."

A bottle of Old Overholt crashed to pieces on a nearby rock, causing the prisoners to turn their heads away from the resultant shower of glass.

Davy heard the brothers Mirabal mutter a brace of Spanish curses, and he himself loosed a volley of home-grown Kansas profanity at the Comanche who had thrown the empty bottle.

The brave heard this and staggered over to stand above him, a fiendish leer upon his face as he weaved back and forth in the ghastly light emanating from the bonfire.

"*Anglo* soon make sport for Comanche," the big brave told Davy and his companions. "Soon Chief Pahanca roast him in fire like young pig."

Davy made a sour face at this, and the Comanche burst into derisive laughter.

"Plenty soon," the brave went on, "be no more *anglo*—no more soldier blue in this land. Soon Comanche rise up and drive 'em all out. Take many scalp, many blue uniform." He chuckled. "Esquival like see that."

"This fella's a reg'lar geyser of conversation," Davy remarked, trying to get a grip on the knot of the rope that bound his hands behind his back.

"No talk!" the big Comanche ordered. "Esquival no finish speak. Say more."

"Indian say too much already," Soaring Hawk suddenly told the drunken brave. "Talk like squaw. Go with women."

This caused the big buck to wheel around and face him.

"You Pawnee," he told Soaring Hawk, glaring at him through bloodshot eyes. "Comanche kill heap many Pawnee. Take heap many scalp."

"Not you," Davy's blood-brother shot back scornfully. "Woman no take scalp."

By this time, a number of Comanches had gathered around the big buck, and when they heard Soaring Hawk's retort, all burst into loud, guffawing laughter.

"You stop talk!" the Comanche bellowed, starting toward the Pawnee with outstretched arms, open hands, and fingers curved like talons. But before he could reach his objective, the buck went sprawling, as Davy Watson thrust out his boot and tripped him.

The other Comanches roared with renewed laughter at this.

The brave hit hard when he landed on the stony ground, and began to flush with embarrassment the moment he rose to his feet.

"White man make Esquival fall," the Comanche muttered. "For that," he added, unsheathing a wicked-looking knife, "I cut off nose."

"Comanche do that," Soaring Hawk called out loudly, just as the big buck grabbed hold of Davy's hair with one hand and brought the knife up to his face with the other, "and he shows everyone that he *is* squaw."

"What?" the Comanche shrieked, infuriated by the Pawnee's taunt. He let go of Davy's hair, spun around, and lurched over to where Soaring Hawk sat.

"You!" he cried, his deep voice croaking under his anger. "You make too much talk. Esquival fix so you talk no more." He raised the big, mean-looking knife, whose blade glittered as it reflected the roaring fire behind Soaring Hawk. "Esquival cut out tongue of Pawnee. Fix him good, so he talk no more."

"You cut out my tongue," Soaring Hawk sneered. "No matter. Everyone still know what a squaw is Comanche brave. By'n by, all Indian see what—"

Whap! The Comanche cut short Soaring Hawk's speech with a hard backhand slap. Then he knelt down in front of the Pawnee and raised his knife in the air.

Frantically, Davy rolled over on the stony earth, as he endeavored to get closer to his blood-brother's attacker. And then, coming out of his roll, the Kansan laid flat on his back and drew back his legs. A second later, his booted feet shot forward and made contact with the back of the Comanche.

Thwack! Davy's boots hit the buck's flesh with a resounding smack, and the drunken man shot forward suddenly, flying toward Soaring Hawk.

Seeing this, the Pawnee brave ducked down, and when the buck was over him, thrust up his shoulder with all the strength he could muster, sending the Comanche flying over him, crying out in surprise.

The other Comanche braves called out in admiration when the man hit the ground and lay there stunned, his knife gone from his hands. The little group broke out into raucous laughter, attracting the attention of the rest of their tribesmen, who had by this time finished their dance around the leaping fire.

It was some time before Esquival tottered to his feet, but when he did, it was to the jeering accompaniment of Comanche laughter. The dazed buck looked around in all directions, but was unable to locate his knife, which had fallen in the shadow of a big rock facing the fire.

The Comanches continued to laugh, and the buck grew livid with shame and rage. He shook from head to toe, as he glared in rapid alternation from the Kansan to Soaring Hawk.

Oh, Jesus—what's he gon' do now? Davy thought, as the enraged buck lurched over to Soaring Hawk and grabbed the Pawnee by his braids.

"Let 'im go, you big, ugly sum'bitch!" he roared, just as Esquival began to drag Soaring Hawk toward the blazing fire.

"Maricón! Pendejo!" the Mirabal brothers shouted at the Comanche, struggling to rise to their feet, as did Davy Watson. But their efforts were to no avail, for their captors thrust them roughly back down to the ground.

"Let 'im go—dadblast you!" Davy shouted, when he looked up once more and saw the huge buck holding the bound Pawnee in his arms, tottering over to the fire with him, about to chuck Soaring Hawk into its blazing heart.

"You bastard—*STOP!*" Davy screamed, suddenly overcome with horror, as a vision of his blood-brother roasting in the flames leapt up in his mind's-eyes.

"Hey-ah-nay!" someone called out over the cries of the drunken braves.

This had the immediate effect of freezing Esquival in his tracks, which was fortunate indeed for Soaring Hawk, whom the huge buck was now holding only feet from the blazing fire.

"Key-hay nata cho-kial," the gruff voice called out once more. Stepping back quickly from the fire, Esquival let go of Soaring Hawk, who then fell backward to the ground.

The Kansan turned to look at the speaker, and saw a lordly Indian of more than average height, slender and tall, rather than the average Comanche body type, which was squat, stocky, and bow-legged. His hair was silver, and his face was as wrinkled as an old piece of hide.

"Kah dayso day?" the imposing Indian asked.

"Kay nah tah-kee-ah, die yay, Pahanca," Esquival replied, glowering down at Soaring Hawk.

At the mention of the name *Pahanca,* Davy Watson realized that he was in the presence of the chief of this particular tribe of Comanches.

"Chief, that damfool was 'bout to chuck my friend there into the fire," Davy angrily told Pahanca, struggling to get to his feet.

The Kansan's speech was immediately translated into Spanish by Anibal Mirabal.

"Hu-uunh," the Comanche chief grunted, turning to look at Davy Watson.

"What the hell's that big sum'bitch want to'go an' do a thing like that fer?" Davy went on, as Pahanca came up to him. "We got no quarrel with the Comanches. An' these here fellas," he indicated Anibal and Vicente with a nod of his head, "is New Mexicans. You know, Chief, *nuevos meh-hee-can-oze.*"

"Hu-uunh," the chief grunted once more, his hot breath breaking over Davy's face in a boozey wave.

Judas Priest, the Kansan thought, staring into Pahanca's dark and bloodshot eyes, *this sum'bitch is walloped, too. Why, he's jus' as drunk as all the rest of 'em.*

"We'd, uh, like to part in friendship, you know, *amigos.* An' we'd like to think of the Comanche nation with pride an' fondness," Davy went on, mustering his eloquence, as Anibal Mirabal did his best to translate the Kansan's rambling words into Spanish.

"Hu-uunh," the chief grunted, in response to Davy Watson's appeal. And then, as all the Comanche braves leaned forward, watching him

with narrowed eyes, Pahanca thrust out an arm
and hit the Kansan square in the chest, sending
him staggering backward toward the roasting
fire.

"Hey! What the hell ya doin?" Davy
protested, skidding to a halt as he dug his
bootheels into the hard, stony ground.

Whump! The Comanche chief straight-armed
him once more, sending the Kansan still closer to
the fire.

"Now, you look here!" he croaked, feeling a
sudden intense heat on his back.

Whump! Another smashing thrust sent Davy
reeling back, to sway at the edge of the fire.

Soaring Hawk was up on his feet, and heading
toward Pahanca, but Esquival suddenly lunged
at the Pawnee and struck him down with a blow
of his big, meaty fist.

Damn! There's no talkin' to this sum'bitch!
Davy told himself, as the Comanche chief
moved in once more, intending this time to pitch
his *anglo* captive straight into the crackling fire.

"Hu-uunh," Pahanca grunted once again, as
he thrust out his right arm and lunged at Davy
Watson.

"Haai-eeee!" he screamed suddenly, startling
the onlookers, as Davy Watson's foot shot out
and the toe of his boot slammed into the
Comanche chief's groin.

"Dah-hayaa!" Esquival cried out angrily, as
Pahanca clutched his testicles, fell to his knees,
and puked out his guts on the ground before
him. The giant reached out his big, clawlike
hands and lunged at Davy Watson, seeking to
finish the job.

BLAM! BLAM! A pistol roared in the
123

darkness beyond the fire, its report heralded by two bright flashes.

Davy heard two flat, smacking sounds, and saw Esquival straighten up all at once—halted in his lunge—and then stagger backward. In another second, the huge Comanche's legs gave way beneath him, and he fell flat on his back with a thud that was heard above the crackling of the campfire. The Kansan looked down at Esquival, and saw two round and bloody holes in his chest and forehead.

Cries of consternation and anger went up from the Comanches, and the drunken braves lurched away from the fire, staggering off to where they had dropped their rifles.

"Git down!" Davy cried, just as Vicente Mirabal said the same thing in Spanish.

All at once, the darkness was ablaze with sudden brief flashes of light, and a thunderous staccato roaring drowned out the sputter and crackle of the fire.

Bam! Blam! Bambam! Blam! Six-guns went off all around the periphery of the Comanche camp, sending in a deadly rain of hot lead that smacked and tore into the bodies of the drunken and panicked Indians, rending flesh and smashing bone.

The Comanches were dropping like flies beneath the withering volleys of their attackers. A handful of braves managed to reach their rifles, and began firing frantically into the darkness before them, attempting to sight on the flashes from the enemy's pistols. But they were too drunk to shoot straight, and only one brief cry indicated that any of the Comanches' bullets had found a mark.

Davy and his companions lay upon the ground, burying their faces in the dust, as the lead flew hot and heavy over their heads. The Comanches continued to fall beneath the onslaught, and by the time a minute had gone by, not a man among them was left standing or firing his rifle.

An occasional shot cracked in the night, and the occasional Comanche who had risen to his knees was soon laid out in the dust, bloody and still.

When the shooting appeared to be over, the Kansan raised his head. "Hoo-wee," he whispered, seeing the ground before him littered with the bodies of his erstwhile captors.

Who had rescued them? he wondered. Who had come to their aid at the last minute, here in the middle of nowhere? He smiled at Soaring Hawk, who responded with a grave and emphatic nod.

"Ay, muchas gracias, compañeros!" Anibal Mirabal cried out in a loud voice, as he rolled over and struggled to stand up.

"If'n it's me you want to thank, pardner," a resonant voice drawled from the darkness, "do it in American."

"Well, whoever you are, *Señor,*" Anibal answered, "I give you my deep gratitude."

"Yep. Thanks a bunch, Mister," Davy said, as a man emerged from the surrounding blackness.

"You might jus' be sorry you said that, *Mister* Watson," the man replied in a jeering voice that was suddenly familiar to the Kansan.

"Judas Priest!" Davy exclaimed as he got to his feet, stunned by the sight of his rescuer.

"You got you a talent for keepin' bad company, now ain't you, Watson?" said Bart Braden, that characteristic cruel and mocking smile upon his lips.

Davy shook his head. "Lord Almighty," he said. "I may not like you a whole helluva lot, Braden. But I do thank ya from the bottom of my heart."

The ramrod chuckled. "Why, don't think nothin' of it, Watson," he told the Kansan. "I'm savin' you fer better things."

"Tejanos," Vicente Mirabal whispered, as the men who had ridden with Bart Braden came into the light. *"Muchos tejanos."*

"What, uh, what was you boys a-doin' out here in the middle of nowhere?" Davy asked Bill Fanshaw's right-hand man.

"What d'ya think them red dogs traded, fer all the damn likker they done swilled down?" Braden replied.

Davy raised his eyebrows. "Cattle," he answered.

Braden nodded, his eyes narrowed now. "Bill Fanshaw's cattle, boy. Well, we wasn't 'bout to play around with them Comanches."

He turned and surveyed the carnage. "How many's still alive an' kickin'?" the ramrod asked his men.

"Oh, 'bout six or seven," one of the Texans called out.

Braden nodded, his smile fading. "Well then," he told the Texans, "git out your ropes, an' le's git busy stringin' them redskin horse thieves up."

"Hey, hold on a spell," Davy said, when he saw the Texans begin to uncoil their lariats.

"You don't mean to tell me you's gonna hang them Injuns here an' now."

"You got the idee," drawled Bart Braden, the mocking smile back on his lips.

"But you can't do that!" the Kansan protested. "Not whilst you can jus' as easily bring them Comanches to justice."

Braden smiled a hangman's smile. "Boy, you're forgettin' where you are," he told Davy in a soft, cold voice. "You're in the New Mexico Territory." He pulled his six-shooter out of its weathered holster and brandished it in the air. "This here's the only law in these parts—ol' Judge Colt."

"*Señor,* I, too, protest," Anibal Mirabal told the Fanshaw ramrod. "This will be nothing more than cold-blooded murder. Those Comanches are wounded and helpless."

Braden shook his head, motioning for his boys to slip a noose around the neck of the first of the six Comanche survivors, who now sat on a horse provided by the Texans.

"They still get hanged," he told Anibal.

"You cannot do this!" cried Vicente Mirabal, struggling with the ropes that bound him.

Braden stared at the young man, a faint sneer coming to his lips. "Well, Mister," he told Vicente, "I reckon you ain't no cattleman. 'Cause if'n you was, you'd see things a mite different, I'm thinkin'."

"But not enough to hang them!" retorted the younger Mirabal.

"Hangin's too good fer them sum'bitches," a Texan on Braden's right chimed in. "Anyone what rustles cattle deserves whatever he gits."

"Damn it, how 'bout untyin' us, Braden?"

127

Davy asked Fanshaw's foreman and trail boss.

The Texan flashed him a bright smile. "No, I'm 'fraid not, Mister Watson. It jus' ain't convenient, right now—leastways, not 'til we get them Comanches strung up."

"You murderin', low-down—"

Davy's words were cut off abruptly, as the Texan beside him jabbed an elbow into his gut.

"Who's these here Spanish boys, anyway?" Braden asked, eyeing Anibal and Vicente curiously. "I know that fella," he added, pointing to Soaring Hawk. "He's the buck what likes to shoot at Texans." He smiled his hangman's smile again. "Mebbe we jus' oughtta string him up with the Comanches."

Anibal stood tall before Braden, looking proud and haughty, despite the fact that he was on foot, bound with a rope, and facing an armed man on horseback.

"I see you do not remember me, *Señor* Braden," Anibal told the ramrod, looking him straight in the eye. "But you and your four *amigos tejanos* were just guests at the *hacienda* of my father."

Braden's narrowed eyes suddenly widened. "Well, I'll be damned," he said slowly, "if it ain't two of the Mirabal boys. Now, how about that?"

He turned to the Texans behind him. "Boys, we jus' found ourselves two humdingers of hostages. These is ol' Don Solomon's boys."

"You cain't do no better'n that," a portly balding Texan agreed.

"We got to talk with Bill Fanshaw, Braden," Davy told the ramrod.

Braden shook his head. "It ain't convenient,

Watson. I tol' you that before."

"What the hell do you mean, it ain't convenient, dammit?" Davy yelled at Braden, his face going red with anger.

The Texan cast a cold eye on the Kansan. "Boy, ol' Bill's leadin' a little army up this-a-way, goin' to kick ol' Solomon Mirabal's ass. We gon' settle this here business once't an' fer all."

"Hey, Bart," one of the Texans called out from the rear of the group of horsemen. "Ol' Terry Duefield jus' rid up, an' he tol' me that Mister Fanshaw an' the rest of the boys is a-comin'."

Braden nodded, and Davy studied his face. The Texan had the look of a man who was doing some fast figuring.

"You tellin' me Bill Fanshaw's a-comin' to start a range war?" the Kansan asked.

Braden looked preoccupied. "Yep. Tha's 'bout the size of it," he mumbled.

"But you can't do that!" Davy cried, evading the man who had elbowed him, and coming up to stand before Bill Fanshaw's ramrod.

The Texan frowned. "What d'ya mean, I cain't do that, Watson?" he asked in a low voice.

Meeting the man's eye, Davy said, "What I mean is that I been on my way to talk with Mr. Fanshaw. Don Solomon, he sorta, uh, empowered me to do business with yer boss."

Braden shot him a suspicious glare. "What kinda business?" he asked.

"Business regardin' his cattle," Davy began. "Don Solomon said—"

"Let 'er rip!" Braden called out suddenly, interrupting Davy Watson. And before the

Kansan could protest, one of the cowboys had slapped the rump of the horse upon which sat the Comanche with the noose around his neck. As Davy looked up, he saw that the other end of the rope was slung over a dark gnarled tree, and attached to a big stone twenty feety away from it.

"Oh Lord," he muttered as the horse streaked off, leaving the Comanche to kick and dance in the air.

"*Braden—what the hell are you doin'?*" Davy screamed up at the mounted man before him.

"Let 'er rip!" Braden called out once more, and the second of the six Comanche survivors began to dance the hanging jig.

"*Are you out'n yer mind?*" Davy roared. "We come to stop any more killin'! We got a offer to make to Bill Fanshaw."

Braden raised his hand in the air, holding it straight above his head for a moment. Then he brought it down sharply.

"*Braden!*" the Kansan roared, struggling against his bonds.

"*Asesino!*" screamed Anibal Mirabal.

"*Cobarde!*" shrieked his brother Vicente.

Standing behind them, his face looking as hard as if it had been carved out of the bedrock which supports the island of Manahatta, Soaring Hawk watched as the third of his race kicked and bobbed grotesquely in the air, eyes bulging and face purpling, the life being strangled out of him by the force of his own body weight, as the thick noose of Texas hemp continued to tighten with each move the struggling Comanche made.

The remaining three Comanches sat slumped

upon the horses which would take them on their last earthly ride. They had pretty much sobered up by now, and one of them was hiccuping violently.

All around the prisoners, leaning forward in their saddles with grim and self-righteous smiles upon their faces, were the Texans. Their blood was up now, and the eyes of each rider blazed with something more than the mere reflection of the firelight.

Davy Watson threw himself against Bart Braden's horse, causing the beast to whinny and shy.

"By Gawd, Braden," he called out hoarsely, "You'll burn in hell for this. Wait 'til Fanshaw gits wind of what you're cookin' up! Now, you jus' hold on an' stop all this killin'. Fer the love of God, man—I'm talking about stoppin' a range war!"

Hearing this, the ramrod's eyes narrowed and he hefted the Colt .45 that he held in his right hand. Then, glancing left to right at his own cowhands for a moment, Bart Braden leaned over in his saddle and brought the butt of his pistol slamming down against the base of Davy Watson's skull.

As the Kansan's body crumpled to the ground, the Texan turned to the men behind him.

"When did Terry Dufield say ol' Bill Fanshaw's due?" he asked, holstering his Colt.

"Why, I reckon jus' 'bout any minute now, Bart," the man told him.

Braden nodded and turned to the man on his left. "Jeff, git these here four boys back to the ranch. Pronto!"

"But ain't you gon' show 'em to Bill hisself?" the hand asked. "Specially the Mirabal boys."

The ramrod shook his head. "Jus' git 'em back there—right away, like I tol' you, Jeff."

"Yessir," the hand replied submissively. "Can I take Ike and J.B.?" he asked.

Braden nodded, and then held up his hands in the air.

"Now, I don't want none of you boys a-goin' an' tellin' Bill Fanshaw what that *hombre* done said." He pointed to the fallen Kansan. "We gon' finish what we done started. I'll take full responsibility fer ever'thin'. Y'all understand me?"

The Texans all nodded and growled in the affirmative, despite the protests of the two Mirabal brothers.

"Seems a pity we cain't string that Pawnee varmint up, while we's at it, Bart," said one of the men Soaring Hawk had originally fired upon when he and Davy had come to the rescue of Jesse Santacruz and Ramon Santiago.

"Ain't got time, right now," the ramrod said in a matter-of-fact tone of voice. "But I'm sure ol' Bill, he'll let you settle up with the redskin, after all the shootin's over."

"I shorely hope so," the Texan whispered fervently, staring at the Pawnee brave the way a weasel stares at a hen.

"Now, git on with yer business, boys," Bart Braden told his men, as Davy Watson's unconscious body was slung over the back of a horse. "An' finish stringin' up them other three Comanches."

7

THE TEXANS STRIKE

While Bill Fanshaw's forces rallied on the western edge of the *Llano Estacado,* preparing to sweep across the lands belonging to Don Solomon Mirabal, Davy Watson and his companions were taken back to the cattle baron's headquarters in the new settlement of Roswell.

What Bart Braden had in mind when he pistol-whipped Davy Watson, no man could say for sure. The ramrod was a close man, one who kept his own counsel, and rarely confided in another living soul. Bill Fanshaw's trail boss and foreman had a high degree of contempt for most men, and consequently would never trouble himself to share his feelings with them.

Men like Bill Fanshaw were the exception to Braden's cynical rule. He considered the rough-riding cattle baron a man among men. Fanshaw, like Charlie Goodnight and others of his ilk, had parlayed a few longhorn steers into an empire that stretched for miles and miles on all sides, running from Texas into the Territory of New Mexico.

Fanshaw had always held his own against all comers, and Bart Braden respected the cattle-man mightily for that. And now, since he was headed for a showdown with Don Solomon

Mirabal, if he won a hands-down decision over the old *patrón,* there would be no stopping the man. Bill Fanshaw would have cut a swath across the heart of the territory, and he would have easy access to the railheads beyond, enabling him to ship his cattle to the eager markets of the North well in advance of his fastest rivals. He would dominate the cattle business in New Mexico, no question about that.

Fanshaw had a high regard for Bart Braden. He admired the ramrod's toughness, doggedness, efficiency, and ability to bend men's wills to his. The cattle baron had great hopes of marrying Samantha off to Bart Braden, thereby taking the first step toward founding a dynasty. He felt that his trail boss and foreman was the perfect man to carry on with the building of his already-mighty empire.

The ramrod had plans of his own, however, and none of them even remotely included settling down with the cattle baron's daughter. Braden was still obsessed with Raquel Mirabal, and he was determined to have her, come hell or high water. In fact, the reason he had clubbed Davy Watson down earlier was because the Kansan's mission on behalf of the sheepmen might have well halted Bill Fanshaw's incursion into the territory of Don Solomon Mirabal.

That was altogether contrary to the ramrod's purpose, for Bart Braden had decided to use the occasion of Fanshaw's raid to seize Raquel Mirabal, and take her away with him.

Of course, there would be hell to pay, once Bill Fanshaw got wind of it, but the ramrod was determined only to leave the Mirabal lands accompanied by the *patrón's* lovely daughter. Not even his affection for, and loyalty toward, the cattle baron could sway the Texan. Braden knew that there was no turning back. Let the chips fall where they may . . . .

When Davy Watson regained consciousness and opened his eyes again, he was well on the way to the settlement of Roswell. His three companions rode beside him, all of them bound as securely as he, and each one of them powerless to avert the bloody range war which loomed over the lands of the sheepmen, like a tidal wave cresting and massing its power, in the instant before it breaks upon the earth below with devastating force.

"Hell, I don't know what-all to do," he complained to Soaring Hawk, once two of the Texans had ridden over to where he lay slung across the back of his horse, and helped him into the saddle.

The Pawnee shook his head. "Not look good," he replied tersely. "But better for us than burn in Comanche fire."

"Well, you're right there, ol' son," the Kansan agreed. "Guess I oughtta look at the bright side. An' if'n it wasn't fer that damn *loco*, Bart Braden, why, we'd be fried crisper'n a couple of pieces of chuck-wagon bacon."

"Too bad Braden shoot Comanche called Esquival," Soaring Hawk told his blood-brother, a faint trace of regret in his voice. "They no kill him, I go back and take his scalp."

"He ain't gon' rustle him no more Texas cattle, tha's fer sure," one of their escorts told them, having overheard their conversation.

"Now, you tell me, Mister," Davy said, turning in his saddle as he appealed to the Texan, "why's that Bart Braden so damn hard-headed? We's come to offer Mr. Fanshaw a deal—straight from Don Solomn an' the other *patróns*—an' the damn fool don't want him to know. Now, what the hell's goin' on here?"

The cowhand shrugged. "Well, I don't rightly know myself, son," he told the Kansan. "But I been through thick an' thin with ol' Bart, an' I ain't ever rode with a better man. So you can be shit-sure he's got him some good reason of his own."

"They's gonna be a passel of folks dyin' thereabouts pretty soon," Davy told the man, in a voice thick with bitterness and disgust.

"Oh, it ain't so bad, son," the man said consolingly. "They's only sheepherders—and greasers, to boot."

The other Texans began to laugh. The Kansan shook his head and clenched his teeth, turning to the Mirabal brothers, whose anguished eyes foretold the suffering with which their home would soon be visited.

Roswell was only settled the year before, in 1869, and it owed its existence to the Texans. For cattle made the place—the business end of cattle, anyway, and even before Charlie Goodnight and Bill Fanshaw located their bases of operations in the area, no less a giant of the cattle trade than John Chisum had chosen to oversee his empire from Roswell.

The hated *tejanos,* possessing over five million head of cattle after the Civil War ended, ran their herds up from downstate, in great drives over the plains, to the railheads of Kansas. This constituted the first successful invasion of New Mexico by the Texans.

As the Texan cattlemen all started north to market, one man drove his to the west. Charlie Goodnight intended to sell his beef to the gold miners of northern New Mexico. He therefore set out, after combining his herds with those of one Oliver Loving, from a point west of Fort Worth, intending to cross the territory.

From the Brazos River to the Pecos, at Horsehead Crossing, Goodnight and Loving drove their herds, entering the territory at Hope's Crossing. And eventually the trail went in several directions: first, through Las Vegas and Raton, then on to Denver; and second, east of Las Vegas, passing by Fort Bascom, and into Colorado at the Trinchera Pass.

Fortune smiled on the progress of Goodnight and Loving, for not only did the miners pay well for their cattle, plunking down gold dust and spot cash, but the many forts throughout the territory provided a ready and huge market, as well. The drive was such a success that Goodnight sped back to Texas, and managed to head another herd before the fall.

Later, the competition grew heavy, and Goodnight, now in full partnership with Oliver Loving, sent his cattle to the ranchers of Colorado and Wyoming, selling the bulk of his herds to John Wesley Iliff, the great Colorado rancher. In three years, Charlie Goodnight delivered over thirty thousand head of cattle to that market, populating the Plains with his longhorns, as well as feeding the miners and railroad crews.

The great Texas cattle drives became a vivid part of New Mexico's history, and the coming of the great herds was an unforgettable sight. One man had this to say about those spectacular migrations:

"To those who took part, accustomed as they became to all the possible incidents of the drive, near as they were with the solitudes over which they passed, each drive was a new adventure and its successful completion always brought to the most experienced something of the thrill of achievement."

". . . to all those who saw that long line of Texas cattle come up over a rise in the prairies, nostrils wide for the smell of water, dust-caked and gaunt, so ready to break from the nervous control of the riders strung out along the flanks of the herd, there came the feeling that in this spectacle there was something elemental, something resistless, something perfectly in keeping about the unconquered land about them."

Soon the Texans brought their herds into New Mexico with an eye to keeping them there. There was grass and water enough for their needs, and cattle had the great advantage over sheep of being able to graze unattended.

The great territorial cattleman of the day was John Chisum, who had originally driven herds to be delivered to Charlie Goodnight. Some accused him of not paying for the cattle he drove, and others called him the greatest cattle rustler of all time. He owned the largest herd in the Southwest, with a range extending up and down the Pecos River for a distance of 150 miles, running from the Texas border to Fort Sumner.

Chisum was the law in his own lands, and he ruled like a feudal king. He set the pattern for the style of subsequent cattle barons, and it was not long before his rival, Bill Fanshaw, settled in the Roswell area, too. And what was more important was the fact that, once Fanshaw got control of part or all of Don Solomon Mirabal's lands, even so great a cattleman as John Chisum himself would be forced to bow to him.

Samantha Fanshaw was on the porch of the main house when the Texans rode in with their prisoners. And the sight of the four bound men—two *chicano*, one white, and one Indian, and all lean and handsome—piqued the curiosity of the cattle baron's sexually obsessed daughter.

She leaned against the hitching post as the band dismounted, tied up the horses, and helped the prisoners out of their saddles. Davy Watson, in particular, fascinated Bill Fanshaw's daughter, for his blond good looks were, she realized with a wry smile, the very counterpart of hers.

"Who are these men, J.B.?" she asked the nearest cowhand.

"Oh, jes' some meddlers. Boys who got in the way of Bart Braden, an' tried to put a crimp in his style."

At the mention of Bart Braden, Samantha's eyes flashed angrily.

"They was a-tryin' to stop him. But ol' Bart, he had other plans."

At the mention of Braden's plans, Samantha's eyes narrowed.

"An' them fellas," the hand went on, indicating the Kansan and his Pawnee blood-brother with a stubby forefinger, "like to shoot at Texans." He chuckled. "We gon' have us some real fun with them two, once't Mr. Fanshaw done gits through a-whuppin' that damn greaser, Solomon Mirabal."

At the mention of the *patrón's* name, Samantha Fanshaw gasped.

"Well, send that one into my daddy's study," she told the hand. "I want to talk to him."

"But this here's serious business, Miss Samantha," the man protested.

"So is what I'm going to speak to him about," she told him. "Send him in there, J.B.—that's an order."

Then, as Samantha turned to face Davy Watson, the Kansan saw the strange and triumphant smile upon her lips.

While Davy Watson went into the study with Samantha, and Soaring Hawk and the two Mirabal brothers were led to the bunkhouse, the Texans under Bart Braden and Bill Fanshaw had joined forces and were now moving in a sweep across the pasturelands of Don Solomon Mirabal.

They were over forty strong, and Bill Fanshaw

had seen his chance. He was going to bring Judge Colt right to the sheepman's door; there was going to be no more lollygagging and farting around with the *ricos* of New Mexico, those courteous *hidalgos* whose Spanish manners and courtesy could tie things up for years. No, this time the old judge would settle the dispute between the cattlemen and the sheepmen, and Bill Fanshaw harbored no doubt about the outcome.

Bart Braden rode by the cattle baron's side, a tight grim smile on his lips. This was his chance, the ramrod told himself, his eyes glittering with a hard and predatory light. It was now or never: Bill Fanshaw might be fighting for dominion over the best grazing lands in all the territory of New Mexico, but Raquel Mirabal was the only prize that the trail boss considered worth the taking.

The horsemen thundered on, covering the miles that lay between them and the Mirabal *hacienda* with the speed of a wind-fanned prairie fire, their clothes coated with dust, and the mouths of their horses flecked with foam. Once more Death rode on horseback through the lawless New Mexico Territory, as it had so often in the past. And once more the Texans came sweeping in, bringing in with them carnage and devastation.

As he rode, Bart Braden flexed the fingers of his gun hand, and loosened his Colt in its holster. It would not be long until the Texans came to the Mirabal *hacienda*. All hell would break loose any hour now, the ramrod told himself. There would be fighting and bloodshed enough for any man, even the most bloodthirsty of the Texans. And Braden made a silent vow, as his horse came over a rise: there was only one way he would return to Texas, and that was with Raquel Mirabal . . . .

"Tell me more of what Bart Braden's up to, Mister Watson," Samantha Fanshaw requested, offering the Kansan a Kentucky bourbon-and-branch-water to drink.

"Thank you, Miss Samantha," Davy Watson muttered, as he took the glass from her. He felt her hand touch his, and brush it lingeringly.

He paused to sip his drink, thinking of his companions who sat in the bunkhouse, under the hard and watchful eyes of the Texans. Samantha Fanshaw had immediately dismissed the guards, thrown the bolt on the door, and untied the rope that bound the Kansan. After that, she sat him in a comfortable chair, made him a drink, and began to pump him for information regarding Bart Braden and his plans.

Once she had learned that the ramrod and her father were headed for a showdown with Don Solomon Mirabal, there was no stopping her.

"And I thought Bart and Daddy were just going after the cattle that the Comanches stole," she said, shaking her head and narrowing her eyes. "So they're going to ol' Don Solomon Mirabal's place, eh?"

She was an extremely beautiful woman, the Kansan observed. But why was she so all-fired curious about the raid on the *patrón's* estate? She was calling the shots, however—at least for the moment, although his hands were free, and the Texans were gone. It would pay to play the game her way for a while.

"What did you have to do with all this sheep business, Mr. Watson?" she asked, sitting on the arm of the big overstuffed chair that held the Kansan.

He felt her body press against his arm, and could not help noticing that her nipples were erect beneath the thin cotton blouse she wore. The smell of her perfume reached his nostrils, and Davy was reminded of honeysuckle in June.

"I, uh, was sent after Bart Braden, Miss Fanshaw," he began, feeling his ears burn.

"Call me Samantha," she told him, leaning over so that he could feel the pressure of her breast upon his shoulder.

"Sure, uh, Samantha," he replied puzzled by the liberties she took with him. "An' uh, you can call me Davy."

"I will. Now, go on . . . Davy."

"Well, I was a-comin' to make yer father an offer. Ol' Don Solomon hisself sent me."

"Were you a guest of his?" Samantha asked, stroking his thick wheat-colored hair.

"Yep, I guess you could say that. Me'n ol' Soaring Hawk, we done rescued two of Don Solomon's boys from a little Texas justice." He flashed Bill Fanshaw's daughter a wry smile. "Some of your daddy's boys was 'bout to lynch them."

"So you shot two of them?" she asked, looking Davy right in the eye.

"Well, they didn't really leave us no choice, Miss—uh, Samantha," he told her. "We jus'

143

fired a few times to warn them boys off—to stop 'em from stringin' up them two sheepherders." He cleared his throat. "Y'see, they done lynched one already. Well sir, they jus' come a-ridin' in at us, firin' their pistols fer all they was worth."

He shrugged and held his big hands out at his sides. "It was them or us."

Samantha Fanshaw nodded, her eyes still on Davy Watson's face. "And how did you meet Bart Braden?" she asked, trying unsuccessfully to mask the anxiety that she felt.

"The next day," he told her. "They was havin' themselves a *fiesta,* this here feast of La . . . I fergit the name, but it was a big one. Braden, he come ridin' in with a bunch of cowhands. We, uh, we didn't git on too well, Samantha," he said, concluding his speech.

"Did you get to know the Mirabal family at all, Davy?" Samantha asked, her fingernails grazing the nape of his neck in slow runs.

"Yep," he answered, as her other hand stroked his shoulder and upper arm.

"I want to know if someone was there, Davy," she purred, leaning over still further, her firm breast again making contact with his arm. He could feel her breath, hot in his ear.

"Do you know Raquel Mirabal, Davy?" Samantha asked, punctuating the sentence by darting her tongue into the Kansan's ear. "Was *she* there?"

"Uh, yes, she was," he said, raising his cool drink to his lips, as he felt a sudden heat and stiffening in his groin.

The next thing he knew, the tall, handsome blonde had undone the top buttons of his flannel

144

shirt, and was running her hand over his hairy chest.

Boy, she sure is one for socializin', Davy told himself, as Samantha Fanshaw lowered her head and brought her full, pink lips down to his mouth. He still didn't know what she wanted, but the Kansan was determined to enjoy her interrogation to the fullest extent.

"Tell me how Bart reacted to Raquel," she murmured just before their lips met.

It was a long, intense kiss. She licked and teased Davy's lips, and he, in turn, nibbled hers and darted his tongue into her mouth. Samantha leaned over and placed her hand upon the bulge in Davy Watson's denims.

"He, uh, couldn't keep his damn eyes off'n that little gal," Davy whispered hoarsely, once the epic kiss had come to an end.

"You mean you think he was interested in her?" Samantha asked him sweetly, as she proceeded to unbutton Davy's fly.

"That's puttin' it mild-like," he said, gasping as her hand went inside his pants. "That sum'bitch—excuse me, Samantha—uh, Braden was gettin' on my nerves."

"You don't like him?" she asked, taking his wrist with her free hand and guiding it to her full, taut-nippled breast.

"That ain't statin' it none too strong," he grunted, as her fingers began to stroke his stiff and throbbing rod.

"Maybe we can help each other, Davy," Samantha whispered, running her nails lightly along the underside of his cock.

"What . . . do . . . you . . . mean?" he asked

between clenched teeth, as he proceeded to help the lissome blonde out of her pants.

"Make love to me first, and then I'll tell you," she whispered in his ear. "But it could mean your freedom, Davy, so make it good . . . ."

They were both naked before he knew it, and Samantha's tall, supple body squirmed in his arms, as they stood on the Persian carpet before the big mahogany desk of Bill Fanshaw.

The Kansan was steamed up now, thanks to the artful stimulation of the cattle baron's daughter, and he kissed and caressed her sweet, golden-hued flesh with fervor and complete abandon.

Samantha rubbed her thick blonde muff up and down against the Kansan's thigh, and she tugged at his lower lip with her even, white teeth as they kissed and hugged, naked and ardent, in Bill Fanshaw's study.

Working on her with his tongue, Davy bowed his head and ran a series of zig-zag trails down from behind Samatha's ear, over her neck, over her breast bone, and then through the cleft of her bosom, until he sidetracked and wound up circling the thick pink nipple of the tall blonde's left breast.

While the Kansan did this, Samantha emitted a series of rapturous gasps, closed her big blue eyes, and leaned back far enough to rest her elbows on the mahogany desk. Davy Watson continued his ardent tracking, and was now heading down in the vicinity of her navel.

"Ooooh," she moaned, as he worked it over after the fashion of a horse at a salt lick. Then, as he resumed his downward course, Samantha leaned back on the desk, opened her long legs, and thrust her pelvis forward in anticipation of pleasures to come.

Davy wanted to make sure that she was happy, for his life and the lives of his companions might well hinge upon the skill of his lovemaking.

Down he went, skimming his tongue over her flat, golden belly, moving it like a butterfly in high grass, suddenly parting the uppermost fringe of her thick, blonde fleece, on its way to the musky ravine of her sex.

"Oooh," Bill Fanshaw's daughter moaned again, as the Kansan's able tongue parted her nether lips. And for a moment, as he lapped at her pink and glistening inner parts, the blonde sobbed once as she thought of Bart Braden, who had made love to her in this same fashion not long ago. But the ramrod's memory left her mind as she stared down at the bobbing head and muscular back of Davy Watson. Samantha closed her eyes and sighed, smiling a strange, cruel smile.

Davy mouthed and tongued, and Samantha tensed and twitched, sending papers on top of her father's desk flying every which way. And when she lay back, her legs suddenly sagging in the aftermath of her orgasm, closing her eyes and resting the back of her head on the top of the big desk, the Kansan rose from where he had been kneeling, and leaned over the long and elegant, golden body.

Grasping Samanth'a trim waist in his two big hands, Davy moved her up until her back and buttocks rested firmly on the desk.

"You had your fun," he told her in a husky voice, smiling down at her, his eyes gleaming as they reflected the light of the kerosene lamp across the room. "Now it's my turn."

"Oh, yes," she murmured eagerly, throwing back her head and tossing her golden mane over the far end of the mahogany desk. "Oh, yes. Come inside me, Davy. Come inside me."

"Hoo-wee," the Kansan grunted, as he stood over Samantha Fanshaw's lithe, golden body, his eyes coursing over its glowing hollows and curves.

Standing over her as he did, as if he were looking down upon some undiscovered land, some valley rich in abundance and delight, Davy Watson felt the thrill of discovery and conquest. It was as if he had scaled some insurmountable height in order to look upon that wild and enthralling spectacle. He felt like a man who had made some great and remarkable discovery, as if he were Balboa, on the day that the worn and footsore *conquistadore* had trudged up a steep hill and suddenly found himself face to face with the vast expanse of rolling blue water that is the great Pacific Ocean. And Davy was no less impressed by the wondrous landscape of the long-limbed blonde's lush body than was the Spaniard with his view of the rolling ocean.

She lay there before him, stretched out across the desk, her golden skin contrasting with the deep, dark tones of the wood beneath her, arms folded over her eyes, making little high-pitched sounds in her throat, sounds that were somewhere between a coo and a whimper.

Her full breasts flowed over onto her ribcage;

her taut nipples stood out above her capped areolae like sentries on twin hillocks. The soft swell of her belly, flecked with tiny golden hairs, ran down to the thick tangle of her muff. The hollows of her thighs gleamed with traceries of sweat, and her nether lips parted in a gentle exclamation of longing and desire.

She murmured words in some unknown tongue, calling in a deep and urgent voice, a voice that rose up from the depths of her passion. Her hair spilled down over the desk top like a cascade of gold; her back arched and her long, elegant body began to shudder.

The Kansan clenched his teeth, narrowed his eyes, grasped his throbbing rod at its base, and guided it between the swollen and golden-fringed outer lips of Samantha's sex, entering her as slowly as he could, inch by inch.

"Ooo-ooo-oooh," she moaned, with a voice like the wind coming up on the eastern plains, as his thick hard maleness penetrated her with an excruciating and delightful slowness.

He did not stop until he had gone to the hilt in her hot, sopping pussy, coming to rest with his pubic hair tangling with hers.

Samantha gave a little gurgling cry and closed her sightless eyes. And then as her thighs tightened around the Kansan's waist, she cried out beneath him.

"Bart," she called, in a voice like the wind running through a canyon. "Oh, Bart . . . ."

8

THE TAKING OF
RAQUEL MIRABAL

When the forty-odd Texans thundered onto the
grounds of Don Solomon Mirabal's *hacienda,*
they were welcomed by the fire of the *patrón* and
a number of his *patridarios* and retainers.

All hell broke loose in the plaza as the riders
came in, blasting away at the defenders of the
two-story *hacienda* where the Don made his
stand. The answering fire was too heavy, and the
horsemen were forced to dismount and seek
shelter throughout the length of the plaza.
Braden and the cattle baron were furious. *Don
Solomon had been warned, and he was ready for
the onslaught of the Texans.*

What had happened was that Fanshaw and his
hands had almost reached the *patrón's* quarters,
when they ran smack into a sheep drive. There
were more than twenty *chicanos* with the herds,
and all were armed. But the Texans had surprise
and determination on their side, and they made
short work of the unwary sheepherders, some of
whom had escaped, riding off to warn the Don.

Now the Texans were all lathered up and out
for blood, having had a foretaste of victory.
And Bill Fanshaw, intoxicated by this initial
success, had sworn not to rest until he sat at the

head of Don Solomon Mirabal's great table, until the choicest lands in all the New Mexico Territory were his by right of conquest.

The *patrón* had managed to call in enough of his *partidarios* to defend the hacienda; and when Bill Fanshaw and Bart Braden rode in at the head of the Texans, they met with unexpectedly stiff resistance.

Bullets whined through the air in the plaza, thick as hornet swarms, and the Texans were forced to dismount and lead their horses to cover. There was heavy fighting by the Don's barns and stables, as well as at the *hacienda* itself.

Several of the cowhands lay sprawled in the plaza, where they had initially been shot off their horses, and several more lay wounded in the stables and behind the draw well. The *hacienda's* defenders continued to blast away with their Winchesters and handguns from its roof and upper story, making it impossible for Fanshaw's forces to take the place without incurring great losses to their number.

"That ol' boy must've got wind of us comin', when we tangled with them greasers afore," Bill Fanshaw grunted, squatting behind the draw well to reload his rifle.

"I reckon," his ramrod said tersely, as he sighted upon a *chicano* firing from the *hacienda's* roof.

KA-BOOM! The mouth of Bart Braden's Winchester flared for an instant, followed by a roar that resounded throughout the small plaza. Above him, a man screamed, and jackknifed off the roof in a shower of *adobe*.

The answering fire was furious, and Braden and Fanshaw curled themselves up in the fetal position behind the well, as bullets spanged off its sides and blew the hanging wooden bucket to smithereens.

"Them boys is pumpin' a lot of lead our way," Braden told his boss through clenched teeth, wincing as fragments of flying *adobe* whizzed past his ear.

"Yep," the cattle baron grunted, after firing at the *hacienda*. "I 'spect ol' Solomon done got him a few boxes of cartridges put by fer jus' such a occasion."

The ramrod fired again. This time, his shot hit a red Spanish tile on the roof top and smashed it into a hundred tiny, whistling fragments.

"Looks to me like that ol' boy could set there fer quite a spell, Bart," Fanshaw told his foreman, as the other man lowered his smoking Winchester.

Bart Braden nodded, a sour smile on his face. "I reckon so, Bill," he agreed. "An' we ain't got all that long to wait. 'Cause they's bound to've been one or two of them greasers who took off once't they seen us a-comin'. An' it ain't but a matter of time, 'til they rides back with some neighbor *patrón* an' his hands."

"Shit, yeah," the cattle baron agreed bitterly. "We done spent all day a-tryin' to take that damn *hacienda.*" He paused to send a large, brown gobbet of tobacco juice flying onto the dust of the plaza. "An' we been havin' us 'bout as much luck as a longhorn steer a-tryin' to mount a Chihuahua dog."

"I don't think we's gon' get anywheres, jus'

bangin' away at all them greasers inside.'' Braden told his boss, in matter-of-fact tones.

Bill Fanshaw scowled as he shook his head. "No, I don't rightly think we can afford to sit here on our butts no longer, son. This ain't nothin' but lollygaggin'. Them damn greasers is wedged in there snugger'n a parson at the dinner table on a Sunday afternoon."

"I reckon we ought to give that there stuff I brung a try, after all, Bill," Braden told the cattle baron.

The man let fly another gobbet of tobacco juice before replying; it hit the ground an instant before a bullet spattered the viscous, brown mass over the side of the draw well.

"I don't know nothin' 'bout such new-fangled stuff," Bill Fanshaw grunted, pumping a cartridge into the firing chamber of his Winchester. "But we ain't got ourselves nothin' to lose by tryin' it out at this point. Go to it, boy."

"Yessir," Bart Braden nodded, squatting down as he began to signal the cowhands behind him to concentrate their fire upon the *hacienda*, thus drawing the defenders' attention away from the well.

"If'n this works," Fanshaw gloated, "we got us one hell of a surprise fer ol' Don Solomon an' his greasers." As Braden got ready to scurry for the wall of an adjoining building, the cattle baron patted him on the rump. "Go to it, boy," he told the man whom he intended to make his successor.

"Oh, if it works, there's gon' be some surprises, all right," Bart Braden muttered

153

between clenched teeth, as he scrambled and zigzagged frantically to the safety of the wall. "An' you gon' be jus' as surprised as the next man, Bill Fanshaw, 'cause you gonna have to git you a new ramrod—right soon!"

Bam-bam-blamblam! The defenders peppered the plaza, as they vainly attempted to draw a bead on the fast-moving Braden. An instant later, he dove behind the wall, and the plaza was still once more.

Pah-whaa-aang! Just as Braden got to his hands and knees, a slug whined loudly as it went by his head. The Texan threw himself down on the ground.

Pah-whaa-aang! P-wow-w-w-w! Another slug whined, coming so close to Braden that it shook his hat and gouged a channel in the wall's *adobe* brick.

The Texan had his pistol out now and was squinting along its barrel, as he tried to get a bead on the unknown marksman.

"Over there, hah?" Braden muttered, as he swept left with his gunhand. He was now sheltered from the guns of the *hacienda,* so the ramrod deduced that he was probably being fired upon from either the barn or the Mirabal stables.

Pah-whaa-aang! P-wow-w-w-w! Chwok! The Texan grunted in pain, as the third shot tore through the back of his leather vest, and ripped open his flannel shirt and several layers of his skin.

"Oooh, shit," Braden groaned, leaning to his left as he finally sighted his assailant. The rifleman had been firing at him from the hayloft in the front of the big barn. He braced his gunhand with his free hand, squinted, and took careful aim.

Pah-whaa-aang! Blamblamblam!

Just as another slug came hurtling his way, the ramrod squeezed off three shots, aiming directly at the brief, bright flash that lit up the gloom of the hayloft.

BWOW! Another flash rent the darkness, but this time it did not issue forth in Bart Braden's direction. The shot had gone up into the air, at an oblique angle, and was followed by a muffled scream.

"Now, I don't think that ol' boy's gon' do him no more sharpshootin' today," the Texan grunted through clenched teeth, as he struggled to his feet, hissing as a searing pain coursed down the right side of his back.

Braden moved on, along the side of the wall, until he came to the back of the building. From that point on, he was sheltered from the *hacienda,* as well as from the barn and stables, and was able to proceed freely on his way.

The rear of that building led along to an alley, where a number of other buildings adjoined. And at the far end of the alley, Bart Braden found what he had been seeking.

A Conestoga wagon—a big canvas-covered rig of the kind used to traverse the American continent by its early settlers, stood in the shade by the end of the short, dusty alley. The late afternoon sun glowed through the wagon's canvas, and set the harness of its team of thickset horses to gleaming with a dull lustre.

A toothless old man with a white goatee and a

bald head sat in the driver's seat, a shotgun cradled in his lap. Beside him sat a teenaged boy with sandy hair and a face full of pimples. The youth held a breech-loading rifle across his thighs.

"Well, lookee here," the toothless old-timer said, his tongue pushing out past his puckered lips as he spoke, "if'n it ain't ol' Bart. What'ch'ee up to, boy?"

"Them damn greasers is dug in real tight," Braden informed the odd-looking pair in the wagon. "So's I reckon I'm jus' gon' have to blow 'em out."

"Gee whillikers, Mr. Braden," the youth said in a voice that cracked, "you gonna use that there stuff," he jerked a thumb over his shoulder, toward the inside of the Conestoga, "an' blow them ol' boys to kingdom come?"

Braden nodded, winking at the boy. "We shorely gonna have us a try, son," he replied, the pain in his back forgotten now. "Now, lemme have a couple of batches of them things." He stood before the wagon and reached up his right hand.

Wide-eyed, the boy gulped. He stared down at the ramrod, gaping in wonder.

Braden smiled a wry smile as he looked up at the awestricken boy's face. No one spoke for several moments, and the only sound the ramrod heard, apart from the occasional bark of guns and whine of bullets in the background, was the stertorous breathing of the toothless old man.

"Well?" he asked, breaking the heavy silence, "How 'bout handin' me the stuff?"

"Consarn it, boy!" the old man whined in a

high-pitched voice, suddenly cuffing the youth on the back of the neck. "Git that stuff fer Mr. Braden—*pronto!*"

"Yessir, Mr. Bevis," the boy muttered, his ears going red as he turned and reached into the dark interior of the Conestoga wagon.

"Now, you go gentle with that there stuff, boy," the old man piped up again. "Y'all better set to handlin' them things as if'n you was a-jugglin' hummin'bird eggs."

The boy gulped. "Yessir, Mr. Bevis," he squawked in his parroty voice, "I shorely will be careful. I shorely will."

" 'Cause if'n you ain't," the old man groused, "you'll be like to blow us straight through the Pearly Gates." He cleared his throat loudly. "An' while I may be somewhat advanced in years, I ain't ready to meet ol' Saint Pete jus' yet. Y'hear me, boy?"

"Yessir, I do, Mr. Bevis," the youth replied, leaning over as he reached into the wagon.

"Shoot, Ernie," Bart Braden told the old-timer, "y'all're one helluva taskmaster. Why, I don't reckon the Israelites done had it any tougher under ol' Pharoah than this here poor lad got it under you."

"Well, sir," the old man whined, holding up his hands in protest, "you *got* to treat 'em that way. Y'see, boys today jus' ain't wuff a shit. T'ain't like it were when I was a lad. Them days, young fellas ⟋ allus minded their elders. Nowadays, they don't give a hoot in hell fer nothin'."

"Here y'are, Mister Braden, sir," the boy said, his voice shooting up into falsetto, as he leaned over and gingerly handed two bundles of bound stick-like objects to the ramrod.

"Thank ya, Bobby Joe," Braden told the boy, taking the bundles in his hands and hefting them lightly, as he turned and began to head back to the plaza.

"Oh say, Bart," the old man piped up suddenly behind him, "what the heck do they call that durn stuff again?"

"Dynamite, Ernie," was the ramrod's terse reply. "Dynamite."

Hooves thundered over the dry hard earth to the southwest of the Staked Plains, as Davy Watson and his three companions sped toward the *hacienda* of Don Solomon Mirabal, riding into the purple twilight that had begun to mantle the land.

Samantha Fanshaw had responded to his loving; there was no question about that, Davy Watson realized. But she'd had other fish to fry . . . and that was what finally won the Kansan and his companions their freedom. Bart Braden was the thread that connected both their lives; and that thread must be severed in order for those lives to run their course.

In the aftermath of their passion, Davy and the cattle baron's daughter had spoken of the ramrod, of how he had suddenly come to have such a drastic effect upon their lives. And when the Kansan described Bart Braden's fixation upon the innocent and virginal person of Raquel Mirabal, Samantha Fanshaw cried out in anguish and rage.

She then told Davy of her love for Braden,

and of her vow to share him with no other woman. He, in turn, was worried about the lovely young *chicana's* safety, and was determined not to lot the ramrod lay hands on her.

"Well, then I reckon we can help each other, Davy," Samantha had told him, staring deep into his eyes as she stroked the hairs of his chest. "You want to stop Bart Braden, and I want him stopped."

He shook his head and spoke in a low, harsh voice. "Oh, him an' me, we got us a little score to settle, all right."

Samantha Fanshaw nodded, a grave expression on her face. "I do believe it's time that score got itself settled." She took his hands in hers. "If I see to it that you get away from here, Davy," she said in a husky whisper, "will you swear by all you hold sacred to settle Bart Braden's hash?"

"You better believe I will," the Kansan growled back, his eyes flashing as he looked up into hers. "I intend to stop him from layin' hands on Raquel Mirabal . . . an' I don't think he's gon' be willin' to let her be." He shook his head. "But if'n I have to claim that gal over Bart Braden's dead body, well, sir, that's jus' what it's gon' take."

"Swear it on your honor as a man, Davy!" the tall blonde urged, squeezing his hands in a grip whose power surprised him.

"I swear it," he told her, a grim look coming over his face. "I aim to take Raquel Mirabal out of harm's way, an' if'n I come up against Bart Braden, well, then I mean to lay him out in the undertaker's parlor.''

Upon hearing this, Samantha Fanshaw smiled a smile as hard and cruel as Bart Braden's.

Putting her clothes back on, Samantha had told Davy where the horses were saddled, and where his companions were held prisoner.

After he had dressed, she reached into one of the drawers of her father's big desk, produced a Colt with six bullets in its chambers, and handed it to Davy. Then, pausing only to peer deeply into the Kansan's eyes, she let him out the back door of her father's study.

Moments later, Davy stood before the bunkhouse where Soaring Hawk and the Mirabal brothers sat in grim silence, watched by two of the three Texans who had escorted them back to Roswell.

The remaining Texan had just rounded the corner of the bunkhouse, on his way to relieve the other guards, when Davy Watson brought the butt of his pistol down upon the base of the man's skull.

As the Texan crumpled to a heap on the dry, dusty ground, the Kansan edged his way up to the bunkhouse door.

Inside the bunkhouse, the captives sat in silence, as the New Mexican twilight seeped through the windows and empurpled the interior of the building.

One of the guards had just stood up, in order to light the kerosene lamp situated directly over the bench upon which he had earlier seated himself. Consequently, his back was turned to the bunkhouse door, as Davy Watson came noiselessly through it.

The second Texan looked up at the creaking of a floor board, only to find himself staring into the black, gaping maw of Davy's revolver.

Holding a finger to his lips, the Kansan motioned with the barrel of his gun for the guard to raise his hands into the air. The man nodded slowly, his eyes still on the gun.

Taking his finger from his lips, Davy pointed to the bench, indicating that he wished the Texan to sit down where the other guard had been seated.

At that instant, the second guard wheeled around, turning where he stood on the bench, the lamp freshly lit, and a match still burning in his hand.

"Jus' hold it, friend," Davy called out to the Texan, training his gun on the man.

The Texan, however, had decided upon his own course of action, and his right hand shot down to the cracked and scarred holster at his side.

Blambam! Two bright flares of light spewed forth from the mouth of Davy Watson's sixgun. The Texan's body slammed into the bunkhouse wall, shaking the lamp and causing it to bathe the room in a dizzying, hallucinatory light. His body began to slide down the wall, and the man coughed, and then opened his bloody lips to moan in a deep, faraway voice.

There was fire in Davy Watson's eye, as he looked at the other Texan. "I got me some more of the same, 'case you got you any ideas 'bout reachin' fer your gun, Mister."

"Shit, no!" the second man growled. "I ain't damnfool enough to go up against a *hombre*

161

what's got a bead drawn on me." He shook his head. "Ain't no way I'm gon' call you, Mister."

"That's good," Davy said in a low, even voice. " 'Cause I ain't a-tall in the mood to play games with any of you Texans. Now, you jus' git yer butt over t'other side of the room, an' untie them three fellas."

"Yep," the Texan growled again, going red in the face as he rose from the bench, his hands still held high in the air. "I think I'll jus' do that little thing."

"You'd best be doin' it," Davy snapped at the man, "if'n you don't want that mangy hide of your'n blowed full of holes. An' don' go a-soundin' as if yer doin' me no favor, neither."

"No need to take offense, Mister," the Texan said placatingly. "I didn't mean nothin' by it."

"Well, jus' quit flappin' yer gums, an' git them fellas untied," the Kansan told him sternly, causing the Texan to scuttle over to Soaring Hawk and the Mirabal brothers.

Several minuters later, the three men were untied and stretching their limbs. Then, Soaring Hawk promptly turned and knocked out the remaining Texan.

"Que diablo!" Vicente Mirabal said with a bright smile, as he clapped Davy Watson on the back. "My fren', what you have done wit' that *muchacha* is a deed worthy of Don Juan Tenorio, himself."

"Ay, coño," Anibal Mirabal muttered. "An' that one was the daughter of *Señor* Fanshaw. *Sagrado corazón de Jesus!"*

The Kansan broke out into a broad grin.

"Big surprise," Soaring Hawk grunted, as he

162

unbuckled the unconscious guard's holster. "Alla time, pussy get us in heap big trouble . . . but this time, get us out."

Davy had to laugh. "Now, hold on, fella," he told them. "What ol' Samantha an' I done could hold its own with the best of 'em, I'll grant ya that. But it warn't that what made her turn me loose. She wants a piece of Bart Braden—'most as bad as we do."

The others nodded.

"And this time, we will pay our respects to *el señor* Braden properly," Vicente muttered ominously.

"That's the ticket," the Kansan told him, putting his gun back in its holster. "Now, le's saddle up, an' git back to Don Solomon's place."

Dynamite was still new to the world, having been invented a mere three years ago, in 1867. It was the second most important invention of Alfred Nobel, who coined the explosive's name from the Greek word for power, *dynamis*.

Nobel was a chemist, and a native of Sweden. There he had worked with his father and brother, studying the commercial potential of the new and dangerously unstable explosive, nitroglycerin, which was first discovered in 1846 by the Italian chemist, Ascanio Sobrero.

The plant at Heleneborg, Sweden, where the Nobels conducted their research, was among the safest and most efficient of the day, but in 1864, it exploded, killing Alfred's younger brother, Emil Oskar. But the chemist persisted in his studies, and in 1865, invented the blasting cap, the greatest advance in the science of explosives since the discovery of the original chemical explosive, black powder (sodium nitrate, charcoal, and sulfur).

The basis for Alfred Nobel's invention of dynamite was his discovery of a safer way to handle and use large quantities of nitroglycerin. Combining 75 percent nitroglycerin with 25 percent *guhr* (*kieselguhr,* a porous siliceous earth which absorbed large quantities of the explosive), Nobel came up with that he called "Dynamite No. 1."

Subsequent improvements (including the use of woodpulp for an absorbent, and sodium nitrate for an oxidizing agent) led to the improved efficiency of dynamite, and the ability to prepare it "straight," that is, in varying strengths. And in 1869, Nobel decided to patent the use of the explosive's active ingredients. Several conflicting patents were similarly established at that time, and the Swede was unable to establish an undisputed claim to his invention.

Dynamite, in its latest and most refined form, was what Bart Braden held in his hands as he made his way back to the plaza. Don Solomon's forces were not going to be able to withstand the power of the new explosive for long, the ramrod told himself. It would all be over in a little while.

Only one thing troubled him: *How could he avoid harming Raquel Mirabal?*

Braden scowled as he peered around the wall that faced the plaza. He couldn't risk endangering Raquel's life, he thought anxiously.

For it was on her account that the ramrod had precipitated the bloody range war.

He waved a hand in the air, summoning a number of cowhands to his side. Then he distributed most of the dynamite sticks among them, keeping three for himself. The Texans huddled around their ramrod, listening to his instructions. And when he had finished, Braden dismissed them with a nod and a mocking smile.

After that, the ramrod ducked his head, clutched the dynamite sticks to his chest, and made a beeline for the draw well in the center of the plaza, where Bill Fanshaw was still crouched, firing into Don Solomon's *hacienda* and waiting for his foreman's return.

Rolling over as he dove into the shadow cast by the well, Bart Braden smiled as he held up the three sticks of dynamite. Bullets spanged off the side of the well, or whined as they sent up jets of dust where they made contact with the ground.

"Good boy," Bill Fanshaw grunted, nodding to his ramrod. "Now, how we gon' work this thing?" he asked.

"You jus' leave that to me, Bill," the ramrod told the cattle baron with an icy smile. "I got it all worked out." He raised a hand in the air. "Jus' look over that-a-way."

Fanshaw looked where his ramrod had indicated, and saw the small building with the cross upon its peaked roof, which served as the Mirabal estate's chapel. Just then, Braden lowered his hand.

BAA-BAH-H-H-BOOM! A huge, flaring explosion rent the chapel's center, obscuring all else from sight with its raw, furious colors, sending torn and splintered sections of board and *adobe* brick flying into the air.

"God A'mighty!" croaked Bill Fanshaw, "what a hellish thing!" He could hear the rubble created by the explosion thudding and pattering onto the ground in all directions. And when the smoke had cleared, the cattleman's eyes went wide, when he saw that the building had been razed to its very foundations.

Braden raised his hand once more, smiling at Bill Fanshaw like a hangman on a busy day, and brought it down sharply.

BUH-BAH-BOO-O-O-M! The end of the barn closest to the Mirabal *hacienda* went up in a furious and churning explosion, in much the same fashion as the chapel. Once again, rubble could be heard falling to the ground in all directions, and the lowing of wounded and panicked animals filled the air.

"Oh, my sweet Jesus!" gasped the Texas cattle baron, as he surveyed the bloody limbs and carcasses which now littered the plaza.

Inside the *hacienda,* a great wailing went up from its occupants, once they had recovered from the shock of witnessing the dreadful spectacle.

Bill Fanshaw gasped as he made out the cries of women and the frightened screams of children over the deeper wailing of the *chicano* men.

"Lord," he said in a husky, quavering voice, "it's like Judgment Day. God help us all."

Bart Braden was smiling a cold, predatory smile of triumph. "Well, I reckon ol' Don Solomon might be 'bout ready to palaver a spell,

Mr. Fanshaw," he told his employer. " 'Cause I got a strong suspicion he jus' realized he ain't holdin' no more high cards."

"Go 'head, boy," Fanshaw croaked. "Talk to 'im. An' le's git this damn business over with."

"Don Solomon!" the ramrod called out suddenly, breaking the ringing, stunned silence which had followed the shock of the explosion. "Don Solomon—Mr. Fanshaw wants to talk turkey with you."

For a long moment, there was silence. Finally, the ramrod saw the Don's silvery mane coming out of one of the upper-story windows of the *hacienda.*

"What does *Señor* Fanshaw want?" the *patrón* said haughtily, despite the fact that his voice quavered and broke.

"He wants you to back down, Don Solomon," the Texan called out. "Whilst you still got the chance."

The *hidalgo* glared down at Bart Braden and Bill Fanshaw. His face was livid now, and his beard quivered as he shook with anger at what he had just been told.

"And if I refuse . . . to 'back down' . . . as you put it?" the Don asked, his eyes narrowing until they were mere slits in his face.

"Well, sir," the ramrod called out loudly, in a clear and ringing voice, for all to hear, "if'n you don't back down, why, we'll jus' have to blow you out of that there *hacienda.*"

He smirked up at the *patrón.* "Now, it'd be a real shame if'n we had to go an' blow that fancy house of yours to smithereens, Don Solomon."

A heavy silence descended upon the plaza.

"Well, sir," Braden called out after a time, "are you gon' listen to sense, an' come out'n there with yer hands up?"

"Never!" the Don cried vehemently. *"Never while I see the light of day!"*

Bill Fanshaw took this all in, goggle-eyed, as he realized with growing horror that Don Solomon Mirabal meant exactly what he said.

"You ain't making this any too easy fer Mister Fanshaw, Don Solomon," Braden called up to the *patrón* in a tired voice. "I'm gon' give you one more chance to reconsider that there decision of yours. Now, don't be hasty." He smiled mockingly. "Why, I'm sure you an' Mr. Fanshaw'll be able to come to terms. Think it over carefully, Don Solomon."

"Gawd, boy," Bill Fanshaw muttered, "you 'bout the cold-bloodest *hombre* I ever did see!"

Bart Braden was grinning from ear to ear as he turned to face his boss. "Well, we ain't here to make ourselves no friends, is we, Bill? We's jus' here to cut 'n shoot."

Fanshaw nodded, impressed by his ramrod's nerveless demeanor. "Well, close the deal, son," he told Braden.

"Don Solomon," the Texan called out once more. "Don Solomon. At least get the womenfolk an' kids out'n the *hacienda* whilst you can. You done seen what can happen."

There was a long silence. And then the *patrón's* voice rang out over the plaza. "All right," he called out. "You are right, there. I will give the order to have all women and children evacuated from the *hacienda*. I want

168

your word that they will not be molested."

"You have Mr. Fanshaw's word," Braden called back.

"I wish to hear it from *Señor* Fanshaw's lips," the Don persisted. "He is the only *tejanos* I will trust at this time."

Bill Fanshaw stood up and cleared his throat. "The womenfolk an' children 'll be well looked after, Don Solomon," he called out in a rasping voice. "I give you my solemn promise on it."

"So be it," the *patrón* called back, nodding as he drew his head inside the window.

"Well, it's all over 'cept for picking up the pieces," Bart Braden said, as he turned to the cattle baron. "Looks like you jus' tied up the New Mexico cattle business, Bill."

The big, gray-haired man with the weather-beaten face shot him an incredulous look. "Well, it's your doin', son. You an' that dynamite of yours. Yessiree. An' you got you one helluva ree-ward comin', Bart," Fanshaw proudly informed him.

"Oh, I got me all the ree-ward I need," the ramrod said cryptically, as he turned back toward the *hacienda,* where women and children had already begun to file out through the front door.

The Texan's spurs jingled as he left the draw well and walked over to the side of Paul Cady, one of his trusted hands.

"Paul," he whispered, glancing quickly back to where Bill Fanshaw stood gaping at the ruins of the Mirabal chapel, "I want you to escort them women an' kids to where we got the Conestoga wagon a-setting'. Leave 'em with ol'

Ernie an' the kid. Take Ben an' Duff an' Cutler to help you."

The hand nodded. "Shore thing, Bart."

"One thing more, Paul," the ramrod added, taking hold of the man's arm and squeezing it until he winced. "When you see young Raquel Mirabal a-comin' through that door, why, you jus' drop ever'thin' an' take that little gal over to where my palomino is saddled."

The cowhand frowned. "I don' folly ya, Bart," he told the ramrod.

"You don't have to folly me, Paul," Braden told him with a fierce smile. "Jus' do like I tell ya. You put that little gal atop the roan stallion what's beside my palomino. An' then you jus' set there, a-holdin' her hand until I come by. You folly *that,* Paul?"

"Uh, why, I guess so, Bart. If'n you say so."

The ramrod nodded. "Attaboy, Paul. Now, you round up them boys, an' git crackin'."

"I shore will, Bart," the man said as he moved off.

"You take care of the details, boy?" Bill Fanshaw asked, as his ramrod returned to the well.

"Yessir," Bart Braden told the cattle baron, smiling an enigmatic smile. "*All* the details."

9

THE KANSAN AND THE TEXAN

BAW-BUH-BOOOM! The large, ironwood door to the Mirabal *hacienda* blew apart, as its center was consumed in a great gout of flame which grew and sent out fiery tentacles, searing and blowing down the surrounding *adobe* of the doorway with its withering force. The *hacienda* itself shook as if hit by an earthquake, and fragments of the ironwood door flew like missiles throughout the plaza.

"Come on now, Solomon," Bill Fanshaw called out, once the effects of dynamite blast had subsided. "You ain't got a snowballs chance in hell. Le's you'n me talk things over."

Crack! Crack! Puh-whaa-aang!

By way of reply, two rifle shots flared down from the upper-story window where the Don had last been seen, sending the cattle baron scurrying for shelter behind the draw well. The second slug ripped the dove-gray Stetson off Fanshaw's head, tearing a hole in its brim the size of a silver dollar.

"Damn your ass, Mirabal," the Texas cattleman bawled angrily, "you committin' suicide! Git out, whilst you still got the chance."

Crack! Puh-whaa-aang! Adobe flew, as another answering slug from the hacienda tore a chunk out of the outside of the well.

The cattle baron shook his head as he turned to Bart Braden, who stood behind a wall at the far end of the plaza. "I cain't do no more with that stupid ol' billy goat," Fanshaw called out to his ramrod, raising his hands aloft in a helpless gesture. "I reckon you git to finish the job, Bart."

Braden's eyes narrowed, and he flashed his boss a wolfish smile. Then he struck a lucifer on the seat of his pants, and raised its sputtering, sulfurous flame to the stick of "straight" dynamite that he held in his other hand.

PUFF-F-FISS-Z-Z-ZIV-V-V! The five-inch fuse whistled as it sputtered, and trailed down to the dynamite stick in a sky-rocket arc.

"Remember the Alamo!" Braden called out, as he wound up and tossed the dynamite at the *hacienda*.

Crack! Crackcrack! Whaa-ang! Puh-whaa-aang! The defenders' frantic volleys blew holes out of the wall behind the suddenly-visible Texan.

GUH-BUH-BOOM! Braden's missile went high and wide, landing upon the roof to the right of the Don's room. Red brick tile flew through the air, along with the bodies of two of the unfortunate *partidarios*.

As usual, after the appalling spectacle of the explosion, an awed and horrified silence fell over the plaza, affecting the besiegers and the besieged equally.

"Oh, sweet Jesus," lamented Bill Fanshaw, as

he knelt behind the draw well. "Whoever invented that stuff done busted open the gates of hell," the cattle baron muttered, shaking his head as he did. "What's gon' happen now—now that a body can blow his enemies to kingdom come that-a-way? . . . The ante's gon' go up that's fer shit-sure. Why, I can see armies a-lobbin' sticks of dynamite at each other, blowin' theyselves to bloody little bits. Lord only know where it'll end."

Behind the wall at the far end of the plaza, Fanshaw's ramrod pointed to the building opposite him and nodded his head. An instant later, a cowhand came out from behind the building's wall, holding a lit stick of dynamite, which he proceeded to chuck at the Mirabal *hacienda.*

Crack! Crack! Crackcrack! Whang! Bwaaaang! The man was not as fast-moving as Bart Braden, and the marksmen in the house cut him down before he could hurl his stick of dynamite.

"Oh, shoot," someone in the vicinity cried. "Lyndon's gone an' took one! Run fer cover!"

BAH-BAA-BOOM! Braden's dynamite sticks all had fast, tightly wound fuses, and the man's words had barely died away when an explosion rocked the plaza.

This time, the bloody limbs and torsos that streaked through the reeking, acrid air were those of the *tejano* enemy. Cheers went up from the defenders, raucous Spanish cries of victory and defiance.

"God damn!" Bill Fanshaw bawled, moved to tears by the sudden loss of three men whom he had known for more than twenty years. "Be careful of that stuff, boys. It's the devil's own work. Watch yer butts."

The cattle baron, hard man that he was, was truly appalled by the destructive potential of Alfred Nobel's explosive. What was going on, he realized with a cold, gnawing feeling of horror in the pit of his stomach, was not a showdown, but butchery—butchery, pure and simple. But he was not in control any more, he sadly acknowledged, he had washed his hands of the whole bloody business. Bart Braden was now running the show.

And run it he did. The ramrod's eyes were a-glitter with bloodlust as he directed his forces to regroup, shoring up his right flank after the disaster which had suddenly visited his ranks. But while he made an outward show of generalship, marshalling the Texans in an efficient manner, Braden's mind's-eye was alight with images of a naked and ardent Raquel Mirabal, bucking and squirming beneath him in the embrace of love.

At the same time, while Bart Braden directed the siege of the *hacienda* and made love to her in fantasy, the corporeal form of Raquel Mirabal sat astride the roan stallion which had been provided for her next to the ramrod's palomino, under the anxious and watchful eye of Paul Cady.

The Fanshaw trail boss and foreman was preparing to make his move. In another few minutes, the Texans would have blasted away the center of the *hacienda;* almost certainly killing the proud Don, and throwing his forces into confusion. At that point, Fanshaw's boys would storm over the smoking ruins, and the ramrod would then seize the opportunity to ride off with his prize, the beautiful and virginal Raquel Mirabal, turning his back upon fortune and position, friends and countrymen. Bart Braden was obsessed with possessing the lovely young *chicana,* and Bart Braden was a man who always got what he wanted.

"Make 'em choke on it, McKillop!" the ramrod bellowed, urging on one of his men on the near end of the plaza. "Let 'er rip, boy!"

The man thus addressed nodded his head, stuck a lucifer on the sole of his boot, touched it to the stick of Number Two dynamite in his hand, and then tossed it toward the *hacienda.*

It floated lazily through the air in a high arc, tumbling end over end, as the defenders blazed away at the dynamite thrower, who scrambled to safety behind the nearest wall, Winchester slugs creasing the soles of his shoes.

You jus' keep a-sittin' on that purty l'il coozy of yours, Raquel, the ramrod soliloquized in the privacy of his thoughts. *'Cause ol' Bart's 'bout to show ya how to use that sweet honey-pot.*

GAB-BAA-BOOM!

The room beside the Don's blew out in a ghastly, flaring blast, which was followed by a raging fire and billows of acrid black smoke. For a moment, the defenders were too shaken even to fire back at the Texans.

"Won't be long, now," Bart Braden muttered through his icy smile, as he raised his hand and went to signal his men.

BOWM-BAH-BOOM!

The ramrod's jaw dropped as he watched the

wall which sheltered his men as the far end of the plaza go up in a great flaming blast. Squinting as he peered through the smoke, Braden cursed his cowhands for their clumsiness in handling the dynamite.

A second explosion—this time, at the opposite end of the plaza—caused the Texan's jaw to drop open once more, as he finally realized what was happening. His men had not fumbled the dynamite at all; *someone was using it against them!*

BAA-BUH-BOOM!

Cheering wildly, the defenders had rallied within the *hacienda,* and were pouring their fire down upon the confused Texans, who had begun to spill out into the plaza as explosions—which grew more frequent—shook their positions.

"What the hell's goin' on here?" Bill Fanshaw bellowed from his position behind the draw well, turning to glare across the plaza at his ramrod.

Bart Braden's face was dark and angry as he looked around the plaza, still unsure as to who was hurling the dynamite at his Texans.

"Git outta there, Bill!" he yelled suddenly, as a stick of dynamite spiralled through the air, heading in an arc which the ramrod calculated would bring it down in the center of the plaza.

"God A'mighty!" the cattle baron squawked, rising clumsily to his feet and turning to run across the plaza, darting an anxious look over his shoulder at the stick of dynamite sailing through the air.

"Look out, yer own self!" a cowhand

screamed, as another stick of dynamite, its fuse sparkling and sputtering wildly, flew through the air, heading right for the building against whose wall Bart Braden was ensconced.

BAW-BUH-BOOM! BOO-BOO-BOOOM!

The draw well blew apart in a gust of flames and black, tossing clouds. A second later, the corner of the *adobe* building where Bart Braden had positioned himself to direct the attack had been blown away. And once more, a strained and horrified silence fell over the scene of combat—an ominous and dreadful silence . . . .

"Shit, I'm outta matches!" Davy Watson growled as he looked around, bouncing up and down upon the balls of his feet as he waited for the smoke to clear, anxious to ascertain whether anything remained of either Bill Fanshaw or Bart Braden.

"Here—take!" Soaring Hawk cried out to his blood-brother, chucking him a box of lucifers.

The defenders had seen their chance, and began to pour out of the smoking and devastated *hacienda*. Davy was relieved to see that Don Solomon Mirabal was with them.

"Look out!" he yelled to Soaring Hawk, just as a brace of Texans came out of the smoke before them and began firing away with their sixguns.

The Kansan's strategy had been to sneak up on the Texans and seize the Conestoga wagon which held the dynamite. The four companions had quickly captured and tied up the young man and the boy who sat on the Conestoga, after which they immediately grabbed all the dynamite they could carry and split up, turning the fearsome explosive upon the besiegers.

This maneuver enabled the defenders to evacuate the death trap of the *hacienda,* buying time for the beleaguered *partidarios.* But the Texans were already rallying, and they still possessed a distinct numerical superiority.

Davy and the Pawnee hit the packed earth of the alley at almost the same time, and each rolled toward the nearest available shelter. The shots fired by the two Texans who had stumbled upon them in the smoky aftermath of the latest series of explosions flew overhead and smacked into the canvas covering of the dynamite-laden Conestoga wagon.

Davy and Soaring Hawk rolled over and came up with their pistols in hand, blazing away at the Texans. The cowhands managed to get off a bullet or two in return, but the Kansan and the Pawnee proved to be the truer shots. Coughing, moaning, and gurgling, the two Texans fell in the dust.

"Texan come start shoot again," Soaring Hawk warned his blood-brother, as they got to their feet. Behind them, the canvas crackled and shuddered, as tongues of flame lapped at the side of the wagon.

"Judas Priest!" the Kansan exclaimed. "The damn wagon's caught fire! Git that ol' man out'n the way. I'll git the kid."

Saying this, Davy darted behind the wagon and dragged the pimply-faced youth around the corner of the nearest *adobe* building. The boy's hands were bound behind his back, as were those of his companion, the old man known as

Ernie, whom Soaring Hawk brought up on the run.

"Consarn it, Injun," the old man groused. "I cain't run that fast!"

"You better run that fast, ol' man," Davy told him, thrusting the old fellow around the corner after the boy. " 'Cause that damn Conestoga's on fire, an' if you don't run, you'll get your scrawny ol' butt blown straight back to Texas."

"Them sum'bitches is gittin' the upper hand again," Davy told Soaring Hawk, shaking his head as he looked around to see the Texans, persistent as ever, regrouping into new positions, where they began to blast away at the *chicanos* with renewed ferocity, peppering them now with heavy fire from both Winchester rifles and Colt six-guns.

Smoke rolled through the plaza in dark, sulfurous clouds, and the gathering dusk added to the low visibility in the area. The only bright spot in the vicinity of the *hacienda* was the burning dynamite wagon.

"Listen, we got to git Raquel outta here, an' away from them Texans" Davy told the Pawnee. "That was my bargain with Samantha Fanshaw." He looked around anxiously. "I don't know where the Mirabal boys has got to," he told the Pawnee, motioning him away from the flaming Conestoga wagon, "but we better git that gal, while the gittin's good. An' besides, they ain't a lot more we can do for Don Solomon an' his boys. They're jus' gonna have to hold on fer a time, 'cause them sheepherds we met comin' over here was a-ridin' like all get-out to rally the other Dons. I reckon they'll be back afore long. An' then Fanshaw's boys'll git what for."

The Indian nodded, as he pulled Davy around the corner. "Move quick. Fire spread through wagon."

"Uh, right you are, ol' son," Davy whispered back, as they started down the dark alley which led to the spot where the Texan named Paul Cady kept watch over Raquel Mirabal.

"Damnation," the Kansan muttered, "if'n I have to shoot it out with that fella, them other Texans 'round the corner'll be on us like a pack of hounds."

"Not worry," the Pawnee told him, drawing a long, gleaming knife out of its sheath. "Soaring Hawk take care of him."

Seated astride the roan stallion which stood twitching its tail, idly chasing flies as men killed each other less than a hundred yards away, Raquel Mirabal looked in the direction of the burning *hacienda* of Don Solomon Mirabal, the expression on her face a commingling of anxiety and exhaustion.

Beside her on his own horse, a bay mare, Paul Cady whistled a tuneless whistle as he slapped the reins of his horse against his saddle horn, a drawn pistol in his free hand.

Davy Watson flattened himself against the *adobe* wall as his blood-brother wound up and stepped past him, about to throw his knife at the unsuspecting Texan.

A brief *whoosh,* like the sound made when a hummingbird darts past a sleeper's ear, was the only herald of death. An instant later, Cady grunted like a poled steer and fell sidewise out of his saddle. By the time his body hit the ground with a thump, the Texan was already in shock. Soaring Hawk's knife had sliced through Cady's jugular vein, burying itself in his neck up to the hilt. In a matter of minutes, the man would bleed to death.

•Having recoiled in surprise as Cady suddenly pitched out of his saddle, Raquel Mirabal had opened her mouth and was about to scream, when she recognized Davy Watson and Soaring Hawk.

"Ay, Dios mio!" she whispered. *"Dah-veed,* it is you."

"Yep, it's me, honey," he whispered back. "An' I've come to take you away from here."

"What were the *tejanos* going to do with me?" she asked, as Soaring Hawk knelt down and retrieved his blade from the Texan's body.

"Well, honey," Davy grunted, as he drew his own knife and began cutting the rawhide thong that bound the dark-eyed beauty's wrists, "it 'pears that our buddy, ol' Bart Braden, done got it in his head to ride off with you."

"Por qué? Why would he do this thing?" She grasped the Kansan's wrist as hers came free, and she drew close to him, shivering in the cold dusk of New Mexico's early spring.

The Kansan looked into her wide, dark eyes as a breeze came up from the distant mountains, bringing him the fragrant scent of her lustrous black hair. The smell of flowers and the closeness of the *chicana's* ripe body stirred Davy Watson deeply, and he felt a surge of heat and a swelling thrust in his groin.

"I reckon he done got him a crush on you, Raquel," he told her in a voice gone suddenly husky. She leaned even closer to him, her moist lips parting, hunger in her eyes. "You *are* a right purty gal."

"*Son of a bitch!*" a voice called out from the darkness at the head of the alley. "*Lookee thar—them fellas is about to run off with Bart's gal!*"

Bam! Bam! Blambam! Shots flared in the dusk and bullets spanged and whined through the alley. The Kansan and his blood-brother hit the dirt, Davy yanking Raquel Mirabal out of the saddle. Then the two men sent back a volley of answering shots.

"Oh, shit—I'm drilled!" a man cried out in a high-pitched voice, indicating that Davy or Soaring Hawk had scored a hit. The subsequent scuffling noises which attended this remark told the two companions that the Texans had dragged their wounded comrade out of the alley.

An instant later, Raquel Mirabal's horse keeled over and hit the ground with a loud thud, its skull shattered by one of the Texans' bullets.

"Le's git to the horses," Davy whispered to Soaring Hawk, helping Raquel to her feet as he spoke.

The moon had been obscured behind a bank of clouds; and the night was dark and starless, indicating that a heavy rain would soon be due. The Kansan and the Pawnee groped along the alleyway, turning off and heading around toward the Mirabal *cantina,* on the way to where their horses had been hitched.

By the time they sat to horse, Soaring Hawk

on his Indian pony and Davy with Raquel Mirabal before him in his saddle, the big, cold moon had begun to emerge from the clouds.

"Stop 'em!" someone cried out in front of them. *"Git that gal!"* Three Texans rounded the corner of the building opposite the *cantina*.

Blambam! Bam! Blam! The blood-brothers sprayed a trail of hot lead across the street, causing the Texans to dive for shelter.

"C'mon, le's vamoose!" Davy told Soaring Hawk, as he reined in his horse and wheeled it around toward the gates of the Mirabal estate.

"But *Dah-veed,*" Raquel protested over the sounds of gunshots in the plaza, "my father is back there!"

"I know, honey," the Kansan told her, grasping the reins and encircling her with his arms. "But there ain't a whole lot we can do fer him. An' I know he'd want me to git you away from them Texans."

Damn them Texans! Davy swore in his thoughts as he saw a number of them in the moonlit plaza, all scrambling onto their horses. He and Soaring Hawk emptied their pistols at the Texans, unhorsing several, and causing a general confusion among them.

"Ride like you never rid before!" he called out to Soaring Hawk as their mounts streaked off, their iron shoes striking sparks on the stones at the edge of the plaza as they disappeared into the chill and moonsilvered night.

The Texans had been thrown into confusion by the quick thinking of the blood-brothers. Two of them would never ride again, and another was sorely wounded. Shooting continued throughout the plaza and the streets that led away from it as the sheepherders, scattered now and fighting *guerilla* style, held out stubbornly. Only three men on horseback could be spared to pursue Davy Watson and Soaring Hawk.

By this time, the Mirabal *hacienda* was a roaring inferno, and its hellish glare lit the plaza, making it almost as bright as it had been by day. Rifles barked and pistols cracked, and the cattlemen found it hard going trying to subdue the scattered and elusive *chicanos,* who had the advantage of knowing the territory upon which they fought.

To add even further to the disorder which had visited the ranks of the Texans, it now appeared that they were leaderless. Bill Fanshaw's body lay broken and twisted at one edge of the plaza, contorted into the grotesque position it had assumed after being picked up and flung into a wall by the force of the dynamite blast.

And Bart Braden, the cowhands in the vicinity realized with shocked surprise, had last been seen behind the wall of a building which had since been reduced to a pile of rubble. And although the Texans wanted to try and dig the ramrod's body out, the gunfire that came at them from the committed defenders was too heavy to permit them to do so.

Old Don Solomon was still alive, however, and the *patrón* was the rallying point for his harried *partidarios*. And to add to the already great ill-luck and misfortune of the Texans, reinforcements suddenly rode in, led by Don

Francisco Guzmán, not more than half an hour after Davy Watson and Soaring Hawk had rescued Raquel Mirabal.

This broke the back of the attack; Don Solomon's lands had been saved. With great losses on their part, the hated *tejanos* were forced to retreat, riding off the Mirabal lands with less than half the men who had ridden on to them. It was a rout—a total defeat for the cattlemen, and an event which would be celebrated in the *jácaras* of New Mexican *troubadores* for some time to come.

The pursuit of Davy and Soaring Hawk continued well into the night, however; the Texans who rode after them had no knowledge of the sudden reversal in their fortunes.

On and on the blood-brothers rode, until they found themselves in the foothills of the mountains to the west of the Mirabal lands. And on came the three Texans behind them, persistent as bloodhounds.

Up they rode into the mountains, higher and higher, up past junipers, into stands of *piñon* and pine, in their desperate attempts to evade their pursuers. But the Texans hung on like grim death.

Finally, in a clever maneuver, the Pawnee dislodged several boulders and blocked the ascent temporarily with a rock slide. After that, he reined his horse in near Davy's and leaned toward his blood-brother.

"Go that way," he whispered, pointing up to an alley between two thick stands of pine. "I keep on trail, lead Texans away from you and woman."

The Kansan darted a quick glance down the side of the mountain and saw that the Texans were already down from their horse, rolling boulders off the trail. If anyone could lead the grim horsemen a merry chase, it would be the Pawnee. Raquel's added weight was beginning to slow Davy's horse down, and he knew that it would otherwise by only a matter of time until the Texans closed in on him.

He nodded, his eyes meeting Soaring Hawk's. "There's a lake up on that peak," he whispered, reaching out to take the brave's hand. "Remember, from the way we come across't country?"

The Pawnee nodded.

"Well, le's meet up there, after you give them boys the slip," Davy went on, gripping his blood-brother's hand tightly in his.

"Two hour, mebbe three," Soaring Hawk said, reining in his horse and wheeling around, after he had let go of the Kansan's hand. In another second, he disappeared in the darkness, while Davy flicked the reins and headed his horse off the trail, up toward the alley between the pines.

Having gained shelter, after a steep ascent of several hundred feet, Davy halted his horse and turned to look back at the moonlit trail below. Raquel shivered in his arms, chilled by the night air. The Kansan drew her closer to his body.

He did not have long to keep his vigil. Several minutes after he had halted in the cover of the pines, Davy heard a growing thunder of hoof beats and saw three grim and ghostly riders flash by in the cold and eerie light of the New Mexican moon.

"Good luck, ol' son," he whispered, as the horsemen disappeared from sight. Then he gave the reins a flick, and sent his stallion up through the sheltering pines.

"Ay, Dah-veed," Raquel murmured, pressing her body against his in the darkness. *"Es muy frio.* It's *so* cold."

"Well, you jus' snuggle up to me, darlin'," Davy whispered huskily in her ear, drawing the eighteen-year-old's firm, supple body still closer to his.

The fragrant scent of her hair intoxicated him, and before he knew what he was doing, the Kansan leaned over and pressed his lips to the sweet flesh upon the side of Raquel Mirabal's neck.

"Ay, querido," she gasped suddenly, passion welling up in her, as the touch of his lips under her flesh loosed a tide of emotion and desire which threatened to overrun the containing levee of her virginal modesty. *"Querido Dah-veed,"* the beautiful young *chicana* murmured, as shock and exhaustion liberated her ardent emotions, and fantasy became reality in the darkness of the pine-studded mountainside.

She leaned back and raised her head, bringing her moist lips up to his. The moment their lips met, her tongue darted hungrily into the Kansan's mouth, and his rod grew hot and stiff as a branding iron at round-up time.

His right arm encircled her waist, while he held the reins in his right hand. Davy stroked and caressed Raquel's firm and stiff-nippled breast with the trembling fingers of his free

187

hand, causing Don Solomon's youngest daughter to moan like a catamount in rut.

"*Oh, Dios mio,*" she gasped, as the stallion continued its course up the side of the mountain. "Take me, *Dah-veed, mi corazón.*"

And take her he did, as the stallion careened up through the pines, turning Raquel around in the saddle and making love to the beautiful young *chicana* in the manner practiced by Plains Indians, Russian Cossacks, and the Huns of Attila, the Scourge of God.

Holding her with his right arm, he helped Raquel out of her underpants with his left hand. Then as they kissed, he unbuckled his belt, unbuttoned his fly, and peeled his pants down over his hard muscular thighs.

For a moment he placed her cool hand on his hot, throbbing rod, and then kissed her for all he was worth. At the same time, he stroked her black, silky pussy and then gently entered her with his middle finger.

The interior of Raquel's lushly forested grotto of delight was sopping wet, and the muscles of her vaginal barrel contracted reflexively. Though technically a virgin, the young *chicana* had torn her hymen through riding or exercise or some accident, as had many young women, and consequently Davy was not confronted with the problem of piercing her hymen. Men subscribed to the belief that each virgin would be deflowered on her honeymoon night, but it was, in a great number of instances, only a myth cherished by jealous and insecure males.

"*Ay, Dah-veed,*" Raquel whispered in a voice both anguished and ecstatic, as the Kansan put his big hands beneath her pert buttocks, lifted her up, and began to lower her onto his rigid and burning member. *"Ay, caramba! Ay, Dios mio!"*

She gripped him snugly as she slid down his pole, registering frequent and intense contractions every inch of the way. And when they finally sat face to face, their groins butted, generating a heat in their midsections that the Kansan thought would send his saddle up in flames, Raquel threw back her head and gave a short, sobbing gasp.

Then she squirmed furiously against him, as he began to clutch her buttocks once more. And when he began to move her sweet, snug pussy up and down, running the length of his shaft in its sopping, musky course, the lovely young daughter of Don Solomon Mirabal, the *gran patrón* of the New Mexico Territory, murmured incoherently, as she gasped out her delight in a torrent of disconnected Spanish words.

Up and down he stroked, faster and faster, while the stallion continued on its way through the pines. Davy's eyes rolled up in his head as he felt a geyser about to erupt in the pit of his groin. Raquel had her sopping, clutching sex plastered up against him, and her straight jet-black pubic hair mingled with his dark blond curls.

"OOO-oooh," he muttered, his pelvis beginning to jerk as he felt an irresistible rush in his groin, and he came in hot, full spurts that made him think of Independence Day Roman candles.

Raquel's own pelvis bucked wildly and she

dug her fingers in his hair, threw back her head, and emitted a long, strangled gasp. Her mouth hung open, and her lips had gone suddenly cold, as if she were sucking ice. She shuddered convulsively once or twice, and then collapsed in his arms.

Davy sighed like a poled steer and fell onto Raquel. They sat together on the saddle, sighing and shuddering, still fused at the groin, while the stallion made its way up to the top of the mountain, their handsome young bodies silvered by the moon.

By the time they had reached the lake at the top, the horse now walking along its eastern shore with grace and dignity, Raquel was nestled in the Kansan's arms, staring lovingly up at him, and cooing like some *paloma* from the woodlands below.

They dismounted at a clearing in the pines which opened out onto the water. There they refreshed themselves, and Davy tended to his lathered horse. Raquel sat on a rock at the lake's edge, pretty as a water nymph, and stared up at the Kansan with her great dark eyes.

For over an hour they sat by the edge of the lake, cradled in each other's arms. Then a rustling in the bushes, at the far end of the clearing, interrupted their long and passionate kiss.

Davy gestured for Raquel to be silent. He got to his feet, easing his Walker Colt out of its holster as he started toward the far end of the clearing. He turned once, to gaze at the starry-eyed *chicana* before he went on. The Kansan held the gun lightly, and there was a smile on his lips as he started on his way, for he was certain that Soaring Hawk had arrived.

A rustling in the pines behind him caused Davy to spin round. The smile on his lips suddenly froze, and his grip on the Colt tightened. There in the underbrush, not fifteen feet away from the Kansan, stood a shadowy figure. And Davy's blood ran cold when he saw that it was not Soaring Hawk.

The man's gun was already trained upon Davy Watson, and its long barrel gleamed in the moonlight. Emitting a grunt of surprise, the Kansan's finger tightened on the trigger.

Blam! Blam! Bam! Bambam!

The clearing was lit for an instant by a succession of bright flashes. Raquel Mirabal screamed and leapt to her feet. Both men fell back onto the ground. Raquel Mirabal gasped as she saw the bloody wound on the left side of the Kansan's head.

Davy Watson's eyes rolled up in his head and he gave out with a long, deep sigh, as he fell over a rock. Then, as his Walker Colt fell from nerveless fingers, he pitched backward off the rock and disappeared with a loud smacking splash into the dark, icy waters of the lake.

At the same time that the Kansan disappeared beneath the surface of the water, Bart Braden lurched dizzily to his feet. Clutching the bloody wound in his left shoulder, the ramrod advanced upon the terrified Raquel Mirabal.

"I come fer you, honey," the Texan told Don Solomon's youngest daughter, smiling like a wolf that has just caught sight of a solitary lamb . . .

Soaring Hawk arrived at the lake forty minutes after Bart Braden had ridden off with an unconscious Raquel Mirabal. For a moment, the Pawnee was unable to locate his blood-brother, but the he saw a figure clinging to a rock by the chill water's edge.

He dragged Davy Watson out of the lake and rolled him over on his back. Bart Braden's bullet had creased the Kansan's skull, tearing a swath of flesh out of his temple. Had Braden's shot been an inch or so to the left, all that the Pawnee brave would have found would have been a corpse bobbing in the icy waters.

"Ooh," Davy groaned as the Plains Indian dressed is wound. "That sum'bitch, Bart Braden, was one of them Texans who come after us. You must've given the other two the slip, but he come up on me'n Raquel."

The Pawnee's eyes narrowed. "He take girl?" he asked Davy.

His blood-brother closed his eyes and nodded his head. "Damn right, he did," he told Soaring Hawk through clenched teeth.

The brave nodded, a sour look on his face. "What we do now?" he asked in a low voice.

"We take us a little trip down Texas-way," the Kansan told him, with a smile that was as sharp as the Pawnee's scalping knife.